Giuseppe Garibaldi

The Life of General Garibaldi, Tr.

From his private papers; with the history of his splendid exploits in Rome,

Lombardy, Sicily and Naples, to the present time. Vol. 1

Giuseppe Garibaldi

The Life of General Garibaldi, Tr.
From his private papers; with the history of his splendid exploits in Rome, Lombardy, Sicily and Naples, to the present time. Vol. 1

ISBN/EAN: 9783337331597

Printed in Europe, USA, Canada, Australia, Japan

Cover: Foto ©Raphael Reischuk / pixelio.de

More available books at **www.hansebooks.com**

THE LI[FE]

OF

GENERAL G[ARIBALDI]

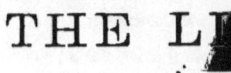

TRANSLATED FROM HIS

WITH

THE HISTORY OF HIS SP[...]

IN ROME, LOMBARDY, SIC[...]

TO THE PRESE[NT]

BY

THEODORE D[WIGHT,]

AUTHOR OF "A TOUR IN ITALY IN 1821," "THE [...]

𝔈𝔪𝔟𝔢𝔩𝔩𝔦𝔰𝔥𝔢𝔡 𝔴𝔦𝔱𝔥 𝔞 𝔉𝔦𝔫𝔢 𝔈𝔫𝔤[...]

AND

AN AUTOGRAPH LETTER TO[...]

NEW YORK[:]
DERBY & JACKSON, 498 B[ROADWAY.]
1861.

THE following pages are principally written by the pen of the hero of our age, that pure-hearted man—that devoted patriot, and noble, generous, and disinterested philanthropist—that spirited, undaunted, and indomitable warrior, whose splendid deeds have dazzled the world, and whose career, according to his own recent declaration, will be brought to its close by a final triumph, for which he is now preparing, to be gained early in the present year.

While General Garibaldi resided in New York and its vicinity, in the years 1850 and '51, the author of this book enjoyed his acquaintance, and the favor of receiving from him his private memoirs, with permission to translate and publish them.* They had just been prepared for the press, when Garibaldi requested that they might be withholden from the public while he remained in this country, probably because he preferred to be unnoticed, being at that time employed in making candles on Staten Island, and naturally fond of retirement.

The first part of this volume, to page 210, contains a literal translation from his original private manuscripts, in which a clear, unadorned English style was adopted, as nearly corresponding, as the translator's abilities would allow, to the manly and pure Italian of the author. No attempt was made to

---

* (TRANSLATION.)

"STATEN ISLAND, 30th October, 1850.

"DEAR MR. THEODORE DWIGHT:

"According to what I have promised you, I send you the first biographical sketch; and do not be surprised that it is that of my wife. She was my constant companion, in good and bad fortune—sharing, as you will see, my greatest dangers, and surpassing the bravest men. I wish you to consult Foresti, respecting the manuscripts and translations, and frankly express to me your opinion.

"Yours,   G. GARIBALDI."

3

change, by dilating or polishing, as the translator believed it to be almost as hopeless to improve his style as to rival him with the sword. That portion of the volume relates to his early life, and the fourteen years he spent in the service of the Republican cause in South America.

The succeeding pages are devoted to his services in Italy in the revolutions of 1849, 1859 and 1860; and a large proportion of their contents is occupied by his proclamations and other documents of his own, in translating which the same efforts have been made to render them correctly.

The author has received assistance from some of the country-men of Garibaldi in New York, for information not otherwise to be obtained, several of whom have been his fellow-soldiers. Many extracts have been taken from the most authentic and interesting descriptions, by intelligent eye-witnesses, of scenes in the two last campaigns in Italy. A personal acquaintance with Italy and Italians has enabled the writer to select, arrange, and explain the vast amount of materials presented by those most extraordinary seasons, in a manner perhaps best adapted for his readers. Some omissions were necessary, in composing a work of this kind, but nothing of essential importance.

The reader can hardly fail to bear in mind, while here re-viewing the life of this wonderful man, the most formidable of modern times, who is at the same time one of the most gentle and amiable at heart, that even now the present pause in his career is a solemn one, as it is speedily to be followed by a scene of excitement, conflict and consequences, perhaps un-equalled by those which are past. The results none can fore-see: but it is evident that they must be momentous and extensive, whether prosperous or adverse; and no intelligent American can anticipate them without deep emotion. Well may we look to heaven for the protection and success of the noble hero of Italian independence and liberty, the avowed enemy of the Papal Anti-Christ, whom he unmasks and de-nounces, and for the diffusion among his countrymen of that pure and undefiled Christianity, of which he declares himself a believer, and which he so earnestly claims for the religion of Italy.

The efforts, sacrifices, and sufferings of thousands of Italians for the independence, freedom, and happiness of their country, have been such, in past years, as to present pages worthy of record in history for the honor of mankind, and lessons for other nations. Many of the purest men have been suffering the pains and sorrows of exile in our own land, some of them after long and cruel punishment in the dungeons of Austria, those of the brutal kings of Naples, or of the Pope of Rome. With a patience and magnanimity astonishing to witness, they have justly excited the respect, love, and admiration of Americans who knew them, and ever showed themselves sincere and cordial friends of our country, our institutions, and state of society. Unlike too many other foreigners, they have been content with the protection which they enjoyed, and never sought for office or power, much less to act as the servants of European despots, to undermine American liberty. Some of these noble men, on returning to Italy, left with us records of their lives, which may, perhaps, hereafter be published, according to their desire, to promote a warm attachment between our countrymen and their own, for which those writings are admirably adapted.

The following pages contain the translation of one of the collections of manuscripts here referred to, and it is most gratifying to the translator to bring before the American public, at this time, so appropriate, interesting, and authentic a biography of the admired man of our age, under his own authority, and from his own pen.

Could there be a character better adapted as a model for American youth, in training them to just views of the value of what has been called the humble virtues of common life? The example of Garibaldi displays those virtues which adorn every pure, honest, and disinterested character, in happy contrast with the false and selfish principles which are too generally approved, admired, and recommended to the young. How much the world owes him, for his disinterested career, his devotion to the good of others, his refusal of rewards of every kind, and his preference of simple life in a lonely, rocky island, with only his son and daughter, and a few true friends, to all the honors, riches, and luxuries of the European capitals!

And how noble an example, also, have the Italians given us of union!

CONTENTS

viii CONTENTS.

CHAPTER VI.

CHAPTER VII.

CHAPTER VIII.

CHAPTER IX.

CHAPTER X.

CHAPTER XI.

CHAPTER XII.

CHAPTER XIII.

CHAPTER XIV.

CHAPTER XV.

CHAPTER XVI.

CHAPTER XVII.

CHAPTER XVIII.

TEN YEARS LATER.

CHAPTER I.

CHAPTER II.

CHAPTER III.

CHAPTER IV.

CHAPTER V.

CHAPTER VI.

CHAPTER VII.

CHAPTER VIII.

CHAPTER IX.

CHAPTER X.

CHAPTER XI.

CHAPTER XII.

CHAPTER XIII.

CHAPTER XIV.

CHAPTER XV.

CHAPTER XVI.

CHAPTER XVII.

CHAPTER XVIII.

CHAPTER XIX.

CHAPTER XX.

CHAPTER XXI.

Caro Sig.r - Teodoro Dwight -

Siccome io vi avevo promesso un
ri-spetto al provino come biografico
e non stupirete che sia della condotta
mia - Essa mi fa compagnia così
an-te, nella buona e contrari fortuna
Accludendo come vedrete e sperando ogni valore -
miei pericoli e sperando ogni valore -
Bramo, condividere foreste circa a
trasmetterla e tradurcome, e francamente
un effronate e genuina nostra - p.ro -

LIFE OF

GENERAL GARIBALDI.

[.... 186/.

CHAPTER I.

MY FATHER—MY MOTHER—HER INFLUENCE ON MY LIFE—INCIDENTS OF
MY CHILDHOOD—MY FIRST SCHOOLMASTERS.

IN commencing an account of my life, it would be un-
pardonable in me to omit speaking of my kind parents.

My father, a sailor, and the son of a sailor, educated
me in the best manner he could in Nice, my native
city, and afterwards trained me to the life of a seaman
in a vessel with himself.   He had navigated vessels of
his own in his youth ; but a change of fortune had
compelled him afterwards to serve in those belonging
to his father.   He used often to tell his children that
he would gladly have left them richer ; but I am fully
convinced that the course which he adopted in our education was the best he possibly could have taken, and
that he procured for us the best instructors he was
able, perhaps sometimes at the expense of his own convenience.   If, therefore, I was not trained in a gymna-
sium, it was by no means owing to his want of desire.

· In mentioning my mother—I speak it with pride—
she was a model for mothers ; and, in saying this, I

have said all that can be said. One of the greatest
sorrows of my life is, that I am not able to brighten
the last days of my good parent, whose path I have
strowed with so many sorrows by my adventurous career. (Her tender affection for me has, perhaps, been
excessive; but do I not owe to her love, to her angel-
like character, the little good that belongs to mine?
To the piety of my mother, to her beneficent and charitable nature, do I not, perhaps, owe that little love of
country which has gained for me the sympathy and af·
fection of my good, but unfortunate fellow-citizens?
Although certainly not superstitious, often, amidst the
most arduous scenes of my tumultuous life, when I have
passed unharmed through the breakers of the ocean, or
the hail-storms of battle, she has seemed present with
me. I have in fancy seen her on her knees before the
Most High—my dear mother!—imploring for the life
of her son; and I have believed in the efficacy of her
prayers.

I spent my childhood in the joys and sorrows familiar to children, without the occurrence of anything
very remarkable. Being more fond of play than of
study, I learned but little, and made but a poor return
for the kind exertions of my parents for my education.
A very simple accident made a deep impression on my
memory. One day, when a very little boy, I caught a
grasshopper, took it into the house, and, in handling
it, broke its leg. Reflecting on the injury I had done
to the harmless insect, I was so much affected with

grief, that I retired to my chamber, mourned over the poor little creature, weeping bitterly for several hours. On another occasion, while accompanying my cousin in hunting, I was standing on the side of a deep ditch, by which the fields were irrigated, when I discovered that a poor woman, while washing clothes, had fallen from the bank, and was in imminent danger. Although I was quite young and small, I jumped down and saved her life; and my success afforded me the highest pleasure. On that occasion, and in various other circumstances of a similar kind, I never hesitated for a moment, or thought of my own safety.

Among my teachers, I retain a grateful recollection of Padre Gianone and Signor Arena. Under the former I made but very little progress, being bent more on play than on learning; but I have often regretted my loss in failing to learn English, whenever I have since been thrown in company with persons speaking that language. To the latter I consider myself greatly indebted for what little I know. The ignorance in which I was kept of the language of Italy, and of subjects connected with her condition and highest interests, was common among the young, and greatly to be lamented. The defect was especially great in Nice, where few men knew how to be Italians, in consequence of the vicinity and influence of France, and still more the neglect of the government to provide a proper education for the people. To the instructions of Padre Gianone, and the incitement given me by my

elder brother Angelo, who wrote to me from America
to study my native language, I acknowledge my obligations for what knowledge I possess of that most beautiful of languages.   To my brother's influence, also, I
owe it, that I then read Roman and Italian history
with much interest.

This sketch of my early youth I must close, with the
narration of a little expedition which I attempted to
carry into effect — my first adventure.   Becoming
weary of school in Genoa, and disgusted with the confinement which I suffered at the desk, I one day proposed to several of my companions to make our escape,
and seek our fortune.   No sooner said than done.   We
got possession of a boat, put some provisions on board,
with fishing tackle, and sailed for the Levant.   But
we had not gone as far as Monaco, when we were pursued and overtaken by a "corsair," commanded by
good father.   We were captured without bloodshed,
and taken back to our homes, exceedingly mortified by
the failure of our enterprise, and disgusted with an
Abbé who had betrayed our flight.   Two of my companions on that occasion were Cesare Tanoli and Raffaele Deandreis.

When I recur to the principles which were inculcated at school, and the motives used to encourage us to
study, I am now able to understand their unsoundness
and their evil tendency.   We were in danger of growing up with only selfish and mercenary views : nothing
was offered us as a reward for anything we could do,
but money.

CHAPTER II.

How everything is embellished by the feelings of youth,
and how beautiful appeared, to my ardent eyes, the
bark in which I was to navigate the Mediterranean,
when I stepped on board as a sailor for the first time!
Her lofty sides, her slender masts, rising so gracefully
and so high above, and the bust of Our Lady which
adorned the bow, all remain as distinctly painted on
my memory at the present day, as on the happy hour
when I became one of her crew. How gracefully
moved the sailors, who were fine young men from San
Remi, and true specimens of the intrepid Ligurians!
With what pleasure I ventured into the forecastle, to
listen to their popular songs, sung by harmonious
choirs! They sang of love, until I was transported;
and they endeavored to excite themselves to patriotism
by singing of Italy! But who, in those days, had ever
taught them how to be patriots and Italians? Who,
indeed, had then ever said, on those shores, to those

2

young men, that there was such a thing as Italy, or
that they had a country to be ameliorated and re
deemed ?

The commander of the Costanza, the vessel in which
I had embarked, was Angelo Pesante. He was the
best sea-captain I ever knew, and ought to have the
command of a ship of war of the first class, as soon as
Italy shall have such a fleet as she deserves,—for a
better commander could not be. He has, indeed, been
captain of an armed vessel. Pesante was able to
make or invent every thing that could be wanted in a
vessel of any kind whatsoever, from a fishing-boat to
a ship of the line ; and, if he were in the service of
the country, she would reap the advantage and the
glory.

My second voyage was made to Rome, in a vessel
of my father's. Rome, once the capital of the world,
now the capital of a sect! The Rome which I had
painted in my imagination, no longer existed. The
future Rome, rising to regenerate the nation, has now
long been a dominant idea in my mind, and inspired
me with hope and energy. Thoughts, springing from
the past, in short, have had a prevailing influence on
me during my life. Rome, which I had before admired and thought of frequently, I ever since have
loved. It has been dear to me beyond all things. I
not only admired her for her former power and the
remains of antiquity, but even the smallest thing connected with her was precious to me. Even in exile,

these feelings were constantly cherished in my heart; and often, very often, have I prayed to the Almighty to permit me to see that city once more. I regarded Rome as the centre of Italy, for the union of which I ardently longed.

I made several voyages with my father, and afterwards one with Captain Guiseppe Gervino, to Caglieri, in a brig named the Emma, during which, on the return passage, I witnessed a melancholy shipwreck, at a distance, in such a storm that it was impossible to render any assistance. In that instance I witnessed, for the first time, that tender sympathy which sailors generally feel for others in distress. We saw Spaniards, in a Catalan felucca, struggling with the waves, who soon sank before our eyes, while my honest and warm-hearted shipmates shed tears over their hard fate. This disaster was caused by a sudden change of wind when the sea and wind were high. A Libaccio, a south-west wind, had been blowing furiously for several days, and a number of vessels were in sight, of all which the felucca seemed to make the best way. We were all steering for Vado, to make that port for shelter, until the storm should subside. A horrible surge unexpectedly broke over the Spanish vessel, and overset it in an instant. We saw the crew clinging to the side, and heard their cries to us for assistance, while we could perceive their signals, but could not launch a boat. They all soon disappeared in the foam of a second surge, more terrible than the first. We afterwards heard that the nine persons thus lost all belonged to one family.

From Vado I went to Genoa, and thence to Nice, whence I commenced a series of voyages to the Levant, in vessels belonging to the house of Givan. In one of these, in the brig Centesi, Captain Carlo Seneria, I was left sick in Constantinople. The vessel sailed; and, as my sickness continued, I found myself in somewhat straitened circumstances. In cases of difficulty or danger, I have never, in all my life, been disheartened. I then had the fortune to meet with persons kindly disposed to assist me, and, among others, I can never forget Signora Luigia Saiyuraiga, of Nice, whom I have ever since regarded as one of the most accomplished of women, in the virtues which distinguish the best and most admirable of her sex.

As mother and wife, she formed the happiness of her husband, who was an excellent man, and of their young and interesting children, whose education she conducted with the greatest care and skill. What contributed to prolong my abode in the capital of Turkey, was the war which at that time commenced between that power and Russia; and I then, for the first time, engaged as a teacher of children. That employment was offered me by Signor Diego, a doctor in medicine, who introduced me to the widow Temoin, who wanted an instructor for her family. I took up my residence in the house, and was placed in charge of her three sons, with a sufficient salary.

I afterwards resumed the nautical life, embarking in the brig Nostra Signora della Grazia, Captain Casabana; and that vessel was the first I ever commanded, being made Captain of it on a subsequent voyage to Mahon and Gibraltar, returning to Constantinople.

Being an ardent lover of Italy from my childhood, I felt a strong desire to become initiated in the mysteries of her restoration; and I sought everywhere for books and writings which might enlighten me on the subject, and for persons animated with feelings corresponding with my own. On a voyage which I made to Tagangog, in Russia, with a young Ligurian, I was first made acquainted with a few things connected with the intentions and plans of the Italian patriots; and surely Columbus did not enjoy so much satisfaction on the discovery of America, as I experienced on hearing that the redemption of our country was meditated. From that time I became entirely devoted to that object, which has since been appropriately my own element for so long a time.

The speedy consequence of my entire devotion to the cause of Italy was, that on the fifth of February, 1834, I was passing out of the gate of Linterna, of Genoa, at seven o'clock in the evening, in the disguise of a peasant—_a proscript_. At that time my public life commenced; and, a few days after, I saw my name, for the first time, in a newspaper: but it was in *a sentence of death!*

I remained in Marseilles, unoccupied, for several months; but at length embarked, as mate, in a vessel commanded by Captain Francesco Gazan. While standing on board, towards evening, one day, dressed in my best suit, and just ready to go on shore, I heard a noise in the water, and, looking below, discovered that some person had fallen into the sea, and was then under the stern of the vessel. Springing into the water, I had the satisfaction to save from drowning a French boy, in the presence of a large collection of people, who expressed their joy aloud, and warmly applauded the act. His name was Joseph Rasbaud, and he was fourteen years of age. His friends soon made their appearance; and I experienced very peculiar feelings excited in my heart, when the tears of his mother dropped, one after another, upon my cheek, while I heard the thanks of the whole family.

Some years before I had a similar good fortune, when I saved the life of my friend, Claudio Terese.

CHAPTER III.

I MADE another voyage to the Black Sea, in the
brig Unione, and afterwards one to Tunis, in a frigate,
built at Marseilles for the Bey. From the latter port
I next sailed for Rio Janeiro, in the Nautonier, a
Nantes brig, Captain Beauregard.

While walking one day in a public place in Rio, I
met a man whose appearance struck me in a very uncommon and very agreeable manner. He fixed his
eyes on me at the same moment, smiled, stopped, and
spoke. Although we found that we had never met
before, our acquaintance immediately commenced, and
we became unreserved and cordial friends for life.
He was Rosetti, the most generous among the warm
lovers of our poor country!

I spent several months in Rio, unoccupied and
ease, and then engaged in commerce, in company with
Rosetti : but a short experience convinced us that
neither of us was born for a merchant.

About this time Zambeccari arrived at Rio, having been sent as a prisoner from Rio Grande, when I became acquainted with the sentiments and situation of the people of that province. Arrangements were soon made for Rosetti and myself to proceed on an expedition for their aid, they having declared their independence. Having obtained the necessary papers, we engaged a small vessel for a crusier, which I named " *The Mazzini.*" I soon after embarked in a garopera, with twenty companions, to aid a people in the south, oppressed by a proud and powerful enemy. The garope is a kind of Brazilian fish, of an exquisite flavor ; and boats employed in taking it are called garoperas. My feelings, at that epoch of my life, were very peculiar. I was enlisted in a new and hazardous enterprize, and, for the first time, turned a helm for the ocean with a warlike flag flying over my head—the flag of a republic—the Republic of Rio Grande. I was at the head of a resolute band, but it was a mere handful, and my enemy was the empire of Brazil.

We sailed until we reached the latitude of Grand Island, off which we met a sumaca, or large coasting boat, named the Luisa, loaded with coffee. We captured her without opposition, and then resolved to take her instead of my own vessel, having no pilot for the high sea, and thinking it necessary to proceed along the coast. I therefore transferred everything from the Mazzini on board the sumaca, and then sunk

the former.   But I soon found that my crew were not
all men like Rosetti, of noble and disinterested character and the purest morals ; and, indeed, I had before
felt some apprehensions, when I saw among them
several physiognomies by no means prepossessing.   I
now found them, when on board the sumaca, affecting
ferocity, to intimidate the poor Brazilian sailors,
whom we had made prisoners.   I took immediate
steps to repress all such conduct, and to tranquilize
the fears which they had excited, assuring the crew
that they should be uninjured and kindly treated, and
set on shore at the first convenient landing-place, with
all their own personal property.   A Brazilian, a pas-
senger in the sumaca, took the first opportunity, after
coming on board, to offer me a casket containing
three valuable diamonds, in a supplicating manner, as
if afraid for his life ; but I refused to receive it, and
gave peremptory orders that none of the effects of the
crew or passengers should be taken from them, under
any pretext whatever.   And this course I pursued on
all subsequent occasions, whenever I took any prizes
from the enemy ; and my orders were always strictly
obeyed.

The passengers and crew were landed north of
Itaparica, the launches of the Luisa being given to
them, with all their movables, and as much brandy as
they chose to take with them.   I then went to the south,
and soon arrived in the port of Maldonado, where
the favorable reception given us by the authorities

and the people, afforded us a very flattering prospect.

Rosetti set off for Montevideo, to arrange things connected with the expedition, leaving us to await his
return ; and during eight days we enjoyed one un-
interrupted festival among the hospitable inhabitants.
The close of that period of gayety would have been
tragical, if the political chief of the town had been less
friendly than he proved himself to be. I received
unexpected notice, quite different from what I had
been led to expect, that the flag of Rio Grande was
not recognized, and that an order had arrived for our
immediate arrest. Thus compelled to depart, although
the weather was threatening, I hoisted sail without
delay, and steered up the river Plata, with scarcely
any plan or object, and almost without opportunity
to communicate to any one that I should await, at the
Point of Jesus Maria, news of the result of Rosetti's
deliberations with his friends in Montevideo. After a
wearisome navigation, I reached that place, having
narrowly escaped shipwreck on the Point of Piedras
Negras, in consequence of a variation of the compass
caused by the muskets placed near it.

I found no news at that place ; and our provisions
were entirely consumed. We had no boat to land
with : but it was indispensable to procure food for the
men. At length, after some deliberation, having discovered a house about four miles distant from the shore,
I determined to get to the land, by some means or

other, and, at any cost, to procure provisions and bring
them on board.   The shore being very difficult of approach, because the wind was blowing from the pampas, the vast plains which extend far and wide, it was
necessary to throw out two anchors to draw up a little
nearer.   I then embarked on the dining table, accompanied by one of my sailors, named Maurizio Garibaldi,
and moved on towards the land, not navigating, but
rolling through the breakers of that dangerous shore.
In spite of the difficulty attending the enterprise we
reached the river's bank in safety, and drew up our
strange craft on the sand.   Then, leaving my companion and namesake to refit, I set off for the house
which I had seen from the vessel.

Walking up the bank I reached the level of the
pampas, and then, for the first time in my life, caught
a view of one of those vast South American plains.
I was struck with admiration :—such a boundless scene
of fertility, where wild horses and cattle were running
free and unrestrained, feeding, resting, and racing at
full speed, at will.   My mind was filled with new, sublime and delightful emotions, as I passed on towards
the solitary habitation to which I was bound.   When
I reached it I found a welcome, and easily obtained a
promise of an abundant supply of food for my crew.
The daughter of the proprietor of that vast estate was
an educated, refined and agreeable young lady, and
even a poetess ; and I spent the remainder of the day

very pleasantly, in company with her and the rest of the family.

The next day I returned to the shore, with the quarters of a fat bullock which had been killed for me out of the immense herd of cattle, at the order of the proprietor. Maurizio and I fastened the meat to the legs of the table, which were in the air, the table itself being placed upside down on the water, and then we launched out into the river to make our way to the vessel. But the weight of the cargo and crew proved entirely too great, and we immediately began to sink until we stood in the water; and on reaching the breakers, the agitation caused so much rocking that it was almost impossible to proceed, or even to keep our footing. Indeed, we were in actual danger of drowning. But, after great exertions, we reached the Luisa with our load of provisions, and were hailed by the shouts of our companions, whose only hope for subsistence depended on our success.

The next day, while passing a small vessel called a Balandra, we thought of purchasing her launch, which we saw on her deck. We therefore made sail, boarded her, and made the purchase for thirty dollars. That day also we spent in sight of Jesus Maria.

13*

CHAPTER IV.

THE day after, while lying a little south of Jesus
Maria, two launches came in sight and approached us
in a friendly manner, with nothing in their appearance
to excite suspicion. I made a signal agreed on with
friends, but it was not answered ; and then I hoisted
sail, had the arms taken from the chests, and prepared
to meet them as enemies. The launches held on
towards us : the larger showed only three men on deck :
but, when she came nearer, called on us to surrender, in
the name of the Oriental Government. The next
instant thirty men suddenly rose, as if by a miracle,
and she ran up on our larboard side. I immediately
gave command to " brace the yards," and then to " fire."
An active engagement then commenced. The launch
being then alongside of us, several of the enemy
attempted to board us, but were driven back by a few
shots and sabre-cuts. All this passed in a few moments. But my order to brace the yards was not
obeyed, for my men were new and in confusion, and
the few who began to haul at the weather braces found
they had not been let go to leeward, and were unable

to move them. Fiorentino, one of the best of the
crew, who was at the helm, sprang forward to cast them
off, when a musket ball struck him in the head and laid
him dead on deck. The helm was now abandoned;
and, as I was standing near, firing at the enemy, I
seized the tiller, but the next moment received a bullet
in my neck, which threw me down senseless, and I
knew nothing more until the action was over. When
I came to myself I found that an hour had elapsed, a
hard fight had been maintained against a superior
force, and a victory won, chiefly by the bravery of the
Italians, the mate, Luigi Carniglia, the second mate,
Pasquale Lodola, and the sailors Giovanni Lamberti
and Maurizio Garibaldi. Two Maltese and all the
Italians, except a Venitian, fought bravely. The
others, with two negroes, sheltered themselves under
the ballast of the vessel.

I found that the enemy had hauled off out of gun-
shot. I ordered that our vessel should proceed up the
river, in search of a place of retreat. When I first
began to recover consciousness, I lay helpless, apparently dead, but felt as if unable to die. I was the
only man on board who had any knowledge of navigation; and, as none of the others had a single idea of
geography, or knew where to go, they at length
brought me the chart. None of us had been in the
waters of the Plata before, except Maurizio, who had
sailed on the Uruguay. When I turned my dying
eyes on the chart, I was unable to see distinctly, but

made out to perceive that one place on the river was printed in large letters, and at length discovered that it was Santà Fé, on the Paraná, and thought we might there make a temporary harbor. So, pointing at it with my finger, and signifying as well as I could the direction and distance, I left the helmsman to him-self.

All the sailors, except the Italians, were frightened by seeing my situation, and the corpse of Fiorentino, and by the apprehension of being treated as pirates wherever they might go. Every countenance wore an expression of terror ; and at the earliest opportunity they deserted. In every bird they observed on the water they imagined they saw an enemy's launch, sent to pursue them. The body of the unfortunate Fiorentino was buried the next day in the river, with the ceremonies usually practised by sailors, as we were unable to anchor anywhere near the land. I was per-haps affected the more by the sad scene, because I was in so feeble a condition. I had never thought much about death, although I knew I was liable to it every moment ; but I mourned deeply at the funeral of my lost friend, who was very dear indeed to me. Among the numerous poetical lines which occurred to my mind, was that beautiful verse of Ugo Foscolo :

> Un sasso che distingue le mie
> Dall' infinite osse, che in terra
> E in mar, semina Morte."

[Let a stone distinguish mine from the innumerable bones which Death sows on land and in the sea.]

My friend had promised me never to bury me in the water : but who can tell whether he would have been able to keep his promise ? I could never have felt sure that my corpse would not feed the sea-wolves and acaves of the great river Plata. If it were so, then I should never have seen Italy again ; never fought for her—which was the great wish of my life : but then, too, I never should have seen her sink into ignominy. Who would have said to the amiable man that, within a year, Garibaldi would see him swallowed up in the surges of the ocean, and that he would search for his corpse, to bury it on a foreign shore, and to mark the spot with a stone, for the eyes of strangers?   He deserved my kind regard ; for he attended me, with the care of a mother, during the whole voyage from Maya-guay. During all my sufferings, which were very severe, I had no relief but what he afforded me, by his constant care and kind services. I wish to express my gratitude to God for sending me such a friend.

CHAPTER V.

OUR vessel arrived at Gualaguay, where we were very
cordially received and kindly treated by Captain
Luca Tartabal, of the schooner Pintoresca, and his
passengers, inhabitants of that town. That vessel had
met ours in the neighborhood of Hiem, and, on being
asked for provisions by Luigi, they had offered to
keep company with us to their destination. They
warmly recommended us to the governor of the prov
ince, Don Pasquale Echague, who was pleased, when
going away, to leave his own surgeon with me, Dr.
Ramon del Orco, a young Argentine. He soon ex-
tracted the ball from my neck and cured me. I resided in the house of Don Jacinto Andreas during the
six months which I spent in that place, and was under
great obligations to him for his kindness and courtesy,
as well as for those which I received from his family.

But I was not free. With all the friendliness of
Echague, and the sympathy shown me by the inhabitants of the town, I was not permitted to leave it without the permission of Rosas, the traitor of Buenos

(33)

Ayres, who never acted for a good reason. My wound being healed, I was allowed to take rides on horseback, even to a distance of twelve miles, and was supplied with a dollar a day for my subsistence, which was a large sum for that country, where there is but little opportunity to spend money. But all this was not liberty. I was then given to understand by certain persons (whether friends or enemies), that it had been ascertained that the government would not wish to prevent my escape if I should attempt it. I therefore determined to gain my freedom, believing that it would be easier than it proved, and that the attempt would not be regarded as a serious offence.

The commandant of Gualaguay was named Millau. He had not treated me ill, but it was very doubtful what his feelings towards me really were, as he had never expressed any interest in me.

Having after a time formed my plan, I began to make preparations. One evening, while the weather was tempestuous, I left home and went in the direction of a good old man, whom I was accustomed to visit at his residence, three miles from Gualaguay. On arriving, I got him to describe with precision the way which I intended to take, and engaged him to find me a guide, with horses, to conduct me to Hueng, where I hoped to find vessels in which I might go, *incognito*, to Buenos Ayres and Montevideo. Horses and a guide were procured. I had fifty-four miles to travel, and that distance I *devoured* in less than half a night, going almost the whole way on the gallop. When day broke, we were at an estancia, within about half a mile of the town. My guide then told me to wait in the bushes where we were, while he went to inquire the news at the house. I complied, and he left me. I dismounted and tied my horse to a tree with the bridle, and waited a long time. At length, not seeing him return, I walked to the edge of the bushes, and looked about in search of him, when I heard behind me a trampling of horses ; and, on turning round, discovered a band of horsemen, who were rushing upon me with their sabres drawn. They were already between me and my horse, and any attempt to escape would have been fruitless—still more any effort at resistance. I was immediately seized and bound, with my hands behind me, and then placed upon a miserable horse, and had my feet tied under him. In that condition I was taken back to Gualaguay, where still worse treatment awaited me.

Such were the impressions made upon my feelings by the barbarous usage which I received at that time, that I have never since been able to recall the circumstances without a peculiar agitation of mind ; and I regard that period as the most painful of my life.

When brought into the presence of Millau, who was waiting for me at the door of the prison, he asked me who had furnished me with the means of escape. When he found that he could draw no information from me on that subject, he began to beat me most brutally with a club which he had in his hand. He then put a rope over a beam in the prison, and hung me up in the air by my hands, bound together as they were. For two hours the wretch kept me suspended in that manner. My whole body was thrown into a high, feverish heat. I felt as if burning in a furnace. I frequently swallowed water, which was allowed me, but without being able to quench my raging thirst. The sufferings which I endured after being unbound were indescribable: yet I did not complain. I lay like a dead man; and it is easy to believe that I must have suffered extremely. I had first travelled fifty-four miles through a marshy country, where the insects are insufferable at that season of the year, and then I had returned the same distance, with my hands and feet bound, and entirely exposed to the terrible stings of the zingara, or mosquito, which assailed me with vigor; and, after all this, I had to undergo the tortures of Millau, who had the heart of an assassin.

Andreas, the man who had assisted me, was put into prison; and all the inhabitants were terrified, so that, had it not been for the generous spirit of a lady, I probably should have lost my life. That lady was Señora Aleman, to whom I love to express my gratitude. She is worthy of the warmest terms of admiration, and deserves the title of "angelo generoso di bontà" (generous angel of goodness). Spurning every suggestion of fear, she came forward to the assistance of the tortured prisoner; and from that time I wanted nothing—thanks to my benefactress!

A few days after, I was removed to Bajada, the capital of the province, and I remained a prisoner in that city for two months. I was then informed, by Governor Echague, that I should be allowed to leave the province. Although I professed different principles from his, and had fought for a different cause, I have ever been ready to acknowledge my obligations to that officer, and always desired an opportunity to prove my gratitude to him for granting me everything that was in his power to give, and, most of all, my liberty.

I took passage in a Genoese brig, commanded by Captain Ventura, a man of such a character that he had risen superior to the principles inculcated in Italian youth by their priestly instructors. From him I received the most gentlemanly treatment on my passage to Guassu. There I embarked for Montevideo in a balandra, commanded by Pascuale Corbona, who likewise treated me with great kindness. Good fortune and misfortune thus often succeeded each other.

CHAPTER VI.

In Montevideo I found a collection of my friends, among whom the chief were Rosetti, Cuneo, and Castellani. The first was on his return from a journey to Rio Grande, where he had been received with the greatest favor by the proud Republicans inhabiting that region. In Montevideo I found myself still under proscription, on account of my affair with the launches of that state, and was obliged to remain in concealment in the house of my friend Pepante, where I spent a month. My retirement was relieved and enlightened by the company of many Italian acquaintances, who, at that time, when Montevideo was not suffering from the calamities it has too often known, and, as is always the case in time of peace, were distinguished by a refinement and hospitality worthy of all praise. The war, and chiefly the late siege, have since embittered the lives of those good-hearted men, and produced great changes in their condition.

After the expiration of a month, I set off for Rio Grande with Rosetti, on horseback ; and that first

long journey I ever made in that manner I highly enjoyed. On reaching Piratimin, we were cordially received by the Governor of the Republic; and the Minister of War, Almeida, treated us with great honor.
The President, Bento Gonzalez, had marched at the
head of a brigade to fight Silva Tavares, an imperial
chief, who was infesting that part of the province.
Piratimin, then the seat of the Republican government, is a small village, but a peaceful place, in a ru-
ral situation, and the chief town of the department of
that name. It is surrounded by a warlike people,
much devoted to the republic.

Being unoccupied in Piratimin, I requested permission to join the column of operations under S. Gonzalez, near the President, and it was granted. I was
introduced to Bento Gonzalez, and well received;
spent some time in his company, and thought him a
man highly favored by nature with some desirable
gifts. But fortune has been almost always favorable
to the Brazilian Empire.

Bento Gonzalez was a specimen of a magnanimous
soldier, though he was at that time nearly sixty years of
age. Being tall and active, he rode a fiery horse with
all the ease and dexterity of his young countrymen.

In Camarino, where we had our arsenal, and whence
the Republican flotilla went out, resided the families
of Bento Gonzalez; and his brothers and numerous
relations inhabited most of the extensive tracts of
country lying along both sides of the river. And on

these beautiful pastures were fed immense herds of cattle, which had been left undisturbed by the war, because they were out of the reach of the troops. The products of agriculture were very abundant; and surely nowhere, in any country on earth, is found more kind and cordial hospitality than among the inhabitants of that part of the Province of Rio Grande. In their houses, in which the beneficent character of the patriarchal system is everywhere perceived in every family, and where the greatest sympathy prevails, in consequence of a general uniformity of opinions, I and my band were received with the warmest welcome. The estancias, to which we chiefly resorted, on account of their proximity to the Lagoon, as well as for the conveniences which it offered us, and the kind reception which always awaited us, were those of Donna Antonia and Donna Anna, sisters of Bento Gonzalez. The former was situated on the Camones, and the latter on the Arroyo Grande.

Whether I was under the influence of my imagination, which at that early age may have been peculiarly sensitive, and inclined me, with my little knowledge of the world, to receive strong impressions from every thing agreeable, or whatever else may have affected me, there is no part of my life on which I look back with greater pleasure, as a period of enjoyment, than that which I spent in that most agreeable society of sincere friends. In the house of Donna Anna, especially, I took peculiar interest. That lady was advanced

in years, but possessed a most amiable disposition, and
was a very attractive acquaintance. She had with her
a family which had migrated from Pilotos, the head of
which was Don Paolo Ferreira. Three young ladies,
all of them agreeable, formed the ornaments of that
happy home. One of these, named Manuela, I most
highly admired, regarding her with that pleasure
which is natural to a young man, who goes into the
world with such a pure and exalted estimate of female
excellence as I had imbibed from my mother, and
who, after enduring great reverses, meets the sympathy
of such a person in a remote land of exile. Signora
Manuela, as I well knew, was betrothed to a son of
the President. In a scene of danger that young lover
displayed his attachment to her, in a manner which
convinced me of the sincerity of the love which he
professed ; and I witnessed it with as much satisfaction
as if I had been her brother. I thenceforth regarded
the President's son as worthy of Manuela, and rejoiced
in the conviction that her happiness was in no danger,
in being entrusted to such faithful hands. The people
of that district are distinguished for beauty ; and
even the slaves seem to partake of the same characteristic.

It may be supposed that an occasional contrary
wind, a storm, or an expedition, whatever else it might
produce, if it threw our vessel on that friendly shore
long enough to allow opportunity to visit their friendly
inhabitants, was not altogether disagreeable. Such an

3

occasion was always a festival. The Grove of Teviva, (a kind of palm growing on the Arroyo Grande,) which was the landmark for the entrance of the stream, was always discovered with lively pleasure, and saluted with redoubled enthusiasm and the loudest acclamations. When the gentle hosts, to whose kindness we felt so much indebted, wished to go to Camacuan to visit Don Antonio and his amiable family, I seized the opportunity with great pleasure, as it afforded me a way to make some return for the many kindnesses they had shown us, while it gave new occasions for the display of their amiable character and refined and pleasing manners, amidst the varying scenes of the little voyage.

Between Arroyo Grande and Camacuan are several sand-banks, called Tuntal, which extend from the west shore of the Lagoon, almost at right angles and nearly across, touching the opposite side, except only the narrow space occupied by the boat channel, called Dos Barcos. To go round these bars would greatly prolong the time necessary for the voyage : but that might be avoided, with some trouble. By throwing themselves into the water and pushing the launches along by main force, with their shoulders, the men could get them over the bars, and then keep along the western side of the Lagoon. This expedient was almost always adopted by us, and especially on the occasions referred to, when the boats were honored with the presence of our welcome guests—that precious freight!

Whatever might be the wind, I was usually sure of getting the launches over the bars ; and, so accustomed were my men to the task, and so prompt in the performance of that laborious service, that the order to take to the water [*"Al aqua, Tatos !"*] was scarcely pronounced before they were overboard and at their posts. And so, on all occasions, the task was performed with alacrity and success, as if the crews had been engaged in some favorite amusement on a day of jubilee, whatever might be the hour or the weather. But when pursued by the enemy in superior force, and suffering in a storm, we were obliged to pass that way, sometimes in the water a whole night, and without protection from the waves, which would break over us, while the temperature of the Lagoon was cooled by the rain, and we were far from land, the exposure, the labor and the sufferings were sometimes very great, and all the fervor of youth was necessary to enable us to endure them.

CHAPTER VII.

AFTER the capture of the Sumaca, the imperial merchant vessels no longer set sail without a convoy, but were always accompanied by vessels of war; and it became a difficult thing to capture them. The expeditions of the launches were, therefore, limited to a few cruises in the Lagoon, and with little success, as we were watched by the Imperialists, both by land and by water. In a surprise made by the chief, Francisco de Abrea, the whole of my band was near being cut off with its leader.

We were at the mouth of the Camacua, with the launches drawn up on land, opposite the Galpon of Charginada,—that is, the magazine or depôt of the estancia, or large estate of that name. We were engaged in salting meat and collecting Yerba Matté, a species of tea, which grows in those parts of South America, and is used as their daily beverage by the inhabitants. The estate belonged to Donna Antonia, sister of the President. In consequence of the war,

(44)

meat was not then salted there ; and the Galpon was
occupied only with Yerba Matté. We used the spacious
establishment as our arsenal, and had drawn up our
launches some distance from the water, between the
magazine and the bank of the river, in order to repair
them. At that spot were the shops of the smiths and
laborers of the establishment, and there was a plenti-
ful supply of charcoal ; for although not then in use,
the place retained something of its former condition
and appearance. There were not wanting pieces of
iron and steel, fit for different purposes in our little
vessels. We could easily visit the distant estancias
by a galloping ride, where we were most cheerfully
supplied with whatever we found deficient in the arsenal.

With courage, cheerfulness, and perseverance, no
enterprise is impossible ; and, for these I must do
justice to my favorite companion and usual forerunner,
John Griggs, who surmounted numerous difficulties,
and patiently endured many disappointments, in the
work of building two new launches.

He was a young man of excellent disposition, un-
questionable courage, and inexhaustible perseverance.
Though he belonged to a rich family, he had devoted
himself disinterestedly to the young Republic ; and,
when letters from his friends in North America invited
him to return home, and offered him a very large
capital, he refused, and remained until he sacrificed
his life for an unhappy, but brave and generous, people.

I had afterwards to contemplate the sad and impressive spectacle, presented by his death, when the body of my friend was suddenly cut down by my side.

While the launches were lying drawn up, as before mentioned, and the repairs were busily going on, some of the sailors were engaged with the sails, and some at other occupations, near them, while several were employed in making charcoal, or keeping watch as sentinels, every one being busy about something,—by some unexpected chance, Francisco de Albera, commonly called Moringue, determined to surprise us; and, although he did not succeed in his design, he gave us not a little trouble. A surprise certainly was effected on that occasion, and in a masterly manner.

We had been on patrols all night, and all the men had been, a short time before, assembled in the Galpon, where the arms were loaded and deposited. It was a beautiful morning, though cloudy; and nothing seemed to be stirring, but all around was silent and apparently lonely. Observations, however, were made around the camp, with the greatest care, without discovering a trace of anything new. About nine o'clock, most of the people were set at work, in cutting wood; and for this purpose were scattered about at considerable distances. I had then about fifty men for the two launches; and it happened that day, by a singular concurrence of circumstances, our wants being peculiar, that only a very few remained near the boats. I was sitting by the fire, where breakfast was cooking, and was just then taking some Matté. Near by was the cook, and no other person.

All on a sudden, and as if just over my head, I heard a tremendous volley of firearms, accompanied by a yell, and saw a company of the enemy's horsemen marching on. I had hardly time to rise and take my stand at the door of the Galpon, for at that instant one of the enemy's lances made a hole through my poncho. It was our good fortune to have our arms al' loaded, as I have before mentioned, and placed in the Galpon, in consequence of our having been in a state of alarm all night. They were placed inside of the building, against the wall, ready and convenient for use. I immediately began to seize the muskets and discharge them in turn, and shot down many of the enemy. Ignacio Bilbao, a brave Biscayan, and Lorenzo N., a courageous Genoese, were at my side in a moment; and then Eduardo Mutru, a native of the country, Rafaele and Procopio, one a mulatto and the other a black, and Francisco. I wish I could remember the names of all my bold companions, who, to the number of thirteen, assembled around me, and fought a hundred and fifty enemies, from nine in the morning until three in the afternoon, killing and wounding many of them, and finally forcing them to retreat.

Among our assailants were eighty Germans, in the infantry, who were accustomed to accompany Maringue in such expeditions, and were skilful soldiers, both on foot and on horseback. When they had reached the spot, they had dismounted and surrounded the house, taking advantage of the ground, and of some rough places, from which they poured upon us a terrible fire from different sides. But, as often happens in surprises, by not completing their operations and closing, men ordinarily act as they please. If, instead of taking positions, the enemy had advanced upon the Galpon, and attacked us resolutely, we should have been entirely lost, without the power to resist their first attack. And we were more exposed than we might ordinarily have been in any other building, because, to allow the frequent passage of carts, the sides of the magazine were left open.

In vain did they attempt to press us more closely, and assemble against the end walls. In vain did they get upon the roofs, break them up and throw upon our heads the fragments and burning thatch. They were driven away by our muskets and lances. Through loop-holes, which I made through the walls, many were killed and many wounded. Then, pretending to be a numerous body in the building, we sang the republican hymn of Rio Grande, raising our voices as loud as possible, and appeared at the doors, flourishing our lances, and by every device endeavoring to make our numbers appear multiplied.

About three o'clock in the afternoon the enemy retired, having many wounded, among whom was their chief. They left six dead near the Galpon, and several others at some distance. We had eight wounded, out of fourteen. Rosetti, and our other comrades, who were separated from us, had not been able to join us. Some of them were obliged to cross the river by swimming; others ran into the forest; and one only, found by the enemy, was killed. That battle, with so many dangers, and with so brilliant a result, gave much confidence to our troops, and to the inhabitants of that coast, who had been for a long time exposed to the inroads of that adroit and enter-prising enemy, Maringue.

We celebrated the victory, rejoicing at our deliverance from a tempest of no small severity. At an estancia, twelve miles distant, when the news of the engagement was received, a young lady inquired, with a pallid cheek and evident anxiety, whether Garibaldi was alive. When I was informed of this, I rejoiced at it more than at the victory itself. Yes! Beautiful daughter of America! (for she was a native of the Province of Rio Grande,) I was proud and happy to enjoy your friendship, though the destined bride of another. Fate reserved for me another Brazilian female—to me the only one in the world whom I now lament, and for whom I shall weep all my days. She knew me when I was in misfortune; and her interest in me, stronger than any merit of my own, conquered her for me, and united us for ever.

3

CHAPTER VIII.

THE Lake or Lagoon Dos Patos is about 45 leagues in length, or 135 miles, and from eleven to twenty miles in medium width. Near its mouth, on the right shore, stands a strong place, called Southern Rio Grande, while Northern Rio Grande is on the opposite side. Both are fortified towns, and were then in possession of the Imperialists, as well as Porto Alegre. The enemy were therefore masters of the lake by water. It was thought impossible for the Republicans to pass through the outlet which leads from the lake to the sea, and as that was the only water passage, we were obliged to prepare to effect a way of communication by land. This could be done only by transporting the launches on carts over the intermediate country. In the northern part of the lake is a deep bay, called Cassibani, which takes its name from a small river that empties in at its further side. That bay was chosen as the place for landing the launches; and the operation was performed on the right bank. An inhabitant of that part of the province, named De Abrea, had prepared wheels of great solidity, connected two and two by axles, proportioned to the weight of the vessels. About two hundred domestic oxen were then collected, with the assistance of the neighboring inhabitants, and, by their labor, the launches were drawn to the shore and got into the water, being carried on wheels, placed at proportionate distances from each other. Care, however, was taken to keep them in such positions that the centre of gravity should be preserved, by supporting the vessels laterally, without disturbing the free action of the wheels. Very strong ropes were, of course, provided, to attach the oxen to the wheels.

Thus the vessels of the Republican squadron started off, navigating across the fields. The oxen worked well, they being well placed and prepared for drawing freely in the most convenient manner. They travelled a distance of fifty-four miles without any difficulty, presenting a curious and unprecedented spectacle in those regions. On the shore of Lake Tramandai the launches were taken from the carts and put into the water, and then loaded with necessaries and rigged for sailing.

Lake Tramandai, which is formed by the streams falling from the chain of Espenasso, empties into the Atlantic, but is very shallow, having only about four feet of water at high tide; besides, on that coast, which is very open and all alluvial, the sea is never tranquil, even in the most favorable weather : but the numerous breakers incessantly stun the ear, and from a distance of many miles their roar sounds like peals of thunder.

Being ready to sail, we awaited the hour of the tide and then ventured out, about four o'clock in the afternoon. In those circumstances, practical skill in guiding vessels among breakers was of great value, and without it it is hard to say how we could ever have succeeded in getting through them, for the propitious hour of the tide was passed, and the water was not deep enough. However, notwithstanding this, at the beginning of the night our exertions were crowned with entire success, and we cast anchor in the open sea, outside of the furious breakers. It should be known here, and borne in mind, that no vessel of any kind had ever before passed out from the mouth of the Tramandai. At about eight in the evening we departed from that place, and at three in the afternoon of the following day were wrecked at the mouth of the Arevingua, with the loss of sixteen of the company in the Atlantic, and with the destruction of the launch Rio Pardo, which was under my command, in the terrible breakers of that coast. The particulars of that sad disaster were as follows :

Early in the evening the wind threatened from the south, preparing for a storm, and beginning to blow with violence. We followed the coast. The launch Rio Pardo, with thirty men on board, a twelve pounder on a pivot, and some extra rigging, taken for precaution, as I was unacquainted with that navigation, seemed strong and well-prepared for us to sail towards the enemy's country. But our vessels lay deep in the water, and sometimes sank so low into the sea, that they were in danger of foundering. They would occasionally remain several minutes under the waves. I determined to approach the land and find out where we were; but, the winds and waves increasing, we had no choice, and were compelled to stand off again, and were soon involved in the frightful breakers. I was at that moment on the top of the mast, hoping to discover some point of the coast less dangerous to approach. By a sudden turn the vessel was rolled violently to starboard, and I was thrown some distance overboard. Although in such a perilous situation, I did not even think of death; but, knowing I had many companions who were not seamen and were suffering from sea sickness, I endeavored to collect as many oars and other buoyant objects as possible, and brought them near the vessel, advising each man to take one to assist him in reaching the shore.

The first one who came near to me, holding to a shroud, was Eduardo Mutru; and to him I gave a dead-light, recommending to him not to let go of it on any account. Carniglia, the courageous man who was at the helm at the moment of the catastrophe, remained confined to the vessel on the windward side, being held down in such a manner, by a Calmuc jacket

which confined his limbs, that he could not free himself. He made me a sign that he wanted my assistance, and I sprang forward to relieve my dear friend.
I had in the pocket of my trowsers a small knife with
a handle; this I took, and with all the strength I was
master of, began to cut the collar, which was made of
velvet. I had just divided it when the miserable
instrument broke,—a surge came over us, and sunk the
vessel and all that it contained.

I struck the bottom of the sea, like a shot; and the
waters, which washed violently around me like whirlpools, half-suffocated me. I rose again: but my unfortunate friend was gone for ever! A portion of the
crew I found dispersed, and making every exertion to
gain the coast by swimming. I succeeded among the
first; and the next thing, after setting my feet upon
the land, was to turn and discover the situation of my
comrades. Eduardo appeared, at a short distance.
He had left the dead-light which I had given him, or,
as is more probable, the violence of the waves had torn
it from his grasp, and was struggling alone, with an
appearance that indicated that he was reduced to an
extremity. I loved Eduardo like a brother, and was
affected beyond measure at his condition. Ah! I was
sensitive in those days! My heart had never been
hardened; and I was generous. I rushed towards my
dear friend, reaching out to him the piece of wood
which had saved me on my way to the shore. I had
got very near him; and, excited by the importance of

the undertaking, should have saved him : but a surge rolled over us both ; and I was under water for a moment. I rallied, and called out, not seeing him appear ; I called in desperation,—but in vain. The friend dear to my heart was sunk in the waves of that ocean which he had not feared, in his desire to join with me in serving the cause of mankind. Another martyr to Italian liberty, without a stone, in a foreign land !

The bodies of sixteen of my companions, drowned in the sea, were transported a distance of thirty miles, to the northern coast, and buried in its immense sands. Several of the remainder were brought to land. There were seven Italians. I can mention Luigi Carniglia, Eduardo Mutru, Luigi Stadirini, Giovanni D.,—but three other names I do not remember. Some were good swimmers. In vain I looked among those who were saved, to discover any Italian faces. All my countrymen were dead. My feelings overpowered me. The world appeared to me like a desert. Many of the company who were neither seamen nor swimmers were saved.

I found a barrel of brandy, which I thought a valuable acquisition, and told Manuel Rodriguez to open it, and give some to each of the survivors, to invigorate them. Efforts were made to open the cask : but, fatigued as we all were, much time was spent in performing the task ; and, in the mean time, the men became so much chilled, that they might have perished, if the thought had not occurred to me to set them all running, in order to restore their strength by keeping their blood in circulation. " Come, let us run !" I said to them ; and then, starting off myself and running as fast as I could towards the north, they would follow me, until unable to go further. I repeated this until I thought they no longer required exercise ; and am sure that my own life, at least, was saved by the expedient, —for without the effort, I must have fallen a victim to fatigue and cold. Thus running along the shore, we encouraged each other, to go further and further. It made a bend, at some distance ; and on the inner side is the Arasingua, which runs almost parallel with the sea at that place, to its mouth, half a mile distant. We then followed the right bank ; and, after going about four miles, found an inhabited house, where we were received with the greatest hospitality.

The Seival, our other launch, commanded by Griggs, being of a different construction from the Rio Pardo, was better able to sustain itself, although but little larger, against the violence of the storm, and had held on her course.

CHAPTER IX.

THAT part of the Province of St. Catharine where
we had been shipwrecked, fortunately had risen in insurrection against the empire on receiving the news of
the approach of the Republican forces ; and therefore
we were well received, found friends, were feasted,
and at once obtained everything necessary, at least
everything which those good people had to offer. We
were soon furnished with what we needed to enable
us to join the vanguard of Canabarro, commanded by
Colonel Terceira, which was setting off on a rapid
march, to surprise Laguna. And, indeed, the enterprise was very successful. The garrison of that little
city, consisting of about four hundred men, took up a
forced march in retreat ; and three small vessels of war
surrendered after a short resistance. I went with my
shipwrecked sailors on board the sloop Itaparica, which
had seven guns. Fortune smiled so much on the Republicans in those first days of the revolution, that it

3*   (67)

seemed as if Providence was pleased to grant us success. The Imperialists, not knowing and not believing that such an expedition could be sent so suddenly to Laguna, but having information that an invasion was meditated by us, had a supply of arms and ammunition then on the way, which, with soldiers and everything, fell into our hands. The inhabitants received us like brothers and liberators : a character which we well merited, and which we sustained during our stay among those very kind and good people.

Canabarro, having fixed his head-quarters in the city of Laguna, called by the Republicans Villa Juliana, (because our entrance was made in July,) promised to establish a Provincial Representative Government, the first president of which was a reverend priest, who had great influence among the people. Rosetti, with the title of Secretary of the Government, was in fact the soul of it. And Rosetti, in truth, was formed for such a station.

At that time occurred one of the most important events of my life. I had never thought of matrimony, but had considered myself incapable of it from being of too independent a disposition, and too much inclined to adventure. To have a wife and children appeared to me decidedly repulsive, as I had devoted my whole life to one principle, which, however good it might be, could not leave me the quietness necessary to the father of a family. But my destiny guided me in a different direction from what I had designed for my-

self. By the loss of Luigi Carniglia, Eduardo and
my other comrades, I was left in a state of complete
isolation, and felt as if alone in the world. Not one
of those friends of my heart remained. I felt the
greatest possible need of them. All the friends I now
had were new ones: good, it is true, but not one of
them really an intimate one. And this change had
been made so unexpectedly, and in so terrible a manner,
that it was impossible to overcome the impressions it
had made upon my feelings. I felt the want of some
one to love me, and a desire that such a one might be
very soon supplied, as my present state of mind seemed
insupportable.

Rosetti was a brother to me: but he could not live
with me, and I could see him but rarely. I desired a
friend of a different character ; for, although still
young, I had considerable knowledge of men, and
knew enough to understand what was necessary for
me in a true friend. One of the other sex, I thought
must supply the vacant place, for I had always regarded woman as the most perfect of creatures, and
believe it far easier to find a loving heart among that
sex.

I walked the deck of the Itaparica, with my mind
revolving these things, and finally came to the conclu-
sion to seek for some lady possessing the character
which I desired. I one day cast a casual glance at
a house in the Burra, (the eastern part of the entrance
of the Jayuna,) and there observed a young female

whose appearance struck me as having something
very extraordinary. So powerful was the impression
made upon me at the moment, though from some cause
which I was not able fully to ascertain, that I gave
orders and was transported towards the house. But
then I knew of no one to whom I could apply for an
introduction. I soon, however, met with a person, an
inhabitant of the town, who had been acquainted with
me from the time of arrival. I soon received an invitation to take coffee with his family, and the first person who entered was the lady whose appearance had
so mysteriously but irresistibly drawn me to the place.
I saluted her; we were soon acquainted; and I found
that the hidden treasure which I had discovered was
of rare and inestimable worth. But I have since reproached myself for removing her from her peaceful
native retirement to scenes of danger, toil and suffering. I felt most deeply self-reproach on that day when,
at the mouth of the Po, having landed, in our retreat
from an Austrian squadron, while still hoping to restore her to life, on taking her pulse I found her a
corpse, and sang the hymn of despair. I prayed for
forgiveness, for I thought of the sin of taking her
from her home.

Little or nothing of importance, after this, took
place in the Lagoon. The building of our launches
was commenced; and the materials were obtained
from the remains of the prizes, and by the assistance
of the neighboring inhabitants, who were always

friendly, and forward in aiding me. Two launches having been completed and armed, the band were called to Itaparica, to coöperate with the army, then besieging the capital of the province, Porto Allegre. The army accomplished nothing ; and the band were unable to effect anything all the time they spent in that part of the Laguna. An expedition was contemplated in the province of St. Catherine ; I was called to join it, and General Canabarro was to accompany me. The two smaller launches remained in the lake, under the command of Zefferino d'Ubrea ; and I went with two others, with the division of Canabarro, which was to appear by land, while I was to approach by water.

I was accompanied by my inseparable friend, John Griggs, and had with me a chosen part of my band, who had assisted in building the launches.

The three vessels which were armed, and destined to make an excursion on the ocean, were the Rio Pardo, which was under my command, and the Casapava, under Griggs—both schooners—and lastly, the Seival, which had come from Rio Grande, commanded by the Italian, Lorenzo. The mouth of the Lagoon was blockaded by Imperial vessels of war ; but we went out by night, without falling in with any of them, and steered north. When we had reached the latitude of Santos, we met an Imperial corvette, which chased us two days in vain,—when we approached the Island of Abrigo, where we captured two Sumacas. This is a kind of vessel, so named by the Brazilians, being a sort of sloop. We then proceeded on the cruise, and took several other prizes. After eight days' sailing we returned towards the Lagoon.

I had conceived a singular presentiment of the state of things in that region, because, before my departure, the people of St. Catherine's had begun to show a bad humor, and it was known that a strong corps of troops was approaching, commanded by General Andrea, who was famous for precipitation, and his atrocious system of warfare, which made him much feared. When off St. Catherine's, on our return, we met a Brazilian patachio, which is a sort of brig-schooner,—the Rio Pardo and the Seival being to-gether, the Casapava having parted company a few nights before, when it was very dark.

We were discovered; and there was no escape We therefore attacked them, and opening a fire. The enemy replied bravely; but the action could produce but little effect, because the sea was very rough. The result, however, was the loss of several of our prizes, the commanders of some of which, being frightened by the superior force of the enemy, struck their flags, while others steered for the neighboring coast. Only one of the prizes was saved, that commanded by the brave Ignacio Bilbao, which went ashore in the port of Imbituba, and remained in our possession. The Seival had her gun dismounted in the engagement, and having sprung aleak, took the same direction, and I was obliged to abandon the prizes.

We entered Imbituba with a northerly wind, which changed to the south in the night, and thus rendered it impossible to enter the Lagoon. It was to be presumed that we would be attacked by the Imperial vessels stationed at the island of St. Catherine's, because information would be carried to them by that with which we had the engagement. It was therefore necessary to make preparations; and the Scival's dismounted gun was placed on a promontory which forms the bay on the eastern side, and a battery was formed of gabions. At daylight three Imperial vessels were discovered approaching. The Rio Pardo, which was at anchor at the bottom of the bay, commenced the action, which was rather a singular one, the Imperialists being in incomparably superior force. The enemy, being favored by the wind in manœuvring, kept under sail, and gave a furious fire, from favorable positions, all of them upon my one poor little schooner. She, however, maintained the fight with resolution, and at close quarters,—even carbines being used on both sides.

But the injuries done were in inverse proportion to the forces of the two parties; for the Republican vessel was soon strewn with dead bodies, while the hull was riddled and the spars destroyed. We had resolved to fight to the last; and this resolution was increased by the Brazilian Amazon on board. My wife not only refused to land, but took an active part in the engagement. If the crew fought with resolution, they

received no little aid from the brave Manuel Rodriguez, who commanded the battery, and kept up a
well-directed and effective fire. The enemy were very
determined, but operated chiefly against the schooner ;
and I several times believed, as they came up, that
they were going to board us,—and was prepared for
everything, except to submit.

At length, after several hours spent in active fight,
the enemy retired, on account, as was said, of the
death of the commander of the Bella Americana, one of
their vessels. We spent the remainder of the day in
burying our dead and in repairing our greatest damages.

During the following day the enemy remained at a
distance, and we made preparations for fighting, and
also for escape by sailing to the Lagoon, the wind being
then more favorable.

[Here occurs a blank in our manuscript.—*Translator.*]

CHAPTER X.

CHANGES were expected to take place at Laguna on
the approach of the enemy, who were very strong on
land ; and little good-will shown by St. Catherine's
induced some of the towns to rise against the Republican authority. Among these was the town of Jamaica,
a place situated at the extremity of the lake. Canabarro gave me a peremptory charge to reduce it, and,
as a punishment, to sack it. The garrison had made
preparations for defence towards the water ; but I
landed at the distance of three miles, and attacked
them unexpectedly from the mountains. The garrison
being discomfited and put to flight, the troops under
my command were soon in possession of the town. I
wish, for myself, and for every other person who has
not forgotten to be a man, to be exempt from the necessity of witnessing the sack of a town. A long and
minute description would not be sufficient to give a
just idea of the baseness and wickedness of such a
deed   May God save me from such a spectacle here-

4   65)

after ! I never spent a day of such wretchedness and in such lamentation. I was filled with horror; and the fatigue I endured in restraining personal violence was excessive. As for preventing robbery, that was impossible. A terrible state of disorder prevailed. The authority of a commander availed nothing; nor could all the exertions made by myself and a few officers control their unbridled cupidity. It had no effect to threaten them that the enemy would return to the fight in much greater numbers, and if they should take them by surprise, disbanded and intoxicated, would make a sacrifice of them,—though that was true to the letter. Nothing would prevent them from engaging in a general scene of pillage. The town, though small, unfortunately contained a vast quantity of spirits; and drunkenness soon became general. The men who were with me were new levies, whom I did not know, and wholly undisciplined. I am sure that if even fifty of the enemy had appeared, in those circumstances, we should have been lost.

After a long time, by threats, blows, and some wounds, those wild beasts were marched out and embarked; several pipes of spirits were shipped for the division, and we returned to the Lagoon, while the Republican vanguard was retiring before the enemy, who were advancing with celerity, and very strong.

When we reached the Lagoon, we took the baggage across to the right shore.

That day I had much to do; for, if the men were

not very numerous, there were many embarrassments, and many horses to be taken care of. And besides, the outlet of the Lagoon was narrow at the entrance, the current was strong, and when this was not found, the shores were not distant. I had to labor, therefore, from morning until near noon, to get the division over, and then stood near the bar to observe the enemy's vessels, which were advancing in combination with the land forces with a great number of troops on board. Before ascending the mountain, I had already sent information to the General that the enemy were preparing to force the passage of the bar, having been able to discover the enemy's vessels while I was effecting the transport. Having reached the other side, I satisfied myself of the fact. The enemy had twenty-two vessels, all adapted to the entrance. I then repeated the message; but either the General was doubtful, or his men wanted to eat or to rest. The fact was, that not a man arrived in time to assist in operating at the point where our infantry had been posted, and where we might have made great havoc with the enemy. Resistance was made by the battery situated on the eastern point, commanded by the brave Captain Capotto; but, in consequence of the want of practice on the part of the cannoniers, very little damage was done. The same result was experienced by the three vessels under my command, the crews of which were very small, many of the men that day being on land; and thus some would rest, and others would not expose themselves to the tremendous battle which was preparing. I was at my post in the Rio Par-lo; and my wife, the incomparable Anita, fired the first shot, putting the match to the gun with her own hand, and animating with her voice the timid and the hesitating.

The battle was short, but a murderous one. Not many were killed, because very few were on board; but I was the only officer in the three vessels left alive. All the enemy's squadron entered, making a tremendous fire, favored by the wind and the current flowing in, by which their velocity was much increased, and anchored at the distance of a cannon-shot from our vessels, still keeping up their cannonade. I asked Canabarro for men to continue the battle; but received, in answer, an order to destroy the vessels and retire, with all the remainder that could be landed. I had sent Anna with the message, directing her to remain on shore; but she returned on board with the answer, showing a coolness and courage which excited my astonishment and highest admiration. To her boldness and exertions was due the saving of the ammunition, which was safely landed. When this was effected, I remained alone on board, having yet to perform the last act of setting the little flotilla on fire. The enemy still continued their severe cannonade. I had to contemplate a terrible spectacle on every vessel, as I visited them all in succession, the decks being strewn with the dead. Captain Enrique, of the Taparica, from Laguna, was found shot through the breast with a grape shot; Griggs, commander of the Cassapava, had been cut in two by a shot, and his trunk was standing against the bulwarks, his face retaining its natural rubicund look, so that he seemed as if living. A few moments afterwards their bodies were sunk in the water : those victims of the empire were lost to human sight.

Night came on, as I collected the survivors, and marched behind the division, on the retreat for Rio Grande, by the same road which they had trodden a few months before, with their hearts filled with hope and confident of victory.

Among the many sufferings of my stormy life, I have not been without happy moments; and among them, I count that in which, at the head of the few men remaining to me after numerous conflicts, and who had gained the character of bravery, I first mounted, and commenced my march, with my wife at my side, in a career which had always attractions for me, even greater than that of the sea. It seemed to me of little importance that my entire property was that which I carried, and that I was in the service of a poor republic, unable to pay anybody. I had a sabre and a carbine, which I carried on the front of my saddle. My wife was my treasure, and no less fervent in the cause of the people than myself; and she looked upon battles as an amusement, and the inconveniences of a life in the field as a pastime.

Then, whatever might happen, I was looked upon with smiles; and the more wild the extensive and desert American plains appeared, the more beautiful and delightful they seemed to our eyes. I thought myself in the performance of my duty, in encountering and overcoming the dangers to which I exposed myself, as the object I had in view was the good of men who needed my aid.

We reached Las Torres, the boundary of the two neighboring provinces, where we established our camp. The enemy contented themselves with being masters of the Lagoon, and did not proceed beyond. But, in combination with the division of Andrea, the division of Acunha advanced by the Serra, having recently come from the province of St. Paul, and being on the way for the Cima da Serra, (meaning the top of the mountains,) a department belonging to Rio Grande. The Serrans, overwhelmed by a superior force, asked assistance of General Canabarro; and he arranged an expedition for their aid, under the command of General Terceira. I, with my companions, formed a part of it; and, having joined the Serrans, who were under Colonel Acunha, we completely beat that division at Santa Victoria. The General was lost in the river Pelotas, and the greater part of his troops were made prisoners.

That victory brought the three provinces of Lages, Vaccaria, and Cima da Serra, under the republic; and, a few days after, the conquerors entered Lages in triumph.

In the meantime the invasion by the Imperialists had restored their party to power in the province of Missiones ; and Colonel Mello, the Imperial General, had increased his corps in that province to about five hundred men. General Bento Manuel, who was to have fought him, was unable, because he had retreated ; and he contented himself with sending Lieutenant-Colonel Portinhos in pursuit of Mello, who was marching in the direction of San Pablo. The position in which I was then placed gave us an opportunity not only to oppose Mello, but also to exterminate his force. But such was not the event.

Colonel Terceira being uncertain whether the enemy would come by Vaccaria, or by the Caritibani, divided his forces into two, sending Colonel Aranha, with the good cavalry of the Serra, to Vaccaria, and marching towards the Caritibani with the infantry, and a part of the cavalry, chiefly composed of prisoners. It was by that point that the enemy approached. This division of the forces proved fatal. Their recent victory, the ardent feelings of the corps, and the information received concerning the enemy, which represented their numbers and spirit as less than they really were, led to their despising them too much.

After a three days' march we reached Caritibani, and went round by the pass of Maromba, by which it was supposed the enemy would march. Guards were placed in the Pass, and at other points, where they were thought necessary. Towards midnight the

guards at the pass were attacked, and compelled to
retreat, so that they had scarcely time to escape after
firing a few shots.   From that moment until the
break of day, the Republican troops stood ready for
action ; and it was not long after that hour that the
enemy appeared, having crossed the river with their
whole force, and drawn up near it ready for action.

Any other officer than Terceira, on seeing their
superiority, would have hastened to effect a junction
with the column of Aranha, and would have occupied
the enemy until he could have accomplished it.   But
the ardent Republican feared that the enemy might
escape him, and deprive him of an opportunity to fight.
He therefore pressed on to the encounter, although the
enemy were in an advantageous position.   Of that
position they took advantage, having formed their line
of battle on a hill of considerable height, opposite
which was a very deep valley, obstructed with thick
bushes.   I had covered our flanks with several platoons of cavalry, which they did not see.   Terceira
ordered to attack, with a band of infantry, taking
advantage of the obstacles in the valley.   The attack
was made, and the enemy made a feint of retreating ;
but, while the whole Republican body, after passing
the valley, was pursuing the enemy under the hill,
within musket-shot, it was charged in flank by a
squadron which had been concealed on the right flank
of the enemy, obliged to retreat in disorder, and to
concentrate anew.   In that encounter fell one of the

bravest of my officers, Manuel N., who was very dear to me. The troops, being now reinforced, and sent forward with greater impetus and resolution, the enemy finally retired, and took up their retreat, leaving one of their men dead on the field.

There were not many wounded on either side, for very few had taken part in the action. The enemy, however, retreated precipitately, and the Republicans pursued them to Aube ; but the infantry were not able to overtake them in nine miles, although they did their utmost to accelerate their march. In the vicinity of the Pass of Maromba, the commander of the Republican vanguard, Major Jacinto, informed the Colonel that the enemy were crossing the Ganado and the Cavaladas,* with indications that they would continue their retreat and not recover from their panic. The brave Terceira did not hesitate for a moment, but ordered the cavalry to proceed on the gallop, and directed me to follow with the infantry as fast as possible.

The watchful enemy, however, had only manœuvred to deceive us, and by the precipitation of their march had got in an advantageous position of which we were not aware, concealed by the ground. One of our platoons had been placed far in advance, and two others

---

* "Ganado" means herds of cattle, and " Cavaladas" herds of horses, which animals abound in those regions, living in the rich pastures. The cattle afford the only food for soldiers, and the horses are indispensable for cavalry—the best troops in South America.

4

near it, but the infantry imprudently left far behind. The enemy suddenly extended their right and made his appearance on our left, running out from a valley which had a small declivity. They bore down upon the Republican platoon with their lances, and gave them this first notice of their error, which there was not time to repair. Attacked in flank, they were completely discomfited. The other platoons of cavalry shared the same fate, notwithstanding the courage and efforts of Terceira and several brave Rio Grande officers. Being taken in detail, they opposed little resistance; and in a short time all were scattered, flying and completely broken. To be so far with the infantry was very painful to me, and the more so because the materials of which it was composed were not good, the greater part being men who had been prisoners in Santa Victoria. I therefore hastened on the infantry as fast as possible to join in the fight, but in vain. Having reached an elevation, I witnessed the slaughter of my friends, and knew there was no time to do anything to turn the tide, and therefore resolved to save as many as possible.

I called to about a dozen of my old companions, whom I saw and recognized; and, on hearing my voice, they hastened towards me. I left an officer, to remain in charge of the body of infantry (Major Peixotto,) and then, with that small band, I took a position, partly sheltered by a few bushes, on an elevated spot of ground. There we began to make a stand against

the enemy, and to teach them that they were not victorious everywhere. In an attack upon us, several
companies of cavalry were repulsed, although they
made great efforts and displayed much courage. The
infantry at last joined us in our position, and then the
defence became powerful, and to the enemy terrible
and murderous.

CHAPTER XI.

IN the meantime, strong in my position, and having
now a band of seventy-three, I fought the enemy with
advantage. As the Impérialists were destitute of infantry, they had little desire to engage with troops of
that arm. Notwithstanding the advantageous ground
possessed by us, however, it was necessary to seek a
more secure cover, to prevent the victorious enemy
from bringing together all their forces, and to avoid
giving time for the courage of the defenders to cool.
I observed a cappon, or island of trees, which was in
sight, at about the distance of a mile, and undertook
a retreat in that direction. The enemy manœuvred
to interrupt us, and every few moments charged with
the advantage of the ground. In such circumstances
it proved highly important that my officers were armed
with carbines; and, as they were all good soldiers,
they repelled the enemy's charges with unshaken firmness. Thus the remains of our conquered party reached
the cappon, where the enemy offered us no further
molestation; while we penetrated a little distance into

(76)

the wood, chose a cleared spot, and collecting together, with our arms ready, waited for night. The enemy were heard calling out to us " Surrender ! Surrender ! " We kept silence and returned no answer.

Night at length came on ; and I made preparations for departure. A few wounded men, who were of our number, presented the greatest difficulty. Among them was Major Peixotto, who had received a ball in his foot. Near ten o'clock in the evening, when the wounded had been accommodated in the best manner possible, the march was commenced, by proceeding along the skirts of the cappon, which we left on the right, endeavoring to find the borders of the Matto, or forest. That forest, perhaps the largest in the world, extends from the alluvial regions of the Plata to those of the Amazon, crowning the crest of the Serra de Espinasso, which forms the backbone of Brazil, over an extent of thirty-four degrees of latitude. The number of degrees of longitude which it embraces we are unable to give. In the midst of that immense wilderness are situated the three departments of Cima da Serra, Vaccaria and Lages, which are surrounded by the forests. The scene of our dangerous operations was now Caritibani, in the last named department, a place which derived its name from Caritiba, a place in the province of Santa Caterina, (St. Catharine,) from which the inhabitants came.

In order to reach the forest, the troops moved along the side of the *cappon*, intending to take the course towards Lages, to find the corps of Aranha, from which they were unfortunately separated. One of those things occurred on their issuing from the wood, which prove how far man is the child of circumstances, and what effect may be produced by a panic, even on the most intrepid soldiers. The Republicans were marching in silence ; and, as may be supposed, prepared for action, in case the enemy should appear in an attitude of opposing them. A horse, which happened to be in that part of the wood, on hearing the little noise made by the cautious soldiers in their march, took to flight, and ran away. One voice was heard to exclaim : " The enemy !" and, in a moment, all those seventy-three men, who had so lately most valiantly fought five hundred, rushed at once into the thickest of the forest ; and, so far did they become separated and scattered, in that moment of fear, that it would have taken many hours to collect them again ; and, as it was impossible for us to wait long enough, several were left behind and lost. The others pursued their way with me ; and when daybreak appeared, we found ourselves on the long wished-for border of the forest, and issuing in the direction of Lages. The next day the enemy approached, but did not reach us. The day of battle was terrible, for its labors, dangers and troubles ; but we fought, and that idea overpowered every other ; but in the forest, where meat, the accustomed food, was in fact wanting, and where no other kind could be obtained, we remained four days without finding anything to eat except the roots of plants. The fatigue we endured was indescribable, in following a retreat where there were no paths, and where nature incomparably prolific and robust, had reared up colossal pines in the immense woods, and the gigantic taquara, (a kind of cane,) which formed insuperable barriers in many places. Many of the company were discouraged, some deserted, and it was a great task, first to collect them, and then to convince them that it was better to accompany the corps than to desert it, though they might absent themselves, if they preferred it, as they should be free to do as they pleased. This manner of proceeding with them proved perfectly successful. From that moment there was no more desertion ; and the hope of safety began to arise in the hearts of the troops.

On the fifth day after the battle we reached the entrance of the Piccada, (a narrow path cut through the forest,) where we found a house and made a halt, killing two oxen. We made two prisoners in the house, who belonged to the enemy, and who had fought us. We then continued our way to Lages, which we reached after a day's march through the rain.

The town of Lages, which had made such rejoicing on our arrival as conquerors, had changed its flag on hearing of our disasters ; and some of the boldest of the inhabitants had established the imperial system. On our approach they fled ; and, as most of them were merchants, numbers left their stores filled with everything necessary to restore the needy soldiers ; and thus their condition was greatly improved.   Terceira wrote to Aranha, in the mean time, ordering him to concentrate again ; as he had notice at that time of the arrival of Lieutenant Colonel Tartinho, who had been sent by Bento Manuel in pursuit of the forces of Mello.

CHAPTER XII.

I HAVE served the cause of the people in America, and
served it with sincerity, as I everywhere fought against
absolutism. Being warmly attached to the system corresponding with my convictions, I was equally opposed
in my feelings to the opposite system. I have always
rather pitied than hated men who have been led to
selfishness by misfortune ; and, when now viewing the
scenes I passed through, from a far distant country,
and long after their occurrence, the accounts contained
in the succeeding pages may be regarded as impartial,
with the care which has been taken in recording facts,
reviewing occurrences, and making allowances for
men and circumstances.

It may be unhesitatingly asserted that " *The Sons
of the Continent*," (the name given to the people of Rio
Grande,) were most ardent and intrepid men. This

4*   (81)

character I claim for them, after having had many opportunities to form a correct opinion. The occupation
of Lages by our troops was therefore a very bold step,
with the intention of defending it against an enemy
ten times superior and victorious, and divided from
them only by the river Canoas, which could not be defended, and far from any auxiliaries who might have
wished to aid the Republicans. Many days passed before the junction of Aranha and Portinho ; and, during
all that time, the enemy were kept at bay by a small
band of men. The reinforcements had no sooner arrived, than the Republicans marched resolutely against
the enemy : but the Imperialists did not accept the
offer of a battle, but retired when we approached, making a stand in the Province of San Paolo, where they
were to be joined by large reinforcements of infantry
and cavalry. The Republicans then felt the defect
and the evils of being composed chiefly of men brave
indeed, but who did not know the importance of keeping their ranks, except when the enemy appeared, and
relaxed in discipline whenever they were either far
distant, or remained near without showing inclination
for a speedy battle.

That fault was almost their ruin, and a more enter-
prising enemy would have known how to take advantage of it. The Serranos, (or people of the neighboring
mountains,) began to leave the files, and throw their
lazos, not only over their own horses, but over those
belonging to the division. Those of Portinho, (the

people of the Province of Missions,) followed their example ; and the force was soon so far reduced, that they were obliged to abandon Lages, and retire to the province of Rio Grande, fearing an attack from the enemy. The rest of the forces, being thus weakened, and in want of necessaries, especially clothing, which was quite indispensable in consequence of the commencement of cold wheater so early in those elevated regions, began to lose their spirits, and demanded, with a loud voice, to return to their homes. Colonel Terceira was then obliged to yield to so many necessities, and ordered me to descend the Serra and rejoin the army, while he prepared to follow me.

That descent was arduous, in consequence of the difficult roads, and the decided hostility of the inhabitants, who were enemies of the Republicans. I proceeded by the Piccada de Peluffo. The troops were only about sixty in number, and they had to confront terrible ambuscades ; but such were their indomitable boldness and perseverance, that they passed in safety. Although the path was very narrow, and everywhere overshadowed by a very thick forest, the enemy, being natives of the country, and therefore perfectly acquainted with every place, chose the most thorny spots for their ambushes, rushed out with fury and tremendous cries upon the Republican troops, who in return poured in their volleys of musketry, and used their sabres. At length, the vigor and perseverance of the latter so far intimidated the mountaineers, that they killed but one horse, and only slightly wounded a few men.

We arrived at the head-quarters, in Malacara, distant twelve miles from Porto Allegre, where was the President, Bento Gonzales, then General-in-chief.

The Republican army were preparing to march. The enemy's army, after losing the battle of Rio Pardo, had recruited in Porto Allegre, and gone out, under command of the old general, Jorge, (George,) and had encamped on the bank of the Cahi, waiting for General Calderon to join him, who had left Rio Grande with a strong body of cavalry and was to effect a junction, by crossing the country. The same defect which has been mentioned above,—that is, the delusive security of the Republican troops when there was no enemy in sight,—facilitated those movements of the enemy : when General Netto, who commanded the country troops, had collected force enough to fight Calderon, the latter, having now joined the main body of the Imperial army, at Cahi, which was threatening the Republicans with superior numbers, while besieging, compelled them to raise the siege. It was indispensable to the President to join the division of Netto, in order to be in a condition to fight the enemy's army ; and that junction, being happily effected, greatly honored the military capacity of Bento Gonzales. They marched with the army from Malacara, taking the direction of San Leopoldo, passing within two miles of the enemy's army ; and in two days and nights, almost without eating, arrived in the neighborhood of Taguary, where they found General Netto, who had come to meet them.

The march had been made, as was just remarked, almost without eating ; and, as soon as the enemy had notice of the movement, they set off, at forced marches, to fight them. By rare fortune they overtook the Republicans when they had halted, and were engaged in cooking their meat,—the only food, as has been remarked, which armies in that country ever have to subsist upon. They were, therefore, obliged to desist, and defer their meal until they could effect the junction designed. They halted again at Pinheirino, six miles from Taguary, and made all the arrangements for a battle. The Republican army, consisting of five thousand cavalry and one thousand infantry, occupied the heights of Pinheirino ; the infantry being in the centre, under the command of the aged Colonel Crescenzio ; the right wing under General Netto ; and the left under General Canabarro. Both wings were wholly composed of cavalry, which, without exaggeration, was the best in the world, although ill-provided. The infantry was excellent; and the desire for fighting was strong and general. Colonel Joaõ Antonio commanded the reserve, which was a corps of artillery.

The enemy had four thousand infantry, and, it was said, three thousand cavalry, with a few pieces of artillery. They had taken positions on the other side of the bed of a little torrent, which divided the two armies ; and their force and position were not to be despised. They were the best troops of the empire, and commanded by a very skilful general, although advanced in years.

The enemy's general had marched in warm pursuit of the Republicans up to that place, and now made every arrangement for a regular attack. Two bat-talions of infantry had crossed the dry bed of the torrent ; and two pieces of artillery, placed on the bank, thundered upon the line of Republican cavalry. On their side, the brave men of the first brigade, under the command of Netto, had drawn their sabres, and waited only for the sound of the trumpet, to launch themselves upon the two battalions which were crossing over. Those warlike sons of the continent felt the certainty of victory. Netto and they had never been conquered. The infantry, échalloned by divisions, on the highest part of the hill, and covered by its verge, were crying out for battle. /The terrible lancers of Canabarro had already made a movement forward, confusing the right flank of the enemy, which was therefore obliged to change front in confusion. The brave freedmen, proud of their force, became more firm and resolute ; and that incomparable corps presented to view a forest of lances, being composed entirely of slaves liberated by the Republic, and chosen from the best horse-tamers in the province, and all of them blacks, even the superior officers. The enemy had never seen the backs of those true sons of liberty. Their lances, which were longer than the common measure, their ebony faces and robust limbs, strengthened by perennial and laborious exercise, and their perfect discipline, struck terror into the enemy./ The animating voice of the General-in-chief had been heard, as he rode along the lines: "Every one of you must fight for four men to-day!". These were the few and only words of that distinguished man, who possessed all the qualities of a great captain, except good fortune. Every heart seemed to feel the palpitation of war, and the confidence of victory. A more beautiful day, or a more splendid scene, was never beheld. The ground was scattered with a few low plants, and offered no obstacle to the view, so that everything was clearly visible, even the slightest movement, and, as it were, all under my feet. In a few minutes was to be decided the fate of the largest part of the American continent, with the destinies of a numerous people. Those bodies of men, so compact, so orderly and steady, in a few moments will be broken up, and some of them thrown into confusion and defeated. Soon, the blood, the mangled limbs, and the corpses of many of those young men will disfigure the beautiful fields. Yes: now all are waiting and panting for the signal of battle.——Yet in vain was all that preparation, vain the expectation; that field was not to be a field of slaughter.

The enemy's general, intimidated at the strong positions occupied by the Republicans, and by their

proud array, made his appearance, and had the two
battalions recalled from the opposite bank, to which
they had crossed without orders, and placed himself
on the defensive.   General Calderon was killed in
making a reconnaissance.   Was that the cause of the
irresolution of General Jorge?   As the Republicans
were not attacked, they ought to have attacked.   This
was the opinion of many; but would it have been
wise?   If they had been attacked in their fine positions, there would have been every probability of
victory; but to descend from them and meet the enemy
on equal ground, it would be necessary to cross the
bed of the torrent, which was somewhat rough and
difficult, although dry, and the superiority in numbers
of the enemy's infantry was by no means small.   In fine,
there was no battle, and the enemies remained all day
in sight of each other, with only a little skirmishing.

In the camp of the Republicans there was a scarcity
of meat, and the infantry especially were famishing.
But, what was still more insupportable, thirst also
prevailed, for there was no water.   But that people
are hardened by a life of privations.   No lamentations
were heard, except for the want of permission to
fight.   Oh, Italians! oh, for the day when you shall
be united and enduring like those children of the
desert.   The stranger shall not then trample upon
your soil; he shall not contaminate your air.   Italy
will then take her proper place among the first nations
of the earth.

That night the old general, Jorge, disappeared, and in the morning the enemy were nowhere to be seen on any side. The early mist remained until ten o'clock ; it then rose, and they were discovered in the strong positions of Taguary. Soon afterwards news arrived that their cavalry were crossing the river. The enemy, therefore, were retreating, and it was necessary to attack them. The Republicans made no hesitation, and the army marched, resolved on a battle. Only the enemy's cavalry, however, had crossed the river, assisted in the passage by several imperial vessels, but the infantry remained on the banks, protected by the woods, having taken the most advantageous positions. The second brigade of Republican infantry, composed of the second and third battalions, was destined to begin the attack. This was performed with all possible bravery, but the numbers of the enemy were very far superior, and those courageous soldiers, after performing feats of valor, were compelled to retire, supported by the first brigade, which consisted of the first battalion of marines and the artillery, who had no cannon.

That was a terrible battle between the infantry in the forest, where the reëchoing of the guns, and the frequent flashes among the thick clouds of smoke seemed like a raging tempest. Not less than five hundred men were wounded and killed on both sides ; and the dead bodies of the Republicans were found on the very bank of the river, to which they had driven

5

their enemies. But all this loss was of no use, for when the second brigade retired the conflict was suspended ; then night came on, and the enemy were able to complete their passage without interruption.

Among many brilliant qualities, General Bento Gonzales had a kind of indecision, the effect of the disasters which had successively befallen him in his enterprises. He would have wished that, because a brigade of infantry, disproportionately inferior in numbers, had thrown itself upon the enemy, the action should be closed by making not only all the infantry take part in it, but also the cavalry on foot.

Such a proceeding might indeed have given him a brilliant victory, if by making the enemy lose their footing it had thrown them into the river ; and such a result might not have been improbable. But the general was determined to adventure everything, and even the only infantry which the Republicans ever possessed. The fact is, that the battle was a real disaster to them, as they had not the ability to supply the loss of their brave infantry, while the enemy chiefly abounded in that kind of forces.

The enemy remained on the right bank of the Taguary, because they were almost wholly masters of the country. The Republicans repassed the road to Porto Allegre, to recommence the siege of that town. The condition of the Republic was now somewhat worse. The army recrossed to San Leopoldo, and then to Settembrino, and afterwards to Malacara, into the old camp. From that place, a few days after, they changed their encampment to Bella Vista ; and at the same time the General planned an operation, the result of which was to restore them to excellent positions.

CHAPTER XIII.

THE enemy, for the purpose of making excursions into
the country, had partly garrisoned with infantry the
strong places.   San Jose del Norte was in such a situation.   That place, which stands on the north shore
of the outlet of the Lake Dos Patos, was one of its
keys ; and the possession of it would have been sufficient to change the face of things.   The town was
taken, and the Republican troops gave themselves up
to pillage and riot.

In the meantime the Imperialists, having recovered
from their surprise, assembled in a strong quarter, and
made head.   The Republicans assaulted them and
were repulsed.   The combatants endeavored to renew the attack, but did not meet, or, if they met, they
were unfit for fighting.   Some had damaged their
muskets by breaking doors, and others had lost their
flints.   The enemy lost no time.   A few vessels of war
lay in the harbor.   They took positions and raked the

(92)

streets occupied by the Republicans, sent to Southern
Rio Grande for aid, and occupied the only fort which
they had not taken. The largest fort, called the Emperor's Fort, situated in the centre of the line of fortifications, and which had cost them a great assault,
was rendered useless by a tremendous explosion, which
killed and wounded a great number. In short, the
greatest triumph was changed, towards noon, to a
shameful retreat, almost to a flight. Good men wept
with anger and disappointment. The loss of the Republicans was comparatively immense. From that
time their infantry was a mere skeleton. A few cavalry belonged to the expedition, and they served as a
protection on the retreat. The division marched to
their barracks of Buena Vista, and I remained at San
Simon with the marine, which was reduced to about
fifty individuals, including officers and soldiers.

My object in staying at that place was to prepare
some canoes, (boats made of single trees,) and to open
communications with the other parts of the lake ; but,
in the months which I spent there, the canoes did not
make their appearance ; and for the reason that they
had existed only in idea. Instead of boats, I therefore
occupied myself with procuring horses, there being an
abundance of wild ones, which furnished much occupation to the sailors, who became so many knights,
though all of them did not manage their steeds with
superior dexterity. And San Simon is a very beautiful and spacious place, although at that time de-

stroyed and abandoned.   It was said to belong to an
exiled Count San Simon, or his exiled heirs, who had
left home because of opinions different from those of
the Republicans.   There being no masters there, we
strangers fed on the cattle and rode the horses.

At that place our first child was born, on the 10th of
September, 1840.   The young mother, although so short
a time before united to her martial husband, had already
passed through many trials and dangers.   After the
terrible affair with the Brazilian men of war, she had
accompanied me on the marches, and even in the battles
described in the preceding pages, and had endured great
fatigue and hunger, and had several falls from her
horse.   During her stay at the house of an inhabitant
of the place, she received the greatest kindness from
the family and their neighbors ; and I shall ever entertain to those who have shown kindness to me, and especially to my wife, "Sarò reconoscientissimo, a
quella buona gente, tutta la mia vita" (I shall be most
thankful to those good people all my life.)   It was of
the highest importance that she had the comforts of
that house and those friends at that time, for the mis-
eries suffered by the army then rose to their height,
and I was absolutely destitute of everything necessary
for my wife and little son ; and in order to procure
some clothes, I determined to make a journey to Settembrina, where I had several friends, particularly the
kind-hearted Blingini, who would cheerfully supply me
with some things I wished to procure for them.   I ac-

cordingly set out to cross the inundated fields of that part of the province, then all drenched by the rains. I travelled day after day in water up to my horse's belly, and crossed the Rossa Velha, (an old cultivated field,) where I met Captain Massimo, of the Free Lancers, who treated me like a true and good friend, as he was. He was posted for the guard of the Cavalladas. I arrived at that place at evening, in a heavy rain, and spent the night; and the next day the storm having increased, the good Captain determined to detain me at all hazards,—but I was too much in haste to accomplish my object, to be willing to defer my journey, and I set off again, in spite of every remonstrance, to brave the flood. After going a few miles, I heard several musket-shots in the direction of the place I had left, which raised some suspicion in my mind, but I could only go on. Having reached Settembrina, I bought some little articles of clothing, and set out on my return towards San Simon. When I had recrossed the Rossa Velha, I learned the cause of the firing I had heard, and the most melancholy accident which happened on the day of my departure.

Moringue, the man who surprised me at Camacua, had now surprised Captain Massimo, and notwithstanding a very brave resistance, left him dead, with almost all his thirty lancers of the garrison. Most of the horses, including the best of them, had been embarked, the remaining ones were almost all killed. Moringue executed the operation with vessels of war and infantry, and then reëmbarked the infantry, going himself by land towards Rio Grande del Norte, alarming all the little forces, which, thinking themselves safe, were scattered about that territory. Among these was my band of sailors, who were obliged to take their clubs and go into the woods, taking my wife with them, who mounted the saddle, to avoid the enemy, with her infant, then only twelve days old, although it was in the midst of the storm.

On my return I could not find any of my men, or any of the friends with whom I had left my family ; but I discovered them at length in the edge of a wood, where they remained without any certain news of the enemy. We went back to San Simon, where I remained some time, and then removed my camp to the left bank of the Capivari.

CHAPTER XIV.

THE river Capivari is formed by the confluence of the different outlets of numerous lakes which garnish the northern border of the Province of Rio Grande, between the sea-coast and the eastern side of the chain of Espinasso. It received its name from the Capivari, a species of amphibious animal, very common in the rivers of South America. We made two canoes, and in them made several voyages to the western shore of Lake Patos, transporting both men and provisions. These voyages we performed from the Capivari and the Sangrador de Abreu, one of the streams in that vicinity, which is an outlet of a pond, connecting it with a lake.

In the meantime the situation of the Republican army grew worse and worse. Every day their necessities became more pressing, while, at the same time, the difficulty of satisfying them became greater. The two battles of Taguare and Norte had destroyed the

5   (97)

infantry, so that the battalions had become mere skele-
tons.   Prevailing wants produced discontent, and that
led to desertions.   The inhabitants, as usually happens
in long wars, were wearied, and looked with indifference upon the forces of the two parties.   In such a
state of things the Imperialists made proposals for an
arrangement which, although advantageous, considering the circumstances of the Republicans, were not
acceptable and not accepted by the most generous
portion of the enemy.   Their rejection much increased the discontent of the extreme and disgusted party,
and finally the abandonment of the siege, and the
retreat were decisive.   The Canabarro division, of
which the marine formed a part, was to begin the
movement, and climb the passes of the Serra, occupied
by General Labattue.   Bento Gonzales, with the rest
of the army, was to march behind, covering the movements.

At that time died Rosetti, an irreparable loss to the
army, and especially to myself.   Having been left
with the Republican garrison of Settembrina, which
was to march last, he was surprised by the famous
Maringue ; and that incomparable Italian perished
fighting bravely.   Having fallen from his horse
wounded, he was called on to surrender,—but he sold
his life dearly.   There is not a spot of ground on
earth in which do not lie the bones of some generous
Italian, for whose sake Italy ought never to cease from
the struggle until free herself.   She will feel the want

of them in the day when she shall rise to drive the ravens from the corpses which they devour.

The retreat was commenced in the worst season, among the broken ridges of the mountain, in an almost unintermitted rain, and was the most disagreeable and terrible which I had ever seen. We had supplied ourselves with a few cows, which we brought with us, there being no animals among the toilsome paths which we were to travel, made impracticable by the rains. The numerous rivers were extremely swollen, and much of the baggage was carried away by the torrents. The troops marched in the rain, and without food ; encamped without food in the rain. Between one river and another, those who were appointed to keep near the cows, had meat, but the others were in a terrible condition, especially the poor infantry, for everything failed them except horse-flesh. There were some dreadful scenes. Many women followed the army, according to the custom of the country, and many children. But few of the latter came out of the forest, and some were picked up by the horsemen, one of whom, here and there, was fortunate enough to save his horse, and with him a poor little creature, left by its dead or dying mother, who had fallen a victim to hunger, fatigue, and cold.

Anna was much distressed by the apprehension of losing her little son, Menotti, who was saved with difficulty, and as if by a miracle. In the most difficult parts of the road, and in crossing rivers, I carried

my poor little child, then three months old, in a handkerchief tied round my neck, contriving to keep him
warm with my breath.   Of about a dozen animals—
horses and mules—with which we entered the woods,
some of them used for the saddle and some for baggage, there remained only two horses and two mules.
The others had tired, and were abandoned. To crown
our misfortunes, the guides had mistaken the road ;
and that was one of the reasons which induced us to
cross the terrible woods of Las Antas.   The word
"Anta" signifies a harmless animal, of the size of an
ass, whose flesh is exquisite, and whose hide serves for
making many strong and many ornamental articles.
This animal, however, I never had the fortune to see.
Although the troops continued to proceed, they could
not find the end of the piccada ; and I remained in
the woods, with two tired mules, and sent Anna,
with her servant and the child, to endeavor to find a
clear place where they might obtain some food for
themselves and the animals.   The two remaining
horses, which were used alternately, with the surprising courage of the mother, overcame every difficulty.
She succeeded in getting beyond the piccada, and
fortunately found some of the soldiers with a fire, a
very rare thing, and then not always to be obtained, on
account of the continued rain, and the miserable condition to which we were all reduced.   The men
warmed some cloths, took the infant and wrapped him
in them, and thus resuscitated him.   The poor mother

who had given up almost every hope of his life, took him again and cherished him with the tenderest care, while the good-hearted soldiers went to seek for some kind of food to restore the exhausted strength of the mother. I labored in vain to save the mules. Being left alone with them, I cut as many as I could of the leaves of the baguara, a species of cane, and gave them to eat; but it was of no use. I was obliged to abandon them, and seek to get out of the forest on foot, and exceedingly fatigued.

Nine days after entering it, the last of the division barely got through the piccada, and only a very few of the horses of the officers were saved. The enemy, who had preceded us in their flight, had left some artillery in the forest of the Antas, which the pursuers were unable to transport, for the want of means, and they were left buried in certain caverns—who knows for how long? In that woody region the storms seemed as if tired out; for, on getting into the open fields of the elevated plain, called the Cima da Serra (or top of the ridge), the troops found good weather. Some oxen, which were discovered there, afforded them a welcome supply of food, and made some amends for the sufferings they had passed through. They then entered the department of Vaccaria, in which they remained several days, waiting for the division of Bento Gonzales, which joined them much broken, and in a miserable state. The indefatigable Maringue, informed of their retreat, had pursued that division and harassed it in every way, aided by the mountaineers, who were always decidedly hostile to the Republicans.

All these things gave Labattue as much time as was required for his retreat and junction with the Imperial army. They arrived, however, almost without men, in consequence of desertions occasioned by the severe and forced march, and privations, and sufferings endured by the other troops.* Beside all these, he had an adventure, which deserves to be mentioned here on account of its remarkable nature.

Labattue being obliged to pass in his march through the two forests known by the names of the Mattos or woods of Portugues and Castellano, met in them several tribes of the Bugre Indians, the most savage in Brazil. These, knowing of the passage of the Imperialists, assailed them, laying ambushes in different places in the bushes, and did them much injury, letting us know, at the same time, that they were friends of the Republicans. In accordance with this profession, my comrades and I myself experienced no inconvenience from them on our march; but we saw the *poge*, or holes, carefully covered with grass, into which the incautious enemy might fall, when the savages would take advantage of his misfortune and assault him. But all these were left open where the Republicans were to pass, that we might not be exposed to the danger.

On one of those days I met a woman, who had been

stolen by the savages in her youth, and profited by the opportunity offered by the neighborhood of the troops. The poor creature was in a most pitiable state.

As we had no enemies to fly from or to pursue in those lofty regions, we proceeded slowly on our march, almost entirely destitute of horses.

CHAPTER XV.

THE corps of Free Lancers, being entirely dismounted,
were obliged to supply themselves with wild colts ; and
it was a fine sight which was presented almost every
day, to see a multitude of those robust young black
men, leaping upon the backs of their wild coursers,
and rushing across the fields like a thunderstorm.
The animal used every exertion to gain his freedom
and to throw off his hated rider ; while the man, with
admirable dexterity, strength and courage, continued
to press him with his legs, drawing in his feet against
his sides like pincers, whip and drive him, until he at
length tired out the superb son of the desert.

In that part of America the colt comes from the field
lassoed, and is saddled, bridled, and rode by the
domator, or horse-breaker, and in a few days obeys
the bit.   Experienced men obtain many excellent
horses in a short time ; but few come out well broken
from the hands of soldiers, especially when they are

on a march, where neither the necessary conveniences can be obtained, nor the necessary care taken to break them well.

Having passed the Mattos Portuguez and Castellano, we descended into the province of " Missiones," proceeding towards Cruz Alta, its chief town. It is a very small place, but well built, situated on a high plain and in a beautiful position ; as fine, indeed, as all that part of the State of Rio Grande. The troops marched from Cruz Alta to San Gabriel, where the head-quarters were established and barracks were constructed for the encampment of the army. I built a cottage, and spent some time in it with my little family ; but six years of a life of dangers and sufferings, far from the company of old friends, my father and mother, from whom I had no news, among that people, isolated by the war with the empire, made me wish to return to some place where I might obtain information concerning my parents. I now found that although, amidst the scenes of bustle and trial through which I had passed, I had been able to banish the recollection of their affection for a time, my love for them remained lively and warm in my heart. It was necessary to improve my circumstances, for the benefit of my wife and child, and I determined to make a journey to Montevideo, even if but for a short time. I asked and obtained permission from the President, who also allowed me to take a small herd of young cattle, to pay the expenses of travelling.

And here I took up the business of a cattle-drover, or *trappiere*. In an Estancia, called the Corral del Piedras, under the authority of the Minister of Finance, I succeeded in collecting, in about twenty days, about nine hundred cattle, after indescribable fatigue. With a still greater degree of labor and weariness they were driven towards Montevideo. Thither, however, I did not succeed in driving them. Insuperable obstacles presented themselves on the way, and, more than all, the Rio Negro, which crossed it, and in which I nearly lost all this capital. From that river, from the effects of my inexperience and from the tricks of some of my hired assistants for managing the drove of animals, I saved about five hundred of the cattle, which, by the long journey, scarcity of food and accidents in crossing streams, were thought unfit to go to Montevideo.

I therefore decided to " *cuercer*" or " *leather*" them,— that is, to kill them for their hides ; and this was done. In fact, after having passed through indescribable fatigue and troubles, for about fifty days, I arrived at Montevideo with a few hides, the only remains of my nine hundred oxen. These I sold for only a few hundred dollars, which served but scantily to clothe my little family.

In Montevideo I spent some of my time in the house of my friend Napoleon Castellani, to whose kindness, and the courtesy of his wife, I felt much indebted. I acknowledge my obligations also to my dear friends, Giovanni Battista Cuneo and Giovanni Risso. Having a family, but my means being exhausted, I felt it necessary to provide for the subsistence of the three individuals of whom it consisted. Other people's bread always seemed to me bitter, whenever in my diversified life I have found it necessary to partake of it; and I have been so happy as never to be dependant on any friend. Two occupations, of small profit, it is true, but which would afford me a subsistence, I assumed for a time. They were those of a broker and a teacher of mathematics, given in the house and to the pupils of the estimable instructor, Signor Paolo Semidei. This manner of life I pursued until I entered the Oriental squadron.

The Rio Grande question was approaching a settlement, and there was nothing more to be thought on that subject. The Oriental Republic soon offered me employment, and I accepted it.

I was appointed to proceed on an expedition, the results of which, through either ignorance or malignity, proved ruinous.

With the sloop Constitucion, of eighteen guns, the brig Terceira, of two eighteen pounders, and a transport, the schooner Procida, I was ordered to proceed to Corrientes, an allied province, to assist in their military operations against the forces of Rosas.

The Oriental Republic of the Uruguay, like the greater part of the Republics of South America, was a prey to intestine disputes; and the occasion then was the pretension of two Generals to the Presidency, viz : Rivera and Ouribes. Rivera, being more successful, succeeded after several victories, in driving away Ouribes, and gained possession of the power which he had held. The latter, being expelled, took refuge in Buenos Ayres, where the Dictator, Rosas, received him, together with many Oriental emigrants, and employed them against his enemy, who were then under the command of General Lavalle. Lavalle being conquered, the ferocious Ex-president of Montevideo undertook to regain his lost power in his own country. In that Rosas found the object most agreeable to his wishes ; that is, the destruction of the Unitarians, or Centralists, his mortal enemies, who were supported by the Oriental State ; and the ruin of a neighboring Republic, his rival, which disputed with him the supremacy of the immense river, by throwing into her bosom the most terrible elements of civil war.

At the time when I embarked on the river, the Oriental army was at San Jose de Uruguay, and that of Ouribes at La Bajada, the capital of the province of Entre Rios, both making preparations for a great conflict. The army of Corrientes then made arrangements for uniting with the Oriental. I was to go up the Parana to Corrientes, pass over a distance of more than six hundred miles, between two banks occupied by the enemy, where I would be unable to anchor, unless at islands and desert places.

CHAPTER XVI.

As has been said, the war in Montevideo was caused by the personal ambition of the two generals, Ouribes and Rivera, who were aspirants for the Presidency of the republic. The former was defeated by the latter, about the year 1840, and obliged to emigrate to Buenos Ayres.

At that time Rosas, the tyrant of Buenos Ayres, was engaged in war with the Centralists, or Unitarians, who were the national and liberal party, and were led by Generals Lavalle and Paz. Rosas received Ouribes and many of his partizans, and gave them immediate employment in his own army, while he conferred the supreme command of it upon the emigrant General. Ouribes, being able to bring many reinforcements to the tyrant's army, which was already strong, defeated Lavalle, who died in the upper provinces of the Argentine Republic, (I think Mendoza,) in a surprise. General Paz, by intrigues and dissensions, was obliged to abandon the struggle, after the brilliant victory of Caguazú, and to return to Montevideo, where the greater part of the Centralists who had fought against Rosas had retreated.

The Argentine Republic being pressed by enemies, Ouribes descended towards Montevideo, and established his camp at Bajada, the capital of the province of Entre-Rios, having under his command an imposing army, and meditating with Rosas, the invasion of the State of Montevideo. Rivera was then on the left bank of the Uruguay, preparing and receiving all the forces which he could dispose of, and doubtless expecting to be attacked.

Wise would have been the resolution to await the enemy in his own positions; but, having much confidence in himself, and strengthened by the junction with the army of Corrientes, he made arrangements to cross the river, and seek the enemy. The Oriental and Corrientes armies amounted to ten thousand men. Ouribes had fourteen thousand, and was much superior in infantry and artillery.

The battle was short; and the combined armies were entirely defeated on the Arroyo Grande. Ouribes passed the Uruguay, invaded the territory of Montevideo, and then laid siege to the capital.

The catastrophe of Arroyo Grande, and the certainty that the implacable ex-president would come, meditating terrible revenge, stimulated the population of the State of Montevideo to take up arms *en masse* and repel the invasion by force. It should here be observed, that the war had changed its character, and it was no longer a personal consideration in favor of Rivera which induced the people to take up arms ; but the fear of becoming subject to the depredations and excesses of a foreign and barbarous enemy, led them to fight for the independence of the country.

The beginning of patriotism, which then animated the people, was the same which led them to so many heroic deeds, and to sustain the most desperate of struggles, at the cost of unheard of sacrifices. Then began the glorious contest carried on by the Montevideans, which still continues, and which will astonish the world, when its events are exactly known.

General Paz, reduced to Montevideo, after the unfortunate occurrences in the Argentine State, was received with acclamation by the government and people, as general of the nascent army ; and to him are certainly due the beginnings of bravery and discipline by which it was distinguished, as well as the system of defence which was adopted.

Rivera kept the field, made skilful movements, and was defeated by Ouribes at India Muerta. The errors of Rivera and his conflicts completed his discredit, and entirely removed him from the scene of events. He is now an emigrant in Rio Janeiro, and I do not think his influence can produce any disturbance on the Rio de la Plata.

The question of Montevideo, therefore, reduces itself to the following, at the present epoch [1850] :

Rosas, the tyrant of Buenos Ayres, and chiefly in-
terested in the humiliation of Montevideo, maintains
an army in besieging that city, in order to destroy it.
That army is commanded by a Montevidean, who
wishes, at any cost, to command in his country ; and
the people of Montevideo are fighting against that
army, because they are not willing to submit to the
hated and abominated domination of Rosas and Ouribes.

Indignant at the sight of such a scene of arrogant
and inhuman oppression as that presented in Buenos
Ayres and the Argentine Republic, I was impelled to
present myself in opposition to the Dictator, and to
adopt the cause of the injured as my own. Having
mingled with the people in my own country, and all
my experience, short as it was, having taught me to
sympathize with them, against the old and hereditary
aristocracy of Europe, I could not regard with indifference the upstart oppressor, Rosas, so treacherous to
the principles of equality and republicanism, which he
pretended to love, while violating them, in the grossest
manner, for his own insatiable ambition. Notwithstanding the depressed condition of the true patriot
party in Montevideo, on my arrival in that city, circumstances ere long proved favorable ; and on their
beginning to renew their movements, I appeared
among them with my native activity and zeal.

I conceived the idea of performing an important
service for my own country, while devoting myself to

that in which I was residing. I soon perceived that the spirit and character of the Italians needed great efforts, to raise them from the depressed state in which they existed in fact, as well as in the opinion of the world ; and I was determined to elevate them, by such a practical training as alone could secure the end.

By means of Napoleon's treachery to the cause of liberty, which he had pretended to espouse on entering Italy, that unhappy country had been led to a ruin more deep and complete than any of the other of his victims ; for she had been, more than any other, reduced to spiritual slavery, as well as temporal. The allies (with Protestant Prussia and England among them,) had restored the papacy along with monarchy and aristocracy ; and yet the Italians were vilified as a degenerate race, and falsely acccused of having brought their misfortunes upon themselves, by their ignorance, fanaticism and pusillanimity.

6

CHAPTER XVII.

THERE were many Italians in Montevideo, whose condition and feelings I soon learned to appreciate. They
were regarded with scorn by many of the other foreign residents, especially the French, who were in
much greater numbers, and seemed to take pleasure in
humiliating my poor and injured countrymen.

This was not the first case, though one of the most
marked and unrighteous, in which the wronged and
suffering party were made to bear the reproach of
those very traits of character displayed by their strong
and false-hearted conquerors. In exile and poverty,
under the bitter and hourly personal experience of their
national misfortunes, and reproached by the world
with having brought them upon themselves, the Italians in South America were depressed and disheartened
by their gloomy recollections, their present sorrows
and their cloudy future. Many of them were occupying
themselves with such labors and business as they could

(114)

find or invent, to obtain the means of subsistence, and laying the foundations of the fortunes which they have since accumulated by industry and economy ; but few formed any sanguine expectations of gaining that distinction for military prowess, which the more numerous and vaunting Frenchmen around them then arrogated to themselves. I, however, ere long, began to indulge in more daring anticipations ; and the sequel will show the results.

I resolved to find employment for some of them, and to raise the courage and hopes of all, and at the same time to prepare them for future service as soldiers in Italy, by bringing them into the service which was offered to myself. My progress and success will be seen in the following chapters.

On my entering the service of the Oriental Republic, I received the command of the sloop of-war " Constitucion." The Oriental squadron was under the command of Colonel Cahe ; the enemy under the orders of General Brown. Several battles had taken place, but with results of but little consequence. At the same time a man named Vidal was appointed Minister General of the Republic,—a person of unfortunate and despicable memory. One of his first and most fatal steps was, to gain the dislike of the squadron, which proved highly injurious to its condition, which had cost the Republic immense sums, and which, if it had been cherished as it might then have been, would have established a marked preëminence in the Rio de la

Plata, but which was completely ruined, by selling the vessels at shamefully low prices.

I proceeded up the river with the vessels. We had an engagement with the batteries of Martin Garcia, which are situated near the confluence of the two great rivers Paraná and Uruguay, near which I had to pass, as there was no other channel for large vessels. I had several killed and wounded, and passed on. Among the dead was the brave Italian officer, Pocaroba, whose head was taken off by a cannon shot.

Three miles beyond Martin Garcia, the Constitucion was careened, but unfortunately at a time when the tide was falling; and it cost an immense amount of labor to get her afloat again. It was only due to the most persevering labor, that the flotilla was saved from being lost in those dangerous circumstances. While employed in removing heavy articles on board the Procida, the enemy's squadron appeared on the other side of the island, approaching under full sail. I was thus placed in a terrible condition,—the larger of my vessels lying on the sand, and deprived of her heaviest guns, which were placed in the Procida; the Procida being in consequence useless; and no vessel remaining except the Terceira, whose brave commander was near me with the greater part of his crew, assisting in his work.

In the meantime the enemy moved on proudly, presenting a superb sight, and hailed by the acclamations of the troops on the island, assured of victory, with seven strong ships of war. But I felt no despair—a feeling which I have never known. The cause I have never pretended to give. I did not think of my life at that moment; that appeared to me of little value: but it seemed that dying would not save honor, and it was impossible to fight in my position. Providence extended his hand over my destiny, and I desired no other. The ship of the Admiral grounded near the island; his pride was humbled, and the Republicans were safe. The enemy's misfortune redoubled their alacrity; in a few hours the Constitucion was afloat, and received her guns and loading. "Misfortunes never come single," says the proverb. A very thick fog concealed us, and everything we did, from the eyes of the enemy; and favored us greatly, by preventing them from knowing which way we went. This was of the greatest advantage: for, when the Imperialists got their ships under way, being ignorant of the direction we had taken, they sailed to pursue us, and went up the Uruguay, which we had not entered, and they consequently lost many days before they learned our course.

In the meantime I had entered the Paraná, under cover of the fog and with the favor of the wind. I had the direction of the whole operation, and must pronounce it one of the most arduous of my life. But certainly, in that day, the pleasure afforded by the escape from that imminent danger, and the solicitude caused by reflecting on the greatness of the enterprise

were embittered by the stupor and disaffection of my
companions, who until that moment had believed they
were going to the Uruguay. All declared that they
were unacquainted with the Paraná, and that they refused all responsibility from that moment. Responsibility was of little importance to me ; but something
was to be done in some way or other. After a few
inquiries, one man confessed that he knew a little of
the river, but that he was confused by his fears ; however, he was soon able to collect himself, and proved
useful. The wind favoring, we soon arrived near San
Nicolas, the first town in the Argentine territory,
which is situated on the right shore of the river.
There we found a few merchant vessels, which were
wanted for transports and other service, and, in a
night expedition with launches, both were obtained.
An Austrian, named Antonio, who had been trading
for a long time in the Paraná, was among the prisoners, and he rendered important services in the voyage.

Proceeding up the river, we met with no obstacle
until we reached Bajada, where was the army of
Ouribes. I operated in the transit. Some landed to
find fresh provisions, which consisted chiefly of oxen,
in which. they were opposed by the inhabitants, and
some troops of cavalry stationed there to guard the
shore. Several partial engagements took place on
that account—with some advantages and losses, sometimes on one side and sometimes on the other—in one
of which I had the great affliction of losing the brave

Italian officer, Lalberga, di Leone, a youth of surprising valor and of most promising genius. Another
monument, therefore, was demanded for another son
of the land of misfortune, who, like so many more, had
hoped to shed his blood for the redemption of his
country.

At Bajada, the capital of Entre Rios, where the army
of Ouribes was stationed, I found the most formidable
preparations on my arrival ; and a battle seemed at
first inevitable : but the wind being favorable, and we
being able to pass at a considerable distance from the
enemy's batteries, but little effect was produced by the
heavy cannonade which was made by them. At Las
Conchas, a few miles above La Bajada, I effected a
landing by night, which procured me fourteen oxen, in
spite of strong opposition made by the enemy. My
men fought with great bravery. The enemy's artillery
followed the coast, and profiting by the contrary wind
and the narrowness of the river, cannonaded us whenever they could. At Cerito, a position on the left bank
of the stream, they established a battery of six guns.
The wind was favorable, but light ; and at that point,
on account of the crookedness of the river, our vessels
had to sail in face of them, so that it was necessary to
go about two miles under a battery, which was as if
suspended over our heads. A resolute battle was
fought at that place. The greater part of my men
seemed unable to rise, and did not show themselves.
The others, at their guns, fought and labored with

great alacrity.   It should be remembered that the enemy belonged to a party rendered proud by their
victory, who soon after conquered, at Arroyo Grande,
the two combined armies of Montevideo and Corrientes.   Every obstacle was overcome with very little
loss ; and after having stopped all the enemy's fire, and
dismounted several pieces of artillery, a number of
merchant vessels, coming from Corrientes and Paraguay, which had been placed under the protection of
the enemy's battery, fell into the power of the Republicans with very little trouble.   Those prizes supplied
us with provisions and means of all kinds.

We then proceeded on our arduous voyage up the
river.   The enemy watched us in order to throw obstacles in our way ; but we arrived at Cavallo-quattia,
(or the White Horse,) where we joined the Argentine
flotilla, composed of two large launches and a balandra armed as a war-vessel.   We were thus supplied
with some fresh provisions, so that our condition was
much improved.   We had good and experienced men,
but a reinforcement was agreeable enough, especially
in its effects on the habits of our men.   Having thus
proceeded as far as the Brava coast, we were obliged
to stop on account of the shallow water, the difference
of which, with the draft of the Constitucion, was four
palms.   These difficulties began to excite some suspicions in my mind, concerning the final result of the expedition.   I had no doubt that the enemy would do
their utmost to defeat it ; for if it should arrive at

Corrientes the injury would have been very great to the enemy, by the Republicans having command of an intermediate part of the river, by holding an intermediate position between the interior provinces, the Paraguay and the capital of the Argentine confederation. It would have been a kind of nest of corsairs, to infest and destroy the enemy's commerce.

The enemy accordingly resorted to every measure for our ruin ; and they were greatly favored by the want of water in the river, which was altogether unexampled for half a century, according to the declaration of Governor Ferri, of Corrientes. It being impossible to proceed further, I determined to put the flotilla in the best possible state for resistance. From the left bank of the Paraná, where the depth of water was greatest, I drew a line of vessels, beginning with a merchant *yate*, in which were placed four guns; the Terceira in the middle, and the Constitucion on the right wing, thus forming a row, at right angles to the shore, and presenting to the enemy all the force possible.

6

CHAPTER XVIII.

THIS arrangement cost much labor, in consequence
of the current, which, although small, in that open
place, required the use of all the chains and cables to
anchor the vessels, especially the Constitucion, the heaviest of all. These labors were not terminated when the
enemy made their appearance with seven vessels, a
superior force, and in a situation where they could receive reinforcements and supplies of every kind. The
Republican flotilla, on the contrary, was far from Corrientes, the only part of the country from which they
could obtain assistance, and where it was almost certain no aid would be received, as the result proved to
be too true. It was thought necessary, however, to
fight, at least for the honor of arms ; and an engagement ensued.

The enemy, under the command of General Brown,

who enjoyed the highest reputation as a maritime officer in South America, and justly, too, proceeded in all
the confidence of their power. They had a favorable
wind though a light one, keeping along the left
bank, the right being impracticable. As I had command of the left bank, on which rested the left flank
of his line, I landed part of my soldiers and sailors, to
dispute the enemy's advance, inch by inch. The Republicans fought bravely, and greatly retarded the enemy's advance; but the superior force of the latter
prevailed, and the former were driven under the protection of their vessels. Major Pedro Rodriguez, who
commanded our force on land, fought that day with all
imaginable skill and valor. He placed the outposts
towards evening; and thus they remained through the
whole night, both parties preparing for battle on the
following day.

The sun had not risen on the 16th of June, when the
enemy began a cannonade, with all the force which they
had been laboring to bring to the front in the night.
The battle was then commenced; and it continued
without interruption till nightfall, being sustained on
both sides with great resolution. The first victim
on board the Constitucion was again an Italian officer,
of great bravery and of the highest promise, Guiseppe
Barzone; and I regretted that I could not take charge
of his remains, in consequence of the fury of the contest. Much damage was done on both sides. The
Republican vessels were riddled and shattered. The

corvette, in consequence of not having her shot-holes accurately stopped, leaked so much that she could not be kept afloat without great difficulty, the pumps being at work without cessation. The commandant of the Terceira had been killed in a most daring enterprise by land against the enemy's vessels. In him I lost my best and bravest companion. The killed were numerous, and still more the wounded. The remaining time I was constantly occupied on account of the sinking condition of the vessels. However, there were still powder and shot on board, and we must fight— not for victory, not to save ourselves, but for honor. Some men laugh at the honors of a soldier ; but Italians have given strong proof of the existence and power of such a principle in their breasts, particularly in other places and at a later period than that to which we are now attending, especially when Rome was surrounded by the armies of four nations, in 1849, and long defended herself. Those who scoff at the idea of honor in an honest soldier who fights for his friends and country, can too often show base respect for men who abuse and assassinate their fellow-beings, or who claim to be the supporters of their political or religious opinions, though they may be monsters in cruelty or infamous in vice, especially if surrounded with the power of the great or the splendor of courts.

We fought for honor, although six hundred miles distant from Montevideo, with enemies from all quarters, after a series of battles, privations and misfortunes, and almost sure of losing everything. In the meantime Vidal, the minister of war of the Republic, squandered doubloons to support his splendid banquets, in the first capitals of Europe. Such is the honor of the world! It is thus that the lives of generous Italians are despised and sacrificed, and they are buried in a land of exile, in the continent of their countryman, Columbus, or in other regions of the earth. Such was Castelli, who was beheaded at Buenos Ayres; Borso di Carminati, shot in Spain;—and this, although they were superior men, and had rendered great services to ungrateful foreigners.

Their sympathy those foreigners have shown for thee, O Italy! when thy aged and venerable head was raised for a moment in Rome, from the lethargy of opprobrium in which thy oppressors had conspired to hold thee, thou Mother, Instructress and Mistress of Nations! When thou once more shalt rouse thyself, they will tremble at the defeat of their united powers, combined in the league of Hell, to oppress and degrade thee. Be great, then, once more, O Italy! and then the powerful voice of the Almighty will be heard by all thy sons; and the hungry and cowardly vultures which destroy thee, will be stunned by its thundering sound.

On the night of the 16th all my men were occupied in preparing cartridges, which were almost entirely exhausted, and in cutting up chains to supply the

want of balls, and in the incessant pumping of the
leaky vessels.   Manuel Rodriguez, the same Cata-
lonian officer who had been saved with me from shipwreck on the coast of Santa Caterina, was occupied,
with a few of the best, in fitting up several merchant
vessels as fireships, with the greatest possible quantity
of combustibles, and directing them towards the
enemy. That expedient incommoded them during the
night, but did not produce the effect desired ; the
chief defect of the Republicans being the extreme
scarcity of men.   Between the various mishaps of that
dreadful night, that which most afflicted me was the
defection of the little squadron of Corrientes. Villegas,
the commandant, like many others whom I have seen
bold in a calm, became so much terrified by approaching danger, that it was impossible to make him useful
in any way to the allied vessels, although they were
manned with good sailors, and fitted for any kind of
service on the river, by their swiftness.   Seeing Villegas not quite self-possessed, I ordered him to take
his place behind the line of battle, where I had placed
the hospital—a small vessel destined to that use.
Towards evening he sent me word that he had changed
his position to a short distance, for what motive I
could not imagine.   Needing his coöperation in the
work of the fireships, I sent for Villegas in the night,
and received the alarming news that he was nowhere
to be found.   Not being willing to think him capable
of so much treachery, I went myself in a light palis-

chermo, to satisfy myself of the truth. Not finding him, I proceeded several miles towards Corrientes, but in vain; and I returned, in bitterness of soul. My fears were unhappily too well founded, for most of the little vessels were destroyed in the service before the engagement began. I had counted on the Correntine vessels to receive the wounded and to contain the provisions necessary for all, as we were still far distant from the inhabited frontier of Corrientes. My last hope was now lost, by a cowardly retreat, which is the greatest of crimes when committed in the moment of danger.

I returned on board my vessel a short time before daybreak. A fight was inevitable, but I saw nothing around me but men lying down overcome with fatigue, and heard no sound except the lamentations of the unfortunate wounded, who had not yet been transported to the hospital. Being now unable to wait any longer, I gave the signal and ordered the men to their stations. I gave the orders and spoke a few words of comfort and encouragement, which were not in vain, as I found my companions, although spent with fatigue, with spirit remaining which could yet be excited. They replied with a general cry for battle, and every man was immediately at his post. The engagement was recommenced when it was hardly light; but, if the advantage appeared to be on our side in the previous affair, we now decidedly had the worst. The new cartridges had been made of bad powder; we had used all the balls of proper size for the calibre of the guns, and those we now had were smaller, and, therefore, in going out, did much injury to the pieces, which had before done such service against the enemy. The latter observed the weakness of our fire, and being then informed of our condition by some deserters, showed great joy, while their vessels, which were unable the day preceding to form a line, now effected it in security. Thus the condition and prospects of the Republicans were growing worse and worse, while those of their enemies every moment improved. At length a retreat became necessary, not with the vessels, for it was impossible to move them from their positions, in consequence of their broken condition, the want of water, and the miserable state of the crews. Nothing could be hoped for but the saving of their lives. I therefore gave orders for landing, in a few small boats which remained, the wounded, the arms, the little ammunition left, and all the provisions which they were able to take. In the meantime the fight continued; although on our part but very feebly, but with redoubled vigor by the victorious enemy.

The matches were then prepared, and the firemen stood ready to burn the vessels. All was ready; and, with the few men remaining with me, I got into the boats. The enemy, on discovering our preparations for debarking, naturally inferred our design of retreating, and put all their infantry on the march, to attack us. I was not disposed to meet them, with such inequality of numbers and arms, and in the condition of the enemy's infantry. Besides, an open river was to be crossed. But the burning of the vessels, by the Santa Barbara operation, blowing-up, was performed in a terrible manner, and gave the enemy clear notice of our movements.

The scene presented by the burning flotilla was very striking. The river lay as clear as crystal; and the burning cinders fell on both its banks, while a terrible noise of explosions was continually heard.

Towards evening, in our little boats, we approached the River Espinillo, and encamped on its right bank. During the voyage to Esquina, the first town in Corrientes, we spent three days, proceeding very painfully among islands and ponds, and reduced to one ration a day, consisting of a single biscuit, without anything else to eat. On reaching Esquina, our condition was considerably improved; the wounded were placed under shelter; and the men had meat in abundance. The inhabitants, who were good Republicans, showed us the greatest hospitality.

We spent some months in the Province of Corrientes, without the occurrence of anything important. At length the Governor formed a plan to arm a flotilla of small vessels; but succeeded in nothing but losing time. I then received orders from Montevideo to march to the scene of revolution in San Francisco, in Uruguay, and place myself and my forces at the dis-

6*

position of General Rivera, who was stationed with an army in that neighborhood.

I then traversed the entire territory of Corrientes, from Santa Lucia to the Pass of Higos, on the Uruguay. Going through the Pass, we arrived at San Francisco, partly by the river and partly by land. At the Falls I had the pleasure of meeting Anzani, then transformed into a merchant. Having reached San Francisco, I there found several vessels of war, of which I took the command. General Rivera had gone into Entre Rios, with the army, where the army of Corrientes was to meet him, and go to attack that of Ouribes. On the 6th of December, 1842, occurred, at Arroyo Grande, the celebrated battle in which the nation fought for their sacred rights; but the power of a tyrant triumphed. Different circumstances led to this result, which would require much time to give in detail : but the chief cause was the discord fomented by the ambition of a few, which plunged all into disaster, and exposed them to extermination by an implacable conqueror. Oh, virtuous and generous people! The same fortune befel Italy at a later day, which was suffered by the provinces of La Plata, and brought about by the same cause, which was sent by Heaven in wrath.

At San Francisco, where I found General Aguyar staying on account of his health, I remained only a short time, when I received orders from him to collect all the disposable forces, and a few hundred militia, called Aguerridos, commanded by Colonel Guerra, and march to the Pass of Vessilles, to coöperate actively with the enemy. I reached that place with the vessels, and there found the remains of the army's residence, but not a single person. I sent scouts, to search the surrounding country; but discovered nothing! That day was the fatal sixth of December; and every man had been called to the field of battle, which was decided at the distance of eighteen miles from the spot, on the bank of the Arroyo Grande. There sometimes seems to be something in the depths of our minds superior to understanding; at least so it seemed to me on that occasion. Without pretending to explain it, I thought I felt its effects; which, although in a confused manner, seemed something like looking into the future.

On that day I felt a solemn impression on my heart, mingled with bitterness, like the feelings of warriors left languishing on a field of battle, and trampled on by the insolent soldier, by the hoof of the war-horse of the cruel, the implacable conqueror. Very few were saved from that terrible battle; and the whole band, with me, experienced feelings difficult to describe, indeed, quite unspeakable. Sadness was mingled with a prevailing presentiment of disaster. Not being able to find any living being who could give information of the army, and having no orders from General Aguyar, I resolved to land all the troops, leaving only a small number in the boats, and to march in search of the army.   It should be remarked, that I always pursued my favorite system of the Rio Grande, and never marched without a contingent of cavalry, taken from my amphibious companions in misfortune, men who had been thrown out of the cavalry of the army, for some fault or perhaps some crime, but who fought well, and whom I severely punished when they deserved it.

Although no human beings were to be found in that region, we caught a number of horses which had been abandoned, and obtained a sufficient supply for the service.   The abundance of horses in those countries greatly facilitates such an operation.   All things were soon ready; and I was on the point of giving the order for marching, when, well for me, an order was received from General Aguiar, recalling me to San Francisco.   But for this, I and my troops would doubtless have fallen victims: for the army was so completely broken up on that day, that it would have been impossible to find anything but the mere wreck of it, while we must have met the victorious enemy, from whom escape would have been very difficult, if not impossible.

The troops, therefore, reëmbarked, without the object being known even to their commander, and without obtaining any news whatever of the events of the day.   On reaching San Francisco, I received a note from Colonel Esteves, beginning with the following terrible words:

" Our army has suffered a reverse !"

General Aguiar had marched along the left bank of the Uruguay, to collect the fugitives, and requested me to stay in San Francisco, to guard the great quantity of materials of every kind remaining there.

CHAPTER XIX.

IN the period which elapsed between the battle of
Arroyo Grande and the beginning of the siege of
Montevideo, that confusion prevailed which is common
in such cases, when plans are by turns formed, rejected,
and again adopted. Fear, desertion, and irresolution
existed ; but they were found only in rare and individual cases. The people stood firm and heroic, at
the voice of noble-hearted men, who proclaimed that
the Republic was in danger, and called upon all to
rise in its defence. In a short time there was a new
army, which, although neither so large nor so well dis-
ciplined as the former, was, at least, more full of energy
and enthusiasm, and more strongly impressed with the
sacred cause which impelled them. It was no longer
the cause of a single man which stimulated the multitude : the star of that man had sunk in the late battle,
and in vain endeavored again to rise. It was the
cause of the nation, in the presence of which personal
hatred and dissention were silenced. Foreigners were
preparing to invade the territory of the Republic ; and

(134)

every citizen came out with arms and horses, to range himself under the banner, to repel him. The danger increased, and with it the zeal and devotion of that generous people. Not a single voice was heard to utter the word "submission," or "accommodation." Since the battle of Novara, in Piedmont, I could never compare my countrymen with the Montevideans without blushing. However, all Italy desired not to submit to foreign dominion, but panted for battle; and I am convinced that Italians, like Montevideans, possess constancy and generous devotion to liberty. But they have so many and such powerful influences to keep them enslaved!

I had then orders to sink the small vessels in the channel of the river, by which the enemy's fleet could come up. The larger vessels of the patriot flotilla were then not to be sunk, but to be burned; I was therefore soon engaged in burning a third fleet, but this was not to be done, as on the two former occasions, while fighting, my sailors having, consequently, once more been transformed into foot soldiers. I remained with them a few days in San Francisco, to allow time to ship for Montevideo the remaining materials of the army; and we then set off on the march for the capital, in the neighborhood of which all the forces were to be collected. Little or nothing of importance occurred on the journey, except my acquaintance with General Pacheco, then a Colonel in Mercedes. That illustrious Oriental commenced, at that dangerous crisis, to display a noble superiority in energy, courage, and capacity. He, beyond all question, was the principal champion of the gigantic struggle sustained by his country against foreign invasion ; a struggle which will serve as an example to future generations, and to all nations who are not willing to submit to force ; and may God protect the Oriental people !

Montevideo presented, at that time, a surprising spectacle. Ourives had conquered, and was advancing at the head of an army, which had passed through the Argentine provinces like a tempest, or rather like a thunderbolt. At the Coriolano of Montevideo, neither the prostrations of the priests would have availed, nor the tears of wives or mothers, to soften the hearts of the soldiers. The idea of chastising that city, which had driven him away, and seen him fly, gratified the soul of that atrocious man. The army of Montevideo had been destroyed, and nothing of it remained except small and disheartened fragments of forces, scattered over the territory of the Republic. The squadrons were cut in pieces, arms and ammunition were very scarce, or entirely wanting, and the treasury ! It is only necessary to imagine it in the hands of such men as Vidal, intent on nothing but on getting doubloons, as the most portable kind of money for a meditated flight. He was Minister General.

It was, however, necessary to defend themselves. There were many men belonging to Rivera's party for whom there was no escape after the arrival of the others, and for whom the defence was an indispensable condition. But they were powerless and trembling, being bound to their employments and property. Yet the nation, the people, did not regard Ourives as the antagonist of Rivera, but as the head of a foreign army, which he led on for invasion, slavery and death; and they ran to the defence with a feeling of their rights. In a short time the army, in companies of cavalry, was made new. An army, chiefly consisting of infantry, was organized in Montevideo, to support the capital, and under the auspices of that man of victories, General Paz. That General Paz, whom envy, but no good cause at all, had driven from the command, replied to the call of his country in a time of danger, appeared at the head of the forces of the capital, and organized, with recruits and freemen, then emancipated by the Republic, that army which, for seven years, was the bulwark of the country, and still maintains itself in the presence of the most powerful enemy in South America.

Many leaders, forgotten and not fond of wars in which only individual interests were engaged, made their appearance in the files of the defenders, and increased the enthusiasm and confidence of the troops. A line of fortifications was to be drawn around the city towards the accessible part from the country, and they labored with alacrity until it was completed. Before the enemy's approach, manufactories of arms and ammunition, foundries of cannon, shops for making clothes and accoutrements for soldiers, all sprang up at once, as if by a miracle. Cannons, which, from the days of the Spaniards, had been judged useless, and placed as guards at the borders of the sidewalks in the streets, were dug out and mounted for defence.

I was appointed to organize a flotilla, for which several small vessels were chosen. A favorable incident proved very valuable to me, by enabling me to commence that armament. The enemy's brig Oscar, in sailing at night in the neighborhood of the coast, ran upon the point of the Cerro. That is the name of a mountain west of Montevideo, which forms, with its base, the western side of the harbor. In spite of every effort made by the enemy to get the vessel afloat, they were obliged to abandon her. We profited much by that shipwreck. From the first the enemy endeavored to prevent our saving her, and sent the sloop of war Palmar to cannonade us; but not obtaining much advantage from this, and the Republicans showing much obstinacy in seizing their prey, they soon left them at liberty to pursue their work.

Among the numerous objects removed from the wreck, were five cannons, which served to arm three small vessels, the first in the new flotilla, and which were immediately put to use in covering the left flank of the line of fortifications. I regarded the loss of the Oscar as a good augury of the terrible defeat which was preparing.

CHAPTER XX.

IT was now the 16th of February, 1843. The fortifications of the city had hardly had time to be completed, and to allow a few cannons to be placed, when
the enemy's army made its appearance on the surrounding heights. General Rivera, at the head of the
cavalry, although not strong enough to be able to
fight them, had gone out and taken the field, turning
the left flank of the enemy, and placing himself in
their rear. That manœuvre, performed in a masterly
manner, placed him again in a state to carry on the
war with advantage. General Paz remained in command of the forces in the capital, which were numerous compared with the extent of wall which was to be
defended. If, however, we regard the materials of
which they were composed, who were raw recruits,
and the pernicious elements at work, they could not be

considered powerful. The constancy of the General, however, was displayed to the utmost, who sustained with them the first and most dangerous battles of the siege ; and notwithstanding the generous spirit displayed by the people, there was no want of disturbers, cowards, and traitors. Vidal, then the Minister-General, had robbed the treasury, and run away. Antuña, colonel of a corps, and head of the police, deserted to the enemy, with many other civil and military officers. A corps, called Aguerridos, composed of foreigners hired by the Republic, in various affairs, had almost entirely deserted ; and one night, when they occupied an advanced post, by their treachery they greatly exposed the security of the city. Such examples also were imitated by single individuals, who, from various motives, abandoned the files of the defenders, to pass over to the enemy.

Affairs did not go on well at first. I never knew why Ourives, who must have been well acquainted with occurrences, did not take advantage of such distrust and the bad state of the fortifications, to make a vigorous attack upon the place. He did nothing but make reconnaissances and false attacks by night. In the meantime foreign legions were organized and armed. In whatever way the spirit of the French and Italian legions may be viewed, it must not be denied that the first call to arms was answered by a generous rising, to repel the invasion of their adopted country : but afterwards individuals were introduced, whose in-terested views were quite on the contrary side. The organizing and arming of those corps, however, certainly availed in securing the safety of the city. The French, being more numerous and more excited by military display, soon had two thousand six hundred men under arms. The Italians assembled, in number five hundred ; and, although they might seem few in proportion to the number in the country, and their education, I was surprised at seeing so many, considering their habits. They were afterwards increased, but never exceeded seven hundred.

General Paz, profiting by the increase of forces, established an exterior line, at the distance of a cannonshot beyond the walls. From that time the system of defence was settled, and the enemy were no more able to approach the city.

While I had charge of the flotilla, with the organizing of which I was proceeding, Angelo Mancini was placed in command of the legion—a man of infamous memory ; and he was accepted. The flotilla performed its first service in a sortie ; and, as might be supposed, made no favorable figure. Italian bravery was despised, and I consequently burned with shame. The Legion was appointed to form part of an expedition to the Cerro ; and I was to accompany it. General Bauza, an experienced and good soldier, but an old man, had the command. He appeared in the presence of the enemy, marching and counter-marching, without accomplishing any effect. It was, perhaps, prudent not to attack an enemy, who, if not more numerous, were more experienced and war-like. I endeavored to excite the veteran general, but in vain, when fortune sent General Pacheco from Montevideo, who was then Minister of War. His appearance gratified me very much, as I knew him to be an enterprising and brave man. We were soon acquainted, and I was treated by the new chief with confidence and familiarity. I requested leave to drive the enemy from a position beyond a ditch, which then served as a dividing line to the besiegers. He not only assented, but ordered General Bauza to support the movement of the Italian Legion. We attacked the left wing of the enemy, who fearlessly awaited us with a firm front and a terrible volley of musketry. But the Italian Legion was victorious that day. Although numbers fell wounded, their comrades pressed on fearlessly, and at length charged with bayonets, when the enemy fled, and were pursued to a considerable distance. The centre and right were also victorious, and took forty-two prisoners, be-sides killed and wounded.

That action, although of little importance in itself, was of very great value in its effects,—greatly strength-ening the spirit of the Republican army, and dimin-ishing that of the enemy, while it established, from that day, the military character of the Italian Legion. It was also the precursor of many great deeds per-formed by that corps, which was never conquered.

The next day the Italian Legion was in the principal square of the metropolis, in view of the whole
population, receiving the praises of the Minister of
War and the acclamations of all the people. The
impressive words of General Pacheco had resounded
among the multitude. I had never heard words more
adapted to rouse a nation.

The Italian Legion had now fought for the first
time and by itself, and there was that same Captain
Giacomo Minuto who was afterwards captain of
cavalry in Rome, and there received a wound in the
breast from a ball, and died in consequence of loosen-
ing the bandages at the news of the entrance of the
French.

Major Pedro Rodriguez also displayed much bravery.

From that day until the appearance of Anzani in
the Legion, I absented myself but little from the corps,
although engaged at sea most of the time. About
that period Anzani was at Buenos Ayres, where,
receiving an invitation from me, he came to Montevideo. The acquisition of Anzani to the Legion was
extremely valuable, especially for instruction and discipline. Although he was much opposed by Manceni
and by the second chief, who could not submit to
acknowledge his superior merit, being perfect in
military knowledge and direction, he systematized the
corps on as regular a footing as circumstances would
permit.

The flotilla, although of little importance, did not

fail to be worth something to the defence of the place. Posted at the left extremity of the line of defence, it not only effectually covered it, but threatened the right flank of the enemy whenever it attempted an attack. It served as a link between the important position of the Cerro and the Island of Libertad, by greatly facilitating and coöperating in the attempts which were continually made upon the right of the enemy, who were besieging the Cerro. The Island of Libertad had been watched by the enemy, who laid a plan to get possession of it. Their squadron, under command of General Brown, was prepared to invade it and gain possession. It was determined that artillery should be placed upon it, and I transported to it two cannon, eighteen pounders.

About ten at night, that operation having been performed, I left the island with a company of my countrymen, and returned towards Montevideo. Then happened one of those unforeseen and important events which, I love to say, are evidently brought about by the hand of Providence. The Island of Libertad, placed in advance of the coast of the Cerro at the distance of less than a cannon-shot, is less than three miles from Montevideo. The wind blew from the South, and caused some agitation of the sea in the bay in proportion to its force, and especially in that passage between the island and the mole. I had embarked in a launch, purchased by the government, and had with me sailors enough to perform the service just executed, and the large lighter in tow, in which the artillery had been transported. Between the waves rolling in from the south and the weight of the boat, which was also exactly square in shape, we proceeded slowly, drifting considerably towards the north end of the bay, when, all at once, several vessels of war were discovered to the leeward, and so near that the sentinels were heard calling to the men, " Keep quiet !" It was doubtless the enemy's squadron.

We wonderfully escaped being captured by them ; but the principal cause of our safety was, that the small vessels and the boats of the enemy had gone to attack the island, and there was nothing left that could pursue us. If this had not been the case, we should doubtless have been taken : but, more than this, the enemy did not fire a shot, though they might easily have sunk our little vessels, for fear of alarming their troops who had gone to the island, to surprise it. But what an escape it appeared to me when I reached the mole, and began to hear a terrible discharge of musketry on the Island of Libertad ! I immediately reported the proceedings to the government, and then went on board my little vessels, to prepare them to go in aid of the troops on the island. They were only about sixty there, not well armed, and with but little ammunition. I set sail at dawn of day, with only two small vessels, called *yates ;* the third, and only remaining one of the flotilla, not being fit for use at that time. We proceeded, and soon entered between the

7

island and the Cerro, uncertain whether the enemy had got possession or not in their night attack. But the brave Italians, although taken unexpectedly, had fought with bravery, and had not only repulsed the enemy, but driven them back with much loss; and the corpses of Rosas' soldiers floated about in the waters of the harbor several days after. Having sent a skiff to the island to ascertain its fate, I soon received welcome intelligence of the successful resistance. I speedily landed the munitions, and one of my officers with some men to serve the guns; and this had hardly been accomplished when the enemy opened their fire, and the island replied with its two cannon. I then, with my two boats, got to windward of the enemy's vessels, and did all I could against them. But the combat was unequal in the extreme. I had against me two brigantines and two schooners, and one of the former had sixteen guns. The cannons on the island had platforms, and were ill-supplied with ammunition, and therefore did not fire well, or produce much effect. Had they been better provided for, they might have done good service. Although the sea was not very rough, it was sufficiently so to prevent the guns of my two little vessels from firing with precision; and, in short, it seemed impossible that the engagement could fail to be to the enemy successful. But once more God provided for us!

Commodore Purvis, then commander of the British station at Montevideo, sent a messenger to Brown, on

account of which he ceased firing. From that moment
the affairs turned to negotiation. The enemy's squadron left the harbor, and the island did not again fall
into the power of another. Whatever the reasons of
the Commodore may have been, it is undeniable that
some degree of chivalrous generosity towards an unfortunate but courageous people entered into the
sympathies and into the act of the philanthropic son
of Albion. From that moment Montevideo knew that
she had in the English Commodore not only a friend,
but a protector.

CHAPTER XXI.

THE affair of the island increased the fame and importance of the arms of the Republic, although its
favorable result was more due to fortune than to anything else, and although nothing more was gained by
defending it. Thus it was, that by insignificant, or at
least small but successful enterprizes, a cause was fos-
'tered and raised up, which had been considered by
many as desperate. A patriotic and excellent administration of the government, at the head of which was
Pacheco; the management of the war by the incomparable General Paz ; the fearless and powerful support
given by the people, then purged from their few
traitors and cowards ; and the arming of the foreign
Legions,—in short, everything promised a happy result.

The Italian Legion, whose formation was ridiculed
by some, and especially by the French, had now acquired so much fame, that they were envied by the best
troops. They had never been beaten, though they had

shared in the most difficult enterprizes and most arduous battles.

At Tres Cruces, (the Three Crosses,) where the fearless Colonel Neva, from an excess of courage, had fallen within the enemy's lines, the Legion sustained one of those Homeric battles described in history, fighting hand to hand, and driving the troops of Ourives from their strongest positions, until they brought away the dead body of the chief of the line. The losses of the Legion on that day were considerable, compared with their small numbers, but on that account they gained more honor. That success, which seemed as if it might exhaust it, on the contrary fostered it exceedingly. It grew in numbers, with new recruits, soldiers of a day, but who fought like veterans! Such is the Italian soldier ; such are the sons of the despised nation, when struck with the generous idea of what is noble.

At the Pass of the Bajada, on the 24th of April, was one of the most serious conflicts. A corps of the army under the command of General Paz, had marched out from Montevideo, passed by the right wing of the enemy, proceeded along the shore of the north bend of the bay to Pantanoso, where, joining the Republican forces of the Cerro, he intended to make a decisive blow on the enemy's army,—who were thus drawn out of their strong positions of the Cerrito,—to surprise two battalions, stationed on the shores of that marshy little stream. As that operation was not successful

in consequence of a want of concert, they were obliged to go through the Pass, involved in a very sharp
action. Of the two divisions comprising the corps,
which were about seven thousand, that which formed
the rearguard was so much pressed by the enemy,
that, when recovered from surprise, they endeavored
to regain their ground. This they would have saved
with the greatest possible effort, in consequence
of the extreme difficulty of the place. I commanded the division of the centre; and the general ordered me to re-pass and support the troops in that
danger. I obeyed, but, to my surprise, found the battle a desperate one.   The Republicans were fighting bravely : but the enemy had surrounded them, and
then occupied a very strong salting establishment,
(called Saladero,) between us and the rearguard, who
had exhausted their ammunition. The head of the Italian column entered the Saladero, just when the head
of one of the enemy's columns had entered. Then
commenced a very warm contest, hand to hand ; and
finally Italian bravery triumphed. At that place the
ground was encumbered with dead bodies ; but my
friends were safe, and the fight proceeded, with advan
tage to our side.   Other corps came in to support
them, and the retreat was effected in admirable order.
The French Legion, on that day, going to operate
simultaneously on the line of the city, was defeated.

The 28th of March, however, was highly honorable to the Republican arms, and to the Italian Legion.

The movement was directed by General Pacheco. The enemy were besieging the Cerro, under the orders of General Nuñez, who had shamefully deserted to the enemy's files, in the beginning of the siege. They showed much boldness, and several times came up under the heavy ramparts of the fortress, threatening to cut off the communications with the city and destroying with musket shots the light-house erected on the upper part of the edifices. General Pacheco ordered several corps to be transported to the Cerro, among which was the Italian Legion. That movement took place during the night; and at the first light it was in ambush in a powder manufactory, half a mile from the battery. That edifice, although in ruins, had the walls standing, and afforded sufficient space to contain the entire Italian Legion, though in a somewhat confined situation. Skirmishing was commenced, and afterwards something more serious. The enemy stood boldly against their opponents, and got possession of a a strong position called the *Quadrado*, or the Square, at the distance of a short cannon-shot from the Powder-house. A number of men had already been wounded among the Republicans, and, among others, Colonel Cajes and Estivao, in my opinion the best of the officers. Such was the state of things, when the signal was given for the Legion to make a sortie, and the conflict became serious, under the command of Colonel Carceres, who had charge of the force engaged. I shall always feel proud of having belonged to that handful of brave men, having always seen them on the high road of victory.

It was proposed to attack the enemy on an eminence, behind the shelter of a ditch and parapet. The space which it was necessary to pass, in order to assault it, was unobstructed by any obstacle, and therefore the enterprise was by no means an easy one. But the Legion, that day, would have faced fiends, if they could have been conjured upon the field; and they marched on against the enemy, without firing a shot and without hesitating for a moment, except to throw themselves into the Pantanoso, three miles distant from the field of battle. Nuñez was killed, and many prisoners were taken. The Oriental corps, in company with the Italians, fought very bravely; and, though the above-mentioned movement was somewhat retarded, the order was given to the column on the right to advance and place itself between the river and the enemy. And certainly not one of the enemy's infantry was saved.

That battle reflects great honor on the skill of General Pacheco.

During the first years of the seige of Montevideo, the Italian Legion sustained innumerable conflicts. They suffered the loss of many killed and wounded; but in no engagement did they disgrace themselves.

General Rivera was defeated at India Muerta; but the capital was not conquered with him. The corps belonging to it were trained to war by daily fighting, and also gained moral advantage over the besiegers. The English and French intervention took place, and then all parties anticipated a happy result of the war.

A project for operations, combined by the government and the admirals of the two allied nations, was an expedition in the Uruguay; and it was placed under my command. In the period now past, the national flotilla had been increased by the addition of several vessels, some of which were chartered, like the first, and others sequestrated from certain enemies of the Republic, and others still were prizes made from the enemy, who sent their vessels to the Bucco and other places on the coast in possession of the forces of Ourives. Then, between the acquisition of the above-mentioned vessels, and of two others of the Argentine squadron, sequestered by the English and French, and placed at the disposition of the Oriental government, the expedition for the Uruguay was composed of about fifteen vessels, the largest of which was the Cagancha, a brig of sixteen guns, and the smallest were several boats.

The landing corps was thus composed: the Italian Legion of about two hundred men, about two hundred Nationals, under command of Colonel Battle, and about a hundred cavalry, with two four pounders and six horses in all.

7*

CHAPTER XXII.

THE EXPEDITION PROCEEDS FOR THE URUGUAY — COLONIA TAKEN BY IT — BURNED—PAGE, A SUSPICIOUS FRENCHMAN — MARTIN GARCIA TAKEN.

IT was near the close of the year 1845 when the expedition left Montevideo for the Uruguay, beginning an honorable campaign with brilliant but fruitless results, for the generous but unfortunate Oriental nation. We arrived at Colonia, where the English and French squadrons were awaiting us, to assail the city. It was not a very arduous enterprise, under the protection of the superfluous guns of the vessels. I landed with my Legionaries; and the enemy opposed no resistance under the walls: but, on getting outside of them, they were found ready for battle. The allies then debarked, and requested their commanders to support me in driving the enemy away. A force of each of the two nations accordingly came out for my assistance. But the Italians had hardly begun to fight, and obtained some advantage, when the allies retired within the city walls. The reason for this unexpected movement was never explained to me; but I was compelled to follow their example, in consequence of the great inferiority of my force compared with that of the enemy.

(154)

When the other party proposed to abandon the city, they obliged the inhabitants to evacuate it, and then endeavored to give it to the flames. From that time, therefore, many of the houses presented the sad spectacle of the effects of conflagration, the furniture having been broken, and everything lying in confusion. When the Legion landed, and the Nationals, they had immediately followed the enemy who were retreating; and the allies, landing afterwards, occupied the empty city, sending out a part of their forces to support them. Now it was difficult, between the obstacles presented by the ruins and the fire, to maintain the discipline necessary to prevent some depredations; and the English and French soldiers, in spite of the severe injunctions of the Admirals, did not fail to take the clothes which were scattered about the streets and in the deserted houses. The Italians followed their example, and, in spite of every exertion made by me and my officers to prevent them, some of them persisted in the work for a time; and I have the mortification of acknowledging that I did not entirely succeed in my efforts to prevent them. The most important articles taken by the Italians, however, were eatables; and this afforded some consolation, as the fact was less discreditable to my countrymen than if they had chosen objects of lasting pecuniary value. I feel also most confident in saying, that nothing of that disgraceful conduct would have happened, but for the beginning made by the allied troops.

A Frenchman, named Page, who then resided in Montevideo, published a description of the scene of plunder. It was said by his contemporaries, that Page was a creature of ˝Guizot, sent out as a fiscal, and to take account of what happened. I could not ascertain whether he was a diplomatic spy or not. It is certain that, in consequence of the French sympathy, I was obliged, on landing on the shore of Colonia, to send the men below, as their ship was thundering, with its cannon well pointed towards us. We had several men wounded, receiving contusions from splinters and fragments of rock. Besides, Page's *elegant* "Narrative of Facts," as he entitled a report which he published, called the Italian Legion " Condoltreri," a term of contempt, in his opinion, but which they were farthest from deserving.

In Colonia I and my troops might have coöperated in an attack on the city ; but they were sent elsewhere, to restore the authority of the Republic on the banks of the Uruguay. The Island of Martin Garcia, where I arrived before Anzani with a small force, yielded without resistance. There I obtained a number of oxen and a few horses.

CHAPTER XXIII.

AT Colonia I met with the first " Martrero" I ever saw. He was named Sivoriña, and was one of the remarkable men known by that title who belonged to the patriot party. The services of that class of brave adventurers were of great value to that expedition.

The " Martrero" is a type of independent man. One of them often rules over an immense extent of country in that part of South America, with the authority of a government, yet without laying taxes, or raising tribute : but he asks and receives from the inhabitants their good will, and what is needful to his wandering life. He demands nothing but what is necessary ; and his wants are limited. A good horse is the first element of a Martrero. His arms, usually consisting of a carbine, a pistol, a sword, and his knife, which are his inseparable companions, are things without which he would think he could not exist. If it is considered that from the ox he obtains the furniture of his saddle; the " *Mancador*," with which to bind his companion to the pasture ; " *Mancas*," to accustom him to remaining bound and not to stray ; the " *Bolas*," which stop the *bagual*, or wild horse, in the midst of his fury, and throw him down, by entangling his legs : the " *Lazo*," not the least useful of his auxiliaries, and which hangs perennially on the right haunch of his steed ; and finally the meat, which is the only food of the Martrero ;—if all these are borne in mind, in the forming and use of which the knife is indispensable, some idea may be conceived of how much he counts on that instrument, which he also employs, with wonderful dexterity, in wounding and cutting the throat of his enemy.   The Martrero is the same as the *Gaucho* of the Pampas, and the *Monarco de la cuchilla*, (*Monarch of the Knife*,) of the Rio Grande, but more free and independent.   He will obey, when the system of government is conformed to his own opinions and sympathies. The field and the wood are his halls ; and the ground is his bed.   To him little appears sufficient.   When he enters his house, the Martrero there finds one who truly loves him, and shares with him his toils and dangers, with courage and fortitude equal to his own.   Woman as the more perfect being, appears to me to be naturally more adventurous and chivalrous than man ; and the servile education to which in that country she is condemned, probably prevents the examples from being more common.

Vivoriña was the first of the Martreros who joined my troops : but he was not the best.   On the banks of

the channel of Inferno, the eastern one, between the
island of Martin Garcia and the continent, he had
seized a boat, and put his pistol to the breast of its
master, and compelled him to transport him to the Island, whither he came and presented himself to me.
Many other Martreros afterwards came in, and rendered
much service in the ulterior operations ; but the man
on whom I love to bestow a high title, and who joined
to the courage and audacity of a Martrero, the valor,
integrity and coolness of a good captain, was Juan de
la Cruz Ledesma, of whom mention will often be
made in this narrative.

Juan de la Cruz, with his black head-dress, his eagle
eyes, noble mien, and beautiful person, was my intrepid
and faithful companion in that Uruguay expedition,
which I consider the most brilliant in which I was
ever engaged ; and he, and Joseph Mundell, equally
brave and better educated, are impressed upon my
mind for life.

In Colonia were assembled Colonel Battle, and the
Nationals of the garrison. In Martin Garcia we had
left some men, and raised the Republican standard.
The expedition then continued the voyage along the
river. Anzani had the vanguard, with some of the
smaller vessels, and took possession of a number of
merchantmen under the enemy's flag. We thus reached the Yaguary, a confluent of the Rio Negro with
the Uruguay.

The Rio Negro, which empties into the Uruguay at

that place, forms several islands of considerable size, covered with woods and pasture-grounds in ordinary times ; but in winter, when the rivers are swollen by the rains, they are almost entirely flooded, so that only animals are able to live there. The troops, however, found enough oxen and some wild horses. The greatest benefit to the expedition there was the landing of the horses, and allowing them relief from the evils of the voyage. Beyond those islands towards the east, and bathed by the Rio Negro on the south, by the Uruguay on the north, is the *Rincon de las Gallinas*. This is a part of the main land, of considerable extent, joined to the neighboring country by an Isthmus ; and it abounded with an immense number of animals, of various kinds, not excepting horses. It was, therefore, one of the favorite spots of the Martreros. One of my first cares was to march, with a part of the landing force, and take a position on the shore of the Rincon, from which I sent out Vivoriña, with Miranda, one of his companions, on horseback. They soon met with several of the Martreros of the place, who joined the expedition, and were soon followed by others ; and, from that time, a beginning was made in forming a body of cavalry, which increased very fast. Meat was abundant ; and in that same night an operation was undertaken against a party of the enemy, which had the most successful issue. A Lieutenant Gallegos, who had accompanied the troops from Montevideo, was intrusted with the command. He surprised the enemy, in number about twenty ; but few were able to escape, and he brought in six prisoners, some of whom were wounded. The affair gained for us several horses, which were a very important acquisition in our circumstances.

The system adopted by the enemy was, to send the inhabitants into the interior, in order to cut off their communications with the troops ; and this induced many of those unfortunate people to join us, among whom they found a kind reception and a safe retreat, in the largest of the islands, to which the soldiers carried a great number of animals, and chiefly sheep, for their subsistence. Thus, in different ways, the expedition gained strength and was favored by circumstances, especially by the arrival of Juan de la Cruz, whose discovery deserves to be mentioned.

The Martreros of the Rincon, who were assembled with me at the time, informed me that Juan de la Cruz, at the head of a few parties of his friends, had fought several bands of the enemy on previous days ; but, overcome by numbers, had been obliged to scatter his men, and take to the woods alone, in the thickest bushes, and even to abandon his horse, and to set off in a canoe, for the most obscure islands of the Uruguay. There he was still an object of the chief persecution to the enemy, who, after the battle of India Muerta, when there were no longer any national corps in the country, could pursue the Martreros at their pleasure. In such a painful situation was he found at that time ;

8

and I intrusted one Saldana, an old companion of Juan de la Cruz, with a few Martreros, to visit his retreat and bring him away. The undertaking was successful; and after a few days spent in the search, they found him, on an island, in a tree, and his canoe tied at its root, floating in the water, it being the time of inundation, and the little island being flooded. He had so placed himself that he could at once have retreated into the woods, if enemies had appeared, instead of friends.

The young Italians in the expedition at that time, learned a lesson of the life they will be called to lead, when they shall see their country redeemed. Juan de la Cruz was an important acquisition to the expedition. From that day forward, we had with us all the Martreros of the surrounding district, and a force of excellent cavalry, without which little or nothing could have been undertaken in those countries.

The Isla del Biscaino, (or the Island of the Biscayan,) the largest in the Yaguary, soon became a colony, peopled by the families which fled from the barbarity of the enemy, and various others, from the capital. Many animals were sent over to it, a number of horses were left there, and an officer was entrusted with the care of everything.

CHAPTER XXIV.

THE expedition then proceeded by the river, and
arrived at a place on its banks named Fray Bento,
where the vessels cast anchor. About eight miles
below, on the opposite bank, in the Province of Entre
Rios, is the mouth of the River Gualeguaychu. The
place is distant about six miles from its mouth. That
province belonged to the enemy. The expedition was
in want of horses for the operation; and good ones
were to be found in that region, as well as materials
needed to make clothing for the troops, and other
necessary articles, with which the province was well
provided. An expedition was therefore formed, to
obtain supplies. I went up the river further, expressly
for the purpose of preventing suspicion; and then, in
the night, the small vessels and boats embarked the
Italian Legionaries, and the cavalry with a few horses,
and proceeded towards the landing-place. At the
mouth of the little river lived a family, and it was

known that several merchant vessels and a small war-vessel were there, which it was necessary to surprise; and this was effected. The troops were so successful, that they reached the very house of the commandant of Gualeguayechu, while he was asleep in his bed. The Colonel commandant of the country was named Villagra. All the authorities, with the National Guards, were soon in our hands; and we garrisoned the strongest places with Republican troops. The expedition then proceeded to recruit horses and obtain other things of the most importance.

We obtained many excellent horses in Gualeguaye-chu, with articles necessary to clothe the men, har-nesses for the cavalry, and some money, which was distributed among the sailors and soldiers. All the prisoners were released at our departure. A party of the enemy's cavalry, in garrison in the town, were found to be absent, on the arrival of the expedition, and returned during our stay. Being seen by the sentinels, a few of the best mounted and equipped of the cavalry were sent out, and an encounter took place, in which the enemy were repulsed. This little affair greatly encouraged the Republicans, especially as it took place in view of all. We had one man badly wounded.

At the mouth of the river was a peninsula, formed by it and a small stream, and there was the residence of the family before mentioned. The infantry em-barked in the small vessels in which they had sailed;

the cavalry marched by land to the peninsula, leading the horses they had taken ; and there they again remained. The labor of embarking and disembarking horses was not new to them ; and in a few days everything was carried away—some to the island of the Biscaino, and some to the other island in the upper part of the river, to serve in future operations.

The expedition then proceeded into the interior, as far as Paysandù, with the occurrence of little or nothing worthy of notice. In that city was a large guard, and the enemy had constructed some batteries and sunk a number of vessels, in different parts of the channel of the river, to obstruct the passage. All obstacles were overcome ; and a few shot in the vessels, and a few wounded men, were the only consequences of a heavy cannonade with the batteries. Two officers deserved my particular notice : one a Frenchman, and the other an Englishman, who commanded two small vessels of war of their nations, and accompanied me in almost the whole of that expedition, although their instructions were not to fight. The English Lieutenant was named Tench ; and he remained but a short time ; the French officer was Hypolite Marier, commander of the schooner L'Eclair. The latter was with me the whole time, and became very dear to me, being an officer of great merit.

We reached Hervidero, formerly a most beautiful establishment, then abandoned and deserted, but still very rich in animals, which were highly valuable to the

expedition all the time of our stay. That point of
the Uruguay was named Hervidero, from the Spanish
word Hervir, which means *to boil;* and indeed it
looks like a boiling cauldron under all circumstances,
but especially when the river is low, abounding in
whirlpools formed by the numerous rocks lying under
water, over which a very rapid current pours all the
year. The passage is very dangerous. A very
spacious house stands on an eminence, built with a
terrace on the roof, called Azotea, and overlooks all
the left bank of the river. Around it was a multitude
of *Ranchos*, or barracks, with roofs of straw, which
attested the great number of slaves possessed by the
masters in more quiet times. When I first approached
the house, I found herds of the *Ganado manso*, or
domestic oxen, near the deserted habitations, in search
of their exiled masters ; and with them a *majada*, or
flock of sheep, amounting to about forty thousand,
while the *ganado cuero* or *alzado,*—that is, the wild
cattle,—of about the same number, were scattered over
the fields. Besides these there were innumerable
horses, ginetes and Poledres, chiefly wild, and many
quadrupeds of various kinds. These few lines may
give some idea of the aspect of that kind of immense
estates in South America, called *Estancias.*

The Hervidero, however, a *Saladero,* or place for
salting meat for exportation, as well as for preparing
hides, tallow, and, in short, everything furnished by the
animals slaughtered in their country. The depth of

the river did not permit them to take any other in larger vessels. Anzani, with the infantry, lodged in the establishment, occupying it in a military manner. The measures taken were very useful in repressing an unexpected attack, arranged between the enemies of Entre Rios, under the command of General Garzon, and those of the Oriental State, under Colonel Lavalleja. That was undertaken while I was not at the Hervidero.

And, in the first place, as for the reason of my absence. Among the cares of Juan de la Cruz, was that of sending some of his martreros to inform the others, who were scattered along the left bank of the river, and those of the Gueguay, who were quite numerous. A certain Magellano, and one José Dominguez were among the most famous of them all. They were then in the neighborhood of the Gueguay. José Mundell had come to that country when a child, and had become identified with the inhabitants and accustomed to their habits. He had a present of an estancia, one of the best in that part of the country. Mundell was one of those privileged persons, who seem to have come into the world to govern all around them. With nothing extraordinary in his physical nature, he was strong and active, "a free cavalier," and of a most generous disposition ; he had gained the hearts of all, on whom he bestowed benefits whenever they were in want, thus securing their love and tempering their natures. He was above all things adventurous. It

may be added that Mundell, although he had spent
the most of his life in the desert, had, from his own
taste, cultivated his mind and acquired by study more
than an ordinary share of information. He had never
taken any part in political affairs, beyond those connected with the.choice of men for the Presidency, etc.
But when the foreigners, under the orders of Ourives,
invaded the territory of the Republic, he regarded
indifference as a crime, and threw himself into the
ranks of the defenders. With the influence which he
had acquired among his brave neighbors, he soon collected several hundred men, and then sent me word
that he was going to join me with them. The bold
fellows, commanded by Juan de la Cruz, had brought
in that news to the Hervidero ; and I immediately
resolved to meet with Mundell in the Arroyo Malo,
about thirty miles below the Salto, or Falls. On the
first night after my departure the attack was made on
the Hervidero. Hearing the cannon and musketry
while I was near Arroyo Malo, I was thrown into the
greatest anxiety, as was very natural ; but I confided
much in the capacity of Anzani, whom I had left in
charge of everything.

The attack on the Hervidero had been conceived
and planned in such a manner that, if the execution
had corresponded, its results must have been fatal.
Garzon, whose forces were not fewer than two
thousand men, most of them infantry, was to have
approached the right bank of the river, while Laval-

leja was to attack the Hervidero. In order that they might strike at the same moment, they had placed two fireships in the Yuy, a small river of Entre Rios, a few miles above, intended, if not to burn the flotilla, at least to occupy the sailors, and render it impossible for them to give any assistance by land. The courage and coolness of Anzani, and the bravery of the troops, rendered all the efforts of the active enemy unavailing. Garzon effected nothing by his steady fire of musketry, because it was too distant, and the side of the river's bank was commanded by the cannon of the flotilla, which opened upon it. The fireships, being abandoned to the current, passed at a distance from the vessels, and were destroyed by their guns. Lavalleja pressed his troops against the brave Legionaries in vain, they being intrenched in the buildings, and terrifying the enemy with their silence and proud resistance.

Anzani had given orders that not a musket should be fired, until the enemy were near enough to have their clothes burnt by the powder ; and this plan succeeded well, for, supposing the houses to have been evacuated, they advanced without apprehension : but a general discharge of musketry, when close at hand, from all quarters, put them immediately to flight, making it impossible to rally again.

Having arranged with Mundell about his entering Salto when occupied by the Republicans, I returned to the Hervidero. I received notice, about that time, from Colonel Baez, who was making arrangements to

8

join me with some men. The only vessel of the enemy stationed in the Yuy deserted to us, with a portion of the crew.

Thus everything smiled on the expedition.

CHAPTER XXV.

THE PROVINCE OF CORRIENTES CALLS GENERAL PAZ FROM MONTEVIDEO
—ALLIANCE WITH PARAGUAY—I GO TO SALTO WITH THE FLOTILLA,
TO RELIEVE IT FROM A SIEGE—WITH LA CRUZ AND MUNDELL, ATTACK
LAVALLEJA—RETURN TO SALTO.

THE Province of Corrientes, after the battle of Arroyo
Grande, had fallen again under the dominion of Rosas :
but the admirable resistance of Montevideo, and some
other favorable circumstances, called the people again
to independence ; and Madariaga and the principal
authorities in that revolution had invited General Paz
from Montevideo, to take command of the army.
That old and virtuous chief, by his own fame and
capacity, induced Paraguay to make an offensive and
defensive alliance ; and that state collected at Corrientes a respectable contingent for the army. Things
thus proceeded wonderfully well for that part of the
country ; and not the least important object was the
opening of communications with those interior provinces, to collect in the Department of Salto the Oriental emigrants who were in Corrientes and Brazil. I
then sent from the Hervidero a *balenera*, on a mission
to General Paz : but, being observed and pursued by
the enemy, the men in it were obliged to abandon the

boat, and take refuge in the woods. I was obliged to repeat the same thing three times; when at length a brave officer of the Italians, Giacomo Casella, taking advantage of a strong flood in the river, succeeded in overcoming every obstacle, and arrived in the Province of Corrientes. During the same flood I arrived at Salto with the flotilla.

The city was governed by Lavalleja, who attacked the Hervidero with a force of about three hundred men, infantry and cavalry. He had been engaged for some days in making the inhabitants evacuate the town; and for them and his troops he formed a camp on the left bank of the Capebi, at the distance of twenty-one miles from Salto.

The Republicans took the town, without any resistance, and designed to make some fortifications. That point being occupied, they remained there, but, of course, besieged on the land-side, as the enemy were superior in cavalry. One of the principal inconveniences which they suffered was the want of meat, all the animals having been driven away. But that evil did not last long.

Mundell, having collected about a hundred and fifty men, drove back a corps of the enemy who were pressing upon him, and arrived safe at Salto. From that moment the Republicans began to make sorties, and to bring in animals enough for the subsistence of the troops. With Mundell's horsemen, and those of Juan de la Cruz, we were able to take the field; and one fine day we went to seek Lavalleja in his own camp. Some deserters from the enemy had given me exact information of his position and the number of his forces; and I determined to attack him. One evening I drew out two hundred of the cavalry and a hundred of the Italian Legionaries, and moved from Salto, intending to surprise the enemy before daybreak. My guides were the deserters; and, although they were acquainted with the country, yet, as there were no roads leading in the direction they took, they got astray, and daylight found us at the distance of three miles from the camp we were seeking. Perhaps it was not prudent to attack an enemy at least equal in force, entrenched, and in their own camp, and which might receive reinforcements, which they had asked for, at any moment; but to turn back would not only have been disgraceful, but would have had a very bad effect on the feelings of the new troops. I was a little troubled by the idea of retreating, and determined to attack. I reached an eminence where the enemy had an advance post. They retired on my approach. I could then see their camp, and observed several groups returning towards it, from various directions. They were detachments which had been sent out in the night to different points, to observe the Republicans, the enemy having heard of our setting out. I then immediately gave orders to Mundell, who had the vanguard, to press on a strong body of cavalry, to prevent their concentration.

The enemy did the same, to repel that movement and protect their troops. Mundell, with great bravery, succeeded, and drove and dispersed several of their detachments ; but he advanced too far, in the warmth of the pursuit, so that his troops soon found themselves surrounded by the enemy, who, recovering from their first fright, came upon them with their lances, threatening to separate them from the main body, which, although at a distance, was approaching for a battle. In the meantime, seeing all this, I at first designed to have the whole little force of the Republicans proceed in a mass, and give a decisive blow. I therefore hastened the march of the infantry, forming the rear guard and reserve, with the cavalry of Juan de la Cruz : but seeing the position of Mundell, which admitted no delay, I left the infantry behind under the command of Marrocchetti, and pressed forward the reserve of cavalry in échellons.

The first échellon, commanded by Gallegas, pushed on, and somewhat restored the resistance of the cavalry. The charge of Juan de la Cruz drove the enemy back ; and they retired towards their camp. I had ordered the échellons of the reserve to charge in a compact mass, so that Mundell and his men, who had fought bravely, might recover their order in a moment. Our troops then moved on towards the enemy's camp, in order of battle,—the infantry in the centre by platoons, and under orders not to fire a shot ; Mundell on the

right, and Juan de la Cruz on the left; while a small
échellon of cavalry formed a reserve.

The enemy's cavalry, after the first encounter, had
formed again behind the infantry, who were covered
by a line of carts; but the firmness and resolution of
the Republicans, now marching on in a close body and
in silence, intimidated them so much that they made but
little resistance. In a moment the action was over;
or, rather, it was not a fight, but a complete discomfiture
and precipitate flight towards the pass of the river.
On reaching that point some of the boldest endeavored
to make a stand; and they might have been able, but
it would have been a very arduous task; although the
Republican cavalry had halted : for the Legionaries, at
the command of " Cartridges on the neck!" threw
themselves into the water with the greatest fury, and
there was no more resistance.

The victory was now complete. All the infantry of
the enemy were in the power of the conquerors, and some
of the cavalry, with all the families of the Salto, who
had been dragged from their homes, and a train containing various objects of merchandize, consisting of thirty-four loaded wagons. Above all, we had captured a
great number of horses, which were the most valuable
of all things in our existing circumstances. A brass
cannon, made in Florence, some ages past, by a certain
Cenni, fell into our hands. It was the same piece
which had been fired upon us at the Hervidero; and

being dismounted on that occasion, was undergoing repair in the enemy's camp. After the action, which lasted only a few hours, we collected everything useful, and set off on our return. Our progress to Salto was quite a triumphal march. The population poured blessings on us from their own houses, to which they had been restored by our means ; and the victory acquired for the army a reputation which was well merited, proving that all the three classes of troops were able to keep the field.

Our celerity was of much importance ; for, as has already been mentioned, the enemy were in expectation of a strong reinforcement ; and that was the entire force of General Urquiza, which had just before been victorious at India Muerta, and was then on the march for Corrientes, to fight the army of that province. Vergara, who had the vanguard of it, came in sight of Salto the day after our return, and captured a few of our horses, which were dispersed in the neighboring pastures. Being in the presence of those forces, which seemed to overwhelm us, we made every exertion to resist it.

A battery, marked out by Anzani, in the centre of the city, made a progress that was quite astonishing. Both soldiers and people worked at it, such houses as were adapted to defence were fortified, and every man had a post assigned him. Several cannon were levelled from the boats, and preparations were made to supply the battery. At that time arrived Colonel Baez, with about sixty cavalry. Urquiza soon after presented himself, who had assured his friends that he would cross the Uruguay at Salto, with the assistance of the Republican flotilla, which he expected to capture. But his predicton was not fulfilled. The attack by the enemy was simultaneous with his appearance.

CHAPTER XXVI.

ON the east of Salto was a hill, distant a musket shot from the first houses; and it commanded the whole town. The Republicans had not fortified it, for the want of sufficient force, as it would be necessary, if occupied, to establish a line of fortifications proportioned to the number of disposable troops. As might have been expected, Urquiza took possession of the hill, and placed on it six pieces of artillery. At the same time he sent forward his infantry, at quick step, against the Republican right. Just at that moment two pieces had been placed in the battery : but there was yet neither platform nor parapet ; and the enemy, after giving their fire, threw themselves upon the ground, which was not even consolidated. The Republican right was really the most vulnerable, as the enemy could reach it under cover, in the hollow of a valley. And this they did ; so that the defenders saw them appear suddenly, and without warning, from that concealment. Immediately the right wing fled, and

(178)

those occupying the houses retreated towards the river.

I was then at the battery; and, in disposing of my troops, had reserved a company of the Italian Legion at that point. I immediately made one-half of that company charge the enemy; and after them sent the second half to do the same. And that duty was executed with so much courage, that the assailants were, in their turn, put to a precipitate flight. The company of Italians which performed that service was under the command of Captain Carone, and its lieutenants were Ramorino and Zaccarello.

The enemy were discouraged by their unsuccessful attempt, which prevented them from making any decisive attack, and all their operations were reduced to a cannonade. In that kind of fighting, although the enemy had come upon the Republicans when ill-prepared, from the want of time, yet we were able to maintain a respectable attitude. I had landed the cannon from the vessels, under the orders of their officers, viz., Scozini, Cogliolo, and José Maria, all of them brave and skilful men; so that the enemy's artillery, although superior in numbers and position, was pretty well opposed, and obliged to be occasionally brought under cover of the hill. The enemy left several men dead, while the Republicans had only a few wounded. The latter, however, lost the greater part of their oxen, which were in a corral, or inclosure; and, as they were wild, as soon as the gate was opened, they poured out, like a torrent, and spread all over the country.

For three days Urquiza continued his attempts; but every day found the besieged better prepared. Not a moment was lost during the night. Five pieces of cannon were placed in the battery, the platform was finished, the parapet, and the "Santa Barbara," or mine for blowing up. A proclamation was circulated at that time, signed by Colonel Bacz and myself, condemning to death any one who might leave his post; and the smaller vessels were forbidden to come near the bank of the river, while all which were there were made to draw off.

At the same time the enemy, seeing that they were gaining nothing, adopted a system of blockade, and shut up the city on the land side, in the closest manner. But in that undertaking also they were frustrated; for we were masters of the river, and could bring in all· necessary supplies of provisions by that water. During the eighteen days which the siege continued, we were not idle, having to bring in hay for the cattle and horses continually; and, as the enemy had formed a circular chain of posts around us, we took advantage of moments of inattention, to attack, and often with advantage. At length Urquiza became weary, and perhaps was called away to other parts of the Uruguay, by more pressing affairs. He withdrew, and marched off, to cross the river above Salto.

The two divisions of Lamas and Vergara now remained to continue the siege, with about seven hundred cavalry : but from that time the enemy were unable to keep it closely, for the Republicans made
sorties now and then, sometimes bringing in oxen or
wild horses, and that kept our cavalry in a pretty
good condition, who had lost almost all their horses,
in consequence of the strictness of the siege. It is to
be observed, that the horses of that part of the country
are not accustomed to eat anything but grass, being
pastured in the open fields ; and therefore but few are
fed with hay and grain.

In those days an operation was performed by the
Republicans, of a superior kind. Garzon, who had
been at Concordia, opposite Salto, had marched, to
unite with Urquiza, for Corrientes, under the orders
of the latter General ; but a cavalry corps of observation remained at Concordia. The sentinels of that
body were visible from Salto, and their *cavalcade*, or
troop of horses, went every day to the river's bank to
feed, (probably finding better pasture,) and at night
returned. A plan was formed to capture those animals; and one day about twenty men prepared,
naked, and with nothing but their sabres ; while
a company of Legionaries, divided among the vessels of the flotilla, waited, ready to embark in the
boats. About mid-day, when the sun shone hottest,
the enemy's sentinels were lying on the ground, having
made a shelter of their ponchos, and were fast asleep.

The river, at the place where it was to be crossed, was only about five hundred paces wide. and not guarded. The appointed signal was given. and the cavalry soldiers marched from behind their coverts on the shore, and threw themselves into the water, while the Legionaries leaped into the boats ; and, when the sentinels awoke, they heard the bullets of their active assailants whistling about their ears ; and the amphibious centaurs pursued them along the hill.

Only the brave South American cavalry are capable of performing such an enterprise. Being excellent swimmers, both men and horses, they can cross a river several miles wide, the men holding by the tails of their animals, or by their manes, and carrying their arms and baggage in their *pelottas*, which are made of the *curona*, a piece of leather, which forms a part of the harness.

Some of the cavalry remained on the hill, watching the enemy, while the others collected their horses which were scattered about the pasture, and led them to the shore, where they hurried them into the water, and got most of them over to the other side. Some of the enemy, who resisted, were bound and carried across by the vessels. In the meantime the Legionaries exchanged a few shots with the enemy, who were increasing their numbers, but did not feel strong enough to charge them. Thus, in a few hours, more than a hundred horses were obtained by the Republicans, without having a single man wounded.

That affair was a very singular and curious one,
and performed in full view from Salto. The horses
of Entre Rios are generally esteemed ; and, for good
reasons, that capture excited a desire to attack the
besiegers

CHAPTER XXVII.

VERGARA, with his division, was pressing the town very
closely, and some persons acquainted with the country
were sent to spy his position, which thus became
known to the defenders. It would have been useless
to make an attack by day, because it was impossible to surprise them, and, therefore, it was necessary
to attack by night. I had given Colonel Baez the
command of the cavalry, and Anzani was with the
infantry. They left Salto after nightfall, and took the
direction towards the enemy's camp, situated about
eight miles off. Although the march of the troops was
as silent and as cautious as possible, they were heard
by the advanced sentinels, and therefore Vergara had
time to mount his horse. The assault was made without loss of time, but only the cavalry of the Republicans were able to fight, as the infantry, in spite of all
their exertions, could not reach the field of battle in
season. The enemy fought with spirit, but at the cry
of "The infantry!" which was raised at a favorable

(184)

moment, they gave ground, and then broke their ranks and took to flight. They were pursued several miles, but, on account of the darkness, little was effected. A few prisoners were made and some horses taken, while there were a small number of killed and wounded on both sides. When daylight appeared, it was difficult to find the field of battle, as the fighting had been done on the march. Several groups of the enemy appeared, scattered on the distant hills, and Colonel Baez remained with the cavalry to pursue them and to collect a herd of oxen, while the other troops returned to Salto.

About that time, which was the beginning of the year 1846, we received news that General Medina, with a number of emigrants from the Oriental, was coming from Corrientes for Salto. The discomfiture of Vergara had given the Republicans an advantage, but had not produced the results that might have been expected. Lamas, who was not far off, and engaged in breaking horses, came up on receiving intelligence of the defeat, and ordered the collecting of men. Both established their camps, and recommenced the siege, driving away the animals. Their superiority in cavalry expedited that proceeding. General Medina then came, who had been appointed head of the army, and it was necessary to secure his entrance. Colonel Baez, as has been mentioned already, had assumed the command of the cavalry, and regularly organized it, skilled as he was in that kind of troops. Being

9

possessed of uncommon activity, he greatly increased
the number of horses, and provided the city and the
troops with cattle.   Mundell and Juan de la Cruz
were at his orders, and at that time both were
detached, with commissions to catch wild horses.
Colonel Baez, better known than General Medina,
was in direct relation with him, and knew that he was
to be in sight of Salto on the 8th of February ; and
it was therefore arranged that I should accompany
him with the cavalry.   At dawn of day on the 8th of
February, 1846, we left Salto, and took the direction
of the little river San Antonio, on the left bank of
which they were to await the approach of General
Medina and his army.   The enemy, according to their
custom in that region, showed several troops of cavalry
on the heights on the right, which approached at times as
if to observe whether they were collecting animals, and
to interrupt them.   Colonel Baez stationed a line of
marksmen of the cavalry against those troops, and
employed himself several hours in skirmishing with
them.   The infantry had halted near the little stream,
at a place called Tapera di Don Vicenzio.   I was
separated from the infantry, and observing the guerrillas, fighting, conducted by Baez.   That kind of warfare afforded the Italians an amusing sight : but the
enemy concealed their " wasp's nest" under that kind
of military game, having put forward so feeble a force
only to deceive their opponents, and give their strong
body, which was behind, opportunity to advance.

The country, in all parts of the department of Salto, is hilly, as is also that of San Antonio. Therefore the large force which was advancing was able to approach within a short distance without being discovered.

When I had reached the place of observation, and cast my eyes on the other side of San Antonio, I was overwhelmed with surprise by discovering, on the west of a neighboring hill, where only a few of the enemy had before been seen, a multitude of troops, as was shown by a forest of lances: seven squadrons of cavalry, with banners displayed, and a corps of infantry, double in size of our own, who, having come up on horseback, within two musket shots, dismounted, formed in line of battle, and were marching, at quick step, to charge with the bayonet. Baez said to me: " Let us retire." But, seeing that to be impossible, I replied: "There is not time enough; and we must fight."

I then ran to the Italian Legionaries; and, in order to destroy, or at least to mitigate the impression which might be produced on them by the appearance of so formidable an enemy, said: " We will fight! The cavalry we are resolved to conquer. To-day we have them, although we are a small body of infantry."

At the place where we took position there were numerous wooden posts standing planted in the ground, which had served in the walls of an old wooden edifice; and to each beam was assigned a Legionary. The remainder, forming three small parties, were

placed in column behind the building, and covered by
walls of masonry of the northern end of the same
building, which was in form of a room, capable of
containing about thirty men, and covering almost the
front of the little column. On the right of the infantry, Baez was posted, with the cavalry, those being
dismounted, who were armed with carbines, while the
lancers remained on horseback. The whole force
comprised about a hundred cavalry, and a hundred
and eighty-six Legionaries. The enemy had nine
hundred cavalry, (some said twelve hundred,) and
three hundred infantry. The Republicans, therefore,
had only one thing left that could be done—to defend
themselves—resist, and repel the charge of the enemy's
infantry. I then ran forward, and gave them all the
attention in my power. If the enemy, instead of
charging in line of battle, forming an extended line,
had charged in column, or in alternate platoons, they
must have destroyed our force. By the impetus of
their column they would certainly have penetrated
into our position, and mingled with the defenders ;
and then their cavalry would have completed our ruin
and exterminated us. Then the fields of San Antonio
would have been, to this day, whitened with Italian
bones ! But, instead of this, the enemy advanced in
line, beating the charge, and bravely withholding their
fire until within a few yards. The Legionaries had
orders not to fire until very near. When the enemy
reached the appointed distance, they halted and gave

a general discharge. The moment was decisive. Many of the defenders fell under that fire : but the assailants were thrown into disorder, being thinned by shots from the Republicans, who fired from behind the timbers, and then charged them, not in order, but yet in a body, and forced them to turn their backs, by falling upon them with bayonets, like mad-men. That there occurred for the Republicans a moment of disorder and hesitation, it cannot be denied. There were among us a number of prisoners, who, not expecting a successful termination to the desperate defence, cast about their eyes to find some way open for escape. But they were prevented from doing anything, by some of our brave men, who then, at the cry of " The enemy run !" threw themselves upon them like lions.

From the moment when I directed my attention upon the enemy's infantry, I saw nothing more of Colonel Baez and the cavalry. Five or six horsemen remained with my men, whom I put there under the command of a brave Oriental officer, Jose Maria.

After the defeat of the enemy's infantry, I had hopes of safety ; and, taking advantage of the momentary calm produced by the stupefaction of the enemy, I put my men again in order. Among the dead remaining on the ground, especially those lying where the enemy halted, we found abundant supplies of cartridges ; and the muskets of the killed and wounded served an important purpose, being taken, to arm those of the soldiers who were in want, and some of the officers.

The enemy, having failed in their first charge, repeated it several times, many of their dragoons dismounting ; and with them and masses of cavalry, they attacked us, but succeeded only in increasing their loss. I was always ready, with some of the bravest of the Legionaries, who awaited the charge ; and, when the enemy had made their attack, invariably charged them in return. The enemy several times endeavored to get a position near us ; but I then posted the best marksmen among our soldiers, and made them harrass them, until they took to flight.

CHAPTER XXVIII.

THE fighting began about one o'clock in the afternoon, and lasted until near nine in the evening. Night
came on, and found us surrounded by many corpses
and wounded men. About nine o'clock preparations
were made for a retreat. The number of wounded
was very large, including almost all the officers, viz.:
Morrochetti, Casana, Sacchi, Ramorino, Rodi, Beruti,
Zaccorello, Amero, and Fereti. Only Carone, Traverse, and a few others, were unhurt. It was an
arduous and painful undertaking to remove them from
the ground where they lay. Some were placed upon
horses, which were numerous, while others, who were
able to stand, were helped on, each by two of his comrades. When the arrangements had been made for
the accommodation of the wounded, the other soldiers
were formed in four platoons; and as fast as they were
put in order, they were made to load themselves with
some remaining ammunition, the less to expose themselves to the continual fire of the enemy. The

retreat was then commenced, and I thought it a fine
sight,—though there was but a handful of men, in close
column, with orders not to fire a single shot before
making the edge of the wood which borders the river
Uruguay. I had directed the vanguard to take the
wounded, feeling confident that the charges of the
enemy would be made on our rear and flanks. As
was natural, those unfortunate men fell into some
disorder, which it was impossible to prevent ; but they
yet went on, all, it is believed, except two. The little
column proceeded in the most admirable manner, so
that I must ever speak of their conduct with pride.
The soldiers fixed their bayonets before setting off ;
and keeping close ranks, they reached the designed
place, though not for want of any exertions, on the
part of the enemy, to hinder them : for every effort was
made, by repeated charges from all quarters, and with
their whole force. In vain did their lancers come up
and give wounds to men in the ranks ; the only return
made was with the bayonet, while the soldiers pressed
themselves more compactly together. On reaching
the verge of the wood, we halted ; and the order was
given, "To the right about !" when immediately a
general volley filled the enemy's files with dead, and
they were all instantly driven back.

One of the most severe sufferings endured that day
was from thirst, especially among the wounded.

Having reached the bank of the river, it may be
imagined with what avidity the soldiers ran to the

water. Some of them stopped to drink, while the others kept the enemy at a distance. The success of the first part of the retreat, now performed, secured the retreating troops less molestation on the remainder of their way. A chain of sharp-shooters was formed to protect the left flank, who kept up a continual fire, almost until they entered the city ; and thus we moved along the bank of the river.

Anzani was waiting for us at the entrance of the city, and could not satiate himself with embracing me and my companions. He had never despaired, al-although the enterprise was so arduous. He had collected the few remaining men in the fortress, and replied to the enemy's summons to surrender, which they made during the battle, with a threat to blow up everything before he would submit. It is to be remarked, that the enemy not only assured him that all the Italians were killed or prisoners, but also the greater part of the soldiers with Baez. Still Anzani did not despair ; and I have mentioned him to those of my fellow-citizens who at different times have despaired of Italy. Ah! there are few like Anzani! But he that despairs is a coward!

Our retreating troops entered Salto at midnight, and even at that hour we found all the soldiers and all the inhabitants awake. The latter came out with alacrity, and gave all possible attention and care to the wounded, bringing everything necessary for their relief and comfort. Poor people! Poor people, who

9

suffered so much in the various vicissitudes of war, I shall never think of you but with a deep sense of gratitude!

I had several severe losses to lament in that remarkable affair, though the enemy were much the greater sufferers.

General Servando Gomez, who was the author of the surprise, and who seemed as if he would annihilate us forever, commenced his retreat on the 9th, hastily taking with him his shattered division towards Paisandu, with a great number of wounded men, and leaving the fields of San Antonio covered with dead. The first day after our arrival was occupied in giving attention to the wounded ; and two French physicians rendered them the most important services. They were the physicians of the French ship L'Eclair, whose names have not been obtained, and Dr. Desroscaux, another young man, then for some time connected with the Italian Legion. He had fought all the way as a common soldier, and then devoted himself to the care of his wounded companions. But what most availed at that painful time were the delicate cares of the ladies of Salto.

The succeeding days were occupied in collecting and burying our dead. The battle had been so extraordinary, that I thought it ought to be commemorated by an unusual mode of interring the victims, and I chose a spot, on the top of the hill which overlooks Salto, and which had been the scene of successful battles. There was dug a trench for all, and then handfuls of earth were thrown in by the soldiers, until a tumulus rose, to stand as a memorial. A cross was then placed on the top, with this inscription on one side:

"*Legione Italiana, Marina e Cavalleria Orientale.*"
On the other side:

"*8th Febbrajo*, 1846."

(The Italian Legion, and the Oriental Marine and Cavalry.—8th February, 1846.")

The names of those killed and wounded in that brave fight have been preserved in the journals kept by Anzani.

CHAPTER XXIX.

GENERAL Medina was now able freely to enter Salto
with his suite; and he retained the superior command
until the revolution made by Rivera's friends in Montevideo. Nothing important, however, took place in
all that period.

The revolution in Montevideo in favor of Rivera
gave a terrible blow to the affairs of the Republic.
The war ceased to be national, and was directed by
miserable factions. About the same time occurred the
revolution in Corrientes, brought about by Madariaga,
against General Paz. Those young chiefs, who had
become illustrious by surprising deeds in delivering their
country from the oppressive dominion of Rosas, now,
for jealousy and thirst of power, debased themselves
by the meanest treachery, and thus ruined the cause of
their people. General Paz was obliged to leave the
army of Corrientes, and retire to Brazil. Paraguay

recalled her army after his departure; the troops of
Madariaga, reduced by neglect to their own resources
alone, were completely beaten by Urquiza; and Corrientes fell into the power of the Dictator.

The affair of Montevideo also proceeded no better,
and few events of importance occurred. The, Italian
Legion, so justly esteemed for their honorable and daring
exploits, had continued their accustomed service of advanced posts, alternating with the other corps of the capital. Anzani was with them; and, although no very
important engagements took place, they never failed to
prove themselves worthy of their fame.

I occupied myself more with the marine, fitting up
some of the vessels which were most needed, and in
cruising on the river Plata, in the schooner "Maypú."

In the meantime the French intervention proceeded
every day, and no more coërcive measure was it proposed to apply to the solution of the problem; but
several diplomatists, whom Rosas deluded and mock-
ed at, were sent to negotiate, but obtained nothing
from him better than insignificant armistices, which
had no effect but to waste the limited means collected
with difficulty in the besieged city. With her change
of policy, France had changed her agents. Such men
as Diffandis and Ouseley for ambassadors, and L'Ainé
and Inglefield for admirals, worthy to sustain a generous policy, and dear to the public, were removed; and
such men were substituted as were devoted to a policy
inevitably ruinous to the people.

The Oriental government, powerless from the want of means, was obliged to submit to the dictates of the intervention. Deplorable situation!

Rivera, being restored to power by his partisans, removed all others. Most of those who had engaged in the noble defense from disinterested love of country, had retired, weary of the enterprise, or were displaced to make room for devotees of Rivera, and unfit men. I found, however, at Montevideo, (that city of marvellous changes,) the new elements of another army, and transported them to Las Vacas, on the left bank of the Uruguay. The soldiers of Montevideo were made for conquerors; and they proved it in their first encounters with the enemy in the country. At Mercedes, especially, they performed prodigies of valor; but the evil influence which misled Rivera at Arroyo Grande and India Muerta, beset him at Paisandu, where, after a victory, he saw his army defeated. At Maldonado he embarked again, to return to Brazil, whether more unfortunate or more culpable, it is difficult to determine.

The government of Montevideo having fallen into the power of Rivera, I was left mourning over it, and apprehending public sufferings. The old General Medina, appointed General-in-chief by the government, with the consent of the former not only yielded to events, but, the better to recommend himself to the favor of the new patron, intrigued against my friend; but they deceived themselves. Both Italians and Orientals loved him in Salto, and he would have been able, without fear of any one, to rise independent of the new and illegal power.   But the cause of that unhappy people was too sacred in his eyes.   He loved them, and ever denominated them as good-hearted and generous.   To increase their distresses, by fomenting their internal dissentions, was wholly incompatible with his views and feelings.

To establish Rivera in power, the public squares of Montevideo were made scenes of bloodshed.   At Salto the same fatal game was planned ; but it proved impracticable.   I contented myself with making reprisals, assuming, as at first, the command of the forces. At that time occurred the successful battle against the troops of Lamas and Vergara, on the 20th of May, 1846.   Those two divisions, after the affair of San Antonio, where they fought under the command of Servando Gomez, had been reformed and reinforced ; and they again occupied their positions around Salto, changing their encampments, but always keeping at some leagues' distance.   We did not fail, now and then, to disturb our enemies as much as we could, especially when they went out to catch animals.   One Major Dominguez, who had been sent for that purpose by General Medina, was completely discomfited, losing all his horses and some men.   I had the positions of the enemy's camp examined by spies, and in the night of May 19th, I marched to attack him.   I had with me about three hundred cavalry and a hundred legionaries—the remains of a battalion.   Poor youths! they have since been sadly decimated! My object was to surprise the enemy's camp at early dawn; and we arrived at the spot, for once, exactly at the desired moment. I had the aid of Captain Pablo, an American Indian, and a brave soldier. His infantry were mounted, and they marched all night, and before break of day came in sight of the enemy's forces in the camp of General Vergara, on the right bank of the Dayman. The infantry then dismounted, and were ordered to attack. The victory was very easily obtained. The troops of Vergara immediately took to flight, and were driven into the river. They left their arms, horses, and a few men, who were taken prisoners. But the triumph was far from being complete; for the troops were to return, and we set off as the daylight increased. The camp of Lamas was separated from that of Vergara by a small stream; and, at the first alarm, the former had taken position on the top of a hill, which commanded both camps. Vergara, with the greater part of his men, had succeeded in joining Lamas. They were warlike and brave soldiers, made at the opening of the war.

Having collected, in the abandoned camp, all the serviceable horses, I pursued the enemy, but without success. Most of my cavalry were mounted on *Rodomones*, that is, horses caught and broken only a few days before; and the enemy were better supplied. It was therefore necessary to desist from pursuing them, and be content with the advantages gained, and take the road to Salto. We were, however, very unexpectedly favored, and in an important manner. While pursuing our march for Salto, we were in the following order : a squadron of cavalry in platoons, at the head ; the infantry in column, in the centre ; the remaining cavalry for the rear guard, likewise in column. Two strong lines of cavalry, commanded by Majors Carvallo and N. Fausto, covered our right flank ; and the *cavallada*, with the horses of the infantry, marched on the left. The enemy, having reörganized, as has been said, and reconcentrated all their detachments, amounted to about five hundred men in cavalry. Being acquainted with my force, the enemy flanked us on the right, at a short distance, so that he seemed disposed to revenge himself.

I had placed Colonel Celesto Centurion in command of the cavalry,—a very brave man ; while Carone commanded the infantry. The latter was particularly urged by me to guard against any confusion or disorder in his ranks, and to prevent it at any sacrifice. He was to preserve their order, which was that of close column, and never to make a movement by conversion, but only by flanks and right-about-face. The infantry was to serve as a point of support to Centurion, and also to re-form in any event that might happen. The enemy were emboldened, being increased by detachments.

Our troops proceeded over beautiful hills, for about two miles from the banks of the Dayman. The grass had but just begun to grow, but was very green ; and

9*

the surface of the ground was undulated like the waves of the ocean, but lay in all the majesty of stillness, while not a tree or a bush formed any obstacle. It offered indeed a battle-field, and for the mightiest hosts.

CHAPTER XXX.

HAVING reached the border of a brook, I thought it better not to cross it, because our small force might be disordered in the passage, and the hill on the right concealed the great body of the enemy, who were not far off, and marching in a direction parallel to our own. I thought we would be attacked at that point; and the result justified my expectation. I halted, and, wishing to discover the enemy's condition, sent orders to Major Carvello, to "charge that line of the enemy quite to the hill." The charge was made, and with bravery, as far as the eminence, where the assailants stopped, and an adjutant came galloping up to me, to inform me that the enemy were marching towards us at a trot, and with their whole force in order of battle. No time was to be lost. The cavalry on the wings wheeled to the right, and were reinforced by the line, suddenly concentrated. The infantry formed on the right flank and towards the enemy. When the line reached the top of the hill, the enemy's line was march ing upon us within pistol shot.

I must confess that the enemy had made a movement of which my troops would not have been capable, and which proved that they were brave, warlike,
and well commanded. Seeing this, without taking
time for reflection, I gave the signal for a charge : for
as soon as I discovered them, the enemy were converg
ing, from the centre to the wings, laterally ; and, after
having made about half a circle beyond our flanks,
they charged our cavalry by platoons in flank, and so
rendered our infantry useless. I did not hesitate, but
ordered my cavalry to close in, and charge, to avoid
losing the advantage of the impetus of the horses.
And indeed they charged well, and fought bravely.

Several charges were made by the cavalry on both
sides, and with different results. It would be difficult
to decide which party displayed most valor. The enemy being superior in numbers, and in the excellence
of their horses, drove back ours upon our infantry,
and soon measured our lances with their bayonets.
The latter, having reformed, with the aid of their numbers, drove them back, fighting them hand to hand.
The young Italians then performed their feats to admiration ; and I remember them, and the 20th of May,
with peculiar pleasure. Compact as a redoubt, ex
ceedingly active, they ran to every point where their
assistance was needed, always putting the assailants to
flight. The enemy fired very few muskets, but those
few were deliberate and sure.

At last the enemy, having become disordered by nu-

merous charges, became only a deranged mass ; while,
on the contrary, our troops, supported by the infantry,
were always able to reörganize for fighting well. The
engagement had lasted about half an hour, in that
manner, when, being no longer approached by organized forces, we were drawn up anew and made a decisive charge. The enemy then broke, disbanded, and
took to flight. A cloud of "*bollas*" whirled about in
the air, and presented a curious spectacle.

The *bolla* is one of the most terrible weapons used
by the South American horsemen. It consists of three
balls, covered with leather, and fastened to three
leathern cords, which are connected. One of the balls
is held in the hand, while the other two are flourished
in the air over the head, when the order is given to
charge. When a horse is struck in the leg with one
of them, it stops him, and sometimes makes him fall ;
and in this way many captures are made. The South
American cavalry soldier is second to none in the
world, in any kind of combat ; and in a defeat, they
retain their superiority in pursuing their enemy. They
are stopped in their course by no obstacles in the field.
If a tree does not allow them to pass while sitting
erect, they throw themselves back upon the crupper of
the half-wild horse, and disappear among the trappings
of the animal. They arrive at a river, and plunge in,
with their arms in their teeth ; and sometimes wound
their enemy in the middle of the stream. Besides the
bolla, they carry the terrible *Coltelo*, or knife, which, as

before has been mentioned, they keep with them all
their lives, and manage with a dexterity peculiar to
themselves. Woe to the soldier whose horse tires!
" Bollado," or struck with the bolla, he cannot defend
himself from the knife of his pursuer, who dismounts to
strike him with it in the throat, and then mounts again,
to overtake others. Such customs prevail among them,
that sometimes, when men of courage meet, even after
a victory, scenes occur which would shock a reader if
they were described.

One of those encounters I witnessed. It occurred
at a short distance from a line, between a party of our
soldiers and one of the enemy, whose horse had been
killed. Having fallen to the ground, he rose and
fought on foot, first with him who had dismounted him,
whom he treated very roughly. Another then came
to his assistance, then another ; and at length he was
engaged with six, when I reached the spot, in order to
save the life of the brave man—but too late.

Our enemy was now entirely routed, and the victory
complete. The pursuit was continued several miles.
The immediate result, however, was not what it might
have been, for the want of good horses, as many of the
enemy escaped. But, notwithstanding this, during the
whole time that the troops remained at Salto, we had
the satisfaction of seeing that department free from
the enemy.

The action of the 20th of May has been described
at length, because of its remarkable success,—the fine,

open field on which it was fought, and the fine climate
and sky, which reminded me of Italy. The struggle
was with a practised enemy, superior in number, and
better provided with horses, which are the principal
element of that kind of warfare; and several single
combats took place on horseback, with great valor.
Our cavalry performed wonders that day, considering
their inferiority. Of the infantry, it will be sufficient
to mention the case of Major Carvallo, who was my
companion at San Antonio and Dayman, and in both
actions fought like a brave man, as he was. In each
of them, also, he had the misfortune to be wounded
in the face by a musket-shot. One struck two inches
below his right eye, and the other, in the same spot on
his left cheek, forming a strange symmetry in his face.
He was wounded the second time in the beginning of
the battle of Dayman; and after its close, he asked
leave to return to Salto, to have his wounds dressed.
Passing under the battery of the city, he was asked
what was the fate of the day, when he replied, although
he was able to speak but little : "The Italian Infantry
are more solid than your battery."

The names of the dead and wounded in the engagement, as has before been said, are given in Anzani's
"Journal of the Italian Legion."

CHAPTER XXXI.

AFTER the battle of the 20th of May, at Dayman, nothing important occurred in the campaign of Uruguay.
I received orders from the government to return to
Montevideo, with the vessels of the flotilla, and the
detachment of the Italian Legion. A few of the
smaller vessels remained at Salto, and the place was
left under the command of Commandant Artigos, a
brave officer, who distinguished himself in the battle
on the 20th of May. A few days after my departure,
Colonel Blanco arrived, and took command of the
place at the orders of General Rivera.

In consequence of errors committed at Corrientes and Montevideo, the cause of Rosas gained
strength very rapidly, and that of the people of the
Plata sunk into a desperate condition. The army of
Corrientes was destroyed by Urquiza in a battle; and

that unfortunate people, after swimming in blood, languished under despotism. Rivera, not profiting by the lessons of misfortune, ended as he had begun, by removing from office men who had executed their duties with faithfulness, and substituting his partisans, destroying the materials of an army of operations, which the courage and constancy of the people had created and maintained with incorruptible heroism, and expatriating himself under the contempt and malediction of all. The English and French intervention was watched by intriguers and faithless men. The positions in the interior fell, one after another, into the power of the enemy. Salto, which had been so honorably acquired and maintained, was taken by assault by Sevando Gomez, and Colonel Gomez perished in the defence—an old and brave soldier—with a considerable number of men. At length the defence of the generous Oriental people was once more reduced to Montevideo; and there were collected all the men who had become bound together like brothers, by six years of danger, exploits and misfortunes. There they had again to erect an edifice, which had been destroyed by mismanagement, almost to its foundations.

Villagran, a veteran of forty years of war, a man of virtue, of the greatest bravery, and reïnvigorated by fighting; Diaz Bojes, shamefully banished by Rivera, because he would not serve him, but his country ; and many other young officers, who have been dismissed by him, returned to their posts, with the conscience

10

and the readiness of good men ; and with them the resolute and the faithful returned to the files of the defenders.

Orientals, French and Italians marched to the succor of the country with alacrity ; and not a word of discouragement was heard from any one. The siege of Montevideo, when better known in its details, will be counted among the noble defences of a people fighting for independence, for courage, constancy, and sacrifices of all kinds. It will prove the power of a nation resolved not to submit to the will of a tyrant ; and, whatever their fate may be, they merit the applause and the commiseration of the world.

From the time of my return to Montevideo, to that of my departure for Italy, in 1848, a period intervened marked by no important event.

OUTLINES

OF

GENERAL GARIBALDI'S CAREER IN ITALY

During the Years 1848 & '9;

CHIEFLY GIVEN IN OFFICIAL DOCUMENTS, COLLECTED AND TRANSLATED
BY THEODORE DWIGHT.

THE translator of the preceding pages applied to
General Garibaldi, while in New York, to write an
account of the Roman Republic ; and afterwards requested several of the most intelligent Italian exiles
here to perform the task. They all declined, partly
for the want of leisure, being all engaged in daily
business for their own support. They, however, furnished valuable communications, some of which were
embodied in " *The Roman Republic of* 1849." The
following pages are chiefly occupied by official documents, which have been collected and translated for
this work, in order to present an authentic document-
ary history of the great events in which General
Garibaldi performed conspicuous parts, through the
momentous struggle for liberty in Rome, in the year
1849.

GARIBALDI'S RETURN TO ITALY FROM SOUTH AMERICA, IN 1848.

The following brief outline of General Garibaldi's movements, after the period terminating with the close of his " Autobiography," and previous to the first French attack on Rome, on the 30th of April, 1849, has been furnished for publication here by Dr. G. Gajani, now a citizen of New York, and then a member of the Roman Constituent Assembly, the author of that highly interesting and instructive work, " The Roman Exile."

In 1848, when the news of the Italian revolution reached Montevideo, General Garibaldi gathered his Italian friends and sailed for Italy. They had arrived in sight of Nice (the native city of Garibaldi), when Colonel Anzani, the most intimate friend of Garibaldi, breathed his last. Colonel Anzani was consumptive, and the emotion excited by seeing Italy again proved too powerful for him.

Garibaldi with his friends proceeded to the field of battle in Lombardy, and offered his services to King Charles Albert, who received him coolly. A few days after, the king was defeated, and signed an armistice with the Austrians. Garibaldi was not included in that armistice, and did not choose to lay down his arms. Pursued by the Austrians, he fought several skirmishes at Como, Varese, Laveno, and other places ; but his troops, being overwhelmed by numbers, disbanded, and he retired into Switzerland--and, after much suffering, finally made good his retreat across the Po, into the Papal State, in October, 1848. General Zucchi, the Minister of War of the Pope, happened to be at Bologna, and wrote to Count Rossi, Secretary of State of Pius IX., that Zucchi had ordered two Swiss regiments (which were at the service of the Pope) to march against Garibaldi, who was then at Ravenna, and " throw him and his followers *into the sea*"—meaning, probably, to compel them to embark. But, before this order was executed, the Pope had fled from Rome, and the popular government which undertook to govern the State, enrolled Garibaldi and his followers, and gave him a commission to increase his band, and protect the eastern boundaries of the Roman State against the King of Naples.

A short time afterwards the elections for the Roman Constituent Assembly took place, and Garibaldi was elected at Macerata, and went to Rome to take his seat in the Assembly, at its opening, on February 9th, 1849.

After that day Garibaldi put himself again at the head of his troops, on the boundaries of Naples, and returned with them to Rome, when the French had landed at Civitavecchia.

PRINCIPLES OF THE ITALIAN REPUBLICANS, IN OPPOSITION TO THE CLAIMS OF POPERY.

The Pope at this time published a long and tiresome " *Encyclic*," filled with true Popish arrogance and subtleties, to which pungent replies were made,—one entitled, " *The Pope Excommunicated.*"

Brief extracts from " Thoughts addressed to the Arch-bishops and Bishops of Italy," " on the .Encyclical Letter of Pope Pius IX.," by Mazzini.

The divorce between the world and him (Pius IX.), between believing people, who are the true Church, and the fornicating aristocracy who usurp its name, is impressed on every syllable of the Pope's letter. For many years the Pope has lost the power to love and bless.   Excited for a moment by the immense spectacle of the resurrection of a people, Pius IX., two years ago, murmured a benediction upon Italy ; and that accent of love sounded so new and unusual on the lips of a Pope, that all Europe imagined a second era for the Papacy, and became intoxicated with enthusiasm, ignorant of the history of past ages respecting him who had pronounced it.   Now the monarchs have been paid. . . .

The few important points which the Pope's letter contains, are :

1st, *A theory* on authority : and 2nd, *A doctrine* respecting the evils of the poverty and ignorance which afflict the people in Italy, and in a great degree else-. where.   Both these deny God, the Word of Christ, and human nature.

. . . . The Israel (of Italy) is the revolutionary party, the national party, who say to Italians, *You are not a race born to be slaves* of the Pope, or of the

Austrian whip; *you are twenty-six millions of people*, created free, equal, brethren, all children of God, and servants of nothing but his law.

The *theory* of the Pope's letter is this : " That the poor exist in consequence of things which cannot and ought not to be changed ; that the Catholic religion preaches to the rich to have charity, which will obtain from God treasures of grace and eternal rewards ; that the poor should thank the Providence which keeps them in misery, and that they know how to bear it in peace and a light mind, as an easier way of salvation in heaven." . . .

And to this *theory* is superadded *the other*, respecting authority : " Every authority comes from God ; every government, *de facto*, is a government of right. Obey, or, resisting, be condemned."

In other words, or comprehending the two theories in one : Earth and heaven constitute a perpetual antagonism—Right, equality and truth reign in heaven; fact, force and inevitable evil reign upon earth. There are two human races : the race of the rich and powerful, and the race of the poor and servants. The poor exist for the benefit of the rich, in order that the latter may obtain heaven by exercising charity ; and the servants, in order that the masters can govern with clemency and the spirit of love. When this is not done, God will give punishments and rewards in heaven ; but, every attempt at melioration on earth, by the efforts of the poor and servile race, *is sin*.

12

And this is the religious doctrine which the church of the Pope teaches to mankind in the nineteenth century ; and she teaches it in the name of the Gospel of Christ, confronting it to the words—

"Thy will be done on earth as it is in heaven :"

the only prayer which Jesus taught to believers ; confronting it to the command, "Thou shalt worship the Lord thy God, and him only shalt thou serve ;" confronting it to, "That all may be one, as thou, Father, art in me and I in thee."

No—it is not true that heaven and earth are in antagonism ; it is not true, that, while in heaven the truth and justice of God reign, submission to fact and reverence for brute force are a law of the earth. It is not true that the salvation of human creatures is secured, as if by expiation, by means of resignation or indifference. The earth is the Lord's ; the earth, on which, and for which, Jesus, first, and after him all the holy martyrs of mankind, shed their tears and their blood.

THE CONDITION OF ROME.

The time approached when all eyes were to be opened to the real designs of the French. A crisis was near, when all the charitable hopes of the sincerity of their amicable professions were to be dispelled. The city was to be attacked by a foreign army for the first time since the days of Charles V., in the period of the Reformation, and for the second time since that of the Northern invasions. In looking back for preceding events of the same kind, the mind had but a single step more to make—the attempt by the Gauls. How different the state of the world since those times! How different the condition of the city; the mode and means of warfare; the principles engaged; the effect to be anticipated on the world!

Never before had the city of Rome been voluntarily deserted by a pope, and brought to a state of order and tranquility by a mere declaration of a republic, and become practically and truly a Protestant city. Never had she been, in the judgment of the world, more certain to be overawed by a powerful host, and more unable to resist. Deeply interesting must have been the situation of many a family.

The negotiations which had been carried on with the Triumvirate, by M. Lesseps, the French agent, had resulted in nothing but the manifest exposure of the double-dealing of Louis Napoleon, and a display of the integrity, ability and patriotism of the Romans.

There was a mixed multitude within the walls, but most of them belonging to the city, or other parts of the Roman States, and many of them soldiers who had been engaged in one or more battles in other parts of Italy. The whole number of Polanders and other foreigners was trifling. Volunteers had been hourly arriving for several weeks, some in regular corps, or companies, others in small bands, and some alone. Col. Manara had entered the city, at the head

10

of his legion of Lombards, raised and paid out of his princely fortune, all which, with his services and his life, he gave an offering to his country.

The following extract from the Roman *Monitore*, the official journal, of June 28th, will give a specimen of the style, and the dignity and intelligence with which the people were daily addressed by the government. After denying, in such terms, and by such arguments as have been used in the preceding pages, the calumnious charges against the character and origin of the defenders of Rome, the *Monitore* enumerates the troops in the city, as follows : " The army of the Republic being ten regiments of infantry, and two of cavalry—*all of them from the Roman States ;* the Medici Legion, of 300 Tuscans ; the Foreign Legion, of 250 men, French and Poles ; the Italian Legion of Garibaldi, about 2,000, *all except* 300 belonging to *the Roman States ;* and, finally, several battalions of the Military Guard Mobile, some of Rome, some of the provinces. . . . The pretended *foreign banditti*, then, who *oppress* the Roman people, amount to 1,650 men, in a city of 150,000 inhabitants, and with 14,000 National Guards. These are the men, too, who for a month have repelled 30,000 French troops, not only from the city, but from the country-seats around it, and defended a circuit of 40 miles ! The most solemn denial that can be given to the accumulated falsehoods of our enemies, is to say to all the people of Europe, " Look, and judge ! Assaulted by four armies at once, in the rushing ruin of Italian misfortunes, the Roman Republic raised her sacred standard on the towers of the Capitol, and guards the sacred fire of liberty."

Day broke on Rome, on the morning of April 30th, 1849, upon a scene which no human foresight could have anticipated, even a few weeks before, and which human ingenuity could scarcely have imagined, even in its principal features. The whole city was in solemn expectation of the arrival of a large French force, which was known to be on the march from Civita Vecchia, and near enough to arrive at the walls in a few hours. Arrangements had been made, and publicly announced, to apprise the inhabitants of their first appearance in sight, by the striking of bells. Preparations for defence had been made, and were still making, by the erecting of works in various places in the squares and streets, to oppose the French if they should enter the walls; while the troops were prepared to fight them from the walls and the ground outside. The elevated positions and buildings were crowded by spectators, some of them foreigners, of different classes, and from different countries. The French had pretended to come as friends and protectors, but persisted in advancing, even after being assured by the Romans that they neither needed nor desired their assistance. The French, then assuming a tone of disdain, had plainly expressed their belief that *the Romans would not fight*. The world was waiting, with anxiety, the result of that day's movements ; and, probably, very few men believed that the French would meet with any great obstacle. They expected to dine that day in Rome, and to remain masters of it as long as they pleased.

Perhaps no news has ever been more unexpected, than that which was that day sent from Rome to all parts of the world : that the Romans had fought the French gallantly, with far inferior forces, for several hours, and driven them twelve miles back towards Civita Vecchia. Such, however, was the surprising truth ; and, had not the Triumvirate peremptorily ordered Garibaldi to pursue them no further, he would have continued to press them, with the resolution which he had formed, of driving them into the sea.

Among the spectators who wrote accounts of what occurred that day, were several intelligent men of different nations, who described the defence as conducted with superior skill, and performed with the greatest vigor and valor by the Roman officers and soldiers. Interesting letters from some of these witnesses may be found in the newspapers of different countries, published soon after ; and many concurrent accounts in various other publications, particularly "Italia del Popolo," a monthly magazine, published by the exiled patriot leaders. We give below the official reports of the principal events, during the period of Roman liberty, in all of which Garibaldi was a conspicuous actor.

OFFICIAL REPORT

OF THE REPULSE OF THE FRENCH ADVANCE OF 8,000 MEN, UNDER
GENERAL OUDINOT, UNDER THE WALLS OF ROME—THE FIRST BATTLE:
APRIL 30TH, 1849.

(Translated for the present work.)

ARRANGEMENTS OF THE BATTLE OF THE 30TH OF APRIL.

THE Triumvirate, with information furnished by the
Minister of War, Citizen General Avezzana, publishes
the following report:

The time necessary to collect, from the different
military chiefs, the particulars relative to the engagement of April 30th, has prevented us from publishing
earlier a precise relation. Now, since such particulars
have been minutely transmitted, we fulfil that duty
with such scrupulous exactness, as is demanded by the
truth of history and the just desires of the public.

From the 29th, the commander in chief of the arms
of the Republic, General Avezzana, who is also the
Minister of War, was fully informed of the enemy's
approach by the numerous scouting parties, whose
reports were confirmed by a French prisoner, who, the
same day, fell into an ambush of our advance-posts.

On the morning of the 30th, the telegraph giving
notice of the advance of the enemy's forces, announced

at nine o'clock, that they were within five miles of
Rome ; and the Minister of War sent a captain of the
general staff to the cupola of St. Peter's, to remain
there until the firing should commence, to observe all
the movements of the enemy, and discover their numbers and their intentions.

In the meantime all measures were taken in the city
to repel the aggression, with such desperate energy as
is inspired by the holiness of right and the justice of the
cause. Strong and numerous barricades, at all the gates
and in all the principal streets, especially on the right
side of the Tiber, forbade all access into the city ; the
bastions, rising above, crowned with cannon, were prepared to fire upon the enemy ; and the young army,
impatient with warlike ardor, placed at the different
points where the attack was expected, was disposed in
the following order : The first brigade, commanded by
General Garibaldi, and composed of the first Italian
Legion, the battalion of the University, the battalion
of the Reduced, the Legion of Exiles, and the Mobilized Finanzieri, occupied, outside of the walls, the
whole line from the Portese Gate to the gate of San
Pancrazio ; the second brigade, composed of two battalions of the Mobilized Civic Troops and the First
Light, commanded by Col. Masi, occupied the wall of
the Gates Cavalleggieri, Vatican and Angelica ; and
finally, the third brigade, commanded by Col. Savini,
and composed of the first and second regiments of
Mounted Dragoons, formed the reserve in Piazza Na-

vona. The fourth brigade, consisting of the first and second regiments of the line, commanded by Colonel Galletti, was in reserve at the Chiesa Nuova and Piazza Cesarini, with all the field cannon not in position. General Giuseppe Galletti, commander of Carabiniers, and Major Manara, with the Lombard battalion, forming separate corps, were held ready to proceed wherever necessity might require.

Everything concurred to indicate that the enemy, who were eight thousand men, with two squadrons of cavalry and twelve field-pieces, divided in two columns, intended to make a double and simultaneous attack at the gates Cavalleggieri and Angelica. In fact, about eleven o'clock in the morning, proceeding by Villa Pamfili, they occupied two houses, from which they commenced an active fire of musketry and artillery against the Cavalleggieri gate. The valiant General Garibaldi moved from the gate of San Pancrazio, to attack them in flank, with all his troops and the University battalion ; and there commenced a murderous and obstinate battle, in which a hundred deeds of personal bravery proved, that the modern Italians are prepared to imitate the ancient glories of their fathers. The French made a determined resistance to the onset of Garibaldi ; and even repulsed their assailants, favored by their superior numbers and by their artillery, which they fired briskly. But, being reinforced by the Legion of Exiles, the Reduced battalion, the Roman Legion, commanded by Col. Galletti, and two companies of the first regiment of the line, charging simultaneously, with the bayonet, they compelled the enemy to retire precipitately, leaving in the hands of our troops about three hundred prisoners, among whom were six officers, with the commander of a battalion, and a great number of killed.

While they were fighting thus at San Pancrazio, other attacks were made on the gardens of the Vatican, and along the entire line, from the Cavalleggieri gate to that of Santa Marta, where the enemy endeavored, with all their power, to silence our artillery, and where they made two furious assaults, but were bravely repulsed by the Masi Brigade and the Mobilized Civic, assisted in good time by the brave and ardent Carabiniers. At all those points our troops sustained the attacks of the enemy with admirable firmness and coolness, and, by fighting with the bravery of veteran soldiers, compelled them to make a precipitate retreat. In that encounter the National Artillery deserve special commemoration, under the command of Colonel Calandrelli, who lost two distinguished officers, besides wounded ; and also the Civic Artillery, who rivalled the former in zeal and ardor.

Thus repulsed on the whole line, the French retired first to Bravella, three miles from the city, whence, after a short stop, they continued their retreat towards Castel di Guido, from which, doubtless, they will go to Civitavecchia.

This battle, which wonderfully consolidated the foundation of our Republic, lasted about seven hours, beginning at ten in the morning and ending at three in the afternoon, without including, as a part of the contest, the little skirmishes which were continued until evening, between our ardent soldiers and the bands of the enemy who were pursued without ceasing. According to facts collected, and the statements made by the prisoners, it appears that the enemy lost more than fifteen hundred men, including killed, wounded and prisoners. On our part we have to lament only fifty killed and two hundred wounded, among whom are many officers, subaltern and superior.

We have only a sentiment of admiration and a word of praise, equal for all, officers, soldiers and people, who took part in the combat of the 30th. All fought like heroes ; all showed that when the love of country is living and ardent, the sacrifice of life is sweet. In such a case we cannot make a better eulogium on the valor of our brave men, than by repeating an extract of a letter written by General Garibaldi to the Minister of War :

"All the corps which have fought this day are extremely well-deserving of the country. A detachment of the line, the first Roman Legion, the University battalion, the Arcioni Legion, the battalion of the Reduced, and the first Italian Legion have been rivals in valor. The chief officers and the soldiers of those corps have merited the gratitude of Italy and the title

of valiant men.   Many arms, drums and other articles
of war have remained in our power."

The merits of the sanitary officers of our ambulances
ought not to be forgotten, who were diligent in collecting
on the field, the wounded, on whom were lavished, as is
done in the hospitals, by the ladies, services truly fra-
ternal ; and in mourning over losses, it is grateful to
say, that among the French themselves, many declared,
before dying, that they left life with remorse for having
fought against brother-republicans ; while those who
were saved, imprecating their government, know not
how to thank us for the assiduous cares of which they
have been the objects, but by repeating as often as
their countrymen are made prisoners, ' *Viva la Republica Romana !* '

In short, a profound sentiment of gratitude requires
us to give to that most truly Italian General, Avezzana,
a word of encomium, though far inferior to that great
love of country which impels him to provide for every
exigency of the onerous ministry entrusted to him,
with a tenacious perseverance, and an indefatigable
alacrity, which would have been prodigious in a young
man.   From the first approach of the enemy, followed
by a portion of his staff, (for many other officers belonging to it were appointed to the gates, to direct the
corps which defended them,) General Avezzana visited
in succession the places attacked, and by his voice and
his example, raising to the highest degree the enthusiasm of the people, until they asked for arms, and with

the soldiers who were fighting bravely, secured the triumph of the day and the honor of the country.

In this aggression, France, sacrificed by a government, the enemy of the true interests of their country, has suffered immense losses, more moral than material; she has lost all political influence; she has no right to our sympathies; and if the justice of our cause has given so much energy to conquer the most warlike soldier, we have now the profound conviction of being able to contest, with glory and success, against all the enemies of the Republic and of Italy.

The Triumvirs,

CARLO ARMELLINI,
GIUSEPPE MAZZINI,
AURELIO SAFFI.

FROM AN ACCOUNT OF THE SAME BATTLE OF APRIL
30TH, BY CARLO RUSCONI.

General Oudinot, who, with 8,000 men and 12 field pieces, wished to raze Rome to the ground, ordered a simultaneous attack on Porta Cavalleggieri and Porta Angelica, and occupied two houses of Villa Pamfili, from which he opened an active fire of musketry and artillery. He presented himself against General Garibaldi, one of those men who serve as types in the creations of art. Beautiful in person, simple in habits, frugal in living, courageous as the heroes celebrated in chivalry, he exerted a fascination on all who surrounded him. He had a thousand men about him, who would

have allowed themselves to be killed a thousand times
at his slightest command.   Concise in manner, sparing
of words, terrible in wrath, you would have said that
Byron must have had this extraordinary man before
his eyes, when he delineated his immortal Conrad ;—
Garibaldi, who was not in his element except when
balls were whistling round his head, moved against
the French, attacked them in flank, and, supported by
Col. Galleti, discomfited them, after many hours
fighting.

Garibaldi, having seen that the engagement with
musketry proceeded too slowly, and impatient at that
mode of fighting, made a charge on the French with
the bayonet, in the most destructive manner, and which
secured him the victory.   Finding that that method
turned out well, he never abandoned it in the successive conflicts ; and this explains the great number of
killed in that obstinate war.

SPIRITED PROCLAMATION TO THE PEOPLE OF ROME, BY
THEIR REPRESENTATIVES, THE DAY AFTER THE FIRST
BATTLE.

People ! yesterday commenced the entrance of the
French into Rome.   They entered by the Porta San
Pancrazio—as prisoners !   To us, people of Rome, this
does not cause much surprise ; but it may excite a
curious sensation in Paris.   That also will be well.

People ! the attack will be renewed.   Let us do as
we did yesterday ; and especially do not be alarmed

if a few batteries should be silenced by their cannonade.   Reports of cannon startle the ears, and
somewhat shake the houses : but, in fact, when they
do not reach united masses of people, they destroy but
very few victims. . . . . .

We request good shopkeepers to keep at their business constantly : that will have a good influence and
be very convenient at the same time.

To-day we have need to fortify Pincio, (the Pincian
Mount ;) be there early, in goodly numbers, and let us
labor together.

PROCLAMATION BY THE COMMITTEE OF THE BARRICADES,
TWO DAYS AFTER THE FIRST BATTLE.

People !   General Oudinot promised to pay all and
all in cash.   Well, let him pay, if he can, for the
Tapestries of Raffaele, shot through with French bullets ; let him pay for the losses—no, not the losses,
but the insult cast on Michael Angelo.   Napoleon at
least carried to Paris our master-pieces, and in a certain way Italian genius received the admiration of the
foreigner, as a recompense for the conquest.   Not so
to-day.   The French government invade our territory, and carry their singular predilection for Rome
so far, as to wish to destroy her, rather than have her
exposed to the impatience of the terrible (General)
Zucchi, and the threats of Radetzky and Gioberti,
who are both at several weeks' distance from the

Tiber. General Oudinot is more hasty than our enemies. The Republic is grateful to him. Do you know why? Because, while the Imperialists occupy Alessandria, without a blow struck by Charles Albert, it is a great Italian glory, that the People's Rome honorably repels the Republicans of France, whom a black government sends against us, after calumniating us as robbers and assassins. And the Popes? Let us preserve, in memory of them, the cannon-balls which solemnly celebrated the anniversary of the Pontifical Encyclic. Enough! Of kingdoms and triple kings let us talk no more. Let us now think of the Barricades. Let us think of our honor, which we must fully vindicate. Rome, like Scævola, has still her arm on the burning torch, and has sworn an oath. The three hundred of Scævola routed Porsenna. The history of Rome is not yet finished.

The Representatives of the People,

E. CARNESUCHI,

V. CATTABENI,

V. CALDESI.

Rome, May 2d.

THE NEAPOLITAN INVASION.

On the same day the following Proclamation was published by the Triumvirate, announcing the approach of the numerous army of the King of Naples. Five days later they announced the arrival of the Spanish army, of 5000 men, on the coast. Both those armies had been raised, in obedience to the call of the

Pope, as well as that of France, which had just been so manfully driven from the walls of Rome.

PROCLAMATIONS OF THE TRIUMVIRATE, AT THE TIME OF THE NEAPOLITAN INVASION.

Rome, May 2d, 1849.—Romans! A corps of the Neapolitan army, having covered the frontier, threatens to move against Rome.

Their intent is to restore the Pope, as absolute master in temporal affairs. Their arms are persecution, ferocity, and pillage. Among their files lurks their king, to whom Europe has decreed the name of *the Bombarder of his own subjects;* and around him stand the most inexorable of the conspirators of Gaeta.

Romans! We have conquered the first assailants: we will conquer the second. The blood of the best Neapolitans, the blood of our brothers of Sicily, lies on the head of the traitor-king. God, who blinds the wicked, and strengthens the defenders of right, chooses you, O Romans, for avengers. Let the will of the country and of God be done.

In the name of the rights which belong to every country; in the name of the duties which belong to Rome, in regard to Italy and Europe; in the name of the Roman mothers, who will bless the defenders of their children; in the name of our liberty, our honor, and our conscience; in the name of God and the people ; let us resist, soldiers and people, capital and province. Let Rome be as inviolable as eternal jus-tice. We have learned that, to conquer, it is enough not to fear death.   THE TRIUMVIRS.

THE BATTLE OF PALESTRINA.

The retreat of the French army back to the sea-shore, and the armistice which occurred after the first battle, of April 30th, afforded a remarkably conven-ient opportunity to attend to the King of Naples and his army, which amounted to about twenty thou-sand men. The following is a description of their position, and the marching of the Roman army against them, translated from the beginning of the report of Gen. Roselli, then commander-in-chief. The report includes the time from his leaving Rome, May 16th, until the occupation of Velletri, May 20th, 1849.

" The Neapolitan army occupied the position of Albano, Velletri and Palestrina, and had their line of operations directed towards Rome.

The army of the Republic left Rome, to attack the enemy, on the 16th and 17th, and manœuvred to turn their flanks and cut off their communications with the Neapolitan State. The point of direction of the army was Monte Fortino, whence it might menace all the enemy's communications.

The Neapolitans had no other way but to retreat, or come out and attack us in the positions we had chosen. The army was composed of five brigades, and one of cavalry, with twelve pieces of cannon. The first brigade, with a squadron of lancers and two pieces of artillery, commenced the march. I left Rome at five o'clock, P. M., and took the direction of Zagarola, by the road of Campanelle, to expose the right flank as little as possible. The march was very rapid; we reached Zagarola at ten before noon. The vanguard passed the town rapidly, and encamped on the hills which defend the roads of Palestrina and Albano. According to instructions, the next day it was intended to attack Palestrina, and then march on Velletri; but we learned, from our patrols and information, that the enemy were no longer in Palestrina, having concentrated their forces in Velletri. It was then immediately decided to occupy Monte Fortino.

The order had been given to put the army in movement before daylight; but, from misunderstanding, and insufficiency of the means of transport, the arrival of provisions having been delayed, our brave soldiers were compelled to lose precious time," &c., &c.

The report of the commander-in-chief being deficient in details, I sought for more particulars from Gen. Garibaldi, and soon obtained the following succinct account, written down from his lips, accompanied with a hasty plan of the battle-ground, drawn by his pen. It now became evident that the common opinion was correct, which attributed the two remarkable victories of Palestrina and Velletri to Garibaldi; as the vanguard, led by him, had all the fighting to do ; and the main body of the Roman army, under Roselli, did not arrive until the result was mainly secured.

GEN. GARIBALDI'S ACCOUNT OF THE BATTLES OF PALES-
TRINA AND VELLETRI.

"My first object," said he, " was to turn the enemy's flank ; for I thought that if the King of Naples once heard that I was in his rear, he would be frightened ; and so it proved."

The following is the substance of his account of the engagements, from notes taken in 1850 :

The Neapolitans occupied the strong positions of Tusculum mountains, with their head-quarters at Velletri, and their advanced guard at Albano. Their extreme left was at Castel Gondolfo, and their extreme right a small village.

The battle of Palestrina was about ten days before that of Velletri. The troops present at the former were a hundred cavalry, under Col. Massina ; 300 Bersaglieri, under Col. Manara ; 200 Finanzieri of the Nationals ; 200 Students, mobilized ; and the Italian Legion, of 1,000—in all, about 1,800 men.

Garibaldi was sent out to harrass and observe the Neapolitans, with his division, and was at Palestrina, when seven thousand of the enemy were sent against him, with the intention of attacking him.

Between the Tusculum Mount and Palestrina is a valley, in one of the projections of the Apennines, in an amphitheatre. When Garibaldi perceived that the enemy had arrived at Valmontone, he sent a detachment to observe them. But it was repulsed, with the videttes, and retired upon the corps. When the Neapolitans reached Palestrina, Garibaldi prepared to defend himself. The enemy advanced, by two roads, against Palestrina, when Garibaldi prepared two companies, to protect the returning soldiers, or to harrass the enemy, if occasion should offer; while he remained in the centre, with a reserve.

The Neapolitans extended in line, and attacked; but were repulsed on the left and the centre. The two companies on the right were driven back, when Garibaldi, being victorious in other parts, proceeded with the reserve to the right, and the rout of the enemy was then completed. A strong body of royal Swiss troops, in the pay of Bomba, was present. The Republicans being destitute of cavalry, and the speedy arrival of night, saved the wrecks of the troops of Bomba.

From Palestrina, Garibaldi returned to Rome.

THE BATTLE OF VELLETRI.

A few days after, he again left Rome, with the Roman army, and was in the vanguard, having under his orders the First Italian Legion, of eleven hundred men; the Third of the line, eight hundred; fifty cavalry, and two light guns.

At Valmontone he received advices that the Neapolitans were sending back their baggage and heavy
artillery, and he therefore concluded that they were
retreating, and pressed forward, sending notice to the
principal corps.   At Monte Fortino he received more
positive information, and continued to advance with
haste.   About eight o'clock A. M. he was in sight of
Velletri, which was on the road, and two miles distant.   He then discovered the enemy's cavalry, in
échellon, on the Appian Way, to protect the retreat of
their army, for which they were preparing.   The
main body of the Neapolitan army was then at Velletri ; and, as soon as Garibaldi's corps was discovered
by them, the Neapolitans moved to attack it.

He drew up the Third of the line, in *échellon*, by
companies, near the road, which was among hills
covered with vineyards, to protect his retreat in case
of necessity, and to act as a reserve in case the enemy
should attack.   He placed the First Italian Legion
on both sides of the road, in the best position he could,
and thus awaited the assault of the enemy, leaving
two companies in column in the road itself.   The
cavalry and artillery he placed in positions adapted
to be most serviceable.

The enemy attacked : but all their attempts were
fruitless.   They had many killed, and were finally
obliged to shut themselves up in the city, on the defensive.

Garibaldi's corps alone was too weak to prevent

the retreat of the enemy, which was finally effected
by night.

The principal corps of the Roman army, of seven
thousand men, under Roselli, arrived late, and tired
with their march.   An attempt, however, was made to
attack the city in front, by charging, at the head of
the First Roman Legion, with the battalion of artillery
placed in a good position upon the road.   The Neapolitans sustained the positions of the city, in which
they remained the rest of the day.   The Republicans
took positions, in order to renew the attack the
next day : but in the morning the Neapolitans retreated, and disappeared from Velletri.

These bold and successful operations, so briefly
described, were of the highest importance, in their results, both by driving back the enemy, by encouraging
the Republicans, and by adding to their reputation.
The rout of the Neapolitans was so decisive, that
they gave no further annoyance, and never appeared again during the war.

As for the poor Spanish army, which had landed on
the coast, in obedience to the call of the poor Pope,
they did nothing but issue a few bombastic proclamations, and kept themselves out of harm's way.

The French, in the meantime, were preparing to
take decisive measures against Rome.   The wounded,
whom they had left behind them on the 30th of April,
had been tenderly nursed by the Roman ladies, who
had volunteered to attend at the hospitals ; and three

or four hundred prisoners had been harangued in the Corso, by the commander-in-chief, addressed as brother-republicans, in the name of the government and people, and dismissed without exchange or parole, with open gates, to return to Civitavecchia. On their arrival there, however, full of their praises of the noble Romans, they were immediately shipped for France, for fear of their influence among the troops.

The French army soon moved, in great force, for Rome, with heavy artillery and all preparations for a siege. But their first step was to violate the amnesty, by suddenly attacking the outposts, the night before the time limited by the armistice, and while they were almost unprotected.

(Translated from the Monitroe Romano, of June 8, 1849.)

GENERAL GARIBALDI'S ACCOUNT OF THE ACTION OF JUNE 3D, 1849,

WITH THE FRENCH, AT VILLAS CORSINI AND VASCELLO.

On leaving the Bastion, the ground on the right rises a little in the direction of the Villa Vascello; and on the left forms, by a gentle descent, a little valley, which leads towards the French camp.

From the gate of San Pancrazio a street leads directly to the Vascello, (two hundred and fifty paces,) and then divides. The principal branch descends on the right along the garden of the Villa Corsini, surrounded by high walls, and goes on to join the great road to Civitavecchia. Another, flanked by hedges, leads directly to the Villa Corsini, which is three hundred paces in front of the Villa Vascello. And the third road turns to the left, and is prolonged, like the first, by the wall of the garden of the Villa Corsini.

The Villa Vascello is a large and massive fabric of three stories, surrounded by gardens and walls. In front of the Villa (fifty paces) is a small house, from which firing may be made against the windows of the Villa Corsini.

On the left road, (one hundred paces,) beyond the point of separation of the streets, are two small houses, one behind the garden of Villa Corsini, the other twenty paces before, on the left of the street.

The Villa Corsini, placed on the highest part of the ground, commands all the neighborhood. It is surrounded by a garden and high wall. The position of the Villa is very strong, and the more so because wishing to attack it without showing any preparation of approach before hand, it is necessary, while passing the concello, which is at the foot of the garden, to bear the concentrated fire which the enemy, defended and covered by the hedges and vases, or within the Villa itself, make upon that point at which the garden-walls meet at an acute angle.

The ground is also very descending; and, besides, the Villa Corsini is very favorable to the enemy, because declining, and being scattered with groves, and crossed by deep streets, they can concentrate their

13

reserves in security from our fire, when the cannon
oblige them to abandon the house.

The first attack made by the Italian Legion was
against the positions Corsini and Quattro Venti, which
had been abandoned by our troops, because surprised,
betrayed, and overpowered by the great number of the
enemy. The attack was made with the bayonet, without firing a single shot; the Legion sustained, for
about three-quarters of an hour, the whole weight of
the enemy; and Colonels Daverio and Massina, and
Commandant Peralta were killed, and most of the
officers wounded.

At that moment arrived the Manara Bersaglieri,
who throwing themselves into the garden, vigorously
attacked the enemy, even under the walls of the Villa.
Here fell Captain Dandolo and many soldiers; and
many officers and soldiers were wounded. But from
that moment the houses on the left were ours. The
enemy had stopped their progressive work, and the
Vascello, strongly occupied, poured on them a fire of
grape shot. The brave artillerymen very soon disturbed the enemy in the Villa Corsini.

The Manara Bersaglieri, from the Casini on the left,
and the Italian Legion from the Vascello, drove the
French Tiraglieurs from the garden and hedges. Both
parties kept up a very warm fire.

The enemy were no more able, although reinforced
and protected by two pieces of artillery, to take from
our troops the position held with so much valor.

The artillery fired upon the Villa Corsini so vigorously, that the enemy were compelled to retreat, after setting it on fire ; while the cannon in the right Bastion, and Bersaglieri, thrown forward of the Vascello, attacked with great ardor the enemy, who were in the Casino Quattro Venti, and who occupied numerous small adjacent houses, from which they made a very heavy but useless fire.

On the left, towards the French camp, two companies of the Manara Bersaglieri were then sent, who went far in advance, to annoy the enemy, hidden among the vines.

A very severe conflict continued all day, always to the advantage of our troops, who were able, even a second time, (the Manara Bersaglieri and Italian Legion,) to charge the enemy beyond the Villa Corsini.

Towards evening several companies of the third regiment of the line were sent to reinforce our troops in the Vascello ; and the Medici Legion was sent to relieve the Manara Bersaglieri in the Casini on the left.

The cannon reduced almost to dust the Villa Corsini and the Casino Quattro Venti, being wonderfully well directed—due praise to the brave Lieut. Col. Ludovico Calandrelli.

The enemy were beaten at all points. Our troops, and especially the Manara Bersaglieri and the Italian Legion, again and again charged the enemy breast to breast.

11

The first company of Manara Bersiglieri threw itself into the Villa Giraud, and made many French prisoners. The Italian Legion several times advanced up to Villa Valentini.

At evening the Medici Legion vigorously charged the enemy among the vineyards on the left.

The night came, leaving to us the field of battle, the enemy admiring our valor, and our troops desirous of renewing the battle, which had been so courageously fought on the first day. This they did on the following morning.

All the officers, and especially the superior and subaltern officers whom I wish to distinguish, are these here recorded, because martyrs and dying as brave men.

Cols. Masina, Daverio, and Ramorino; Adj. Major Peralta; Lieuts. Bonnet, Cavalleri and Grassi; Capts. Dandalo and David, Lieut. Scarani, Col. Polline, Lieuts. Larete and Gazzaniga.

GARIBALDI,
Commander of the Division.

[The siege and resistance continued : but the particulars must be omitted here. Passing over three weeks we come to the last great, but unsuccessful attack on the Vascello.]

Translated from the " Monitore Romano" (Roman Monitor), of June 26th, 1848.

OFFICIAL BULLETIN OF EVENTS WHICH TOOK PLACE ON THE 25TH AND 26TH OF JUNE, 1849.

In the last night the enemy made an attack, to dislodge our troops from the Casino, outside the gate San Pancrazio, called the Vascello, but were repulsed with great loss. For the particulars of that action, glorious to our arms, I publish the following extract from a report sent to me by the brave general of division, Garibaldi :

GEN. GARIBALDI'S REPORT TO ROSELLI, THE GENERAL-IN-CHIEF.

CITIZEN GENERAL-IN-CHIEF :

One hour after midnight the enemy tried a second attack, and assaulted our right flank, breaking in towards the Vascello, which is under the command of Lieutenant-Colonel Medici, and on the left side of the Casetta, which is under the command of Major Cenni.

With lively pleasure I communicate to you how heroically our troops sustained themselves, and powerfully repulsed them.

The very deep mist, which involved everything, rendered the conflict the more interesting. Our soldiers gave proofs of their diligence and love for the cause.

Many dead, who still lie unburied on the enemy's ground, bear them witness. And the highest encomium is due in general to the detachments Medici and Melara, and to the Manara Bersaglieri, on the right wing, and on the left to Major Cenni, of the staff of the division; and, of the Arcioni legion, to Captains Joanny, Baily, Romagnori; 1st Lieutenant Carlotti; 2d Lieutenant Bellonghi; and to all the soldiers of that corps. Of the Regiment of the Union, Capt. Colombani and Lieut. Dezzi distinguished themselves. The soldiers are the same as those who so lately defended the Casetta, near the Vascello.

And the detachment of the line should not be forgotten, commanded by Sub-Lieutenant Ferrandi, of the 3d regiment, who showed themselves openly, and intrepid under fire. When the firing had ceased, in consequence of the repulse of the enemy, there was an almost perfect silence, interrupted only by a few exchanges of shot, chiefly harmless. Nothing important occurred before daybreak, and things still remain as yesterday.

Salutation and brotherhood!

General Head-quarters, morning of June 26th, 1849.

GARIBALDI.
General commanding the 1st Division.

The following editorial passage follows the preceding report, in the same paper, the *Monitore Romano.* As it relates to a subject of which much use was afterwards made by the French and Popish writers, to justify themselves, and falsely to accuse the Romans, it seems proper to insert it here, for the information of the reader. In spite of what is here said (greatly to the disgrace of the French invaders), many of the statues, buildings, pictures, and other valuable "monuments of the city," were injured, and some destroyed, by their bullets, grape-shot, cannon-balls and bombshells. They chose their point of attack near St. Peter's church and the Vatican palace, and sometimes appeared to aim their artillery for the wanton destruction or injury of those and other edifices.

From the Monitore Roman of June 26th, 1849.

The Paris *Constitutionnel*, and all the other journals of the (French) government, make known the reason why General Oudinot has not yet entered Rome, in the following passage:—

" It is wrong to believe that Rome can be, in a few days, rescued from the state of defence in which it has been placed by the *foreigners who occupy it.* Even if the possibility of success in an attack by main force were demonstrated, with the use of all the means authorized by war, other considerations should prescribe the greatest circumspection to our general-in-chief. In reality, the order to attack, which was sent to Gen. Oudinot, contains an express recommendation to adopt the most complete measures to avoid the exposure of the monuments of the city, which are now placed under the safeguard of France. Considerations of humanity are no less in the plans of our generals, who in no case will confound the Roman population with the bands of adventurers who ruin and oppress it. For all these reasons, the besieging forces will confine themselves to the attack of exterior works, and of positions from which the city and the monuments can not receive any injury."

[Remarks on the preceding extract from the *Constitutionnel*, by the editors of the *Monitore Romano*.]

" This, it cannot be denied, is an ingenious expedient to justify the slowness of the *brilliant successes* of Oudinot under the walls of Rome. It is not a posthumous expedient, but a witty one, invented *after the act*. The General had first to think how to let his bomb-shells by hundreds fall, not upon the *foreigners* who defend Rome, but upon the heads of the harmless population whom he has come to *protect*. He must think first how to ruin the edifices of Raffaelle, the Aurora of Guido, the temple of Fortuna Virilis, and, only yesterday, the most beautiful fresco of Poussin, in the palace Costaguli, now irreparably lost, because it has never been copied or engraved.

" But this does not prevent the Roman monuments from being placed *under the safeguard* of the French arms! This did not prevent them from having within their scope the defence of the liberty of the people, oppressed by foreigners! Hypocrites and wretches! you do not possess even the brutal frankness of Austria!"

The following brief notices of events in Paris, published in the same number of the *Monitore Romano*, convey striking hints of the condition to which Louis Napoleon was reducing France, while his army was attempting to overthrow the Roman Republic, and fabricating excuses for his ill success.

Paris, June 15th.—The members of the Legislative Assembly under trial for revolutionary proceedings exceeds twenty ; and the list is not yet complete, (Ledru Rolin was at the head of these.)

The Moniteur publishes two decrees of the President of the Republic. By the first, considering that the existing condition of Paris renders necessary the union in one hand of all the disposable forces of the national guard and of the army, it is decreed, that General Changarnier shall unite the superior command of the national guard of the Seine with the command of the troops of the first military division, until the public tranquillity shall be restored in the capital. By the second, the city of Lyons and all the circuit comprised in the sixth military division are placed in the state of siege.

Arrests continue to-day. The whole number is three hundred. . . . . . Letters and papers seized will lead to other arrests.

By a decree of the Executive the following newspapers are suppressed, (naming six.)

THE BATTLE OF JUNE 30TH.

GENERAL GARIBALDI'S LAST OFFICIAL REPORT IN ROME.

*General Head-quarters, San Pietro in Montorio,
July* 1, 1849.—Yesterday was a day fruitful in deeds
of arms: losses and advantages. Yesterday Italy
counted new martyrs. Colonel Manara leaves a void in
the Republican files, difficult to be supplied. Young,
of surprising merit and valor, he was struck by an enemy's ball, while courageously defending the Villa Spada against an enemy very superior. America yesterday
gave, with the blood of a valiant son, Andrea Aghiar,
a pledge of the love of liberal men of all countries for
our fair and unfortunate Italy.

Lieutenant Colonel Medici distinguished himself by
skill and courage, in the defence of the first bastion
on the right of the gate of San Pancrazio, and of the
position Savorelli. He was distinguished in the company of the brave Colonel Ghilardi, commandant of
that line.

The Medici Legion and the first of the line fought
like lions. They several times repelled assaults in the
breach, and paid with the precious life of many young
men, the hope of the country, the sacred debt of all.

Part of the Manara Legion fought at the point of

11*   249

the bayonet with their accustomed courage, in union with the companies of the regiment Massi.

The Italian Legion, under the command of Colonel Manara, showed itself worthy of its fame in the defence of the Villa Spada. The Third of the Line, in defending the positions which were confided to it, covered itself with glory.

GARIBALDI.

THE CITY TO CEASE HER RESISTANCE.

It was now decided that the further defence of Rome was impossible, without exposing the city to destruction. The enemy were within the walls, and could not be dislodged. They were indeed so strong, that the Romans would be obliged at least to abandon their line, and retire to this side of the Tiber, which General Avezzana and Garibaldi proposed to defend with obstinacy. But the inhabitants apprehended, from such a step, the speedy ruin of their houses by the French cannon and shells; and, after a Council which they held with the Assembly, it was resolved to cease resistance. Garibaldi saw that his work was done in the capital; and, with feelings which we may in some degree realize, he resolved not to witness the disgrace brought upon his noble cause, nor to leave his gallant companions to be disarmed and remain useless to the country. He doubtless foresaw that many of them would follow wherever he would lead; and then certainly, not less than at other times, he felt an impulse to lead where only courageous men would follow. He thought of the city of Venice, then besieged by the Austrians, by sea and land, and indulged the flattering hope of being able to reach her, and join her brave defenders. The wide space to be passed over, and the far superior force which the enemy could send to oppose him, were insufficient to discourage him; and he resolved to go. But one obstacle was in his way. His wife was urgent to accompany him, which he opposed; but in vain.

The government issued the following proclamations :—

[Translated from the Monitore Romano, of Monday, July 2, 1849.]

ROMAN REPUBLIC :

The Constituent Assembly, in the name of God and the people, *decrees* :

The Triumvirs, Armellini, Mazzini, and Saffi have deserved well of the country.

ALLOCALETTI, *President.*

SANTARGES,
COCCHI,
ZAMBIANCH,
Rome, July 1st, 1849.   PINNACCHI.

The following was published yesterday :—

Romans! The Triumvirate is voluntarily dissolved. The Constituent Assembly will communicate to you the names of our successors.

The Assembly, deeply affected, after the act of yesterday, performed by the enemy, with a desire to deliver Rome from extreme dangers, and to prevent the fruitless sacrifice of any more lives for the defence, have decreed the cessation of hostilities. The men who were in the right during the contest, could not well continue to govern in the new times which are preparing. The mandate sent to them has ceased *de facto*, and they hasten to resign it to the hands of the Assembly.

Romans! Brothers! you have written a page which will remain in history, a proof of the power and energy which slept in you, and of your future deeds, of which no force can deprive you. . . . . . Assembled under the Republican banner, you have redeemed the honor of the common country, elsewhere contaminated by deeds of evil men, and overthrown by monarchical impotency. Your Triumvirs, becoming simple citizens among you, carry with them the highest comfort in their consciousness of pure intentions, and the honor of having their names associated with your bravest deeds.

A cloud is rising to-day over your prospects and you. It is the cloud of an hour. Remain firm in the consciousness of your rectitude, and with the faith in which many armed apostles among you have died. God, who has treasured up their blood, is surely for you. God wills that Rome shall be great; and she will be. Yours is not a defeat; it is a victory of the

martyrs, to whom the tomb is the passage to heaven. . . .
Viva la Republica Romana!

> The Triumvirs,
>
> > GIUSEPPE MAZZINI,
> > CARLO ARMELLINI,
> > AURELIO SAFFI.

THE CONSTITUTION OF THE ROMAN REPUBLIC ADOPTED —THE CONSTITUENT ASSEMBLY DISSOLVED.

The Constituent Roman Assembly, in their session of yesterday, definitively voted, with unanimity, and *viva voce*, the Constitution of the Republic.

Having fulfilled, by this act, the essential part of its high mission, the Assembly decreed, on motion of the Deputy Agostini, that the law be engraved on two marble tables and placed on the capitol, as an eternal monument of the unanimous will of the people, legitimately represented by their Deputies. Woe to him who shall touch those tables of the new civil and political compact which the Roman People form with themselves before God, in the view of all civilized nations! This compact has been sealed with the blood of martyrs, with the blood of all those who, following the voice of their hearts, hastened to Rome, as to the ancient Mother, to defend the honor and the liberty of Italy, and to lay the first stone of her future and inevitable independence.

Whatever may be the present results of measures which foreign supremacy is preparing, the Assembly, the People, the National Guard and the Roman Army have the consciousness of having fulfilled their duty.

(From the same paper.)

Before dissolving the solemn session, the Assembly decreed a funeral in the Basilica of St. Peter, to all the heroes who have offered their lives for the country and for the Republic, under the walls of Rome. As to the wounded, as no less worthy of honor, and in need of care, the Assembly voted a Hospital, and appropriated for the purpose one of the national palaces.

Finally, that nothing might be wanting to the harmony which always prevails among the people, the Constituent Assembly and the citizens in whom, in the last moments, they had entrusted the salvation of the country, the Assembly declared, by a solemn decree, well deserving of the country, the Triumvirs, Armellini, Mazzini, and Saffi.

(From the same paper.)

We have said it, and we repeat it, and we will repeat it always : The Republic arose in Rome by universal suffrage ; rose on the ruins of the throne of the Popes, which the cry of all Europe, the maledictions of all civilized nations, and the spirit of the Gospel, had crumbled into dust. To-day, when on that throne, stigmatized by civilization, flows the blood of so many victims, who will dare to raise it again? A mountain of corpses shuts up, to the Pontiff, the way to that throne ; and to ascend it again, the white stole of the priest must be dyed with human blood! Can the Pope, like the tyrants, sit upon a seat of bayonets? But it is not in the power of France, it is not in the power of Europe conspiring, to restore the Pope to the minds of citizens, after the enormous events which have occurred. The sceptre of the Popes is morally broken for ever.

PROCLAMATION OF THE MINISTER OF WAR.

Romans! The last word of the Minister of War is a mark of admiration of your valor, and an urgent request to you, to persevere in the sacred enterprise of the redemption of Italy.

Your martyrs died with this name upon their lips.

Difficulties of your condition—adversity of destiny—diplomatic snares—deceitful words—let them never arrest you.

The legacy of the valiant who have fallen for you on the walls of the Eternal City, is holy and inviolate! They have reöpened Roman history—Do you continue its fame.   G. AVEZZANA.

GARIBALDI'S DEPARTURE FROM ROME

WITH HIS REMAINING TROOPS, AND HIS CELEBRATED RETREAT TO THE ADRIATIC.

Garibaldi collected his troops after the government had determined to cease resistance, and addressed them in his Spartan speech, which has been so much admired ; then proceeding out of the gates, followed by a considerable portion of his troops, he took his course across the Campagna, his wife accompanying him on horseback, notwithstanding all his affectionate remonstrances. He had resolved to make a desperate effort, to avoid the necessity of submitting to the enemy.

The retreat of Garibaldi from Rome to the little port of Cesenatico, on the Adriatic, while pursued by an Austrian and a French army, has been much admired for the boldness, skill and judgment which were displayed, through a daily change of dangers, discouragements and sufferings, which would seem too great to be so long endured. His route lay through Forli and Cantalupo to Terni, then declined to the left to Todi, Capretto and Orvieto, where the French troops showed themselves; then on to the frontier of Tuscany, after which they passed Arezzo, and crossing a mountain, reached Cisterna; then, passing on to Borgo, Santangelo in Vado, and Montefeltro, he arrived at San Marino, near the close of July, and left there on the night of the 31st for Cesenatico, where they embarked in several boats, and sailed for Venice. Several of these were captured or sunk, and others driven to the shore, among which last was that which contained Garibaldi, his wife, Bassi, Cicerouacchio, and his two sons, whose fate has been mentioned in the preceding pages.

TEN YEARS LATER.

———•••———

CHAPTER I.

"In thy bosom, fair Italia,
Fire is cherish'd warm and bright,
Ling'ring time alone delays it;
Hour expected—day of light!
Three long centuries we've waited;
Lo! it dawns—a glorious sight!"
            "*Banks of Dora*"—*an Italian Song of* 1846.

GARIBALDI WAITING HIS TIME—THE ISLAND OF CAPRERA—HIS
CONFIDENCE IN THE APPROACH OF ITALIAN DELIVERANCE, EX-
PRESSED IN HIS PRECEDING AUTOBIOGRAPHY, AND AT NEW
YORK—HIS PERSONAL APPEARANCE—INJUSTICE DONE TO HIS
CHARACTER AND STYLE OF WRITING—M. DUMAS' BOOK—PRE-
PARATION OF THE ITALIAN PEOPLE FOR UNION AND LIBERTY,
BY SECRET SOCIETIES—CHANGES OF POLICY—THE PRINCIPLES
OF THE ITALIAN PATRIOTS ADOPTED BY FRANCE AND ENGLAND
—CONSEQUENCES.

THE portion of Garibaldi's life recorded in the preceding
pages, interesting and important as it was, now proves to
have been but the prelude and preparation of the mighty
and momentous scenes which Providence had in reserve for
an extraordinary man like him, fitted by such a long, arduous, and perilous training as he had received, under the super-
vision of heaven. A war like that of Armageddon, so
awfully depicted in the Book of Revelation, was now preparing; and all the effects of the persevering labors and pious
prayers of Italian patriots, devoted to the liberation of their

country, were now to be seen in the spirit of harmony and bravery which had been inculcated by the secret societies, fostered by the experience gained in the revolutions of 1820, '31, and '46, and many insurrections attempted ; and now for the first time, under a leader long known for his unequalled, noble, pure, and exalted character, as well as for his incomparable skill and boldness, and his astonishing success in the field.   And what unexpected changes in the situations of Europe, and especially of Italy, were brought about by events whose tendency was not discovered by human eyes, until war commenced between Sardinia and France on the one side, and Austria on the other.

Only a short time before, peace might have been expected to continue, and the oppression of Italians to be prolonged by Austria, the Pope, and the King of Naples.   There were no uncommon signs of approaching disturbance ; and Garibaldi, in his favorite island retreat, was quietly cultivating his farm, and seemed likely to reap in peace the little field which he was sowing.

THE ISLAND OF CAPRERA.

This little rocky island, near the northeastern coast of Sardinia, has now a peculiar interest, on account of its connection with Garibaldi.   Its greatest length is five miles, and its greatest breadth three.   Its name intimates the nature of its soil and surface, it being rough, rocky, and barren, and well fitted for goats.

It belonged to the government, and a portion of it was purchased by Garibaldi, it is believed, about the year 1856, when he made it his residence, took a number of his fellow-exiles thither, and founded a small colony, directing his attention to the cultivation of the ground.   He afterward sent to New York for some American implements, and prosecuted his design with diligence, until a vessel, which he had loaded with necessaries, especially a quantity of lime, was lost on the voyage, and left him without requisite means to proceed

with his buildings and other improvements.   He still, however, regarded that little secluded island as his home, and
has returned to it at every interval of peace and leisure.

There was Garibaldi, waiting for the day to arrive, which
he had so many years anticipated, hoped and prepared for,
and which he had endeavored to make as visible to the eyes
of his countrymen as it seemed to be to his own.   Yes, the
day was near at hand which he had written down in his
preceding autobiography, pages 112, 115, etc.   On page
125 he said : " Be great, once more, O Italy, and then the
powerful voice of the Almighty will be heard by all thy sons ;
and the hungry, cowardly vultures which destroy thee, will
be stunned by its thundering sound."

Such, also, was the expectation which he expressed in
1850, in his note of courteous but decided refusal of the
honors of a public reception in the city of New York, and
which we here translate from his refined Italian original,
addressed to the committee :

GARIBALDI'S REPLY TO THE NEW YORK COMMITTEE, AUGUST 3D,
1850.

" GENTLEMEN : I much regret that my very poor health does not allow
me to take part in the demonstration which you have appointed for
next Saturday.   The length of my convalescence, and the uncertainty of the time of my recovery, still render it impossible for me
to fix a day when I may be able to yield to the wishes of your affectionate and flattering invitation.   I hope you will allow me to repeat,
more warmly than at first, the desire which I have often expressed to
you, that you will entirely abandon the proposed demonstration.

" Such a public exhibition is not necessary to secure for me the
sympathy of my countrymen, of the American people, and of all true
republicans, for the misfortunes which I have suffered, and for the
cause which has occasioned them.

" Although a public manifestation of that affection would be most
grateful to me, exiled from my native land, separated from my children, and weeping over the fall of the liberty of my country by foreign intervention ; yet believe me, I would rather avoid it, content
that it is allowed me, tranquilly and humbly, to become a citizen of

this great Republic of free men, to sail under its flag, to engage in commerce in order to earn my livelihood, and to wait for a moment more favorable for the redemption of my country from oppressors, both domestic and foreign.

" In regard to the cause to which I have consecrated myself, I esteem nothing more than the approbation of this great people; and I believe it will be sufficient for them to know, how I have honestly and faithfully served the cause of liberty, in which they themselves have given a great and noble example to the world.

"G. GARIBALDI."

The committee published their reply to this letter, and closed it with these words : •

"We lament the modesty of Gen. Garibaldi, which, more than his imperfect convalescence, has prevented the success of our urgent requests."

A small volume has been published by Alexander Dumas, a French novel-writer, of which different opinions have been expressed. It was asserted, last summer, by the " Philadelphia Press," that it was pirated from the first edition of this book, in the French language, and had been translated into English and sold to an American bookseller for five hundred dollars. There are many passages in it which might appear to countenance such an assertion ; but there are numerous passages, and even entire chapters, which are wholly unlike anything in the latter ; and a large part of the volume contains views, sentiments and expressions quite the opposite of Garibaldi's. Indeed, of the 337 small duodecimo pages in the English translation, only 203 are claimed by M. Dumas to be Garibaldi's, other writers being credited for the remaining 134. The 203 pages contain passages which magnify Garibaldi's deeds or spirit much more than he was ever known to do, (for he is always as modest as brave,) with some of his most forcible expressions and passages greatly weakened by useless amplifications. The English translation is in a very loose and inferior style ; and various cases occur in both Dumas and his translators, in which ignorant blunders are made in interpreting the standard before them, whatever it may have been. The motto of chapter 6th Dumas gives in his French, "Le Dieu des Bons Gens : "and his English translator : "*The God of Good People.*" And this is afterward repeated, showing a surprising and laughable mistake in the import of the motto of the Italian Republicans, "*Dio e Popolo*"—God and the People.

The personal appearance of Garibaldi, his mien, address, and manners, are so remarkably accordant with his character, that clear impressions of them seem necessary to a distinct apprehension of the spirit with which he lays his plans, and commences and accomplishes his great deeds. A stranger may obtain such impressions, in a considerable degree, by contemplating the fine steel engraving which forms the frontispiece of this volume, and reading some of the descriptions written by different observers on various occasions. That portrait is accurately copied from a daguerrotype, for which he obligingly sat, at the request of the author, soon after his arrival in New York in 1850; and has been pronounced by many of his friends the best likeness they have ever seen. It certainly is exactly like the daguerrotype, not only in the features, but in the expression of the face.

Any one who would form a correct opinion of the state of preparation in which the people of Italy stood waiting for the time of their emancipation, must recur to the labors of the patriotic leaders who had been constantly laboring to enlighten and inspirit them during the last forty years. Their efforts had been principally through secret societies, formed and conducted somewhat on the plan of freemasonry. The Carbonari (literally, colliers—the makers of charcoal in the mountains, where the patriots often found refuge) were dissolved, after their archives had been seized. The society of Giovane Italia (Young Italy) was then formed, and directed by Mazzini and his friends, from foreign countries, safe from the reach of the enemy. One striking case of their sagacious and successful operations is described in that most interesting and instructive work on Italy, "The Roman Exile," by G. Gajani, formerly an eminent Roman jurist, an officer under Garibaldi in 1849, and now a respected citizen of New York. Thousands of other instances might be mentioned, to prove the powerful influence of those efforts.

The union of Italians was the great object aimed at, and *non-interference by foreign powers* was the principle claimed of Europe. The Republicans of 1849 declared that monarchy was opposed to both these ends ; but, since Sardinia, England and France have all proved by their actions that they have adopted these principles, the Republicans have joined their old opponents, the constitutional monarchists, and ranged themselves under the banner of Victor Emanuel. Garibaldi was a Republican in South America, Rome, and everywhere, until he became convinced of this change of policy ; and now he is devoted to Victor Emanuel—because Victor Emanuel is devoted to Italy. When the voice of calumny shall have ceased, justice will be done to men who are now iniquitously stigmatized.

And what men those were, who then, like lions suddenly roused, sprang from their lairs and rushed to the fight in May, 1859. Those alone who knew them, can form an adequate conception of their feelings, because each had passed through trials which none of us have known, or witnessed among our own happier countrymen. Many of them had been exiles in America, and a number had been residents in New York, and personally known, respected and loved.

A large collection of manuscripts now at hand, in various forms, of various kinds, and of different dates, recall the characters and histories of their authors ; and what may hereafter be published from them will be strictly true, except some changes of names, which propriety may require. Among the papers are letters, notices of friends in need, warnings against plotting enemies—Jesuits in disguise, and long histories of romantic adventures.

CHAPTER II.

" Shouting—' Shame on chains and slavery !'
Brothers, rouse and arm for war ;
All united : now, Barbarians,
'Tis your retribution hour !"—*Banks of Dora.*

POLICY OF LOUIS NAPOLEON SINCE 1849—HIS POSITION IN 1859
—CAUSES OF THE WAR IN LOMBARDY—AUSTRIAN ARMY THREAT-
ENS PIEDMONT—FRENCH TROOPS SENT TO THE AID OF VICTOR
EMANUEL—GARIBALDI CALLED INTO SERVICE—MARCHES NORTH
—APPREHENSIONS OF HIS FRIENDS—HIS BRILLIANT SUCCESSES
AT VARESE AND COMO.

LOUIS NAPOLEON, in 1848, when a candidate for the presidency of the French Republic, solicited the assistance of the
clergy, saying that, if elected, he would reinstate the Pope
in Rome. Afterward, in April, 1849, Louis Napoleon sent an
expedition against Rome, under the command of General
Oudinot. That general, on his arrival before Civita Vecchia,
published a proclamation, printed in France, by which it was
announced that France would occupy Rome, in order to
prevent Austria from doing so.

It seems that Louis Napoleon was not so much guided by
his promise, or by religious devotion, as by the shrewd
design of securing to himself the influence of the Pope,
which Austria would have turned against him. The Pope,
however, continued to lean toward Austria ; and, by her
advice, opposed all the suggestions of Louis Napoleon, and
placed him in a false position.

From 1849 to '59 was a period of secret intrigue and
struggles at Rome, between France and Austria. The
Crimean war added a new element of hostility between the
two courts. Napoleon, as a threat to Austria, invited the

263

king of Sardinia to participate in that war, and afterward allowed Count Cavour to speak in the name of oppressed Italy, in spite of the protest of the Austrian minister.

At this, Austria became more active in preparing and countenancing the ruin of Napoleon in France; and the Pope used his influence with the clergy and the legitimists of that country. Napoleon was thus laid under the necessity of striking a blow at Austria, in self-defence. This explains his league with the king of Sardinia. But Napoleon neither designed nor foresaw all that happened afterward. The complete liberation of Italy and the downfall of the papacy were not in his plan; because he feared that a general convulsion of Europe would be the consequence of such events. In justice to him, however, we must acknowledge, that he has countenanced and aided those events, since he has seen that they were accomplished in a wonderfully quiet manner. There can be but little doubt that Napoleon prefers to see the political influence of the Pope dead forever, instead of being compelled to court it, in competition with Austria.

Early in 1859, the Emperor of Austria began to threaten Sardinia with 100,000 men, demanding that she should disarm, which was refused. The Emperor of the French showed himself ready to sustain Victor Emanuel in his position; and then the Emperor of Austria made an effort to gain time by an artifice, and pressed a powerful army on to the frontiers. With surprising promptitude, Louis Napoleon sent a very large force into Piedmont, partly across Mount Cenis and partly by water to Genoa, availing himself of the facilities offered by the railroads and steam vessels, and armed with the most improved military weapons and implements of modern warfare.

Then commenced one of the most important and sanguinary conflicts of modern times, and one most decisive of results in favor of Italian liberty. The armies on both sides were very large and powerful, and included many of the chiefs, officers, and soldiers who had been trained in Africa and the Crimea, as well as in the European wars ten and twelve years preceding. The sudden and rapid advance of the Austrians was checked by the vigorous stand made by the Piedmontese, and the still more rapid movements of the troops from France. We have not room to give all the details of the battles which ensued, and with which the public are acquainted. The service which our hero rendered in it was of the utmost importance ; and not only fully justified the high reputation he had long enjoyed, but raised him to an eminence proportioned to the magnitude of the immense military operations in which he acted a leading, and we might say almost the decisive part.

When Garibaldi was called by the king to engage in the war, he accepted the office proposed, but, it has been reported, on two conditions : that he should be allowed to act according to his own judgment, and as far from the French as possible. We do not pretend to give credence to this rumor, and can only say, on the one hand, that he showed some symptoms, while in this country, of retaining a bitter recollection of the siege and humiliation of Rome ; but, on the other hand, that he is charitable, generous, and forgiving beyond most other men who ever lived on earth. No sooner was it known that Garibaldi was forming a band to act against the Austrians, than patriots hastened from all parts of Italy to join his banner. Such were their numbers and their enthusiasm, that the authorities in vain attempted to detain them ; and even from the Pope's territories, and from the cruelly oppressed kingdom of Naples, volunteers poured like torrents on toward Piedmont. Promptly a corps was formed under Garibaldi's peculiar tactics, denominated, "*I Cacciatori delle Alpi*" (The Huntsmen of the Alps), and, led by their spirited and fearless leader, started toward the north, and disappeared among the mountain passes of the Alps. No sooner was this news received in the United States, than his friends here foretold that his aim would prove to be, to turn the right wing of the Austrians, get into their rear, and raise Lombardy in insurrection. With anxious solicitude the first inquiries of all seemed to be first for Garibaldi ; and the deeds of daring, labor, fatigue, and skill which he performed were repeated through that great and bloody campaign with skill and perseverance equalled only in his uniform success.

Those who have seen enough of Garibaldi to form a just estimate of his character and powers, can never be at a loss in drawing a picture of him in their imaginations, when they hear that he has been placed in a new scene fitted to call forth his energy. So it was when the news was received that he marched from Turin with 3,700 men, his chosen band, to Biella and Borgomanero, toward the northeast, and had moved with such promptitude and rapidity, and by such secluded and difficult paths, that no certain information could be obtained of his route, plans, or objects. Those who knew him at once declared that his former practices compelled them confidently to predict that he had gone among the mountains to turn the right wing of the Austrians, and raise the country in insurrection in their rear. Many days passed, however, before the truth was known, though various reports came through different channels. At length it was published as certain that he had been successful in a laborious march, and in the accomplishment of a sudden and bold attack upon the Austrians at Varese. By ingenious arrangements he had deceived the enemy, whose spies, as he had expected, carried them true reports of his past movements, present position, and possible preparations, but drew false conclusions of his intentions.

THE BATTLE OF VARESE.

The Canton Ticino is a narrow part of Switzerland, lying along a small river of that name, and extending down far into the north of Italy. The interesting history of that small and rude territory deserves to be much better known, especially on account of the devotion of its virtuous inhabitants to the principles of the Reformation, and the persecutions which they have at different periods endured for their faith. The river Ticino is difficult of passage, and, as the Austrians were strong in their position at Varese, beyond it, it was important to prevent them from meeting him at that stream. At Borgomanero he prepared his plans, and put them in harmony with the instructions given him at headquarters. The principal object was to cross the Ticino and effect the passage and invasion without danger to himself or his men. Garibaldi knew that all these men risked their lives, inasmuch as before becoming soldiers they were refugees, and by bearing arms they incurred, according to the Austrian code, the penalty of death. He accordingly spread the report that he intended to stop at Arona, and he even himself wrote orders to have stores and lodgings prepared there, and the churches fitted up for the reception of horses.

No sooner had he sent off these orders by special messengers to Arona, which is on the Lago Maggiore, than he gave orders to his men, each of whom carried two muskets, to leave for Castelletto, where they crossed the Ticino in a ferry-boat to Sesto Calende, and by an astonishing forced march of two days, proceeded to Varese.

The Austrians, on learning how they had been tricked, assembled at Camerlata, and intercepted the line of the Ticino at Varese, believing that they would thereby cut off the retreat of the force and surprise it. Garibaldi troubled himself little about that proceeding, and induced the towns and villages to revolt.

A proclamation was issued by the general, inviting the whole of the Varesotto province to rise against their oppressors. The appeal was generally listened to, and men of every age and condition hastened to the official residence of Marquis Visconti, the extraordinary commissioner sent by Count Cavour as the coadjutor of the Italian general. In less than two hours the whole of the surrounding country was in arms. Old men, children, and even women, came to the Town Hall, with all sorts of weapons, ready to help the small band (3,000) of their brethren. Varese was soon fortified, barricades erected, means of defence carefully ordered. Bands of peasants were pouring into the town from the numberless hamlets, villas, and villages which deck the picturesque hills of that beautiful country—the finest in Lombardy, and, perhaps of Europe. Garibaldi, who is always to be found everywhere when danger is coming, began to array in companies the new comers, and gave the necessary orders for the defence of the country, as he supposed that the Austrians posted at Gallarate would attack him the next day.

He was not deceived in his expectation, for on Wednesday morning, at dawn three hundred Croats and one hundred and thirty Hussars, with a field battery, marched from Gallarate to Sesto Calende, where the advance guard of Italian Chasseurs was posted. This advance guard was commanded by Capt. Decristoforis, a young man of great military ability, who only two months before was in England, and kept a first-rate military school at Putney. After a fight, which lasted two hours, the enemy was completely defeated, leaving some prisoners. The Austrians were obliged to retire on Somma, and nothing was heard of them till next morning at four o'clock.

This second attack was of a more serious character. It was effected by a brigade, five thousand strong, with ten field pieces, and two squadrons of Uhlans. After a first discharge of their muskets, the Italian volunteers assaulted the enemy with the bayonet, and with so much impetuosity that the Austrian centre was obliged to fall back on its left wing, then engaged by a battalion of the Italian right. Now the fight became general—a tremendous hand-to-hand fight, in which every inch of ground was bravely disputed by both armies. The enemy's artillery was of no more use, because Garibaldi, having none, had ordered his men to fight hand-to-hand with swords and bayonets. At the report of the musketry and artillery, the country people hastened to the scene of action with pitchforks, half-pikes, and cleavers. " It was a dreadful scene of slaughter," said an eye-witness, " which lasted three hours." Nothing can give an idea of the impetuosity of those Italians who could at last revenge so many wrongs, so many cruelities. It was almost madness. Two brothers Strambio, one captain and the other lieutenant, were seen to leap into the inside of a hedge of bayonets, and cut down Croats as if they had been puppets. A Count Montanari, from Verona, whose brother had been hanged, in 1853, by Radetsky's order, was running up and down the bloody field, striking right and left with his powerful sword.

At 7 o'clock, the Austrian general was obliged to give the order for a retreat, as his men were falling in all directions. Garibaldi was close at their heels till they reached the strong position of Malnate, where they stopped to repair their losses.

This is a short but faithful sketch of Garibaldi's exploit. It will always be recorded as one of the most brilliant actions of the war, because he had no artillery, and his soldiers were but volunteers, scarcely drilled, and unaccustomed to camp life.

Garibaldi then went to Como, on the celebrated lake of that name, where he received a positive ovation from the population. All the country was in full insurrection. Young men were putting themselves in uniform, and arming themselves. All classes, without distinction—nobles, peasants, citizens, men, women, and children—were prepared for resistance. Garibaldi had taken the precaution of being able to supply the population with arms and ammunition.

CHAPTER III.

"Morn is breaking! Rise, Italia!
He whose yoke thou still dost wear,
Soon will shake at sight of danger;
Well his coward heart may fear."

" *The Banks of Dora.*"   T. D.

COMO—APPROACH OF GENERAL URBAN WITH 40,000 AUSTRIANS—
GARIBALDI RETIRES—COMO TAKEN—COUNT RAIMONDI'S DAUGH-
TER—GARIBALDI RETURNS AND EXPELS THE AUSTRIANS—THE
BATTLE OF CAMERLATA—THE AUSTRIANS DEMAND THE DIS-
BANDING OF GARIBALDI'S TROOPS—REFUSED—THEY ADVANCE—
THE CANALS OPENED—THEY RETIRE—THE BATTLES OF PALES-
TRO, MONTEBELLO, AND MAGENTA—THE MINCIO AND ITS BANKS
—THE BATTLE OF SOLFERINO.

COMO is a city beautifully situated on the northern end of
Lake Como ; but on the low land near the margin, and over-
looked by the mountains, which rise beyond and around.

The enthusiasm which prevailed on Garibaldi's arrival was
extreme ; and the alarm bells were rung in all the communes of
the Varesotto, Tramezzo, Como and Lecco districts.   The
volunteers were pouring in from every village and hamlet.
In this manner the insurrection gained ground in Upper
Lombardy.   At the first appearance of the braves, all the
civil authorities of Como and Lecco recognized the government of King Victor Emanuel, which in those towns was
represented by Count Visconti Venosta, a young nobleman
from Valtellina of great determination.   His spirited proclamations roused the enthusiasm of country folks and citizens,
who hastened to the scene of action with an ardor never witnessed in 1848.   Money, so much wanted, poured into Garibaldi's military treasury, together with gold necklaces and
other valuable trinkets from fair Lombard ladies.   The sum
thus collected in two days reached 2,000,000 francs.

270

Garibaldi had been instructed to move in the direction of Varese by slow marches, keeping himself in constant
communication with Cialdini's division, which did not follow.
By the necessity of strategetical combinations, Gen. Cialdini
was obliged to march to and fro from Vercelli and Stroppiana,
guarding the right bank of the Upper Sesia, as far as Gat-
tinara.   The necessary result of this constant marching and
countermarching was that of retarding the projects of Garibaldi.   He moved slowly for two days, but he could not
stand it any longer ; and hastening from Romagnana to the
headquarters of the king, he begged him to observe that he
did not and could not understand the scientific principles of a
regular war, and that he wished to be left to his daring
inspiration.

Victor Emanuel saw directly that it was of no use to keep
such a bird in the cage of strategic rules, and, letting him
loose, said : " Go where you like, do what you like.   I have
only one regret—that of not being able to follow you."

While occupying the place, amidst the enthusiasm of the
inhabitants, he learned that General Urban was approaching
with forty thousand Austrians.   He immediately retired
from the city, leaving two hundred men, with orders to hold
the place, with the aid of the inhabitants, to the last extremity.   The enemy came on, attacked, and were bravely
resisted, but succeeded in taking the town.   Supposing that
Garibaldi had retreated into Switzerland, without any intention of returning, they appeared to entertain no apprehensions
of danger from that quarter.   It then became highly important that he should be apprised of the condition of things.
Every effort was made to procure a messenger, and high
rewards were offered ; but the hazards were so great that no
one could be found willing to run the desperate risk of his
life, or rather to go to certain death, as the Austrians were
believed to hold and watch every avenue to the country.

Garibaldi, who was waiting in the mountains for an opportunity to make a sudden descent upon the enemy, but cut off

from communication, and in ignorance of their situation, was surprised in his wild retreat by the arrival of a lady, who had come from Como alone, on horseback, by pursuing by-paths, and with great skill and boldness, finding her way between and around the various points which were guarded by the enemy. Although only twenty-four years of age, brought up in refined society, and of aristocratic family—a daughter of Count Raimondi—this fair and youthful stranger appeared before Garibaldi like a vision, and, with an air corresponding with the spirit which had inspired her through her wild and perilous expedition, presented to him the dispatches with which she had been intrusted, at her earnest petition, in Como. Garibaldi learned from them the position of the enemy, and the readiness of the people to receive him again. Without a moment's delay, he set out on his return, and by a forced march, conducted with the greatest skill, suddenly returned to the Lake of Como, with his resolute band.

Como was occupied after a hard fight of two hours at San Fermo and Camerlata. This last-mentioned position is to be considered as the key of the picturesque barrier of Como, for its elevated ground enables a small body of men to oppose a long resistance even to an army of 15,000 strong. The positions were carried at the point of the bayonet, for the Cacciatori delle Alpi could not fire their muskets, so much inferior in range to those of the enemy. It was a hard and bloody fight, which may, without exaggeration, be compared to the struggles of old, when Roman and Carthaginian legions met together.

The news of the organizing of a corps by the celebrated Garibaldi, had induced the Austrians to make their last demand upon Piedmont, which was a very extraordinary one, and indicated the interesting truth that they duly appreciated Garibaldi. It was, that, unless his band was immediately dispersed, they would march forward in three days. This demand was not complied with, but the King of Sardinia prepared to receive the threatened invaders. With excellent

judgment, however, he did not attempt to occupy the line of
the Mincio ; he chose a stronger one within his own territory,
and occupied that extending from Alessandria to the Apennines, toward Genoa, leaving the road to Turin open to the
enemy.   The Austrians moved ; but, as soon as they had
crossed the Ticino, the engineer who had charge of the canals
which irrigate the extensive valley, was ordered to open them
and make an inundation.   The Austrians soon discovered
that the water was rising, and the general sent word to the
engineer in terms like these :

" Your brother is a prisoner in my hands ; if you do not immediately stop the inundation, I will cut off his head."

The engineer, with the greatest resolution, pressed the
work with redoubled vigor that night ; and by employing
two hundred more men, completed it before morning.   The
Austrians, finding that they were likely to be caught in a
kind of trap, with the inundation rising on their right, and
the Piedmontese army on their left, soon retreated, and recrossed the Ticino.

THE BATTLE OF PALESTRO.

This action was important, not only on account of its re-
sulting in the first victory against the Austrians, but also because
of the excellence of the Piedmontese troops, which had been
denied, and was certainly seriously doubted by Louis Napoleon, who had given to Victor Emanuel four battalions of
French Zouaves for his body-guard.   These were the only
French troops in that battle ; and they so much admired the
conduct of the King of Sardinia, that they elected him
" Corporal" on the field.   This is esteemed the highest
military honor which can be in any way acquired ; and it is
one which Louis Napoleon himself has never yet received,
even from his own troops.

The battle of Montebello was the first ever decided by a

railroad. When the action commenced, there was only a single regiment to resist the Austrians. This was a French regiment, which was so soon, so rapidly, and so greatly reinforced by other French troops, transported on the railroad, that the day was soon decided in their favor. The importance and effect of this manner of conveying the troops was acknowledged by the Austrians, in their official report of the battle.

THE BATTLE OF MAGENTA.

This was fought about twenty miles beyond the last engagement, that of Montebello; and the chief honor of the day belongs to the French. That battle was the first in which rifled cannon and electrical telegraphs were ever brought into use; and both were proved successful in the highest degree. Louis Napoleon was the inventor of the former; and their efficiency was strongly doubted and even denied by many scientific and practical men; but it was established beyond future question by the experiment of that day. The French had also a corps of electricians among them, with apparatus prepared for the establishment and change of lines of telegraphic wires wherever troops were stationed; and these proved of eminent service in conveying orders and information between the positions.

THE RIVER MINCIO.

The banks of the Mincio are, as it were, formed for military scenes. From the source of the river, down almost as far as Pozzolo, the river winds through a succession of hills, rushing close to their base on one side, and leaving fine open meadows on the other. At some points the hills approach on both sides, and form a kind of gorge or neutral ground, where the river is kept within proper bounds, and not allowed to encroach on either side. Perhaps the most picturesque spot on the whole river is here, between Borghetto

and Vallegio.   Two large semi-circles of hills are opposed to
each other, the direction of them being the bend of the river
on this spot; they intersect each other about their centre,
and a little below this point are the two villages of Borghetto and Vallegio.   The latter is behind the hills on the left
bank; only two mills, a church, and a little mediæval tower,
erected on one of the lower spurs, stand close to the water's
edge.   Borghetto has, likewise, only a few detached houses
on the banks of the river, the rest of the village being built
on the hill which skirts the right bank.   On the highest
point of the Vallegio side rises a most picturesque group of
towers of pure Italian castellated architecture, slender and
high like campaniles, with a gallery on their summit, built on
a succession of small arches springing out of the body of the
building.   From these towers, an old wall runs down to the
banks of the river, where two other lower, but more massive,
towers stand, with the ruins of a bridge over the river between them.   From the second of these towers, the wall
runs up to the hill where Borghetto stands, and ends there
in another square tower.   This castle, as well as the surrounding domain, belongs to the Visconti family, and the
fortifications were evidently intended to close the passage of
the river, which they may have done at one time; now they
form only a picturesque feature in the scenery.   The road
from Volta to this place descends along the hillside in a gentle slope, and, after traversing the river, winds up in a similar but much steeper rise, so that you can keep in view the
whole passage through the valley.   On the right bank of the
river extends a fine meadow, through which the road leads.
It was now the camping-ground of the Cavalry of the Guard,
and was, during the passage, a chaos of troops, horses, carts,
and mules, which were huddled together there, waiting for a
passage across one of the four bridges which span the narrow
but rapid little stream.   It was like the emigration of one of
those nomadic tribes of which history tells us.   It seemed for
a moment as if it were impossible to disentangle that mass,

and yet it kept moving, and passed over the river without accident or delay. As all the bridges which had been broken down on the river behind had been repaired, the pontoon train of the whole army became available for the Mincio passage, and there must have been, at the very least, from 12 to 15 bridges on this short line.

THE BATTLE OF SOLFERINO.

The Austrian army, after occupying the right bank of the Mincio, had retired across the stream, in order to lead the French and Sardinians to believe that they were retreating. When the latter had extended their lines, the Austrians suddenly returned and reoccupied their old formidable positions on the heights of Solferino, San Cassiano, and Cavriana, and onward to Volta, all crowned with cannon. Their lines extended five leagues. This movement was made in the night of June 23d, and at three o'clock in the morning they were discovered, in large bodies, marching across the plain to attack the allies.

On the 24th, the emperor, who had arrived just before, ordered the Sardinian army (which formed the left wing) to occupy Pozzolengo, and the French to occupy Solferino and Cavriana. The king also sent a detachment toward Peschiera. The Austrians resisted them powerfully. At ten o'clock the battle became general, and was continued during a severe storm. After twelve hours fighting, the Austrians brought up their reserve of 80,000 men, and the allies theirs of 50,000. After three more hours of severe fighting, the heights were taken by the allies, and the Austrians retreated.

In 1796, Solferino was the point most strenuously contested and won by Augereau. On this occasion that position was taken three times by the French, and the last time at the point of the bayonet. The Emperor of Austria commanded in person, and greatly animated his troops, who fought well. After they had been driven from Solferino, they made a powerful concentrated attack on the right wing of the allies, but were repulsed by a dash of cavalry.

Although the allies were victorious, they were unable to pursue the enemy, who retreated in good order.

THE AUSTRIAN OFFICIAL ACCOUNT OF THE BATTLE OF SOLFERINO.

The official journal at Vienna, of June 26, published the following official dispatch from the seat of war :

"VERONA, *Saturday, June* 25.

"On the 23d inst., the imperial royal army crossed at four places to the right bank of the Mincio. The right wing of the army occupied Pozzolengo, Solferino, and Cavriana. The left wing marched on the 24th inst. to Guidizzolo and Castel-Goffredo, and repulsed the advancing enemy on all sides. As the Imperial Royal army continued its advance toward the Chiese, the enemy—who had also assumed the offensive with his whole force—pushed forward such large bodies of troops, that there was a general engagement between the two armies at ten o'clock, or thereabouts, in the morning of the 24th instant.

"The right wing, which was formed by the second army, under the general of cavalry, Count Schlick, maintained possession of the place which it had originally occupied in the first line of battle until 2 o'clock in the afternoon, and the first army (the left wing), under the general of artillery, Count Wimpffen, continually gained ground in the direction of the Chiese. Toward 3 o'clock the enemy made a vehement attack on Solferino, and after several hours' hard fighting, obtained possession of the place, which had been heroically defended by the fifth *corps d'armée*. An attack was then made on Cavriana, which place was courageously defended until the evening by the first and seventh *corps d'armée*, but was eventually left in the hands of the enemy.

"While the struggle for Solferino and Cavriana was going on, the eighth *corps d'armée*, which was on the outer flank of the right wing, advanced and repulsed the Sardinian troops opposed to it : but this advantage did not enable the Imperial Royal army to recover the positions that had been lost in the centre. The third and ninth corps, which were supported by the eleventh corps, were engaged on the left wing, and the reserve cavalry attached to this wing made several brilliant attacks. Unusually heavy losses, and the fact that the left wing of the first army was unable to make progress on the right flank of the enemy, who directed his main force in the centre against Volta, led to the retreat of the Imperial Royal army. It began late in the evening, during a violent storm. Yesterday evening Pozzolengo, Monzambano, Volta and Goito, were still occupied by our troops."

CHAPTER IV.

THE STATE OF THE CONTENDING PARTIES—SPECIMEN OF THE
BARBARITY OF SOME OF THE AUSTRIAN OFFICERS — THE
ARMISTICE.

THE Austrian army, with its imposing numbers, high military
reputation, and menacing attitude a few weeks before, when
threatening and afterward invading Piedmont, from the line
of the Mincio, had now become vastly weakened, reduced,
and disheartened by the successive conflicts and defeats which
have been briefly described. The causes of its misfortunes
have been accounted for, by an eye-witness, in remarks which
we abridge as follows :

"The Austrian military system has been changed completely within
the last six or seven years ; yet the change in part explains the short-
comings of the past few weeks. The Austrian army, up to this date,
has been an army of very young soldiers, not long under training.
According to the regulations, a fixed number of corps has to be maintained throughout the Austrian empire. At a fixed period of every
year the youth of that empire are drafted into the army, and distributed among the corps. The arrival of these new drafts liberates an
equal number of men who have already served. The latter, after one, or
two, or three years' service, at the option of the colonels of regiments,
retire to their homes on a furlough of indefinite duration, and are
only called out again in the event of a war. The Austrian army at
Montebello, Palestro, Magenta, and Cavriana was thus composed of
young soldiers. It would have been wiser, doubtless, had the Austrians thought of this matter in time. They were aware that Louis
Napoleon would move, if he moved at all, with the flower of his
army. They knew that he had paid high premiums to induce old
soldiers to remain in the ranks after the expiration of their usual time,
and that the picked men of the French army, tried under the fierce
sun of Africa, and in the hard campaign of the Crimea, would be
opposed to them, and be assisted besides by an artillery of a novel
and most effective kind. They did not take sufficient heed of these

important facts, any more than they considered that generals who, ten years ago, fought with ability and success in the campaigns of Italy might possibly have lost some of their original vigor. The result has been such as to open their eyes to the necessity of supplying defects. The question, as far as the present war is concerned, is this : Which is best, to risk all the tried men first, and trust to recruits after, or employ first the young soldiers, and bring up reserves after ? As far as the present campaign is concerned, the results favor the first of these alternatives.

"The advisers of his Imperial Majesty Francis Joseph, at last made up their minds that it was impossible, under present circumstances, to defend the line of the Mincio. Accordingly, the headquarters of the 2d Army, under Count Schlick, came into Verona from Villafranca ; the headquarters of the 1st Army, under Wimpffen, being transferred to Mantua. Verona, Mantua, and the other strongholds of this great military quadrangle are very much stronger than they were ten years ago. There are great field works to be taken before any approach can be made to the main defences, and in the meanwhile Austria may have brought together again an army capable of risking another general action. The soldiers had one moment of enthusiasm ; that was when the emperor led them in person on the 23d to the advanced position from which he intended to attack the enemy ; but the events of the 24th seriously affected the *morale* of the army. Instead of attacking, as they were led to expect, they had to repel the assaults of the Allies, who knowing what was before them, had halted for a meal at two o'clock in the morning. The Austrians, whose baggage and cooking utensils accompany the columns even in the advance, bivouacked on the night of the 23d, and were attacked before they could get their breakfast. The baggage and cooking-carts were obliged to return to the rear out of the fire of the Allies, and the result was that the army of the Kaiser had to fight on empty stomachs. Hunger and hard knocks have a tendency to discourage even the bravest soldier. I was astonished to see men from the field of Solferino retiring unwounded, and lying down exhausted when out of the reach of the enemy's fire. I am told that many so exhausted laid themselves down only to die. The mystery is explained when one considers that these cases arose from want of ordinary sustenance.

"Lichtenstein's corps (the 2d) which should have taken part in the action of the day, was halted in consequence of the approach of some French cavalry in its vicinity, and Prince Lichtenstein, for reasons which he will doubtless have to explain, returned to Mantua. Again, General Zedwitz, commanding the cavalry brigade of the 1st

Army, instead of advancing, as he should have done, fell back on Goito, thus depriving the emperor of six regiments of horse and a considerable amount of artillery. Thus, while on the part of the allies all the available guns that could be brought into action were used, on the side of the Austrians the artillery was weak and utterly unable to oppose an effectual fire to that of the enemy. It is true, on the other hand, that the French artillery did not commit the havoc which it might have done had its fire throughout the day been true to the mark, instead of being over it. Still, the effect of the inferiority under which the Austrians suffered in this respect, was disastrous, as it prevented them from repelling the advance of the infantry opposed to them. Among the wounded, to the number of 4,000 or 5,000 in Verona and the surrounding villages, it is remarkable how few suffered from wounds inflicted by artillery."

In contrast with the condition of the Austrian army, those of Piedmont and France were in most respects superior, and still more in the principles for which they fought. To mention again Napoleon's rifled cannon, in the words of a late writer :

"The superiority of the French artillery during the late Italian campaign was obvious to every one who made himself acquainted with the details of the great battles. At Solferino the heavy and very dangerous Austrian cavalry was thrown into disorder and rendered almost useless at distances to which their own batteries, more favorably placed, would not carry. The Austrians never yielded a foot on the hill of Solferino, till a battery of French rifled cannon was brought to bear upon them at a distance at which their own balls fell short. The Tower could not have otherwise been taken but with an infinitely greater slaughter than that which occurred. When Niel and McMahon had driven the Austrians back as far as the large open space known as the plain of Guidizzolo, there was a fair trial of artillery, which cost the Austrians dear; it was the last stand made by the immense left wing of the Austrian army, and one can well imagine how officers and men grew dispirited in face of artillery that silenced their own wherever it showed itself."

The following remarks on the plans and conduct of the war we abridge from the "London Times," of July 8th, 1860 :

"As far as the Allies are concerned, their aim was driving the Austrians out of Italy. With this aim clearly and distinctly before them, the difficulties and chances could be more or less calculated in advance, and all that vagueness and uncertainty avoided which gives rise to those useless moves in two armies, neither of which knows what it is to do next.

" The Austrians were in this latter case when they began the war, nobody knew why, and while they were allowed to amuse themselves with their harmless offensive movements you saw all those insignificant skirmishes occur on the Sesia, which were put a speedy end to by the advance of the Allies. Since that time the war has been rolling along in great waves. The Allies went straight toward their aim, and the Austrians were so hard pressed, that they endeavored to oppose to a grand plan, executed with the most determined will, equally grand operations.

"Thus, when the Austrians found themselves outwitted by the flank movement on the Ticino, they brought up their troops in all haste to oppose the advance. They were beaten, and immediately resolved to withdraw behind the Mincio. The fight at Malegnano only took place in order to insure this retreat, but from that time they avoided opposing the advance of the Allies, by making a stand at the river lines. On the other hand, the Allies, intent only on carrying out their own great plans, did not think for one moment of molesting their retreat.

" After the Allies had crossed the Chiese, and made preparations for the passage of the Mincio, the Austrians attempted one great blow ; and, collecting all their forces, tried an offensive movement, which was speedily checked by the battle of Solferino. The battle lost, the French, whose preparations were not completed, did not press the retreating Austrians very hard ; while these latter, instead of trying a desultory defence of the Mincio, opposed no resistance to the passage of it, but, without wasting any forces, retired between Peschiera and Verona, to await there the attack of the Allies, or perhaps watch their time for another great offensive movement.

"This avoiding on both sides of those little encounters, deprives the war considerably of its picturesque element—of its individual features, as it were. This whole campaign resolves itself into an alternation between preparations and great decisive blows.

" The Mincio passage was effected without any difficulty, offering by its good arrangements matter of thought to the military, but otherwise being a subject rather for a landscape painter than for a painter of battles. Although the Austrians had gone back from the river, all the precautions were taken as if there had been a constant danger from an attack. The whole had very much the appearance of a field manœuvre in peaceable times, with the difference, however, that even the thin line representing the hostile forces on such occasions, was entirely wanting.   But the movements had to be so combined, that the army should be in readiness to receive the enemy in case he came down from his position between Verona and Peschiera.   The enemy's position was on the left flank of the allied armies, facing the Mincio, with Peschiera just at the angle formed by the intersection of the Mincio with his extreme right.   The Allies were thus obliged, while crossing the Mincio, to change their front and face to the left.   For this purpose the Sardinians, who had kept the position of San Martino, took up the line from Rivoltella, on the lake, in the neighborhood of Pozzolengo.   The 1st French corps, which had been next to them in the *ordre de bataille* of the 27th, marched to Pozzolengo, and, occupying Ponti, faced against Peschiera.   The 2d corps, next to it, kept its original direction toward the Mincio, joining the 1st corps at Castellaro, where the road leads down to Monzambano. To the right of this corps was the 4th, at Volta, likewise facing the Mincio, and the 3d at Goito.   The crossing took place at almost all points simultaneously, with just sufficient interval between the corps to allow time for that furthest to the right to accomplish its change of front, and come into the same direction with the others.   Thus, the 4th corps, which was furthest, with the exception of the 3d, detached toward Goito, was the first to cross at Borghetto and Vallegio, to gain the high road to Verona, and take up its position toward Villafranca.   This was on the morning of the 29th.   Since that time, all the corps have crossed successively, changing their direction from west to east, and making front against the Austrian position.

" While we are discussing the progress of the plot and speculating as to the nature of the catastrophe, the curtain falls.   Yesterday France and Austria were upon the point of joining in another desperate battle.   The celebrated fortified Quadrangle had been reached, Peschiera had been invested, Mantua had been masked, Verona was upon the point of being summoned, Venice was threatened, and Garibaldi was manœuvering upon the rear of the great fortresses.   The waves of warfare were undulating and vibrating to another great burst in foam.   To-day the Spirit of Peace has breathed upon the waters, and the storm is for the moment at an end.   Three months ago we expected peace and were surprised by war.   To-day Europe was waiting in breathless expectation for a great battle, fought in the very fortresses of Austria, and is again surprised by the calm announcement that an armistice has been concluded, and that the two great armies are for the moment no longer enemies."

The cruelties practised by Austrians in Italy will be disgraceful to the memory of their government, its officers and soldiers. A single instance of the crimes of General Urban, in Lombardy, in 1859, will suffice. By his order, a whole family were butchered. It consisted of seven persons, including a grandfather, eighty-two years of age, a boy of fourteen, and a girl of twelve. Merely for the purpose of striking terror into the people, it appears, and without any pretext of fault in them, he had them all put to death, and left their mangled corpses unburied. This atrocious act has been denied; but the king's government have since instituted a regular legal investigation, ascertained its truth, and erected a monument in memory of it.

THE ARMISTICE.

The war, its progress, results, and prospects were not less unexpected or surprising than the armistice which Louis Napoleon, without any warning, suddenly concluded, in an interview with the Emperor of Austria, on the 11th of July. The cause of it still remains a matter of conjecture. It was followed by a treaty, by which the war was terminated and harmony restored, but the promise of Louis not fulfilled, of driving out the foreigners from Italy. Austria was left in possession of the four great fortresses of Lombardy, as well as of Venetia.

The armistice was first announced to France by the following telegram :

"VALLEGIO, *July* 11, 1859.

"THE EMPEROR TO THE EMPRESS.

"Peace has been signed between the Emperor of Austria and myself.

"The bases agreed to are an Italian confederation, under the honorary Presidentship of the Pope.

"The Emperor of Austria cedes his rights over Lombardy to the

Emperor of the French, who hands them over to the King of Sardinia.

" The Emperor of Austria preserves Venetia, but that country forms an integral part of the Italian Confederation.

" General armistice."

It was made known to the army on the following day, by this proclamation :

" SOLDIERS—The bases of peace have been arranged with the Emperor of Austria ; the principal object of the war has been obtained ; Italy is about to become for the first time a nation. A confederation of all the Italian States under the honorary Presidency of the Holy Father, will unite them together as the members of one family. Venetia, it is true, remains under the sceptre of Austria. It will, nevertheless, be an Italian province, constituting a part of the confederation.

" The union of Lombardy with Piedmont creates for us on this side of the Alps a powerful ally, who will owe to us his independence. The governments unconnected with this movement, (*en dehors du mouvement*), or recalled to their possessions, will comprehend the necessity of salutary reforms. A general amnesty will cause to disappear the traces of civil discord. Italy, henceforth mistress of her destinies, will only have to blame herself if she do not regularly progress in order and liberty.

" You will soon return to France. The grateful country will welcome with transport those soldiers who have borne so high the glory of our arms at Montebello, Palestro, Turbigo, Magenta, Mariguan, and Solferino, who in two months have emancipated Piedmont and Lombardy, and only paused because the struggle was about to assume proportions inconsistent with the interests of France in connection with this formidable war.

" Be also proud of your success, proud of the results obtained, proud, above all, of being the well beloved children of that France which will ever continue a great nation, so long as it shall have a heart to comprehend noble causes, and men like yourselves to defend them.

" At the Imperial Headquarters of Vallegio, 12th of July, 1859.

" NAPOLEON."

The following considerations are suggested by the peace just concluded :

The cession of Lombardy to Piedmont comprehends that of the two fortresses, Mantua and Peschiera. The superfices of Lombardy is 8,538 square miles. Its population is 2,800,000 souls. Lombardy has hitherto been divided, administratively, into nine provinces or delegations, viz. :— Milan, Pavia, Lodi, Corma, Cremona, Como, Mantua, Sondrio, Breschia, and Bergamo. The fortified towns of Mantua and Peschiera form part of the province of Mantua. The fortress of Pezzighettone is comprised in the province of Cremona. After the annexation of Lombardy and Piedmont, this kingdom (the island of Sardinia both included) will contain a superfices of 37,640 square miles, with a population of 7,800,000. As regards territorial extent, it will occupy a tenth rank in Europe, and will come immediately after the kingdom of the Two Sicilies, and before Portugal and Bavaria. With respect to population, Sardinia will stand in the ninth rank, on a level with Naples, and will be above Sweden and Norway, Belgium, and Bavaria.

The following table completes the comparison as regards Italy :

	Area Sq. M.	Population.
New kingdom	37,640	7,800,000
Venetia	9,525	2,200,000
Papal States	17,218	2,900,000
Tuscany	8,741	1,750,000
Parma	2,268	500,000
Modena	2,090	410,000
Two Sicilies	42,000	8,400,000

Although disappointed, by the imperfect accomplishment of the work of securing all Italy to the Italians, there was much reason to rejoice, that the overflowing fountains of human blood, which had exhibited a spectacle shocking to humanity, had been stopped. The terms of peace were settled by the Treaty of Villafranca.

CHAPTER V.

"A brighter course has never
A hero true display'd ;
Unblemish'd in the hour of peace,
In danger undismay'd."—*Lines to Garibaldi.*

THE CHARACTER OF ITALIAN PATRIOTS—HOW IT HAS BEEN DIS-
PLAYED BY EXILES IN THE UNITED STATES—IGNORANCE OF
ITALY IN AMERICA—GARIBALDI'S APPEARANCE AND CHAR-
ACTER—HIS BAND—HIS "ENGLISHMAN," COL. PEARD.

AND now that we have arrived at another peaceful interval
in the life of this extraordinary man, the astonishing effects
of his superior skill, bravery, and success, having broken the
arm of Austria in Italy, and nothing but the shield of Louis
Napoleon having sheltered her head, a sudden suspension of
hostilities left the world at leisure to admire the past, feel
astounded at the unexpected present state of things, and
look with interest, but painful uncertainty, for the future.
All observers, who had not before made Italy or Italians
their attentive study, were anxious to know more of the
people who had suddenly sprung from a low general estima-
tion as patriots and soldiers, to the rank due to the conquerors at Palestro, Montebello, and Solferino, and had furnished the files of the heroic and irresistible hunters of the
Alps, and their leader, Garibaldi himself. Let us turn a
few moments to inquiries of the same kind ; for even at the
present time, there is too much reason to fear, there are few,
even of our most intelligent countrymen, who have paid
sufficient attention to the affairs of Italy during the past
half century, to give full and clear replies to these questions.

Few indeed have had the best opportunities to learn the

287

general truths, and fewer still have had access to many of those details, by which alone the causes can be well understood, and the effects clearly accounted for. The published accounts of Italians and their affairs have been presented to the world in a detached, uncertain and often confused and even contradictory form, which most readers had neither the disposition, the time, nor the means to unravel, reconcile and correct. There have always been, however, intelligent and virtuous patriotic Italians residing in the United States, and especially in New York, who were able and ready to communicate real facts and just opinions on every event and question of importance. And to such are justly due some portion of the facts contained in this volume, and of the views and spirit under which they are now laid before the American people. With their assistance, and at their urgent request also, was done the little which has ever been effected in this country in past years, to explain and vindicate their cause, to relieve its exiled victims, to expose the insidious intrigues of their enemies against American institutions, and to invite and foster mutual acquaintance, and brotherly affection and coöperation between us and the noble patriots of Italy.

Americans have but one excuse to give for their neglect of Italy in her more triumphant struggle against her combined enemies and oppressors The intrigues of her enemies and their insidious calumnies were sufficient to mislead the incautious and the honest. But we have long since lost the spirit of our Protestant ancestors, who were men of clearer sight, greater knowledge, stronger judgment, and more resolution, bravery and perseverance than their descendants. They distinguished, as we do not, between great truths and great falsehoods ; between great rights and great wrongs ; and acted with promptitude and vigor whenever the time arrived to vindicate or secure the one, and to expose and counteract the other. And such a spirit was displayed by the Italian exiles on our soil. They set us examples of similar ways of thinking, speaking and acting ; and well would it have been if we had rightly appreciated the knowledge which they possessed, the manly views which they entertained, and the plans which they proposed for our mutual benefit.

The following description of Garibaldi we translate from the " History of the Glorious Campaign of the Cacciatori delle Alpi, in the war of 1859," by one of his officers, Col. Francesco Corrano :

" Giuseppe Garibaldi is of middle stature, with broad and square shoulders, herculean limbs, long brownish hair, and beard slightly grey ; a heavy and strong step, sailor-like air, look, and manner of speaking ; his vest buttoned up to his throat, a hat with a broad brim, in the Calabrian style, and large trousers. The noises of the city annoy and disturb him. Commanding mountains please him, covered with evergreen trees, and the sight of the vast horizon and the boundless sea.

" His nose is straight and almost vertical, and his aspect at once vivacious and sweet. Often, under his very heavy beard, his lips are gently moved by a natural and fascinating smile. He converses frankly and unaffectedly, condemns with decision, and praises warmly but briefly ; but he is ever animated, fluent, and even eloquent, whenever the conversation turns on Italy, liberty, and deeds of daring and skill ; to overcome the enemy, and to overdo them (*sopraffare*), his favorite word. Above all things, he prizes faithfulness and valor in chivalrous warfare, though it be not accompanied by fame or popular applause. Proud despiser of pay and money, he loves Italy above all things.

" Cuneo, who is called his friend for life, by Garibaldi himself, writes of him : ' A man of humanity, he is laboring to secure in the future the brotherhood of the people ; but at the banquet of nations he will sit only as an equal, or not sit at all.' He is by nature tolerant of every suggestion. He has trust and sympathy in discipline produced by love, more than by the rigor of laws.

" It would be difficult to find a successor to Garibaldi. His name is popular in Italy, through all Europe, and in America also, as no other is in our day ; and it was owing chiefly to his name, that ten thousand Italians, from every province in the country, and in a short space of time, hastened to join him, and to write their names as ' Cacciatori delle Alpi.' But, more than to command battalions, he is fitted to lead them in fine order; prepared to fight, and with ten-fold moral force, by his terrible name, to overcome and scatter the enemy; to conquer or to fall with signal honor."

The intelligence and respectability of Garibaldi's soldiers were attested by an English gentleman who visited his camp at Firano, August 5th.   He wrote :

" You are already aware that in this singular corps the soldier generally belongs to the best class of Italian society. In consequence of this peculiarity, each of this gallant band is a politician of the first class. The doings of our ministers are sensibly discussed in these bivouacs.

" The only Englishman who is among them has become the lion of this singular corps. In my former letter I had occasion to speak of Captain Peard, the gentleman in question. He comes from Cornwall, and belongs to a militia regiment, whose uniform he wears with a decidedly martial bearing. He is a man of tall and colossal frame, nearer sixty than fifty, and is considered the best shot in the party. Although he has been attached to Garibaldi's staff, he makes war at his own expense, and he was always to be found in the thick of the fray. Whenever he had killed an Austrian, he was seen to mark him down in his pocket-book. A few days ago I met Captain Peard at Brescia, and he was kind enough to show me his book, from which it was apparent that twenty-five Austrians were killed by him during the campaign, besides ten who were under the head of ' uncertain.'

" These are also with Garibaldi two rather eccentric young Frenchmen, dressed in a peculiar costume of their own, who are members of the Paris Jockey Club. These two gentlemen have been so charmed by the gallant general, that I am told they will share his fate, whatever it may be. *Five American citizens*, and a few Germans, are going to do the same, together with a Chinese, who, were I to believe what he told me, is one of the few who escaped the slaughter of Commissioner Yeh at Canton. Most of Garibaldi's officers belong to the upper classes of Lombardy, and have borne arms with him either in South America or in Rome."

The interval which occurred between the day of Garibaldi's departure from Turin, with his *Alpine Huntsmen,* and the dispersion of the forty thousand Austrians at Calatrava, is one of the most interesting and important in modern history. While the most anxious fears prevailed among his friends,

and the most alarming reports were circulated by his enemies ; while the promise of being supported by the number
of troops which he had thought indispensable was entirely
disappointed, by the inability of Cialdini to cross the rivers,
Garibaldi, as we have seen, undismayed by that and other
difficulties, pursued his way with unfailing resolution and
complete success. He raised the country in insurrection
wherever he went ; kindled a flame in every heart from the
electric fire which had so long been cherished in his own ;
unhesitatingly attacked the opposing hosts of the enemy, and
put them all to flight. Thus he alarmed, weakened, and
terrified the invaders, and animated the Allies, whose precursor he was ; gave an impulse to the war at the commencement, and a most powerful support to it till the close, which
will ever secure to him an indisputable claim to a large, a
very large, share of the victory and its results. This claim,
we may surely foretell, will never be made by himself. It
will, however, be made by the world—by mankind—on whom
he has conferred the inestimable benefits of his great deeds,
and his pure and noble example. Such concurrences and
successions of events, such men as have been employed in the
various scenes, and especially such a heroic leader, could have
been devised only by infinite wisdom, and conducted to such
results only by an Almighty hand.

CHAPTER VI.

"Italia ! I thank thee for life, and for pow'r
To fight with the foes of thyself and mankind."

Lines on the death of Anna.

AFTER the interesting scenes described in the last chapter, Garibaldi went to Rimini, and took command of an army which had been collected there, to resist General Lamoricière, who was at Pesaro, 22 miles distant, that French general, commanding the Pope's troops, being menaced by Garibaldi's position, who was said to be urgent for permission to pass at once through the Pope's territory into the Abruzzo, and raise the Neapolitans in insurrection against their cruel old king, Bomba.

Victor Emanuel, disapproving such a movement at that time, wrote to Garibaldi, requesting him to resign his command, with which he complied ; and General Fanti received it in his stead. He then proceeded to Piedmont, where he published the following manifesto :

"TO MY COMPANIONS IN ARMS IN CENTRAL ITALY.

"Let not my temporary absence cool your ardor for the holy cause that we defend.

"In separating myself from you, whom I love as the representatives of a sublime idea—the idea of Italian deliverance—I am excited and sad ; but consolation comes in the certainty that I shall very soon

292

be among you again, to aid you in finishing the work so gloriously begun.

"For you, as for me, the greatest of all possible misfortunes would be not to be present wherever there is fighting for Italy. Young men who have sworn to be faithful to Italy and to the chief who will lead you to victory, lay not down your arms; remain firm at your post—continue your exercises—persevere in the soldier's discipline.

"The truce will not last long; old diplomacy seems but little disposed to see things as they really are. Diplomacy still looks upon you as the handful of malcontents which she had been accustomed to despise. She does not know that in you there are the elements of a great nation, and that in your free and independent hearts there germinate the seeds of a world-wide revolution if our rights shall not be recognized, and if people will not allow us to be masters in our own home.

"We desire to invade no foreign soil; let us remain unmolested on our own. Whosoever attempts to gainsay this our determination will find that we will never be slaves, unless they succeed in crushing by force an entire people ready to die for liberty.

"But, even should we all fall, we shall bequeath to future generations a legacy of hatred and vengeance against foreign domination; the inheritance of each of our sons will be a rifle, and the consciousness of his rights; and by the blessing of God, the oppressor will never sleep soundly.

"Italians, I say again, do not lay down your arms; rally more closely than ever to your chiefs, and maintain the strictest discipline. Fellow-citizens, let not a man in Italy omit to contribute his mite to the national subscription; let not one fail to clean his gun, so as to be ready, perhaps to-morrow, to obtain by force that which to-day they hesitate to grant to our just rights.

"GARIBALDI.

"GENOA, *Nov.* 23, 1859."

Garibaldi then proceeded to Turin, and took his seat as a member of the Sardinian Parliament, to which he had been elected two years before, as the representative of Nice, his native country.

Louis Napoleon having proposed that Savoy and Nice should be ceded to France, the subject was brought before the Parliament and discussed at length, Garibaldi opposing the project with great zeal in several very animated speeches.

The conduct of Napoleon, in 1849, against Rome, may easily account for his feelings on that occasion. He soon withdrew from the chamber, and departed for Caprera, where he remained until a new scene was opened to him in another quarter, where Providence was preparing for him to make that display of his noble character and superior powers, which now has gained him the warmest love, as well as the highest admiration, of the world.

The Sicilians, unable any longer to suppress their discontent under the cruel government of the king, began, in April, 1860, once more to show signs of rebellion. An insurrection was made in Palermo, when the people raised barricades in the streets, and fought the troops with resolution. The combat was very bloody, but the citizens were soon overcome, and most of the insurgents perished at the barricades. Several monks of the convents were seized and imprisoned. Reinforcements had been sent into Sicily. The commercial steamboats had been put into requisition, and the army in Sicily was to be augmented to 30,000 men.

Prince Castilcicala had returned to his post as governor of the island. The panic at Naples on the 6th instant was general, but without consequence. On the evening of the 6th an immense crowd, estimated to number 80,000, blocked up the Rue Tolede at Naples, and raised numerous shouts of "*Viva la Constituzione*" before the residence of the Papal Nuncio. The street was quickly cleared by the patrols.

Palermo had been placed in a state of siege. The insurgents were said to number 10,000 well armed men.

The insurrection at Messina broke out on Sunday morning, April 11th. The popular movement commenced by shots being fired in the strada Ferdinando. Pieces of furniture were thrown from the windows at the troops.

Count Cavour had telegraphed to Legborn, ordering two steam frigates to proceed at once toward the coast of Sicily, and shelter all fugitives from political vengeance. The cry at Palermo, as well as at Messina, was for union with the Italian kingdom.

The disturbances increased, and the Sicilians rose in different places, fought bravely, and maintained themselves with great resolution.

Garibaldi was urgently called to their assistance, and was soon in Piedmont collecting men for an expedition. Great enthusiasm was displayed. Many volunteers pressed forward, and considerable numbers of soldiers deserted from the king's army to join their favorite leader. The government and its agents affected not to perceive the movement, and no impediment was thrown in its way. Vessels were prepared at the little port of Cagliari, and the volunteers, collected at convenient points not far distant, marched quietly to the shore, embarked, and sailed in the night of the 6th of May.

As the events which followed this first step in the last grand drama of Italian history are fresh in the minds of all, the following brief review of them, recently published by the Paris "Siècle," may not be out of place here :

"A man, accompanied by a few volunteers, sails from the environs of Genoa in the night of the 6th of May, on board of a vessel which is not even his own property. He goes to liberate several millions of oppressed people, and to overthrow a powerful monarchy ; he is stigmatized as a brigand, and all the penalties inflicted on pirates are invoked on his devoted head; the cry is raised that both he and his followers might be hanged from the yard-arms of their vessel. On the 7th of September this man has almost accomplished the task he had undertaken ; the monarchy he assailed is *de facto* overthrown. A nation is delivered. Now, which are the wise counsellors? Those who advise sovereigns to make concessions to the spirit of the age, or the flatterers who promise them a protracted reign if they will but resist all progress ? The answer is easy now. The king of Naples is a fugitive. Another dynasty has fallen, though surrounded by soldiers, and well provided with cannon and gold; another hope of the counter-revolutionists has fallen away. But the men bent on the ruin of princes still persist in giving the same pernicious counsels. 'The King of Naples has fallen,' say they, 'but General de Lamoricière still remains; he will fight, he will; he is ready, and the revolution will be overcome.' Wretched counsellors! They are not yet satisfied with their work; they want more catastrophes. Nevertheless, how easy the dynasty of Naples might have escaped destruction! Warnings were not wanting. Four years ago, during the Conferences of Paris, did not Europe, by the voice of her diplomatists, unanimously declare to the King of Naples that he was courting destruction by his bad government—that he was gathering around him all the elements of revolution? Was he not, in a manner, implored to adopt a different policy? Was he not duly informed of the abyss that lay before him?

"The general success of the Italian leader is thus summed up: Five marvellous stages—Marsala, Palermo, Milazzo, Reggio and Naples—performed in the short space of three months, have been all that Garibaldi required, supported as he is by the national sentiment, to overthrow a monarchy deemed immovable; which, not yet four years since, defied France and England; which, in the face of the naval preparations of the two greatest powers in the world, had determined to persevere in its resistance."

The modern history of Sicily requires a particular study before the sufferings and the spirit of its inhabitants can be well understood. The cruelty of the government and its agents have surpassed belief. The people, although few, compared with the numbers which that large and fertile island might sustain under a better government, have made repeated and strenuous efforts to obtain their freedom, and submitted only to overwhelming and irresistible force. They commenced the Italian revolution in 1820; and on several subsequent occasions they boldly commenced insurrections, but always with ill success. The king of the Two Sicilies would send troops from Naples, and then his immediate subjects would endeavor to take advantage of the opportunity. Sometimes the Sicilians rose against the king's troops, in secret concert with arrangements made in other parts of Italy, and sometimes, as it seemed, independently. Bloody scenes followed the victories of the king's troops, but some fugitives were always able to escape, and numbers lived in New York and other parts of the United States—some ever since 1820 or 1822.

Sicily, as described by recent Italian authorities, contains about two thirds as many inhabitants as the State of New York, or a little over two millions, and a territory of 26,582,59 kilometers. A chain of mountains through the northern part appears to be a continuation of the Appenines, and the highest peak is the volcano of Etna, otherwise called Mongibello. The island is the largest in the Mediterranean, extending from N. latitude 36° to 38° 8′, and E. longitude 10°5′ to 13°20′. It has always been celebrated for the fertility of its soil, and was long called the granary of Rome. It contains several provinces, named from their chief cities Palermo, Messina, Catania, Trappani, Syracuse or Boto, Girgenti and Caltanissetta. The city of Palermo has 483,206 inhabitants ; Catania, 56,515 ; Messina, 93,822 ; and Syracuse, 16,916. The land is but little divided, and all the province of Trappani is possessed by only three proprietors. In consequence of bad government, Sicily has only 126 persons to a square kilometer, and the rest of the late kingdom of Naples 87, while Tuscany has 126. In 20 years, under a free government, it may double its population. There were, last year, in Sicily, 17,000 secular priests, 7,591 monks, and 8,675 nuns. Total, 33,976 drones in the hive. Many of those joyfully joined the revolution on Garibaldi's appearance, and gave money from their treasures, and offered their church bells to melt into cannon, preached, and even fought for liberty and Victor Emanuel.

CHAPTER VII.

" Native hills and plains are ringing,
With the sounds of joy once more;
Charming echos send the music,
From Alps to far Sicilia's shore."—

Banks of Dora.

For the following interesting accounts of Garibaldi's expedition to Sicily, its arrival and operations, we copy from some letters published in English papers. Being written on the spot, by intelligent eye-witnesses, they are well adapted to our use :

DEPARTURE OF THE EXPEDITION.

" Garibaldi left the neighborhood of Genoa on the night of the 5th of May. His intention had been to leave the day before, but owing to the non-arrival of one of the steamers singled out for the expedition, he had to defer it to the next day. It is useless to say that the thorny part of the transaction had been arranged beforehand with the owners of the steamers, and that Garibaldi merely consented to take upon himself the responsibility of carrying off the steamers. The captain, engineers and crew had received notice to leave them, the gallant general being himself a good sailor, and having plenty of men of his own to sail and handle the ships. On the 7th a landing took place on the coast of Tuscany, at Talamone, and on the 8th, another, at Orbitello, which detained the expedition the next day. On the evening of the 9th, the expedition set out for the coast of Sicily direct. The Neapolitan government was perfectly well informed, and the fleet was cruising about in all directions except the right one. Little squadrons of two or more steamers had been concentrated in the chief seaport towns of the island, and tried by cruising to keep a *cordon* round the island. The south and southwesterly coasts were, above all, a point of their attention, for some of their ships reported having seen the expedition going toward Tunis. Two steamers, the Capri and Stromboli, were lying at Marsala, and not two hours before the arrival of the expedition, had gone out for a cruise."

THE LANDING.

"The place for landing had not been fixed beforehand; an inspiration of the moment induced Garibaldi to choose the most frequented part of that side of the island, and his star led him there just in the interval which occurred between the going out and returning of the steamers. Had it not been for this the landing might have failed. One of the steamers struck on a rock just at the entrance of the port, while the other went in as close as possible. The information received, was that there was a garrison of 600 men at Marsala, and the orders had already been given to land a small party and dislodge them from the barracks, when the boats from the shore came off with the news that no one was there. This made the landing easy enough; large barges were brought alongside, and took everything ashore; but when everything was landed, the Neapolitans made their appearance, and began firing to their hearts' content, without doing more than wounding slightly two men.

"The first thing was to cut the telegraph wire, but it was too late to prevent it from transmitting the news of the landing to Palermo. The last two messages were : 'Two steamers in sight making for the port; suspicious, as they carry no flag;' and then: 'The two steamers having hoisted the Sardinian flag, have come in and are landing their men.'"

Another eye-witness, writing from Marsala, May 12th, thus describes the landing :

"The extraordinary event which happened here yesterday—which still looks more like a dream than a reality—namely, the landing in this harbor of Garibaldi with a band of about 1,500 as fine looking fellows as you can well imagine, from two Sardinian steamers. The landing was effected in gallant style, and with most extraordinary celerity and order, and part of the time under the guns of a Neapolitan frigate and two steamers. One of the Sardinian vessels was run aground and scuttled by themselves in the harbor, and the other was taken outside by the Neapolitans; but after the landing had been fully effected. I believe the brave adventurers did not lose a man— only two or three wounded. We were all in a state of alarm during the firing, as the shot and shell from the frigate went flying about in a most awkward manner—some into the town, some into Wood-house's stores, some into Wood's *baglio* (factory), and one actually over our heads here on the *baglio* terrace, which fell into the sea beyond the Salinella.

"Our Vice-Consul, with the captains of the Intrepid and Argus (both here fortunately for us at the time), went on board the frigate during the firing to inquire into the meaning of their missiles, so capriciously injuring our factories, on each of which the English flag was flying, and to inculcate more caution and accuracy in their opera-tions. The Neapolitan commanders, wisely considering that it was their duty to expend a certain quantity of powder and shot on such an important occasion, gave the town the benefit of the residuary dose, after the enemy was snug within the walls, and laughing at this exhibition of impotent rage. It was, however, no laughing matter to the poor inhabitants, who, not accustomed to such phenomena, took to flight in all directions to avoid the effects of the shell, which did considerable damage about the Porta di Mare and the Grazzia Vecchia, but fortunately without loss of life, as many families were in the country for their spring trip. A considerable number, high and low, flocked under the protection of our flag here, and the old *baglio* is as crowded as Noah's Ark, only the animals are all human."

MARCH INTO THE INTERIOR.

"In the morning the whole of Garibaldi's party set off for Salemi, reinforced by a good many Marsalese volunteers, and well provided with horses for the officers, carts for their spare arms and ammunition, and mules for the few field-pieces they brought with them. Every-thing was managed with admirable order, and apparently to the satis-faction of General Garibaldi; though under the effect of the bom-bardment from the Neapolitan vessels the poor Marsalese did not show an enthusiastic welcome to their unexpected visitors.

MAY 14.—At Salemi they were received with open arms, after hav-ing been joined on their march by several large armed bands under Coppola, of the Monte, Baron Sant Anna, of Alcamo, etc. Other two bands of armed countrymen have set off from this place to join the brave general, and with the reinforcements expected from Castelve-trano, Santa Ninfa, and other neighboring towns, they will soon mus-ter a very formidable force. Even their artillery is increasing, as some light brass field-pieces, buried since 1849, have been brought out, and found in good condition. Several Franciscan monks have put themselves at the head, with the cross in one hand and the sword in the other."

FIRST EFFECTS OF THE ARRIVAL OF GARIBALDI.

"The arrival of Garibaldi changed the nature of the insurrection in Sicily completely. Until then the different *squadre* (bands) of *picciotti* (youngsters) had carried on a kind of desultory guerrilla warfare without much connection between them. The landowner, if influential enough, or else some popular man more energetic than the rest, collected for this purpose whoever wanted to come and had some sort or other of arms. Their tactics were to appear and disappear in different parts of the country, and harass from safe places the royal troops passing through the interior, but as for concerting a plan or meeting the royalists in the open field, no one would ever have dreamed of it. The mountainous country, and the want of roads, greatly facilitated this kind of warfare, while the absence of danger and fatigue was sufficient inducement even for those who were not driven there by their hatred against the Neapolitans. The country between Palermo, Trapani, Marsala, and Corleone was the chief seat of these *squadre*, not a few of which were collected at the time in the mountain chain above Palermo.

"Garibaldi's name and prestige, and the succors which he brought, became a link between these different squadre, which placed themselves under his orders. Scarce had the news of his landing spread, when the bands from Trapani, Corleone, and one or two other places joined. It was to meet this force, which was every day swelling, that Brigadier-General Landi was sent in the direction of Marsala and Trapani. The road to these places is the same as far as Calata Fimi, situated on the top of an elevated plateau; from thence it separates. A force, therefore, stationed at the intersection, shuts off all communication by regular roads from Palermo to Trapani and Marsala. It was on the lower slopes of the plateau that General Landi had taken his position, with four battalions, one of them riflemen, and four mountain guns. The road from Marsala, after passing Salemi, descends one of those long terraced plateaus which are a characteristic feature of this part of Sicily, and after crossing a little valley, rises up to the other plateau, where Calata Fimi is situate. The position was, therefore, one of the most difficult to carry. Like all soldiers of the same kind, the Neapolitans, whose muskets are excellent, rely altogether on their fire, especially if it can be carried on from afar. The reception, therefore, of Garibaldi and his troops was so hot that the *squadre* soon sought shelter where they could, leaving all the work to the troops Garibaldi had brought with him. The Cacciatori delle Alpi justified their renown, and in spite of the heat of the day, the advantage of position and numbers, drove the Neapolitans, at the point of the bayonet, from one position to another, taking one of the mountain guns. One of the students from Pavia, a youth certainly not more than eighteen, was the first to lay hands on it. In less than two hours, the Neapolitans were driven from all their positions and flying back toward Palermo. A letter, written by General Landi, was found in the village. In it he writes to the commander of Palermo to send him reinforcements, as he could not hold the place. He excuses at the same time the loss of the gun, by saying that the mule which carried it was shot—a falsehood, for the gun carriage was taken with it, as well as the two mules, which are in perfect health.

" The retreat of the brigade, which had lost considerably, was not molested at first, and they passed Alcamo without being attacked, but at Partenico, where they had sacked, burned, and murdered promiscuously, throwing women and children into the fire, the people were up and had occupied the houses, from which they fired on the troops, converting their flight into a regular route, the eleventh regiment losing its colors. Garibaldi is not the man to lose much time, but still the necessity of concerting a common action with the bands in the neighborhood of Palermo, prevented him from taking the position of Monreale by surprise."

PALERMO.

"In order to understand the importance of this position, as well as the rest of the operations, I must say something about the topography of the basin of Palermo. Long before you arrive at Palermo by sea, you have before you a bold limestone mountain, standing there isolated, and resembling somewhat the rock of Gibraltar, but not so lofty. This rock forms the northern limit of the Bay of Palermo and of the Conca d'Oro (Gold Shell), the fertile plain in which the town lies. The plain stretches out in a northwesterly and southeasterly direction, which is likewise followed in a circular sweep by the mountain chain.

" The plain may be about twelve miles in its greatest length, and from four to five in its greatest width. Between the isolated Monte Pellegrino and the rest of the chain the plain runs up to La Favorita, over which a carriage road goes to Carini ; on the opposite side of the plain, skirting the sea-shore runs the highroad to Messina, passing through Bazaria, and close to the ruins of Solento. These are the two easiest outlets of the plain. Everywhere else a continued chain of mountains seems to close all outlet. Nearest to La Favorita a bad mountain road leads in a straight line by San Martino to Carini. To the left of this road rises a rugged, magnificent mountain, looking like the worn side of an extinct crater; it protrudes somewhat into the plain, and throws out a high spur in the same direction as the main chain. This spur is Monreale, and you can see the famous convent and church, as well as the greatest part of the village. Over this plateau passes the high road to Trapani. Behind the spur and plateau of Monreale, the mountain forms a kind of amphitheatre on a colossal scale, the terraced cultivation helping to keep up the illusion. Where it ends, and the mountain begins again to protrude into the plain, you can see on the slopes two white villages; they are Parco and Madonna delle Grazie, over which a carriage road leads to the Piana del Greci and Corleone, two old Albanian colonies, established, like a good number in this part of Sicily by emigration after the death of Skandorbeg. Another spur runs out into the plain, and forms another amphitheatre, more rugged and picturesque than that of Monreale, and dominated by the Gebel-Rosso. In the dip a rugged horse-path ascends, called the Passo della Mezzagna, leading down to the village of Misilmeri, situate on the only highroad into the interior and to Catania. The Gebel-Rosso falls off toward the sea and Cape Zaffarano, and in the lower depression is the highroad from Palermo to Catania. It runs almost parallel to the road on the sea-shore as far as Abate, and then cuts across to the south. From this description you will see that the Neapolitans, possessing the command of the sea, had all the advantages of a concentric position, especially with an enemy who was weak in artillery, and who was chiefly formidable in the mountains. A general concentration of their forces in the plain was clearly indicated, with the single exception of the plateau of Monreale, which is a position in itself, and commands the road from the interior for some distance. The disadvantage of him who attacked was considerably increased by the difficult nature of the mountains, which makes all lateral communication between the roads almost impossible, so that any change of the attack implied a great circuit. The Neapolitans, who had studied the thing for years, were fully aware of these advantages, and concentrated their forces in the plain, merely occupying the plateau of Monreale.

"Garibaldi could not unite his forces in time to arrive at Monreale before the Neapolitans had occupied it in great force, and when he arrived in the neighborhood of the position, four days after the victory of Calata Fimi, he saw that the taking of Monreale could only be effected with great loss. He therefore determined to change his plans. The first thing was to surround and watch all the outlets, and for this purpose the different *squadri* of the insurgents took up positions all round the chain of mountains which inclose the bay. It was one of the finest sights you could see when their fires blazed up at night, and mingled their red glare with the pale light of the moon. They were watched by the inhabitants like the holy fire by the Parsee, and the sole occupation during the last eight days or so seemed to be to observe and comment on their meaning. Now they seemed stronger on one peak, now more spread and continuous on the slope of another mountain, and on the hope kindled by these fires the uninitiated lived. Palermo was in a state of excitement and ferment impossible to describe, and strong enough to brave the state of siege which had been proclaimed. The Secret Committee, which had maintained itself in spite of the vigilance and suspicion of the police, always found means to communicate with Garibaldi, in spite of the military authorities. The committee was known to exist, and it circulated printed bulletins almost daily, but it was so organized that the police, although aware of its existence, could never discover the members. It was a kind of freemasonry, with different degrees of initiation. No one not a member knew more than one member. The houses where the meetings were held were continually changed, and all obeyed blindly.

"The committee informed Garibaldi that Palermo was ready to rise, but it imposed the condition that he should appear before the gates of the town. He accepted this condition, and made his plans accordingly. Seeing that he had come too late for Monreale, he left a party of the native insurgents to keep up the fires and engage the Neapolitans, while he took off the mass of the force, and, by an almost incredible march along the mountain chain, where the guns had to be carried by the men, he appeared all at once at Parco, on the road to Piana, on the 23d. As soon as the Neapolitans saw their mistake, they sent up in hot haste toward Parco whatever they could muster of forces without exposing their position in the town. They did not think them sufficient; for, after some skirmishing on that day, they withdrew again to their position on two lower plateaus, the Piana Borazzo and Santa Theresa. The next day, 24th, they got up some of the troops from Monreale, and thus strengthened, made another attack—the same I witnessed from on board ship. The purpose was gained; they had got another change. Garibaldi withdrew, leaving just a few of the bands behind. These latter did not wait long to follow, and the 'Regii,' as the soldiers are called, entered both Madonna delle Grazie and Parco the same afternoon, and pillaged and burned the place, according to time-honored custom, killing a number of the peaceful inhabitants, and publishing as usual next day, a splendid bulletin, announcing the defeat of the bands of Garibaldi, and promising their speedy subjection. Although Neapolitan bulletins are not much believed, yet there were many in the town whose hearts sank when they saw Garibaldi retire a second time.

"They little knew the man with whom they had to do, nor did the Neapolitans either—although they ought to have remembered Velletri. It was *reculer pour mieux sauter.* In order the better to deceive the Neapolitans, he went back to Piana, and sent his artillery even farther back, while he himself, with his chosen band, made his way over the mountains again, and, while the Neapolitans followed his track to Piana, he had arrived yesterday morning at Misilmeri, on the high-road to Catania, where he had given rendezvous to all the chieftains or captains on that side of the mountain chain.

"I was sick of uncertain rumors, which alone were to be got at in town, and which would leave your readers in darkness about the true state of things. Besides knowing a little of the gallant general's tactics, I had a strong suspicion that something was impending which could be better seen from without than from inside the town, so I determined to see whether I could not get there. Some English and American officers had been out in that direction, and had seen one of the captains, a popular man of this place, called La Maza, so I determined likewise to have a trial. Some friends in the town indicated the way, and I set off in the carriage of one of them. The road to Messina, starting from the Marina and the Villa Giulia at the end of it, skirts the sea as far as Abate, where it unites with the highroad to Misilmeri and Catania. I was advised to take this last, as the least infested by soldiers. What with their confidence in their navy, and what with the stratagem of Garibaldi, the Neapolitans had paid little attention to this road and the southeasterly side in general. Two sentries before the corner of the Villa Giulia, and a post of a score of men a little further, in the *octroi* building, were all that were in the neighborhood of the town. Straggling houses continue for some distance up to a bridge leading ever a little stream or torrent called Orveto, which flows into the sea about a quarter of a mile further on. All along these houses there is a chain of sentries, and in the vicinity of the bridge a post of perhaps eighty men who furnish these sentries.

"I passed them without an inquiry, and was free. There had been the Neapolitan steamers cruising about every day all along this coast; no necessity was therefore felt for any further precaution. I rolled along fast enough with my two Calabrese horses, and passed some American officers, probably bound for Solento. At the very gates of the town the people had joined the insurrection, but there was a kind of neutral ground between the two, which ended in a village beyond Abate, the name of which I cannot recollect. If the Regii were careless, the insurgents were not, and at the entrance of the village one of their armed men asked me for permission to be my guide, a thing which exactly suited me. As we drove through the village the people rushed forward, and trying to kiss my hands, asked me for arms. They were all ready to join, but had no arms, which did not prevent their raising shouts for Italy, Victor Emanuel, and Garibaldi. We had to gallop off in order not to be stopped at every step. A drive of half an hour or more in a gentle descent, with a lovely valley beneath, and beautiful mountain scenery in front, brought me to the town of Misilmeri, a wretched little place, altogether wanting in character. In the little square held out on one side the committee, which forms a kind of provisional government, and on the other, up some wooden steps fixed outside, was enthroned the chief of the staff of Garibaldi's expedition in primitive simplicity. Colonel Sirtori was just giving a pass to two young American officers from the United State's steamship Iroquois, without which no one was allowed to enter the camp. As he had likewise given them an officer as guide, I joined them, and up we sauntered toward the heights leading to the Gebel Rosso and the pass the Mezzagna. We had soon left behind us the few remaining houses, and the ruins of the feudal castle to the left, the white limestone walls of which had something in them which reminded you of a skeleton. The ground all about is planted with olive-trees, vines, and different sorts of grain, which all grow luxuriantly in spite of the stony nature of the place. The general had pitched his camp on a tolerably extensive plateau just above the ruins, looking down on one side toward the plain and the range which ends at Cape Zaffarana, while on the other the peaks of the Gebel Rosso and the pass of Mezzagna were visible across a depression in the ground, looking very much like an extinct crater, and now partially filled with water, owing to the copious rains which had fallen during the last few days. It was one of those panoramas which suggest naturally your pitching your tent there—that is, if you have one. The word tent is erased from the military dictionary of Garibaldi. However, a popular general has to yield at times to his soldiers, and so he could not prevent them from sticking into the ground four of the lances with which the squadron, who have no muskets, are armed, and from throwing over them a blanket. Under the tent you could see the guacha saddle arranged as a pillow, and the black sheepskin covering as a bed. As for every one else, there were

the olive-trees affording shade, plenty of stones for pillows, and perhaps for every tenth man a cloak or blanket. All around were
picketed the horses, most of them entire, and behaving accordingly.
The general himself was not there when we arrived; he had taken one
of his morning strolls, but in front of his tent there were all his trusty
followers—Colonel Turr, the Hungarian, although still suffering from
the shot in his arm, received in last year's campaign, yet always ready
where there is danger; Colonel Bixio, another trusty follower and
well-known officer of the Cacciatori delle Alpi; Colonel Carini, the
bravest of Sicilians, likewise an officer of that corps, besides a number
of others, all brave like him, among them Garibaldi's young son, with
a shot wound in his wrist, received at Calata Fimi, and the son of
Daniel Manin, wounded in the thigh.   There was the ex-priest Guz-
maroli, a Romagnole, who has vowed the most enthusiastic worship
to his hero, and follows him like his shadow, providing for his comforts, and watching his person in the moment of danger.   There was
a small cluster of guides, most of them of good Lombard families,
meant to serve on horseback, but now on foot, and the foremost in
the battle.   Not the least remarkable among all these figures was the
Sicilian monk, Frate Pantaleone—jolly, like the picture of a monk of
the middle ages, but full of fire and patriotism, and as brave as any
of the others.   He had joined the force at Salemi, and did his best
to encourage and comfort them.   Several among the leading men
from Palermo and its vicinity were likewise present among them,
with several priests and monks, who are among the most sincere and
energetic promoters of the movement.   They were a strange sight,
indeed, in this by no means very Catholic army; but I assure you
their behavior has been such that the wildest among these youths
honor and respect them, and in them their order.

"Well, all this motley crowd, increased now by the two young
American naval men, and soon after joined by three British naval
officers, was collected around a common nucleus—a smoking kettle,
with the larger part of a calf in it, and a liberal allowance of onions,
a basket with heaps of fresh bread, and a barrel containing Marsala.
Every one helped himself in the most communistic manner, using
fingers and knife, and drinking out of the solitary tin pot.   It is only
in this irregular warfare that you see these scenes in their greatest
perfection.   The long marches and countermarches, rains, fights,
and sleeping on the ground, had made almost every one worthy to
figure in a picture by Murillo, with all those grand Sicilian mountains, not unlike those of Greece, forming a background such as no
picture can reproduce."

GARIBALDI IN COUNCIL.

" Soon after my arrival, Garibaldi made his appearance, and received
his foreign visitors with that charming, quiet simplicity which cha-
racterizes him, lending himself with great complaisance to the invariably recurring demands of autographs, and answering the numerous
questions which were naturally put to him. It was only after the
departure of his guests that the general resumed business. The question debated was nothing more nor less than to venture on a *coup de
main* on Palermo the same night. There was no doubt, all the information went to show, that the Neapolitans had taken the bait
thrown out for them—that they had taken a feigned retreat for a
defeat, and the sending back of the guns toward the interior as a
sign of discouragement. As to the flank movement to Misilmeri,
they seemed to have no idea of it, for men come from Piani stated
that they were in force in that place. Another considerable body of
men was at Parco, and on the road beyond it. In Monreale, the
reports spoke likewise of several thousand. In fact, the approaches
to these two last-named places, called the Piana di Borazzo and the
Theresa, both of which are close to the Palazzo Reale, in the south-
west part of the town, were the points of concentration, while the
outlets from the southerly and the southeasterly parts of the town
were comparatively undefended. Former events had forced the
Neapolitans to pay attention to the topography of the town, so as to
remain masters of it in case of a popular rising. This was not very
easy in such a town as Palermo, which, like a true southern town,
forms a labyrinth of small and tortuous streets, flanked by high
houses all provided with balconies. This was a serious drawback for
the troops in a street fight. The Neapolitans did their best to repair
the disadvantage. There are two streets, evidently of Spanish origin,
which form the main arteries of the town. The first, called Via di
Toledo, starting from the Marina at Porta Felice, traverse the town
in a straight line from northeast to southwest, passing close to the
Cathedral of Santa Rosalia, and ending at the Piazza Reale, the largest square of Palermo, on the opposite side of the town from which
the roads start to Monreale and Parco. Besides the royal palace,
supposed to be on the site of the old palace of the Emirs of Sicily,
there are several large public buildings which line the square, the
Archivescovado forming one corner, and the large convent of St.
Elizabetha the other. The ground rises gently toward this part,
which commands the whole town. At right angles to the Via di
Toledo runs another street equally straight, the Strada Moquerada,

which, starting from the Porto San Antonino, and traversing the whole town, leads out the road to La Favorita and to the Mole. The two intersect each other right in the centre of the town, where the octagonal place is called the Piazzi Bologni. The lower half of the town, from the sea to this place, had been almost abandoned, or rather committed to the tender care of the shipping and the Castello, which occupies a projecting height on the seashore, near the north-easterly corner of the town. A few posts at the gates of the town on this side, rather points of observation than of action, and a company or so in the building of the Finanze, situated in this part of the town, were all that remained of troops on that side.

" In order to establish and keep up the communication between the upper half of the town, the real point of defence, and the sea-shore, two large *stradoni* have been opened outside of the town, both of them starting from the neighborhood of the royal palace, and running down to the sea, near to the Villa Giulia, a large public garden adjoining the Marina, and the other passing through the Quartiere dei Quatri Venti, to the Mole. This latter *stradone* has always been considered as the line of retreat to the place of embarkation, and is flanked by large buildings, the political prison, some barracks, the criminal prison, and finally the works on the Mole itself.

" The plan which Garibaldi conceived from these dispositions, was to surprise the posts in the lower and comparatively ill-defended part of the town, to throw himself into the town, and then gradually work his way from street to street. The two roads leading to this part of the town run almost parallel, and not far from each other. That close to the sea-shore was the least guarded, containing merely a company or so, altogether cut off from all communication. The task would have been easier from this side, had it not been for the fear of the march of a long column being discovered, and thus an alarm given. The second, the high-road from the interior, was therefore chosen as the line of operations. It crosses, about half a mile from the town, the route Del Ammiraglio, leads through a large open street to the *stradone* on this side of the town, and enters the town at the Porta di Termini. At this gate the Neapolitans had made a sandbag barricade, which was occupied by two companies. The *stradone* before it was enfiladed by a couple of mountain guns, placed at the gate of Sant' Antonino. Beyond the *stradone* small forts extended all along the road up to the bridge, and the outposts were just on the other side of the bridge.

" With that just *coup d'œil* which Garibaldi certainly possesses, he had singled out this point as the most practicable. Having, with the exception of the troops he had brought with him, but rough, undisciplined guerrillas at his disposal, he saw that the best chance was to concentrate all his forces, and surprise or break through by main force. The operation was to be assisted by a general rise of the people in the town.

" Having sketched out his plan, he convoked the different guerrilla chiefs and informed them of his intention. He told them that it was not his custom to have councils of war, but he thought it for once good to consult them, as upon the resolution taken must depend the fate of Sicily, and perhaps of Italy. There were only two things to be done—either to try and get possession of Palermo by a *coup de main*, or else to withdraw and begin a regular organization in the interior, and form an army. He, for his part, was for a *coup de main*, which would at once settle the fate of the island. He told them to be brief in their remarks, and not deliberate long. Most were utterly astonished at the boldness of this plan, and some made remarks about the want of ammunition for their men. They were told for the hundredth time, that it was not long shots which imposed on the well-armed Neapolitans, but a determined rush in advance—that they ought not to waste their ammunition and fire off their guns for sport, and were promised whatever could be spared. This objection being waived, all expressed more or less loudly their approbation of the plan, and were dismissed with the injunction to animate their people and keep up their courage."

CHAPTER VIII.

"I saw Garibaldi, and watch'd him nigh;
I saw the lightnings that flash from his eye:
He's not of the dust of which mortals are made,
And what reaches his heart will not be of lead."

Dall' Ongaro. T. D.

PREPARATIONS TO ATTACK PALERMO—NIGHT MARCH—ATTACK—
BATTLE—THE BOMBARDMENT.

"THE first idea was to make the attack in the middle of the night —the Neapolitans don't like to stir at night, and there was every chance of a panic among them; but there was some danger that way likewise for the Sicilian insurgents, and it was thought best to make such arrangements as would bring the force at dawn to the gates of the town. According to the original and better plan of the general himself and his adjutant-general, Colonel Turr, the movement was to have been made along the main road from Misilmeri, broad enough to admit of considerable development of the columns, and commodious in every respect. The native captains, however, suggested the Pass of Mezzagna, which descends from the heights behind Gebel-Rosso into the plain of Palermo. According to their statements, it was much shorter and by no means difficult. Their statements were believed, and the whole force received orders to be concentrated by nightfall on the summit of the pass, crowned with a church.

"According to the first disposition, the troops brought by the general himself were to lead the way, and the *squadre* to follow; but some of the chiefs begged it as a favor for their corps to have the honor of being first in the town—a claim which could not be very well refused. The plan was, therefore, modified. The guides and three men from each company of the Cacciatori delle Alpi, were formed into an *avant-garde*, confided to Major Tüköri, a Hungarian, an officer who distinguished himself under General Kméty on the 29th of September, at Kars. Behind this *avant-garde* followed the Sicilians, commanded by La Maga, an emigrant, who had come over with Garibaldi. The second line was led by the riflemen of Genoa—excellent shots, all armed with the Swiss carbine. Behind them came the two battalions of Cacciatori delle Alpi, and in the rear the rest of the Sicilians.

" The order having been distributed, the different bands gradually worked their way toward the summit of the pass.   The packing up at headquarters did not take much time ; it soon after broke up its camp and followed the troops.   I was mounted on a regular Rosinante, with a halter passed round the jaw, and provided with a saddle which seemed to have been formed to fit on the vertebræ of my lean black charger.   A blanket was, however, found in due time, and on the whole I cannot complain.   The road up to the pass winds along rows of gigantic cactus hedges, which give a thoroughly eastern character to the country.   It was just sunset when we arrived on the top, where, through a gap, we could see the bay and town of Palermo and the sea beyond, looking more like a fairy picture than reality. All the mountains, with their rugged points naturally of a reddish tint, seemed to have drunk in the rays of the setting sun, and exhibited that rosy color which I had thought hitherto a special gift of the plain of Attica.   While you had this charming scene before you, you looked behind, as it were, into the hearts of the mountains.   It was one of the finest spots I ever saw, and all the country was fragrant with spring flowers, the perfume of which came out with redoubled vigor as soon as the sun had set.   It proved a bad road for the expedition, that mountain pass, but it was lovely to look upon.

" In order to entertain the Neapolitans with the idea that all was safe on that side, the usual large fires were kindled on the tops of the mountains, and kept up long after our departure by men left behind for that purpose.   Garibaldi went up to look at the position underneath, or, perhaps, to indulge in that kind of reverie to which he is subject in such solemn moments, and which ends in a concentration of all his faculties on the sole aim he has before him.

" The evening gun in the fort had been long reëchoed by the mountains, and the moon had risen clear and bright above our heads, giving a new charm to this lovely scenery, before we stirred."

THE NIGHT MARCH.

" During this interval the *picciotti* (youngsters), as the patriots are called, were put into some kind of order, which, you will believe me, was no easy matter in the comparative darkness which prevailed ; no chief knowing his men, and the men not recognizing their chief— every one acting for some one else, and no one able to give an answer.   With the exception of the troops brought over by Garibaldi, all the rest seemed an entangled mass almost impossible to unravel.

However, by degrees, those belonging to the same chief found themselves together, and the march began about ten, P.M. Either the Sicilian chieftains had never looked at the Pass of Mezzagna, or else they have curious ideas of a road; the whole is nothing but a track among big stones, crossing and recrossing the bed of a mountain torrent, following not unfrequently the bed of the torrent, leading over smooth masses of stones and across most awkward gaps—all this at an angle of twenty-five degrees, to be passed on horseback at night! Even the men could only go singly, which made our line a frightful length, and caused continual delays and stoppages. The general vowed never to believe another Sicilian report on the state of a mountain road. However, in the end, we reached the plain and came in among the olive-trees below, with few falls among the sure-footed horses. A halt was made until all the columns had descended, and during this halt an incident occurred which did not promise much for the future behavior of our *picciotti*. The horses in Sicily are left for the most part entire, hence continual fighting and considerable neighing, which was so inconvenient in a night expedition of this kind that several of the most vicious steeds had to be sent back. One of them still remained, and began its antics; the rider lost patience, which made matters worse. Those nearest threw themselves back in haste, and communicated the movement to those behind. These, many of whom had sat down and began to doze, mistook in their dreams, probably, the trees for Neapolitans, the stars for so many shells, and the moon for a colossal fireball; at any rate, the majority of them were, with one bound, in the thickets on both sides of the road, several fired off their muskets in their fright, and very little was wanting to cause a general panic. Every one did what he could to restore confidence, but the effect was produced and reacted, as you will see by and by. Another incident occurred, which might have led to the failure of the whole expedition. The Sicilian guides who were with the *avant-garde* missed the road, and instead of taking a by-road which led into the main road we had to pursue, they continued on the road near the hill-side, which would have brought us just where the Neapolitans were in the greatest strength. The mistake was perceived in time and repaired, but not without considerable loss of time. At last the column emerged on to the main road, which is broad and skirted by high garden walls. As we had lost considerable time with all these *contretemps*, and as dawn was approaching, we had to make haste, but whether from fatigue or the impression of the night panic, the *picciotti* could not be brought to move very fast. It was just the first glimmer of dawn when we

passed the first houses, which extend in this direction a long way out
of the town of Palermo. The *squadre*, who ought to have known
the locality better, began shouting and ' evviváing,' just as if we had
been close to the gates. Had it not been for this blunder, the *avant-
garde* might have surprised the post on the bridge of the Ammirag-
liato, and probably penetrated into the town without the loss of a man.
As it was, the shouting not only roused those on guard on the bridge,
but likewise gave an opportunity to the Neapolitans to strengthen
the force at the gate of Termini, and to make all their dispositions
for a defence from the flank.

"Instead, therefore, of surprising the post on the bridge, the
avant-garde was received by a well-sustained fire, not only in front,
but from the houses in their flanks. At the first sound of the musketry, most of the *picciotti* were across the garden walls, but not
with the view of firing from behind them, leaving thus the 30 or 40
men of the *avant-garde* all isolated in the large exposed street which
leads to the bridge. The first battalion of the Cacciatori was sent
up, and as it did not carry the position fast enough, the second was
sent after it soon after. While these were driving back the Neapolitans, every one did his best to drive the *picciotti* forward. It was
not so easy, in the beginning especially, when the sound of cannon
was heard in front, although its effects were scarcely visible. However, the *picciotti*, who remind me very much of Arnout Bashi-
bazouks, can be led on after the first unpleasant sensation has passed
away, especially when they see that it is not all shots that kill or
wound—not even the cannon-shots, which make so formidable a
noise. They could see this to perfection this morning, for although
the Neapolitan rifles are scarcely inferior to the best fire-arms, I
never saw so little damage done by so much shooting. Every one
put himself, therefore, to work to lead and urge on the *picciotti*,
driving them out of the sheltered places by all kinds of contrivances,
and often by blows and main force. After some trouble, most of
them were safely brought through the open space before the bridge,
but the general tendency was to go under rather than above the
bridge, which is, like all bridges over torrents, high, and was, in this
instance, exposed to a heavy cross fire from the Piana di Borazzo,
where the Neapolitans had a loopholed wall and some guns mounted,
which threw a few ill-aimed shells. While the general himself, and
many of his staff, did their best to make them leave this shelter
again and proceed, the *avant-garde* had chased back the Neapolitans
to the *stradone* which runs down to the sea just in front of the Porta
di Termini. The Neapolitan fort at the gate, considerably rein-

forced, opened a hot fire, which swept down the long avenue of houses leading to the bridge, while at the same time the two guns and the troops posted at the Porta Sant' Antonino, brought a cross fire to bear on the attackers. But this was no obstacle to the brave fellows who led the way. They did not lose time with firing, but rushed on with the bayonet. The commander of the *avant-garde*, who was a Hungarian major, and three of the guides, were the first across the sand-bag barricade in the town, but the leader was wounded by a shot which shattered his left knee. Otherwise the loss had been trifling. While the *avant-garde* and the Cacciatori chased the Neapolitans from spot to spot, the Palermitans began likewise to stir, but, justice compels me to say, only in the parts which the troops had left.

" The same scene as at the bridge was repeated at the crossing of the *stradone* by the *picciotti*, who followed in a straggling movement. And yet it was important to get into the town, in order not to be outflanked or taken in the rear by the Neapolitans holding the Piana di Borazzo. In order to avert this danger, the order was given to some of the bands to get behind the garden walls which line the road by which the Neapolitans might have come down on our left. These diversions, and probably the dislike to fight in open field, were sufficient to parry this danger until the greatest part of the stragglers had passed. At the same time a barricade was thrown up in the rear with anything which could be laid hold of. This work pleased the *picciotti* so well, that they began throwing up a barricade in front likewise. At any rate, they blocked up a part of the road before they could be prevented.

" But the most critical thing was decidedly the crossing of the *stradone*, where the cross fire was kept up, and all kinds of dodges were resorted to to make them risk this *salto*, which they thought mortal. I and one of the followers of Garibaldi held out one of the men by main force exposed to the fire, which soon made him run across. It was here, above all, that the bad firing of the Neapolitans told. I was looking on for some time, and did not see a single man even wounded. In order to encourage the *picciotti*, one of the Genoese riflemen took four or five chairs, planted the tricolor on one of them, and sat down upon it for some time. The thing took at last decidedly, and you saw the *picciotti* stopping on the road to fire off their muskets.

" Close to the Porta di Termini is the Vecchia Fiera—the old market-place. One must know these Sicilians to have an idea of the

frenzy, screaming, shouting, crying, and hugging : all would kiss Garibaldi's hand and embrace his knees.   Every moment brought new
masses, which debouched in troops from one of the streets, anxious to
have their turn.   As the Cacciatori gradually cleared the lower part
of the town, most of the inhabitants came to have a look, and give a
greeting to the Liberator of Palermo and Sicily.   The entrance was
effected about half-past 5 A.M., and by noon more than one-half of
the town was clear of the troops.   But two hours before this was
effected, the citadel had opened its fire on the town, at first mode-
rately enough, but soon after with great vigor, firing large 13-inch
shell, red-hot shot, and every other projectile calculated to do the
greatest possible damage.   About noon or so, the ships in the harbor opened their fire, and between the two they contrived to destroy
a great number of houses in the lower part of the town, killing and
wounding a great number of people of all ages and both sexes.   Two
of the large shells were sent right into the hospital, and exploded in
one of the wards.   Everywhere you perceived ruins and conflagra-
tions, dead and wounded, not a few of whom must have perished among
the ruins of their houses.   It was especially the part of the town
near the Piazzi Bologni, and some of the adjoining streets which was
ill-treated.   If the object of the Neapolitans was to inspire terror,
they certainly succeeded.   Whoever could, took refuge in whatever
he thought the most bomb-proof place, and those who could not, you
saw crying, praying, and wringing their hands in the streets.   It was
a pitiable sight, indeed, and it did more harm to inoffensive people
than to those who might have retaliated.   Before opening the fire,
the commodore sent a polite message to all the men-of-war which
were in the way to get out of it, and all the vessels which were
moored inside the Mole had to shift their berths and take up positions
outside."

THE BOMBARDMENT.

" Evening.

"The bombardment is still kept up, with only short intervals,
especially from the Castle, where the *alter ego* of King Bomba II.
reigns.   There is no doubt that Admiral Mundy made very strong
representations to the Neapolitan commodore about the bombardment, but they have not been listened to.   Some parts of the town
will have to be entirely rebuilt, the large shells having passed right
through from top to bottom, shaking those ill-built constructions.
Several of the churches have come in for their share ; yet all this

useless bombardment has not prevented the soldiers from being, by degrees dislodged from all their positions in the town, with the exception of the parts about the royal palace and their line of communication with the Mole. In the lower part of the town they possess only the Castello Amare and the Finanze, which is held by a company or so of soldiers. Most of the foreign subjects have taken refuge on board the men-of-war, and all the consuls, with the exception of Mr. Goodwin, our own, who sticks like a true Briton to his consular flag. According to all accounts, there is no comparison between the bombardment in 1848 and the present one. Then the Neapolitans were satisfied with sending one or two shells every half hour, while now they take just time enough to let their guns and mortars cool.

"All those who came in this morning with Garibaldi are dead beat, having had no sleep last night, and plenty of work since. The general himself is reposing on the platform which surrounds the large fountain in the Piazza del Pretorio, where the committee is sitting *en permanence*. This committee, the same which carried on the whole movement from the beginning, has constituted itself as a provisional government, under the dictatorship of Garibaldi. It has appointed several special committees for the different branches of its operations, and provides as well as possible for the many wants which occur every moment. Considering the oppression under which the people have been, very little preparation could be made for the emergency, and everything has to be provided now under the pressure of the moment—arms, as far as possible, ammunition, provisions for the troops, hospital wants and arrangements, besides the great fact of satisfying every one who wants, or thinks he wants, something, and listening to every one who has something to say, or thinks he has. There is a great deal of good-will on the part of the committee, but I must say it is not so energetically seconded by the Palermitans as one could have expected from their enthusiasm. There is a semi-oriental *laissez aller* about them, which only produces fits of activity scarcely equal to the moment.

"At our first entrance into the town, there was a good deal of haste made about the barricades, but as the extension of the occupation constantly requires new barricades, there is some difficulty in keeping them up to the work; a great many *evvivas*, but all preferred to run about the streets to laying hand to the work. Even the ringing of the bells, the most demoralizing sound to an army in a populous town, can, in spite of all injunctions, be only kept

up in fits and starts.   It is the southern indolence, which soon
gets the better of all good dispositions.

" The town is illuminated, and presents, during the intervals of
the bombardment, an animated appearance ; but all the shops are
still closed.   The illumination, with the antique-shaped glass lamps
suspended from the balconies, presents a very pretty effect, rather
heightened by the shells flying through the clear sky."

CHAPTER IX.

"A nun of Sicily said to me :
 'He must brother be to Saint Rosalie :
 For there's a wild brilliancy beams in his eyes,
 Sent down by his sister from Paradise.'"
          Dall' Ongaro's lines on Garibaldi. T. D.

JOURNAL OF AN EYE-WITNESS CONTINUED—PALERMO AFTER THE
  CAPTURE—GARIBALDI IN A DANGEROUS CRISIS—THE ARCH-
  BISHOP OF PALERMO AND MANY OF THE HEADS OF CONVENTS
  WITH GARIBALDI—ADDRESS OF THE CORPORATION—INCIDENTS
  IN PALERMO—GARIBALDI'S DECREE FOR POOR SOLDIERS AND
  THEIR FAMILIES.

"The taking of Palermo has had decidedly its effect on the country around. There is no end of the *squadre* which are approaching in all directions and hovering about the Regii. As soon as these latter had left Monreale, the insurgents in the neighborhood descended to occupy it as well as San Martino. All about Piana and Corleone they are swarming and skirmishing, so that the column of 1,500 or 1,600 men which has been sent in that direction is rather compromised. They hoped to destroy Garibaldi and his partisans, and the fate they prepared for them may await themselves.

"But while thus the general march of events is decidedly favorable, I must say the Palermitans are scarcely up to the mark. They are all well-intentioned, but they are distressingly indolent, and want that general coöperation which is most calculated to insure success. There is no initiative or activity on their part, and their sole occupation seems to be to invent and spread rumors. Not a quarter of an hour passes without some fellow or other coming in out of breath and announcing the advance of the royal troops ; now they are from one, now from the other side. Above all, horses and cavalry seem to be the nightmare of the Palermitans. They see the solitary regiment of Neapolitan cavalry everywhere. It is in vain that their noses are thrust against the barricades with which the whole town is blocked up, they *will* see the cavalry. But, although they are thus haunted by the royal troops, few seem to think that they ought to do some thing for themselves—making preparations for the defence of their

319

houses and streets, and being always ready to meet an attack. It never occurs to them, as it did to the Lombards last year, that it is their duty to think day and night how to alleviate the sufferings of those who bleed in their cause. It is not the want of will, but a deficiency in acting otherwise than by order. The only thing which they do spontaneously, is to cry " Evviva," and promenade the streets, eager for news and gossip.

" The irregulars are decidedly improving. They are getting a taste for barricade and street fighting; they still blaze away their ammunition in a frantic manner, but they are beginning to keep to their posts and even to advance, if not too much exposed. This is our advantage in these street fights; the longer they last, the more they increase the confidence of the irregulars, and destroy the discipline of the regular troops.

" Every hour brings new proofs of this in the shape of prisoners and deserters from the Neapolitan forces. With those taken in the hospitals, there must be above 1,000. There is an order from the general to treat them well, and there is no animosity prevailing against them, but so much the greater is that against the *sbirri* and ' *compagni d'armi*,' a kind of local police, who have committed great horrors. They are picked out everywhere, and brought up in gangs of five and six to the committee, trembling for their lives; but only one of them has been killed hitherto, having been taken in the act of firing at those who wanted to arrest him.

" The ceasing of the bombardment, or rather the diminishing of it, has brought people out into the streets again."

GARIBALDI IN A DANGEROUS CRISIS.

"*May* 29—6 P.M.

" About 3 P.M. one of those panics suddenly broke out again which occur every moment, and serve more than anything else to demoralize the town and the *squadre*. The steamers which had gone off yesterday came back, and the rumor was that they were disembarking their troops before the Porta dei Greci;—great running and movement, great confusion, all caused by a column of dust on the road running along the sea-shore. In the afternoon there was some heavy firing, both toward the Piazza Reale and on the left of it, where the Neapolitans have a bastion which flanks the palace and is itself defended from the Castello. All yesterday and to-day the object on that side was to get possession of a cluster of houses, so as to isolate that bastion, and force them out of this, as from that of

Sant' Agata. The town is too large, and Garibaldi's immediate followers are too few to be sent everywhere, and too precious to be exposed, except in the greatest necessity. Thus it is the *squadre* who form the mass in most places.

"The Archbishop of Palermo, and many heads of religious orders, paid a visit to Garibaldi, and returned, delighted with the simplicity and modesty of his bearing. Garibaldi finds himself more at home with the Sicilian clergy than with any other, because it has never made common cause with tyranny, or lost the manly virtues of the citizen. 'It was worth while to come to Sicily,' he said, 'if only to find out that there is still an Italian clergy.' Garibaldi, on the other hand, must contrast favorably in their eyes with the Neapolitan generals who have profaned their churches and plundered them of their sacred vessels, as General Clary did at the sack of Catania, in the confident expectation that the Pope would absolve him as he absolved the Swiss, who, in sacking Perugia, laid ecclesiastical as well as lay property under contribution."

ADDRESS OF THE PALERMO CORPORATION TO GARIBALDI.

"A deputation of the municipality of Palermo presented an address to Garibaldi, expressing its thanks to the liberator of Sicily. The address contains the resolution that the Porta Termini, by which the forces of Garibaldi entered, is to be called henceforth Porta Garibaldi, and the Piazza Vecchia the Piazza di Vittorio Emmanuell. A statue has been likewise decreed to Garibaldi. It is to be erected by subscription.

"Garibaldi answered the deputation by one of those heart-stirring speeches that he knows how to make, reminding them that all was not done, and that every effort must be concentrated to complete the work. He gave them good advice about their duty to organize the people; that there was but one choice between the Neapolitans and a general armament; that Sicily could only be free as part of Italy. He told them that they ought to work for this, but that the time for annexation had not come. It would lead to foreign interference, which ought to be avoided. When the time came, he would be the first to lead in this matter, to which he had devoted his life. Cheering and an enthusiastic expression of thorough confidence was the answer."

Thus it was that Garibaldi, after a brief career, marked by wonderful success at every step, entered Palermo by the eastern gates, and between daybreak and ten o'clock in the morning, had possession of the greater part of the city.

The Neapolitans were driven into a number of strong positions round the royal palace, to the southwest of the town, and to the northwest toward the Mole, their line of retreat, and, not being able to do anything more, the ships opened their fire, always the last remedy. Almost all the civilized nations had representatives of their fleets on the spot to witness and approve by their presence this noble proceeding —English, French, American, Sardinian, Austrian—none of them were wanting ; nay, they anchored in a way which might not hinder the movements of the brave Neapolitan fleet.

The. young King of Naples, though only twenty-three years old, has shown so much of the spirit of his father, recently deceased, that he has been justly named Bomba Junior, or the young Bomb-shell. When the landing of Garibaldi produced the first fit of terror at Naples, the youthful Bourbon sent to his brave fleet concentrated in the Bay of Palermo the order to bombard his faithful Palermitans, and reduce their town to ashes if they should dare to rise against his paternal authority. The Palermitans had been treated once already in this paternal manner by the illustrious father of the present sovereign, who figures in history as King Bomba, for having given these souvenirs of his love to every large town of his kingdom.

During the latter part of the fighting between Garibaldi's troops and those of the king, when the latter were nearly driven from the streets of Palermo, the ammunition of the *picciotti* (or little boys, as the patriot recruits were called) was exhausted at that point, one party of them fell back in one of the streets, and thus allowed the royalists to shut in a street of houses in which another party of them was still holding out.

Garibaldi was at dinner when the news arrived. There had been so many rumors of an advance of the Neapolitans during the day, that the first impression was that this was merely another of those wild rumors ; but Captain Niva, who brought it, was one of the Garibaldians, and there could be no doubt about its truth. .Garibaldi jumped up from his chair, saying, "Well, then, I suppose I must go there myself." He saw it was one of those moments when the chief must be at the head of his troops to restore their confidence. He went downstairs, and took with him whatever troops he found on the road to that exposed point, and proceeded to retake the lost ground.

"His presence (wrote a person who was in the city at the time), not onl soon checked the advance of the royalists, but made them lik wise lose the advantage they had gained a moment before. With that marvellous ascendency which he exercises over those around him, he succeeded in a short time in making the *picciotti* fight, and even in animating the population which had remained in the houses."

In spite of the urgent entreaties of his followers not to expose himself, he remained in the open street, without any shelter, haranguing and encouraging the men ; the enemy seeing this, issued out from the houses and from behind the barricade. One of the *picciotti* was shot through the head just before Garibaldi, who, seeing him falling, held him up for a moment ; and Colonel Turr, at his side, got a ricochet ball against his leg as he took hold of the general and dragged him by main force under shelter. But the effect was produced. One rush brought the party close enough to throw one of Orsini's shells, which prostrated seven or eight men. The bugler, who is always at Garibaldi's side, sounded the charge, and the Neapolitans ran. The sound of this bugle seems to act formidably on the nerves of the Neapolitan troops ; they know they have to do with Garibaldi's men, and at Calata Fimi they ran before even the charge took place.

Royal troops were disembarked in the night of the 29th of May, went out of the Castello toward the Mole, and then by a circuit, rejoined the troops on the other side, anxious to hold their ground in and about the royal palace, rather than to make an attack on the town.

The news from the country could not have been better. Everywhere the people were rising and the troops withdrawing. On the evening of the 23d, General Alfan di Heisia abandoned Girgenti. As soon as the troops left, the population hoisted the Italian flag. A committee was formed, and a national guard. The cries were, as everywhere else, " *Viva l'Italia*," " *Viva Vittorio Emmanuele*," and "*Viva Garibaldi*." The civil authorities were respected, and although the prisoners, two hundred in number, were let out, no disturbance occurred. The whole province there, as everywhere else, followed the example, rising, instituting a committee, and arming itself. The province of Catania rose, with the exception of the town, which was still held by the military, as well as that of Trapani. And all this occurred before the taking of Palermo.

GARIBALDI'S PROCLAMATION IN PALERMO, AS DICTATOR, JUNE 2.

" *Italy and Victor Emanuel!*
" JOSEPH GARIBALDI,
                " Commander-in-Chief of the national forces in Italy,
" In virtue of the power conferred on him, decrees :

" Art. 1.—Whoever shall have fought for the country shall have a certain quota of land from the communal national domain, to be divided by law among the citizens of the commune. In case of the death of a soldier, this right shall belong to his heirs.

" Art. 2.—The said quota shall be equal to that which shall be established for all heads of poor families not proprietors, and said quotas shall be drawn by lot. If, however, the lands of the commune are more than sufficient for the wants of the population, the soldiers and their heirs shall receive a quota double that of other participants.

" Art. 3.—Where the communes shall not have a domain of their own, they shall be supplied with lands belonging to the domain of the state or the crown.

" Art. 4.—The Secretary of State shall be charged with the execution of this decree.

                " The Dictator, GIUSEPPE GARIBALDI.
                " Secretary of State—(Signed)—FRANCESCO CRISPI.
" PALERMO, *June* 2, 1860."

This is a characteristic act of Garibaldi, in whom sympathy and compassion for the poor, weak, and defenceless, form the basis of his character, and have ever given the impulse to his great enterprises, his perseverance, dauntless heroism, splendid successes, and disinterested rejection of honors and rewards. (See these traits, as displayed in childhood, on pages 14 and 15 of this volume, and recorded by his own pen.) Oh, when shall we see such principles ruling our legislators and our citizens? When will they rule in the early education of our families? When all our mothers and fathers are more like Garibaldi's !

CHAPTER X.

"There are some good priests in Italy, but so few, that we call them *Mosche Bianche* (White Flies)."—*Adventures of Rinaldo.*

GARIBALDI SOLICITED BY THE SICILIANS TO ACCEPT THE DIC-
TATORSHIP—DEMAND FOR ARMS—GARIBALDI'S PROCLAMATIONS
ESTABLISHING A GOVERNMENT, ETC.—HIS DIFFERENT WAYS OF
TREATING GOOD PRIESTS AND JESUITS—REASONS—THE KING
OF NAPLES' LIBERAL DECREE—REJECTED.

As soon as Garibaldi landed and went a little way into the interior, all the most influential members of the aristocracy, as well as the free communities, asked him to assume the dictatorship in the name of Victor Emanuel, king of Italy, and the command in chief of the national army.

The first thing, of course, was to organize the military forces. Until then it was an affair of volunteers, who collected round one or another influential man of their town or district, all independent of each other, and remaining together or going home, as they pleased. A decree of the 19th May, from Salemi, instituted a militia, to which all belong from 17 to 50; those from 17 to 30 for active service in the field all over the country; those from 30 to 40 in their provinces, and those from 40 to 50 in their communes. The officers for the active army are named by the commander-in-chief, on the proposal of the commanders of the battalions; those of the second and third categories, only liable to local service, are chosen by the men themselves. But it is rather difficult to act up to this decree under the circumstances. Still, the thing in and about Palermo made progress. The *squadre* were now regularly paid, and probably they could not be kept together if they were not. They are called "Cacciatori del Etna" (Hunters of Etna).

The Sicilian patriots received pay, while the enthusiastic North Italians, who came to help, had not received a farthing, and did not expect to receive anything.

The native militia wore their brown fustian suit, which is generally worn all over the country, and is so alike that it made a very good uniform.

Not two months after the last disarmament took place, it was astonishing what a quantity of guns seemed to be still in the country. They were, for the most part, short guns, looking rather like old-fashioned single-barrelled fowling pieces than muskets. Most of them were percussion, however, and only a few with the old flint-lock. The longing for arms was extraordinary.

It might be said of Sicily, at that time, as was said of Piedmont in central Italy about the same time, by a writer in Turin :

" There is no pen able to describe, nor imagination strong enough to conceive, the nature of the present Italian movement. It is a nation in the struggles of its second birth. Half the youth of the towns are under arms ; young boys of 12 or 13 break their parents' hearts by declaring themselves, every one of them, irrevocably bent on becoming soldiers. There are fourteen universities, and at least four times as many lyceums in the North Italy kingdom, and all of them are virtually closed, for nearly all the students, and many of the professors, are under arms. Those scholars whom mature age unfits for warlike purposes, either sit in parliament, or go out to Palermo to lend a hand to the provisional Italian government. They are everywhere organizing themselves into committees, instituting clubs, or ' circoli,' and other political associations, inundating the country with an evanescent but not inefficient press. There is a universal migration and transmigration. Venetia and the Marches pour into the Emilia and Lombardy. The freed provinces muster up volunteers for Sicily. From Sicily ghost-like or corpse-like state prisoners—the victims of Bourbon tyranny, the remnants of the wholesale batches of 1844 and 1848, the old, long-forgotten companions of the Bandiera, the friends of Poerio, the adventurers of the ill-fated Pisacane's expedition—creep forth from the battered doors of their prison, stretch their long-numbed limbs in the sun, gasp in their first inhala tions of free air; then they embark for Genoa, where the warm sympathy of an applauding multitude awaiting them at their landing greets their ears, still stunned with the yells and curses of the fellow-galley-slaves they have left behind. Such a sudden and universal swarming and blending together of the long-severed tribes of the same race the world never witnessed. Under the Turin porticoes you hear the pure, sharp Tuscan, the rich, drawling Roman, the lisping · Venetian, the close ringing Neapolitan, as often as the harsh, guttural, vernacular Piedmontese."

GARIBALDI'S PROCLAMATIONS ESTABLISHING A PROVISIONAL GOVERNMENT, ETC.

" *Italy and Victor Emanuel!*

" JOSEPH GARIBALDI, Commander-in-Chief of the National forces in Sicily, etc., considering the decree of May 14, on the Dictatorship, decrees :

" ART. 1.—A governor is instituted for each of the 24 districts of Sicily.

" ART. 2.—The governor will reside in the chief place of the district, and wherever circumstances may require his presence in the commune that shall be deemed by him best adapted for serving as a centre of his operations.

" ART. 3.—The governor will reëstablish in every commune the Council and all the functionaries, such as they were before the Bourbonic occupation. He will replace by other individuals such as are deceased, or who from other causes may not appear.

" ART. 4.—The following will be excluded from the civic council, and cannot be members of the corporation, or communal judges, or agents of the public administration :

" (*a.*) All such as shall favor, directly or indirectly, the restoration of the Bourbons.

" (*b.*) All such as have filled or do fill public situations in the name of the Power now tormenting Sicily.

" (*c.*) All such as are notoriously opposed to the emancipation of the country.

" ART. 5.—The governor will have to decide on the grounds of incapacity as stated in the foregoing article, and in case of need will exercise the powers conferred on the district committees by the decrees of July 22, 1848, and Feb. 22, 1849.

" ART. 6.—The governor will appoint in each chief place of the district a quæstor, and in each commune a delegate for the public safety; in the cities of Palermo, Messina, and Catania, an assessor for each quarter.

"The delegates and assessors will be, in the exercise of their functions, dependent on the quæstor, and the quæstor on the governor.

"ART. 7.—The governor will preside over all the public branches of the administration, and direct their proceedings.

"ART. 8.—The sentences, decisions and public acts will be headed with the phrase, 'In the name of VICTOR EMANUEL, King of Italy.'

"ART. 9.—The laws, decrees and regulations, as they existed down to the 15th of May, 1859, will continue in force.

"ART. 10.—All regulations contrary to the present one are cancelled.   "G. GARIBALDI,

"F. CRISPI, Secretary of State.

"ALCAMO, *May* 17, 1860."

"*Italy and Victor Emanuel !*

"JOSEPH GARIBALDI, Commander-in-Chief, etc., decrees:

"1. In every free commune of Sicily the municipality will have to ascertain the state of the local treasuries, and what small sums are there. A report of the same, signed by the Municipal Chief, the Treasurer, and Municipal Chancellor, will have to be drawn up.

"2. The tax on the articles of food, and every kind of tax imposed by Bourbonic authority since May 15, 1849, are abolished.

"6. In the communes occupied by the enemy's forces, every citizen is bound to refuse to the Bourbonic government payment of the taxes, which taxes from this day henceforth belong to the nation.

"G. GARIBALDI.

"FRANCESCO CRISPI, Secretary of State.

"ALCAMO, *May* 19, 1860."

To account for the different ways in which Garibaldi treated some of the ecclesiastics in Sicily, two or three facts should be borne in mind. Innumerable instances have proved, in our day, as well as in various past ages, that some of the orders of monks and nuns are naturally predisposed to be liberal, humane and inoffensive, by the doctrines which they are taught, their inert state of life, the manner in which they are brought into partial contact with the world, or the oppression which they endure from their superiors, while other classes are inclined in opposite directions by influences of a contrary nature. Luther probably owed some of his freedom of thought, and his attachment to the doctrine of justification by faith, to the system to which he was trained in his convent, and became acquainted with some of the good traits of common people, by receiving their daily charity when a poor boy. The mendicant monks in Palermo, because they daily mingled with the people and received their bounty, took a leading part in the insurrection, and were forward and faithful aids of Garibaldi. The Italian patriots know how to discriminate between good and bad priests, many of whom are their enemies, either open or secret, but some of whom have always been their staunch friends. Several of the Sicilian exiles in America have acknowledged their obligations to priests for assistance or for life.

But the Jesuits! Of them there is never any doubt. They are always regarded as deadly foes, and are generally treated very summarily. Exile—immediate expulsion—is the rule toward them ; and this short method, like the suppression of their society, has been forced upon those whom they operate against by the necessities of the Jesuits' own creating. While, therefore, Garibaldi treated some of the clergy with friendliness and confidence, he turned the Jesuits out of Sicily almost the first day.

The King of Naples, as his father did in the previous revolution, issued a decree on the 28th of June, promising privileges to his subjects, and concord with Victor Emanuel : but his word was utterly despised by the people.

NAPLES.

The following is the text of the royal decree :

" 1. General amnesty.

" 2. The formation of a new ministry which shall, in the briefest possible time, draw up a statute on the basis of the Italian and national representative constitutions. The formation of this ministry is confided to Commendatore Spinelli.

" 3. Concord shall be established with the king of Sardinia, for the interest of both crowns and of Italy.

" 4. The flag of the kingdom shall be the Italian tricolor with the royal arms of Naples in the middle.

" 5. Sicily shall receive analogous institutions, capable of satisfying the wants of the populations, and shall have a prince of the royal house for Viceroy.

" The Commendatore Spinelli is reported to have laid down the following conditions for his acceptance of the Presidentship of the ministry: The immediate banishment of the Queen Mother; impeachment of the displaced ministry; an immediate publication of the electoral law, in order to the prompt convocation of parliament; lastly, an alliance offensive and defensive with Piedmont, with reciprocal guarantees.

" On receiving the dispatches announcing that the king had proclaimed a constitution at Naples, Garibaldi decided that the Sicilian committee should assemble on the 18th inst. to vote on a *plebiscitum* (universal suffrage,) proposing immediate annexation to Piedmont.

" The fundamental point of the programme of the commander Spinelli, was the formation of an Italian Confederation, as recommended by the emperor of the French. This confederation to be essentially of a defensive character, and the independence of every State to be maintained, although national unity may be favored."

CHAPTER XI.

" All unfurl the same bright banner,
    All one army rush to form,
    Pious lips shout one hozanna,
    With one fire all hearts are warm."

                            The Banks of Dora.

MEDICI'S EXPEDITIONS FROM PIEDMONT TO AID GARIBALDI—PRE-
PARATIONS, DEPARTURE, VOYAGE, ARRIVAL, ETC.—CAPITULA-
TION OF MESSINA, ETC.—GARIBALDI AT MESSINA—HIS RECEP-
TION, MANNERS, AND SIMPLE HABITS — DIFFICULTIES IN
ARRANGING HIS GOVERNMENT—LETTER FROM VICTOR EMANUEL
FORBIDDING HIM TO INVADE NAPLES—GARIBALDI'S REPLY.

COLONEL MEDICI, who had been an officer of Garibaldi in
South America, and afterward in Rome and Lombardy,
raised and directed several corps of volunteers, who in June
enthusiastically enlisted under the country's standard in
Piedmont, and hastened to Sicily at different times. The
following account of the expedition of the 8th of that month,
is abridged from a private letter, written in the form of a
journal, by one of the volunteers. It begins on " Thursday,
the 14th of June, on board the ship Washington, lying off
Cagliari," a small port of Piedmont a little east from Genoa :

" I little thought on Friday night, as I went to Cornigliano to witness the departure of the 1,200 volunteers, in the clipper Charles and
Jane, that on the following night we ourselves should be *en route* to
Sicily. Yet so it was. Our intention had been to wait for the third
expedition. On the 8th of June came dispatches from Garibaldi,
quite different from any previous ones, asking for men ; so at 3, P.M.,
on the 9th, A—— went to Medici, and was at once accepted. I followed, and with the same success. Our rendezvous was for 9, P.M.,
at Cornigliano. Toward evening we learned from fresh dispatches
that the Neapolitan troops had evacuated Palermo ; this made us
hesitate, as for a thousand and one reasons we should prefer the third

expedition : but calculating that if there should be nothing to do in Sicily, we could return, we took a carriage at midnight and drove off to Cornigliano. The gardens of the Villa della Ponsona, where was the rendezvous for the volunteers, were deserted, and we could see the two steamers lying at anchor off Sestri. A little fishing-boat was lying on the shore, so we coaxed the men to push off, and entered ; we found it ankle deep in water, and in about ten minutes were climbing up the vessel's side. Medici had furnished us with a letter to the commander, who gave us a first-rate cabin, and told us that we were the first on board. Some delay had been occasioned by the little steamer Oregon jostling against the Washington in coming out of the port of Genoa ; but with the exception of smashing the wood-work near the paddle-box, and breaking away a portion of the rails of the upper deck, no great damage was done. For a while we sat on deck, watching the volunteers coming up. Genoa looked more beautiful than ever, the moonlight flooding her marble palaces and spires ; and almost the only constellation visible between the fleecy clouds was Cassiopeia, Garibaldi's star, by whose light he wended his way at night-time across the mountains that divide Genoa from Nice, when condemned to death by Charles Albert, in 1834.

" The expedition was composed of—ship Charles and Jane, of Bath (U.S.), left Genoa at midnight, 8th June, in tow of steamer L'Utile, with 1,200 men, under command of Major Corti.

" Steamship Franklin, left Genoa at 10, P.M., 9th June, for Leghorn, to receive on board 800 men, under command of Colonel Malenchini.

" Steamer Oregon, left Genoa 10th June, 4, P.M., with 200 men, under command of Major Caldesi.

" Steamship Washington, of New York, flag ship, Captain Wm. De Rohan, of Philadelphia, with 1,400 men, under command of Lieutenant-Colonel Baldisseratto, an officer of the Sardinian navy, left Genoa at half-past three, A.M., 10th June.

" Total effective force of 3,600 men, well equipped and armed, the whole under the command of Colonel Medici, accompanied by a full staff.

" There was plenty of food on board, but no getting at it. No one murmured ; indeed the patience and cheerfulness of the volunteers are beyond all praise. Some of them, many of them, are from the first Italian families, who have never known a hardship in their lives ; here they cannot even lie down to sleep, but huddle together, rolled up like balls ; many have to stand all night. We had a long chat with twenty of the famous Carabinieri of Genoa, who are going out to reinforce their company, of whom, out of thirty-five in one attack, six were killed and fifteen wounded. These twenty seem to dream of naught save a like fate.

> " 'Chi per la patria muoja vissuto ha assai,'
> (" He who dies for his country has lived long enough,")

they sing. One's faith in humanity increases wonderfully here.

"On the morning of the 11th, we passed Caprera, Garibaldi's Island, coasted along Sardinia all the day, and at 6, A.M., on the 12th, anchored off Cagliari. Medici hired two brigs, and dividing the volunteers into three portions, gave them breathing room. They looked extremely well in their simple uniform, white trousers and grey or blue blouse, faced with red. It is a pity, considering the heat of Sicily, they have not retained the regular Garibaldi hat, which would have sheltered the face somewhat. By the way, we have the famous Englishman, Captain Peard, on board; he missed Garibaldi's expedition, and is now going to join him; he is captain of the 2d Pavia brigade—a handsome man, with long hair, beard tinged with grey; blue, English eyes, and an honest English heart, much amused at the absurd stories that have been told about him—a true military man, and a worshipper of Garibaldi, intent on doing his utmost for Italian independence.

"Captain De Rohan, too, is a character. I am not at liberty to tell you how much we owe to him for his exertions and pecuniary sacrifices in this expedition. If the Neapolitans respect these 3,600 Sicilian exiles going home, we may thank the stars and stripes under which we sail.

"Medici would be in trouble, as he has positive orders from Cavour not to go; and this is natural. Cavour could not act otherwise since his advice was asked. Medici, had he wanted to do it, should. Medici is a splendid soldier and a good patriot.

"Before quitting Milazzo, I must tell you that I visited the citadel, the field of battle, and other places of interest, besides making the personal acquaintance of Garibaldi, and all the persons of note and interest staying here. Among others, none possess a larger share of the latter, for our countrymen at least, than Captain Peard, 'Garibaldi's Englishman,' a fine English gentleman, and not the melo-dramatic hero that people at home are fondly led to believe. I saw him for the first time under circumstances highly contributing to enhance the interest with which reputation and curiosity have invested him. He had left the café where he had taken up his quarters, and was walking quietly toward the shore, accompanied by his friends, and a few other persons."

Captain Peard was frequently mentioned, as a volunteer in the corps of Garibaldi, or at least in his company, during his daring and perilous, but successful career in Lombardy in 1859. The public have never been informed whether he was actually an officer and soldier of the Cacciatori delle Alpi, or only accompanied that incomparable band.

Garibaldi's Englishman, Captain J. W. Peard, wrote as follows to a friend at Florence, from Palermo, June 22d :

"Here we are, all safe, although I hear the papers say the contrary. We left Genoa with three steamers, one of which ran on to Leghorn, to embark laborers for the Isthmus of Suez, and after a good passage, got into Cagliari. Not so the American clipper, with a battalion on board, that sailed 24 hours before us. The Neapolitans fell in with her off Cape Corso, and captured her. She is now, with all her cargo, both alive and dead, at Naples. Yesterday the American man-of-war on the station sailed for that port to demand her peremptorily. She was taken on the high seas, not in Neapolitan waters —therefore her capture is an act of piracy by the law of nations. Notwithstanding that loss, we landed 2,500 men and large supplies of Enfield rifles and ammunition.

"Palermo is in a frightful state from the bombardment. Accounts vary as to the number of shells thrown into the city ; but the best report I can get gives them at about 800. The Toledo is in places quite blocked up with ruins. Near the palace nearly an entire street is burned. In other parts ruins meet you at every step. At present the people are hard at work removing the barricades and levelling the Castellamare, from which the shells were thrown. All the works toward the city are to be razed to the ground. The people are wild with joy at their deliverance. A friend of mine asked a man yesterday if it was a festa. 'Yes, signore, every day is a festa now,' he said, with tears rising to his eyes. Those who were present tell me never was anything like Garibaldi's entry into the city. He had not above 600 available men, besides the Sicilian levies, and the enemy was 20,000 strong. Extraordinary are the ravages of the royal troops —villas sacked and burned. I was in one yesterday that belonged to the Neapolitan minister, Cavona. They had destroyed everything they could not carry away. The floor was strewed with broken mirrors, chandeliers, marbles, busts, vases, etc. His own room they had piled up with furniture, and tried to set the building on fire. In another villa a valuable library was totally destroyed, the torn books being as high as a man's waist. I saw some Spanish MSS., royal decrees, etc., which would be invaluable to Sicilian historians, torn to pieces. After the armistice the royalists sacked upward of a thousand houses, and committed numberless murders."

Messina, the second city in Sicily, capitulated to General Medici, on the 28th of June. The commander, Field Marshal De Clary, stated that he was animated by sentiments of humanity, and wished to avoid the bloodshed which would have been caused on the one hand by the occupation of Messina, and on the other by the defence of the town and forts. The terms were :

"1. That the royal troops shall abandon the town of Messina, without being disturbed, and the town shall be occupied by the Sicilian troops, without the latter, on their part, being disturbed by the royal troops.

"2. The royal troops shall evacuate Gonzaga and Castellaccio after a delay of two days, to commence from the date of the signature of the present convention. Each of the two contracting parties shall appoint two officers and a commissioner to make an inventory of the cannon, stores and provisions; in short, of everything in the above-named forts at the time of their evacuation.

"3. The embarkation of the royal troops shall take place without disturbance from the Sicilians.

"4. The royal troops shall remain in possession of the citadel, and the forts of Don Blasco, Santerna, and San Salvadore, but shall have no power to do damage to the town, except in the event of those works being attacked, or of works of attack being constructed in the town itself.

"5. A strip of ground parallel and contiguous to the military zone shall be neutralized.

"6. Communication by sea remains completely free to both sides, etc.

"In the last place, the signers of the present convention shall have the liberty of agreeing on the subject of the inherent necessities of civil life which will have to be satisfied and provided for in the town of Messina, in respect of the royal troops.

"Done, read, and concluded at the house of Signor Francesco Fiorentino, banker, at the Quattro Fontaine.

"TOMMASO DE CLARY.
"G. MEDICI."

Messina and other cities of Italy were all captured or otherwise secured by the patriots, under various and highly interesting circumstances ; but the particulars cannot be here recounted for want of space. The following account of Garibaldi's reception in Messina is from the pen of an eye-witness, and contains a just description of the simple manners and habits which he retains under all circumstances :

"At the appointed hour we went to the palace, where about forty or fifty persons were assembled. The banquet passed off very quietly and happily. Garibaldi, as I had noticed before, is very temperate at his meals, drinks water only, and very quickly rises immediately after he has finished, and returning to his office, resumes his business, which he dispatches with remarkable promptitude and ease—no hurry, no confusion, no excitement, even in the most pressing emergencies. On the present occasion he spent a little more time over his dinner, and after dessert he wrote, and chatted with those present. While at dinner a public band of music, improvised for the occasion, playing in the street in front, where a large number of people had assembled, who kept up a round of cheering when anything occurred, such as an arrival of a detachment of volunteers or some public favorite, to excite their curiosity and interest.

"The great event of the evening, however, came off some time later, when the palace having been illuminated, Garibaldi went on the balcony leading out of the banqueting room, for the purpose of showing himself to the people and addressing them. On making his appearance, a tremendous ovation was offered to the liberator by the Messinians. The applause, the cheering—genuine cheering—the clapping of hands, and the manifestations of joy and approbation, were of the most hearty and enthusiastic character. When this demonstration had quite subsided, which required great perseverance and some time to effect, Garibaldi proceeded to address the people. The thousands of upturned faces were all directed toward him, and amid a silence as still as the grave he spoke. The substance of his speech was to this effect : He said that he presented himself to them because they wished it, but that he himself objected to such exhibitions. He did not play the comedian ; he was for deeds, not words. They had achieved a great triumph, but the time was come when they must achieve still greater. He thanked the Sicilians for the courage and enthusiasm they displayed in effecting their own deliverance, and said if they were true to themselves, not Sicily only, but,

with the blessing of Providence, the whole of Italy, would be liberated. He therefore urged upon them the necessity of still following
up the good work, and invited them to come forward and enroll themselves in the ranks of their liberators. I need not dwell on the enthusiasm which this address excited; it was of the most vehement
character I ever witnessed. After acknowledging its cordial reception for a few moments, Garibaldi withdrew."

Garibaldi had various difficulties in arranging his government, the causes of which may, perhaps, not yet have been
fully explained. We will, therefore, only mention some of
the leading facts. Farina, Grasselli, and Toti, whom Garibaldi had found very troublesome to him in Palermo,
were sent out of the island, because, according to the
official journal, they were " affiliated to the police of the
continent," and had " conspired against order." The ministry resigned in consequence, and a new one was formed,
including Messrs. Amari, the historian, Emeranti, and the
following members of the old : Logothe, Laporta, and
Orsini. Reports were published, from time to time, in
Sicily, as afterward in Naples, accusing Republicans of
efforts to counteract Garibaldi : but as the enemies of Italy
have long showed their malice chiefly against the Republicans, of whom Garibaldi has been one, and as Mazzini himself had declared his ardent adhesion to the cause of united
Italy under Victor Emanuel, such accusations are generally
suspicious.

The following letter from Victor Emanuel to Garibaldi,
and the reply, brief as they are, are two of the most important documents connected with the war, and, indeed, with
the lives of their two distinguished writers. It is a most
impressive truth, and must ever be regarded as a proof of
Garibaldi's sound judgment, independence, resolution and
impregnable firmness, in a great and glorious cause, at an
epoch of his career when nothing else gave the right turn to
the results then pending. On which side the " statesman-
ship " then lay, when the king wrote such a veto, with

Cavour sitting at his right hand, and Garibaldi disobeyed it, standing alone, the world can determine, both now and hereafter.

LETTER FROM VICTOR EMANUEL TO GARIBALDI.

"DEAR GENERAL: You know that when you started for Sicily you did not have my approbation. To-day, considering the gravity of existing circumstances, I decide upon giving you a warning, being aware of the sincerity of your sentiments for me.

" In order to put an end to a war between Italians and Italians, I counsel you to renounce the idea of passing with your valorous troops to the Neapolitan mainland, provided that the King of Naples consents to evacuate the whole of the island, and to leave the Sicilians free to deliberate upon and to settle their destinies.

"I would reserve to myself full liberty of action relative to Sicily in the event of the King of Naples being unable to accept this condition. General, follow my advice, and you will see that it is useful to Italy, whose power of augmenting her merits you would facilitate by showing to Europe that even as she knows how to conquer, so does she know how to make a good use of her victory."

Garibaldi replied to the king as follows :

SIRE : Your majesty knows the high esteem and the devotion which I feel toward your majesty ; but such is the present state of things in Italy, that, at the present moment, I cannot obey your majesty's injunctions, much as I should like it. I am called for and urged on by the people of Naples. I have tried in vain, with what influence I had, to restrain them, feeling, as I do, that a more favorable moment would be desirable. But if I should now hesitate, I should endanger the cause of Italy, and not fulfill my duty as an Italian. May your majesty, therefore, permit me this time not to obey ! As soon as I shall have done with the task imposed upon me by the wishes of the people, who groan under the tyranny of the Neapolitan Bourbon, I shall lay down my sword at your majesty's feet, and shall obey your majesty for the remainder of my lifetime.

" GARIBALDI."

The letter is dated Milazzo, the 27th of July.

CHAPTER XII.

"And with such care his busy work he plied,
   That to naught else his acting thoughts he bent.
In young Rinaldo fierce desires he spied,
   And noble heart of rest impatient,
To wealth or sov'reign power he naught applied
   His wits, but all to virtue excellent."

Fairfax's Tasso.

GARIBALDI'S POSITION—A PAUSE IN HOSTILITIES—A PERIOD OF
PREPARATION—PUBLIC ANXIETY—THE SICILIAN FORTRESSES—
CATANIA—MILAZZO—BOATS, MEN AND ARMS COLLECTED AT
FARO—LANDING ATTEMPTED AT SCYLLA—A SMALL BODY SUC-
CEED.

GARIBALDI had now been forbidden by the king to attempt
any further conquests, and warned not to attempt to dethrone
the King of Naples ; and he had declared that he should do
both. From that moment Victor Emanuel was virtually
proclaimed "King of Italy," in spite of his own will and
word. What induced Victor to write that letter may
easily be imagined ; what induced his prime minister to
dictate it, will probably be always a matter of conjecture.
Garibaldi's reply, and the measures which he subsequently
adopted, with the results to which they led, will ever stand
on record, where they can be read by the present and succeeding generations ; and the world will form their own
opinions of his character and capacity, without the aid of
many comments or explanations.

Much was said and conjectured respecting the dissension
which had existed before this time, between Garibaldi and
Farina, a particular friend of Count Cavour. Garibaldi had
appointed Farina counsellor at Palermo, and afterward dismissed him. It appears, even from Farina's own statement,
that it did not arise from any disposition in Garibaldi to

340

establish a republic, or otherwise to prevent the final annexation of Sicily to the kingdom of Sardinia, but was merely
to postpone it for a time which he thought more favorable.
It appears from other evidence, that Farina wished to have
severe measures taken against some of the Republicans, but
that Garibaldi rejected the proposal with noble scorn ; and
to prevent his further interference, banished him and two
others from Sicily, by the following decree :

"'Signor La Farina, Grasselli and Toti, are affiliated to the police
of the Continent. The three were expelled for having conspired
against order. The government, which watches over public tranquillity, could not tolerate the presence of such individuals.'

"The 'Opinione National' of Turin, stated that Farina had full
power from the Sardinian government to assume the title of royal
commissioner, as soon as annexation was declared. Garibaldi, while
advocating annexation, thought it advisable that his dictatorship should
continue till the whole island was subjected, and finding that the
presence of Farina was detrimental to the cause, he ordered him off."

La Farina afterward published the following explanation :

"The causes of my difference with General Garibaldi were as follow : I believed, and still believe, that the only salvation for Sicily is
immediate annexation to the constitutional kingdom of Victor
Emanuel, the most ardent wish of all the Sicilians, already manifested
by the chiefs of more than three hundred municipal bodies. General
Garibaldi believed that the annexation should be postponed till the
liberation of all Italy, including Venetia and Rome, had been effected.
I believed that it was a great act of imprudence to confide a share of
authority and of the public forces to unpopular ministers, etc."

There was now a general suspension of hostilities. The
entire island of Sicily was quiet, and none of the king's
troops remained, except in a few of the fortresses. The circumstances under which some of these had been captured, or
been forced to cease resistance, are interesting, but with the
exception of Palermo, they have not been given for want of
room.

The strait between Sicily and Calabria has been invested

with peculiar interest to readers of history from early ages.
The rocks and quicksands of Scylla and Charybdis, with the
fabulous sirens of which we read in Virgil in our youth,
give us impressions which are never lost. But there are
more modern associations with that arm of the sea and its
shores, of more real importance in the view of persons acquainted with them. American ships have long visited Palermo, Messina, Catania, and some of the other ports of Sicily,
and oranges are brought to us from that fruitful island,
many of which grow on the opposite coast of Calabria, or
Magna Grecia, as it was formerly called. Hills arise from
near the water, and mountains appear behind them, where
scenes of rocky barrenness are intermingled with valleys of
verdure and fertility, inhabited by a population in a simple
state of society, the descendants of ancient Greeks, mingled
with races which at successive periods came in from different
countries. These had been for ages subject to the degrading influences of Romish spiritual rule, and of the despots
of various countries, especially those of Spain and the Bourbons. But the seeds of intelligence have been assiduously
sown and cherished of late years by the patriotic societies
of Italy, who by their cautious, yet often daring and hazardous efforts, have long since brought many of the poor and
rude, but brave and faithful Calabrians into the band of
Italian unity. The events of late years had proved that the
people of that part of the peninsula were to some extent
connected with the great union ; but the approach of Garibaldi and his reception have since shown that the influences so
long and so secretly at work had not been justly appreciated.
There was no considerable insurrection in Calabria during the
conquest of Sicily, and it might have been presumed, from
the general quietness of the population, that they were
unable or unwilling to join with the patriots against the
government of the King of Naples. Some practised observers of Italian affairs, however, regarded that general
tranquillity as the best evidence of a general concert, and

looked for a general rising of the people when the hour should arrive, and the signal should be given. Garibaldi, in the whole course of his proceedings, acted as if he had information not known to others ; and a review of events, since they have passed, and are now fresh in our memory, is calculated to confirm us in this opinion.

In the long and anxious suspense which occurred before any movement was made against Calabria, questions were asked, how the flotilla of boats, which Garibaldi was collecting on the coast of Sicily, could be risked across the strait without a single ship of war to convoy them, and with only two small steamers and one larger one to tow them, while a squadron of the king's steamers was cruising between the shores, and the landing-place was strongly defended by three forts, with heavy cannon, and the whole Calabrian coast was occupied by royal troops. The currents, so terrible to mariners in ancient times, are still violent and irregular.

It was natural to ask, What is coming ? What is about to happen ? Are the apprehensions of Victor to be realized ? Has the king a clearer sight than his gallant precursor, who has hitherto proved his prudence an equal match with his valor ? Is this famous strait to prove its fatal character, so long ago recorded in fable ; and is this passage then, so dreadful to mariners, to be the destruction of our noble sailor ? Will he pass safely between Scylla and Charybdis, or meet his end on one or the other ? On which and how will he be wrecked ; and by what unfortunate circumstances ? Not far distant from this spot, on a point on the coast of Calabria, the two Bandieras, sons of an Austrian admiral, but true Italian patriots, were decoyed to their death, by means of letters violated in the British postoffice. Has Garibaldi been made a dupe, by any artifice ; and has Victor been apprised of danger? Has Louis Napoleon once more changed his policy, and, after favoring Italy in her " latest victories," as Garibaldi recently acknowledged, has he prepared, in consistency with his conduct in 1849, a scheme for something on the opposite side ?

These, and many other questions, naturally disturbed the minds of the friends of Italy, while standing in reality or in fancy on the shore of Sicily, and looking in vain for any sign of the fate which awaited him on the other coast ? But, when we turned, even in imagination, to observe Garibaldi, there was, as ever, something to dispel apprehension, and to encourage the highest hopes ; for, as that patriot priest-poet, Dall' Ongaro wrote :

> " O, well you might say that a saint was his mother,
> For there a mild brilliancy beams in his eyes,
> Which sure was sent down from Paradise "

But on the morning of the 8th of August, Garibaldi began to collect his troops near Faro, which amounted to 15,000 or 18,000 men, without counting the garrison of Messina. The Point of Faro had the appearance of a vast fortified camp, being covered with cannon of all sizes, from mountain howitzers to English 68-pounders, ready to be embarked in the three steamers, which were under steam ; while 300 boats were drawn up ready to receive Garibaldi's troops.

About midnight twenty-five or thirty boats sailed from the coast of Sicily. They were going to attempt a first landing. In three quarters of an hour they crossed to the other side. Unfortunately the current did not permit them to keep the order of their position. Some were driven toward Faro, others swept under the forts of Scylla ; some ran fast on sandbanks further south, while others again were thrown toward Pizzo. The soldiers, however, did not lose their courage at this misfortune. Two or three hundred were landed in all haste, and the flotilla returned to Faro without accident.

On the morning of the 10th a new attempt was made, under the command of an old officer of the French marine service, M. Deflotte : but scarcely had this expedition appeared on the coast, when the enemy rushed upon them from a thousand ambuscades, vineyards, gardens, ditches, and houses. A sharp firing ensued : two Garibaldians were wounded, and the expedition was compelled to return, not, however, without having vigorously responded to the fire of the Neapolitans.

On the night of the 10th and 11th, another landing was vainly attempted. The Neapolitan squadron came up nearer to Faro, and watched every movement of the Garibaldians. The day of the 11th was passed in embarking the artillery. A desperate attempt was spoken of for the next night. At seven o'clock in the evening the Garibaldian steamers began to fire up, and the troops placed themselves in readiness for embarking ; but at eleven o'clock a counter-order arrived. About one o'clock in the night was heard a loud cannonade ; the firing extended from the forts of Scylla to the fortifications of Pizzo. The squadron remained silent ; the engagement had therefore taken place on the land.

It seemed to be evident that the forts were simultaneously attacked by the volunteers and the Calabrians. At a quarter past two the firing ceased : it recommenced after a quarter of an hour in order to cease again after a few minutes. At daybreak, a small boat, chased by a Neapolitan corvette, sought protection under the guns of Faro.

The small party destined to land first in Calabria were under Major Missori, and had been picked from the different volunteer corps. They had been ordered to land on the opposite coast between Scylla and Forte del Cavallo. It is on the extreme point of the Calabrian shore that these forts are situate, at a little distance one from the other. The castle of Scylla stands upon a rock, quite inaccessible from the seaside. Forte del Cavallo is a little further to the left of it, and its walls and fortifications slope gradually down toward the road which skirts the sea, very much like that from Nice to Genoa, which is called the Corniche Road.

On Wednesday evening, the sky so generally blue and bright in this country, was covered with dense whitish clouds, and the night, therefore, was very dark. Garibaldi, who knows how to take advantage even of the smallest incident, at once ordered Missori to sail. Major Missori, having embarked his men on board of large fishing vessels, consequently started at half-past nine o'clock from the Sicilian shore. The Neapolitan cruisers steaming up and down the straits, though numerous and powerful, did not seem to possess the eyes of Argus, and therefore the little expedition was able to land at the intended point. Before reaching the Calabrian coast, however, one of the boats parted company from the other, and sailed a little down toward Scylla Point, just where a Neapolitan battery had been erected. The men on guard in this battery gave the alarm, and the boat was fired at and one English volunteer wounded. Garibaldi had ordered Missori to endeavor to surprise the garrison of Fort Scylla, and to capture the fort. But on hearing the rattling of musketry, and the report of a gun on his left, Missori rightly thought that it would be impossible to seize Fort Scylla by surprise. He therefore hastened to make the concerted signal, informing the Dictator that he had safely landed, and he and his men ascended the rough paths into the Calabrian mountains. As for his companions in the boat which had missed its way, they returned to the Sicilian shore to relate the cause of their failure.

Menotti, Garibaldi's eldest son, arrived at night from Palermo with 800 of the volunteers of Bertani's last expedition. The Dictator had then 20,000 or 25,000 men. His army had been formed into four divisions. That of Medici was at Messina, watching the movements of the Neapolitans, who still held the citadel; the other three were partly concentrated at Faro, a brigade posted at Milazzo and Barcelona, and another, under Bixio, was sent to Bronte, in the province of Catania.

Through the evening of August 11th, fires were seen on the Calabrian mountains behind Pizzo. They were evidently signals made to Garibaldi by the Calabrian bands which had joined the expedition of Major Missori. From about half-past ten, firing was heard in the direction of Fort Scylla; but as that place is hidden from view by the land about Torre del Cavallo, nothing could be clearly distinguished except the heavy boom of artillery. The Neapolitan steam-ers were cruizing all night, as usual; but they did not fire, and only made signals with rockets. It is supposed that the firing was caused by an attack made by Major Missori's party on Fort Scylla.

The following proclamations appeared the next day:

ORDER OF THE DAY.

" FARO, *Aug.* 12.

" OFFICERS AND SOLDIERS OF THE LAND AND SEA FORCES: The General Dictator having for a short time quitted headquarters, left me the following Order :

" GENERAL SIRTORI : I leave to you the command of the land and sea forces, being obliged to leave for a few days.

" G. GARIBALDI.

" OFFICERS AND SOLDIERS : My greatest title to your confidence is the confidence which the man reposes in me who represents your noblest aspirations. I trust that you will obey me as you would obey Gen. Garibaldi.

" G. SIRTORI, Chief of the Staff."

CHAPTER XIII.

" Two seas and the Alps shall Italy bound,
   The oppressors no more in our land shall be found
   The banner of freedom we'll spread to the air,
   And from Apennines rush in a chariot of fire."
                                    Garibaldi's National Hymn.

THE UNCERTAINTY OF THE PROSPECT—APPREHENSIONS—GARI-
BALDI'S MYSTERIOUS DISAPPEARANCE—THE EXPEDITION PRE-
PARED IN SARDINIA—HIS CHANGE OF PLANS—SAILS FROM
GIARDINI, AND LANDS AT REGGIO.

A NEW epoch in the war had now arrived, and one of the
highest interest. What might be the results none could
easily conjecture with any degree of confidence, because the
grounds of calculation were known only to Garibaldi. His
friends in America as well as in Europe were anxious, fearing
that some great disappointment might then await him, after
all his brilliant successes. He was about to land on a wild
coast, lined with strong forts, garrisoned with numerous
troops, and guarded by war-steamers, while not a sign could
be discovered of any friends prepared to join him. He, it
was to be presumed, had secret information, on which he
was acting ; but might not that be erroneous or deceptive ?
Reliance, however, was generally placed on his prudence and
skill, and all waited impatiently to see whether he would
succeed in this independent enterprise, undertaken against
the command of his friend and king.

But, just when things appeared to be all prepared for a
descent upon the Calabrian coast, new anxiety and great
surprise were caused by the sudden disappearance of the
chief. Garibaldi had disappeared, leaving behind him the
proclamation which closes the last chapter. He had left his
trusted and faithful friend Sirtori in his place ; but why

or whither had he gone, or when he would return, no one
could even conjecture. The explanation is now easily given ;
for the facts were known after the reasons for concealing them
had ceased. Garibaldi, it now appears, had been acting in
a manner quite consistent with himself.

About the middle of August, 6,000 men were collected
by Dr. Bertani, Garibaldi's agent in Genoa, for an expedition to the states of the Pope. They were sent in
detachments to the little retired Golfo d'Orangio, on the
eastern side of the island of Sardinia. Bertani went to
Messina for orders from Garibaldi, having been urged by
Farina and Major Trecchi not to complicate matters by
invading the Papal territories before the question of Naples
was settled. It was to Golfo d'Orangio that Garibaldi
went secretly on the 12th. The "chivalrous regard" which
he has been said to have for Victor Emanuel, as the head
of Italian unity, seems to have induced him to consent, and
the 6,000 men were ordered to Sicily. One thousand of them
were therefore sent round the island of Sicily, to Taormina,
with the intention of invading Calabria with the brigade
Bixio, on the south coast. This was a characteristic plan
of Garibaldi, when all eyes were turned to the Straits, as
he is fond of making surprises, especially to attack in the
rear.

Garibaldi therefore left Messina on the 18th of August,
for Giardini, by land, where the troops arrived before him ;
and the materiel and horses were shipped at night, in the
two steamers, Torino and Franklin, which had transported
thither about 2,800 soldiers. These and others—9,000 in all
—were embarked in these steamers and two sail vessels, which
were taken in tow. Garibaldi and his son accompanied this
first brigade, which was to be followed by the second, and
both were to act in combination with the expedition across
the Strait.

At dawn of day the two steamers entered the harbor of
Melito, without opposition, about twelve miles south of Reg-

gio, and east of Capo dell' Armi. But, unfortunately on approaching the shore, one of them, the Torino, got aground, and efforts were made in vain to get her off. Garibaldi, seeing that the case was a serious one, said that he was needed to examine the bottom, and began to throw off his clothes, preparatory to diving. But his sailors were too quick, for ten or twelve of them leaped over the side of the vessel into the sea.

As he intended to take Reggio by surprise, he hastened on shore, and effected a landing, with three cannon, in a wonderfully short time. Knowing that almost all the enemy's troops were down at the forts on the west coast, from Scylla onward, he lost no time, expected no assistance, and gave them not time to learn of his arrival in their rear, but speedily gained the neighboring heights. A frigate and corvette in the King of Naples' service were posted on the watch exactly off the spot at which Garibaldi landed, but, wonderful to relate, they not only did not sink his ship, but opposed no serious obstacle to his disembarkation, although they fired some shots which killed a few of the Garibaldians. Four thousand insurrectionists in the Calabrias fraternized with Garibaldi almost on the moment of his landing. It was rumored also, that the defection of the army of Naples was extremely probable.

We now return to Faro, where the army was left still anxiously looking across the strait :

"Nothing was heard of Missori's expedition till it was reported in the camp that he had established himself at Aspromonte, a small village in the mountains near the Calabrian shore But before reaching this place, he had to fight a company of Neapolitan riflemen, which was dispatched from Villa San Giovanni to stop his march. The skirmish was a sharp one, but at last Missori had the best of it, and was enabled to make his way through the mountains without much difficulty. In this affair, however, he had seven men wounded, and one was made a prisoner by the Neapolitans, as he was so severely hurt that he could not move. In spite of the remonstrances of the surgeon, who told the Neapolitan officer that the man would die if he were taken to Reggio, he was removed, and died on the road. Missori held Aspromonte, and Calabrian patriots joined him from the neighboring villages of the coast: 150 men of Villa San Giovanni, commanded by a Calabrian baron, were among the number.

"During the course of the night, other small expeditions sailed from Sicily, notwithstanding the shining moon which made the night as clear and bright as the day.

"The first of them was directed to land between Azzerello and Villa San Giovanni. The second successfully landed at Fiumara Zaccherella. The third reached Cannamiele. In all, these three expeditions did not number more than 300 men."

Few scenes in history can be found, to be compared with those which soon followed the landing of Garibaldi and his troops, in the manner and at the different points, above mentioned. His combined movements show the wisdom, as well as the ingenuity of his plans ; and the results were probably more favorable even than his anticipations. While amusing the enemy with his preparations, and making his repeated essays to land on the near parts of the coast, he had suddenly got in their rear with a powerful force ; and while the line of forts along the shore were expecting an attack in front, they suddenly discovered the hills behind and above them covered with Garibaldi's army. Their consternation may be imagined, and some idea may be formed, by an active fancy, of the feelings of the soldiers of freedom, as they showed themselves on the lofty heights, which they had attained unperceived, and from which they now looked down into the enemy's forts, and saw what passed, being able to distinguish minute objects and the positions and motions of the men.

Garibaldi sent a summons to the enemy, demanding an immediate surrender. A flag of truce soon appeared, proceeding from below, with a request for an armistice of a few hours, until orders could be received from the commander-in-chief. "You will never receive them," replied Garibaldi. "I have cut off all communications."   "What do you require ?" was the next question.   "Surrender."   "On what terms ?   May we march out with our arms ?"   " Certainly ; and all the troops will be at liberty to return to their homes."

When the messenger returned to the fortress, there was a commotion visible—men running about to spread the news ; and a moment after, a loud shout arose, of " Viva Garibaldi !"   But little time was required to arrange the capitulation, and then Garibaldi descended the heights and entered the place, where he was received with acclamations, and the warmest expressions of joy.   The soldiers crowded round, kissed his hands and hailed him as their friend.   Thus relieved from all their apprehensions in a moment, and, instead of a scene of battle and bloodshed, of which they had expectations, and the forebodings of defeat and its consequences, they found themselves treated with the humanity and tenderness so universally displayed by their conqueror, and at liberty to leave their hard and miserable military life, and to return to their homes and families.   The Calabrians, who had already joined the patriot army in great numbers, were continually pouring in from the country ; and they, being in want of arms and ammunition to equip them for the ranks of the liberator, purchased those of the disbanded soldiers, who having no intention of remaining in the service of the king, were glad to sell what they no more desired to use against their brethren.

The capture of the forts was thus a scene of peaceful jubilee, and effected without shedding a drop of blood.   The results of Garibaldi's proceedings now showed that he must have laid his plans and pursued his movements on information before received, and which fully justified them at every step.   His progress, from that part of Calabria toward Naples, afforded equal evidence of his sagacity and of the preparations made to facilitate and secure it.   The people rose in his favor wherever he came, and insurrections were made in different and some distant parts of the country, often with a boldness and success which proved extensive and well-laid combinations. To secret societies and the patriotism of the people belongs the credit of that great and almost blood-less revolution. The following brief account of proceedings in several places may serve as a specimen of the movements in the country.

"Three thousand men, assembled from Polla, Sant' Angelo, San Rufo, and a number of other places, marched into Sala, commanded by Colonel Fabrizii. There, in the presence of an enthusiastic population, the downfall of the Bourbons was declared, and the government of Victor Emanuel established, with Garibaldi as dictator, and Giovanni Matina as pro-dictator. A *procès verbal* of the whole affair was made, and signed by the authorities. In western Lucania, under the direction of Stefano Passaro, a committee was appointed to collect arms and ammunition, another to collect voluntary offerings, and a third to provide for public security. Three of the four districts of the province of Salerno, Campagna Vallo, and Sala, had already risen. Of the insurrection, or rather of the popular festivity in Vallo, we have these details: that on the 29th the ~~tambour~~ was beaten at 2 P.M., when the male population rushed in arms to the *piazza* of the city. They were shortly after joined by many of the youth of the neighboring communes, and, forming themselves into a column, with music at their head, they went through the streets, taking down the arms of the Bourbons and substituting those of Victor Emanuel. All the women of the place accompanied them, scattering flowers and confetti, and thus, amid tears of joy, they all marched toward Goi.

"The scene is described as having been one of marvellous enthusiasm, and it is added that not a single quarrel or theft took place. Life, order, and property were religiously respected."

CHAPTER XIV.

" Oh, short be his joy in our sorrow and pain,
I see his dark fate writ by destiny's pen."

Eco di Savonarola.

THE excitement in Naples, in consequence of the movements
in Central Italy, had been very great so early as in June, and
a crisis ere long occurred in the cabinet. At a meeting of
the Council of State, the Count of Aquila advocated liberal
principles, and the Count of Frani resisted him. Concessions
were afterward agreed to, and after a conference of six hours,
between Baron Brenier and the Count of Aquila, the following decree was published :

" SOVEREIGN ACT.

" Desiring to give to our most beloved subjects a mark of our sovereign benevolence, we have determined to grant constitutional and
representative institutions to our kingdom, in harmony with national
and Italian principles, so as to guarantee future security and prosperity, and to draw always closer the bonds which unite us to the people
whom Providence has called us to govern. For this object we have
arrived at the following determinations :

" 1. We grant a general amnesty for all political offenders up to this
day.

" 2. We have charged the Commander, Don Antonio Spinelli, with
the formation of a new ministry, who shall compile, in the shortest
possible time, the articles of the statute, on the basis of representative, Italian, and national institutions.

" 3. An agreement will be established with the King of Sardinia
for the common interests of the two crowns in Italy.

" 4. Our flag shall be from this day forward adorned with the national colors in vertical bands, preserving always the arms of our dynasty in the centre.

"5. As regards Sicily, we will grant it analogous representative institutions, such as to satisfy the wants of the island; and one of the princes of our royal house shall be our viceroy.

"PORTICI, *June* 25, 1860."

A letter from Naples of that date, said:

"Wrung from the sovereign as have been these concessions, against his inclinations and convictions, if his majesty can be said to have any, and known as all these facts are, the decree was received with the greatest indifference. People read it on the walls and passed on. I have not heard one cry of pleasure raised, but I have heard official people say, 'Too late! What a pity that it was not given six months ago." It was the concession of one with his back to the wall, and who may hereafter say, as Ferdinand II. said, that he yielded on compulsion, and it was not binding.

"An order was given for the immediate release of the political prisoners in Santa Maria Apparente, and a steamer, hired by their friends, went to Capri to-day to bring back the victims of a long and cruel persecution."

Everywhere this decree was regarded in the same manner. The celebrated Poerio, who had been released from a long and cruel imprisonment a few months before, for supporting the constitution to which the father of the present King of Naples had himself sworn, was at this time a member of the House of Deputies of Sardinia, and in a speech said:

"The traditions of the Neapolitan government are hereditary perjury. The new king, almost to prove the legitimacy of his descent, is preparing to perjure himself; and, in order to qualify himself for the task of forswearing himself, he must first swear. It is with that view that he declares himself ready to swear constitutions and alliances. His object in proposing an alliance with the king's government is obvious. He is only meditating the reconquest of Sicily These are the old fox-like wiles of the Neapolitan government. As these have thrice availed them, they hope, even now, from the same arts, to attain the same results. But if these are very clearly the intentions of the government of Naples, there is also no doubt but the

government of the king—of that king who for the last twelve years
has held aloft the banner of Italian nationality, will never desert his
post, never will associate itself with a faith-breaking government, a
government by the nature of its very institutions an implacable foe to
Italian regeneration."

The following is an extract from the letter of an English
lady in Florence :

"The details that have reached here, through both private and
public information, of the horrible sufferings endured by the Sicilians,
are enough to account for the fiendish hatred excited by the Neapolitans, whose conduct to the unfortunate islanders is almost a repeti-
tion of the frightful barbarities of the Indians during the late war, for
neither sex, age, nor innocence, are any protection against the perpe-
tration of the most awful atrocities.   It is beyond belief that, in the
nineteenth century, in a Christian part of Europe, there have been
scenes enacted within the last few months that renew the days of the
Inquisition.   A gentleman, residing in Florence, has received intelligence of his family in Sicily, giving details of the sufferings of his
brother, who was subjected to a 'torture' that even surpassed all the
refined cruelty that was ever imagined by Ximenes and his inquisito-
rial establishment, having been chained to a copper chair, under the
seat of which was lighted a charcoal fire!   This is only one of the
many incidents that have taken place—incidents that make the cheek
grow pale, even to hear of.   No wonder there has been such a burst
of enthusiasm throughout all Europe for Garibaldi and his noble expedition.   Every civilized land has echoed the bell which has been
tolled in Italy for the annihilation of despotism.   There has not been
raised one sympathetic voice to cry to Francis of Naples, 'Hear it not
Duncan, for it summons thee' to join the circle of deposed tyrants
that have sought asylums within such short distances of each other,
imitating the instinct of the featherly tribe, who only seek society with
companions of the same color."

The feelings of the people of Naples cannot be imagined,
without some knowledge of the cruelties of the government.
The following shocking account of the cruelty practised on a
man who was called an American, by the priests of Rome
and Italy, is from a letter written in Naples, just after the
revolution, by a person who saw him and obtained from him
since his own story :

BARBAROUS TREATMENT OF A POLITICAL PRISONER.

"Amongst the many cases of brutal and illegal imprisonment which have been brought before the public during the last ten days, none has been worse than that of Francisco Casanova, *calling himself an American.* He was confined in San Francisco, and some young men who had formerly been placed in the same prison, though not in the same room, remembering his case, went, on the amnesty being proclaimed, to deliver him; but he was all but naked, and he could not leave until an advocate called Arene, who has acted with great benevolence, sent him some clothes, and has since received him in his house and fed him. Last night I went to see him, and I cannot tell you whether indignation against this most Christian government or compassion for the victim was the strongest feeling. 'When he entered my house,' said Arene, 'he was supported by two persons, for he was unable to walk. He looked like a ghost.' 'Where am I?' he exclaimed, as he looked confusedly around; and well he might, after six years and a half of confinement from all intercourse with man. But I give you his own description of his sufferings, as nearly as possible in his own words, premising merely that there were witnesses of all that I relate, in Arene himself, a Neapolitan friend, and a foreign consul.

"I landed in Genoa from Boston some time in 1853, and wishing to see the south of Italy, travelled till I came near to Viterbo, when I was cautioned not to go to Rome; but I still persevered in my intention of doing so, when I was arrested as not having a passport, and carried to the Eternal City, where I was placed in the Carcere Nuova. Not satisfied with the report I gave of myself, I was tortured for three months as follows. My hands and arms were bound together, and then, by ropes tied round the upper part of the arms, they were drawn back till my breast protruded, and my bones sounded, 'crick, crick.' There was another species of torture practised upon me, which was this: At night, whilst sleeping, the door was secretly opened, and buckets of water were thrown over my body. How I survived it I cannot tell; the keepers were astonished, and said they never had such an instance; 'but you will never get out alive,' I was told. I replied that I never expected to do so, and prayed for the angel of death to come. The worst torture of all, however, was the prison itself—a room into which a few rays of light struggled from above, and the stench of which was as bad as death. For three months I suffered thus, and then, without any reason assigned, was taken from it and placed, always alone, in a room called 'Salon del

Preti,' a large airy room, and was well fed and well treated for
twenty-one months more. I was a prisoner of the Cardinal Secretary
Antonelli. About the middle of 1855 again, without any reason
being given, I was sent off to Naples, was placed first in the Vicaria
and afterward in San Francisco, in a small, close room, where I was
detained for four years and a half. I was questioned on several
occasions, and at last refused to answer, saying that my persecutors
already knew what I had to say, that I was unjustly and illegally confined, and nothing could compel me to utter another word. On
another occasion I was called before Bianchini, the director of police,
who interrogated me. I appealed against my sufferings, and all the
reply I received was, 'Va bene, va bene,' from a Christian man to
one suffering as I was, but my invariable answer was, I will die first;
never will I ask anything of this government. When first I arrived
here I had a little money, which for a short time procured me better
food than prison fare, and then by degrees I sold my clothes. At
last I sold my black bread to have a little salt to sprinkle over my
beans, and sometimes to procure some incense to relieve the horrid
stench of my prison. As for water for purposes of cleanliness, it was
never supplied me, and all that I could do, was to dip one of my own
rags in a jug of drinking water, and wash some portions of my body.
During the day I could repose, but at night I was covered with black
beetles, fleas, lice, and every conceivable species of vermin. I
expected death, and desired and prayed for it as a relief, but it never
came. My clothes were at last so reduced, that I was all but naked,
and so I have passed four summers and winters, pacing up and down
my narrow chamber.

"'I will show you my prison-dress,' said he; and going out,
returned in a few moments. He might have stood as a model for
Lazarus risen from the tomb. The lower part of his body was
covered with a thin pair of linen drawers, nothing more. On his feet
was a pair of shoes, with soles and upper leather all in holes. He
had no shirt, but over the upper part of his body, was thrown a rag,
something like a common kitchen-towel, one corner of which he had
placed on his head, as the long elfin locks which had not been cut
for many years hung down over his neck and shoulders. He appeared
more like a brute than a Christian man. 'See this rag,' said he,
' how I have botched it. This was my dress, and so clad, I paced up
and down my solitary den.'

"There is much that Casanova reports of himself that I do not
repeat, for it is so mysterious that I require further evidence of its cor-
rectness There can, however, be no doubt of his sufferings and

imprisonment in Naples. It has long been whispered about here that an unknown individual was lying in the prisons of San Francisco, but nothing was known of him. He was one of the mysteries of the dungeon, and even now there is much to unravel. Who is he?— what secret motives led to his double confinement here and in Rome?—why was he transferred from the hands of a Christian cardinal to the mercies of De Spagnoli? What he said I report, and time must unravel his story; but the world will know how to appreciate the influence of a priesthood under whose eye such enormities have been committed."

In Naples, on the 26th of June, assemblages of the population commenced. The populace shouted " GARIBALDI forever !" " Annexation forever !" " Death to the police !" The following day a panic took place ; the police were maltreated, and disappeared as soon as the same cries were raised by the populace.

The king had twice sent Signor Aquila to Baron Brenier, and had promised to make a strict investigation.

On the 28th of June all the police stations were pillaged in open day; forty of the agents were surprised, and either killed or wounded. The archives were burnt. The spoils were carried about in triumph by the populace.

The king had arrived at Naples, and had ordered the immediate formation of a national guard.

A proclamation was issued, prohibiting seditious shouts, and recommending the military to disperse assemblages of the population with moderation.

As the successes of Garibaldi in Calabria became known in the city of Naples, and his unimpeded advance toward that capital, the excitement daily increased. A letter, dated there on the 5th of September, said :

" Seven-league boots must be in fashion again, and Garibaldi must have a pair. It was but yesterday he was at Faro ; then we find him at Pezzo, Tiriola, Nicastro, Paolo, until, by a series of gigantic strides, by last reports he was at Campagna, the capital of one of the four districts of Salerno. I shall expect at any hour to meet the great dictator in the Toledo. His march has been a continual triumph

-—war in its severer aspects he has not seen in the kingdom of Naples, but wreathed with flowers scattering confections and weeping tears of welcome and joy. Apart from a hatred of the Bourbons, Garibaldi is worshipped as a demi-god, and I believe that the veriest reactionist in the kingdom would sheathe his sword to look at him. It is hero-worship which has smoothed the passage of the dictator rather than anything more definite or settled in principle."

The priests, the same letter declared, were much connected with the two last revolutionary attempts:

"For that of Prince Luigi (Count of Aquila), the vicars of some parishes, just before the outbreak was to have occurred, placarded the doors of the houses of their faithful followers with little bills, one of which is in my possession, bearing this inscription:

" 'Viva Jesu Christo!
Viva la Madonna Immacolata!
Viva San Francesco!'

"This was to protect those houses.
"Naples is in a state of the greatest excitement. It is one great heart without a head, and the most singular contrasts present themselves at every step. I left a scene of wild confusion in the Toledo late last night, when the names only of Garibaldi and Victor Emanuel were heard, and, going down to Santa Lucia, I found every house illuminated, torches burning, and fagots borne by a crowd of rabble, a small bell tinkling, and a priest bearing the host, surrounded by hundreds of devotees. They stop, and the vast crowd fall upon their knees. Silence! not a sound was heard, except the indistinct roar of voices from the Toledo. On the walls close behind were the cannon of the Bourbons, and in the offing the fleets of many nations, all brought out as distinctly as possible by the gorgeous moonlight of our southern sky. What a host of conflicting ideas were here brought into juxtaposition and contrast!

"Last night it was decided that the king should leave immediately; at midnight it was deferred, but *only* deferred. The throne has well nigh fallen."

The following Address to the Clergy of the Kingdom was issued by the Ecclesiastical Committee of Union:

"THE CLERGY OF THE KINGDOM.

"*Viva Italian Independence!*
"*Viva Victor Emanuel!*
"*Viva Giuseppe Garibaldi!*

" PROGRAMME.

" Italianism, Activity, Catholicity—these are the duties demanded of every good Neapolitan Christian, whether priest or layman; these he is called upon to practise both in thought and action for the benefit of the country. Such, in fact, is the speculative and practical principle which in Naples animates the Union Ecclesiastical Committee in order to arrive at the most holy object of independence, in the noble undertaking of Italian redemption. For these reasons the committee are intent on the union of ideas with facts; they profess it to be their indispensable duty to labor unweariedly, so as not to go in opposition to the orthodox faith, which rests in Christ and his vicar on earth—in Christ as God-man, in his vicar as the first religious and the first civil power of the world. Hence, taking its stand on these axioms, the committee declares its intention of realizing the evangelical maxim that spiritually the state is in the church, as temporarily the church is in the state; and so it labors to establish the unity of Italy in the order of religion and civilization; in the order of religion, of which the pontiff of Rome is the œcumenical moderator; in the order of civilization, of which Victor Emanuel is the the only regulator in the Italian kingdom."

CHAPTER XV.

" Expect not, O Pope ! a second retreat
  To find in Gaeta, or a stool for your feet :
  A worse fate than even your own may await
  The felon to you who once open'd the gate."
                                    G. ROSETTI. T. D.

THE CONDITION OF NAPLES SINCE THE REIGN OF TERROR IN APRIL
—AGITATION ON GARIBALDI'S APPROACH.

THERE was a reign of terror in Naples in April, 1860, in consequence of numerous arrests and imprisonments of persons of all classes, many of them on the merest suspicion. The British minister in that city, who had repeatedly distinguished himself by his humane exposure and protest against the cruelties of the old savage, Bomba, now made new representations to his government, that these measures were taken by the Intendants in compliance with a circular from the Minister of Police. On the 1st of March they arrested numbers who were not suspected at all, and among them several dukes, marquises, counts, and princes. Other evidences were given by the government of their great fear of an insurrection.

The following is from the letter addressed to the King of Naples by the Count of Syracuse :

" Civil war, which is already spreading over the provinces of the continent, will carry away the dynasty into that ultimate ruin which the iniquitous arts of perverse advisers have long been preparing for the descendants of Charles III. of Bourbon ; the blood of the citizens, uselessly spilt, will again flood the thousand towns of the kingdom, and you, once the hope and love of the popele, will be regarded with horror as the sole cause of a fratricidal war.

" Sire, while it is yet time, save our house from the curses of all Italy ! Follow the noble example of our royal kinswoman of Parma, who, on the breaking out of civil war, released her subjects from their allegiance, and left them to be arbiters of their own destinies. Europe and your subjects will take your sublime sacrifice into account, and you, sire, will be able to raise your brow in confidence up to God, who will reward the magnanimous act of your majesty. Your heart, tempered by adversity, will become accessible to the noble aspirations of patriotism, and you will bless the day when you generously sacrificed yourself for the greatness of Italy.

"With these words, sire, I fulfill the sacred duty which my experience imposes upon me, and I pray to God that he may enlighten you, and render you deserving of His blessings.

"Your majesty's affectionate uncle,

"Leopold, Count of Syracuse.

"Naples, *Aug.* 24."

In the latter part of August, reports of the nearer approach of Garibaldi, and of risings in different parts of the country, were multiplied daily; and the secret patriotic committee more openly and freely circulated their publications, which were to be seen in every house. Movements had been made, before the 25th, in Matera, the Capitanata, Bari, Monopolo, and Sassinoro, and in Potenza and Corleta provisional governments were formed in favor of Victor Emanuel. Indeed, the kingdom was in a state of general revolution, and a pro-dictatorial committee held its sessions to direct "the great Lucanian insurrection." An order was also published in Naples, in the name of Garibaldi, Dictator of the Two Sicilies, providing that all authorities should remain at their posts; that acts of the government should be published in the name of Victor Emanuel; that a committee of public security and a commission of engineers should be formed to barricade the city; and that all capable of bearing arms should join the National Guard. Committees were also formed for looking after the commissariat, and attending to the sick and wounded, on which committee were the names of seven ecclesiastics. The headquarters of the insurrectionists were at Potenza, in the province of Basilicata, and to this point were crowding hundreds and thousands of volunteers. The people of the country itself had taken up arms.　All business was suspended; one thought alone occupied the public mind.　The great fear of many was of pillage; and the want of occupation, and the almost general famine among the lower classes, gave such a fear yet greater appearance of reasonableness.

The landing of several detachments of the Garibaldians was now a confirmed fact.

The following account of the revolution in the Basilicata will afford an idea of the changes then made in the country :

"The province of Basilicata had long been agitated ; it is a mountainous country, subject to earthquakes.　The war of Italy, the adventures of Garibaldi, the constitution of Francis II., precipitated the crisis. The reactionary attempts at Matera gave the signal for the movement. Potenza, the chief town of the province, was only defended by gendarmes.　They were apparently on good terms with the national guard, and their chief, Captain Castagna, had given his word of honor that he would not be the first to commence the attack.

"On the morning of the 18th of October, the gendarmes formed in column, left the town, and took up a position within musket shot of the houses on the Monte.　Castagna removed his men in this way to tranquillize the country, as he said.　However, a picket of national guards at the Salsa gate watched the movements of the gendarmes. It was well they did, for Captain Castagna all at once returned with his men at double-quick pace, dividing them into two columns, one of which was to attack the post held by the national guard, and the other to open the prisons.

"The first discharge of the royalists took place before the men attacked had time to cry 'To arms!'　A bullet struck Captain Asselta in the temple.　He had firmly stood the charge with some fifty of the national guardsmen.　Not till then did the latter open fire, and the gendarmes were put to flight.　They disbanded about the town and the open country, striking at random, pursued and hunted everywhere by the peasants, who were armed with hatchets.　They also lost some fifty prisoners : about fifty were wounded, and more than twenty slain.

"Besides the wound of Captain Asselta, the insurgents had to deplore the loss of two young men, and count both women and children among the wounded.　Nevertheless, this strange insurrection, provoked, hastened at least, and justified like the Italian war of last year, by the attack of the gendarmes, was entirely successful, and it spread

most rapidly. Clouds of armed mountaineers came down from all
parts of the heights to help their brethren in the town. The wounded
and royal prisoners were not only spared, at the simple command of a
chief, but received every assistance, just as if they had been fighting
for the good cause.

"On the 19th, at Tito, the national guard drove out the gendarmes;
on the 20th there were more than 10,000 armed men at Potenza; on
the 22d 16,000 were mustered. All the nobility, the landowners, the
chief inhabitants, the educated citizens, even the priests, were on the
side of the insurgents. The peasants took up arms spontaneously to
the cry of 'Long live Victor Emanuel.' The cross of Savoy floated
everywhere on the tri-color flag. The forces were commanded by a
Neapolitan, who had already figured in two former Italian wars—Colonel Boldoni.

"Strong detachments were stationed *en échelons* around the town
and upon the mountains. Good positions were occupied, amongst
others that of Marmo, whence a handful of men can keep in check an
army, and renew the defence of Mazagran. The insurrection assumed
such proportions that it kept the royal forces at a distance. Neapolitans and Bavarians had been sent against it; the former stopped at
Auletta, the latter at Salerno.

"Potenza was barricaded, and preparing to resist to the death. It
had already a provisional government, whose two first acts the
National Committee published, headed :

"'VICTOR EMANUEL, KING OF ITALY. GENERAL GARIBALDI, DICTATOR
OF THE TWO SICILIES.

"'A pro-dictatorial government has been formed to direct the
great Lucanian insurrection. (Basilicata is the ancient Lucania).

"'The members sit permanently in the old hall of Intendants.

"'POTENZA, *August* 19, 1860.'

"'FOR THE DICTATOR, GARIBALDI.

"'*The pro-dictators, N. Mignona, G. Albini; the secretaries, Gae-
tano, Cascini, etc.*

"'It is ordained: 1. That the authorities shall remain at their
posts and actively assist in maintaining order, providing for the proper
carrying on of the judicial and civil administration. 2. The acts of
the government relating to the civil and judicial administration shall
be headed: Victor Emanuel, King of Italy; Joseph Garibaldi, Dictator of the two Sicilies. 3. A committee of public safety is established
and a committee of engineers for barricading the town.'

"The fifth article nominates the majors and captains of the national guard. The sixth directs them to form the several corps. The seventh appoints a deputation to see to the conveyance of provisions, etc. The eighth appoints a deputation for providing quarters. The ninth names a committee for attending to the sick, wounded, and prisoners.

"Rumors of the defection of the king's officers were repeated every moment. It was asserted in Naples that General Nunziante had just gone over to Garibaldi. The Duchess of Mignano, the wife of the exiled general, having been ordered to quit Naples, proudly refused to go, and defied the ministers to remove her by force."

During a few days about the beginning of September, the king's ministers, his army and the city, were in a state of the greatest agitation. On the 3d, General Cotrufiano sent in his resignation, but expressed his hope that the ministry would remain in power. The National Guard, who had before communicated with them, then told them that if they did not remain they would commence the revolution in the city.

As circumstances, however, were, the ministers considered it impossible to remain with dignity or advantage to the country, and, *en masse*, again sent in their written resignation. "We have been called traitors," they said. "We have the troops against us, and no longer enjoy the confidence of the sovereign; we are supported by the National Guard and the people, it is true, and are their ministers rather than the king's; but this is not according to the principles of the Constitution, and we therefore earnestly beg your majesty to choose a transition ministry. Besides, we will not undertake the responsibility of the war against Garibaldi and his followers, for it will be altogether useless." Such, remarks a writer who was at that time in Naples, was the manner in which the ministers addressed his majesty, and put into plain English, it means this: "*If your majesty will abandon all self-defence, we will serve you, but if you are determined to risk an action, we will persist in resigning, and then barricades will be formed directly.*" The choice left to Francis II., then, was revolution or abdication, and this is the end of that vast structure of despotism which Ferdinand II. reared with so much labor, and cemented with so much blood. On Sunday morning, the ministers met in the council chamber, and waited for some decision on the part of his majesty, but none came; but later in the day, De Martino was sent for by the king, and requested to form an administration. This, however, De Martino declined doing, and the king exclaimed, in great sadness, "Then I am abandoned by all." So stood the matter on Sunday night. It was clear that the ministers had no hopes or intentions, even if they remained in power, of doing anything more than keep things together till Garibaldi came. To them, as to all in Naples, it was evident enough that the game was up, and that all they could do for the country was to make the fall, or transition, as easy as possible. Up to that time their conduct was beyond all praise. There was an impression in the city that the ministerial difficulties had been arranged, and, in consequence, on Saturday and Sunday night there was a partial illumination of the city, and bills were placarded bearing the inscription, "*Viva Garibaldi!*" "*Viva Romano!*"—the chief minister.

It is impossible for any generous mind to contemplate the position of Francis II. without compassion. Not gifted by nature with much intelligence, kept in gross ignorance, and reared in a school of political despotism and religious bigotry by his father, misguided and betrayed by evil counsellors in the early part of his reign, and finally abandoned by his oldest uncle, and by the contemptible nobility and parasites who supported or tolerated the corruptions of the government so long as they were to their own advantage, he sat alone in his palace, the last sovereign of his family, hesitating as to the moment when he is to lay down both crown and sceptre. Close to his palace crowds were reading and rejoicing in the latest dispatches from the camp of the enemy, who was advancing by rapid marches—an enemy whom he had no force to repel; and not much more distant resided the minister of a sovereign who subscribed himself the "beloved cousin" (or by some similar hypocrisy) of Francis II., at the same time that he was doing all that in him lay to drive him from the throne. The position was a hard one, created by the Bourbons themselves—a fulfillment of the great decree, that the sins of the fathers shall be visited on the children.

What a contrast was then presented between the cold, bloody cruelty of the Bourbons and the noble moderation of this long oppressed people! Thousands in the city had in some form or other been victims of revenge or suspicion; and it is truly wonderful that not a hand, nor even a voice, was raised against the unprotected king.

As for placing himself at the head of the army, his majesty had no army to command. During the whole of Sunday night, boats were going backward and forward between the land and the Spanish vessels with royal property. The queen mother was already in Albano, near Rome.

There was in the bay a most imposing fleet, representing every nation in Europe. Even the Pope had his flag lying off the Villa. On that side of the city there were fourteen vessels of war, and as many off Santa Lucia.

FLIGHT OF THE KING OF NAPLES.

"At 6 o'clock in the evening of September, his majesty went on board a Spanish vessel, and at 8 o'clock left Neapolitan waters. Before leaving, his majesty published his protest, which is given below.

"It would appear that the French admiral thought, with the prefect, that some precautions were necessary, and he therefore called on the British Admiral Mundy in the course of the evening, and announced his intention of sending some men on shore. Admiral M. replied that he saw no necessity for the step, as the city was perfectly tranquil."

PROTEST OF FRANCIS II.

"Since a reckless adventurer, possessing all the force of which revolutionary Europe can dispose, has attacked our dominions, under the name of an Italian sovereign who is both a relation and a friend, we have striven for five months long, with all the means in our power, on behalf of the sacred independence of our states.

" The fortune of war has proved contrary to us. The reckless enterprise of which the above sovereign protested his ignorance in the most formal manner, and which, nevertheless, at the moment when negotiations were going on for an intimate alliance between us, received in his own states its principal support and assistance, that enterprise at which the whole of Europe assisted with indifference, after having proclaimed the principle of non-intervention, leaving us alone to fight against the common enemy, is now upon the point of extending its disastrous effects to our own capital. The forces of the enemy are now approaching this neighborhood.

"On the other hand, both Sicily and the provinces of the continent, which for a long time have been agitated in every manner by a revolution, rising in insurrection under so great an excitement, have formed provisional governments under the title and nominal protection of the above sovereign, and have confided to a pretended dictator full authority and the decision of their destiny.

"Strong in our rights, founded upon history, in international treaty, and in the public law of Europe, we intend to prolong our defence, while it is possible ; yet we are no less determined upon every sacrifice in order to save this vast metropolis, the glorious home of the most ancient memories, the birthplace of national art and civilization, from the horrors of anarchy and civil war.

" In consequence, we shall retire beyond the walls with our army, confiding in the loyalty and the love of our subjects for the preservation of order and for respect being shown to authority.

"In taking this determination we are conscious of a duty which our ancient and uncontested rights, our honor, the interest of our heirs and successors, and more than all, the welfare of our most beloved subjects, have imposed upon us, and therefore we protest loudly against all acts which have been accomplished up to this time, and against the events which are on the point of completion, or which may be accomplished in future. We reserve, then, all our rights and privileges, arising from the most sacred and incontestable laws of succession as well as from the force of treaties, and we declare solemnly that all the aforesaid acts and events are null, void, and of no effect. For what concerns us we leave our cause, and the cause of our people, in the hands of Almighty God, under the firm conviction that during the short space of our reign we have not entertained a single thought that was not devoted to the happiness and the good of our subjects. The institutions which we have irrevocably guaranteed are the proof of this.

" This protest of ours will be transmitted to every court, and we desire that, signed by us, provided with the seal of our royal arms, and countersigned by our minister of foreign affairs, it should be preserved in our royal offices of the exterior, of the privy council and of grace of justice, as a record of our firm resolution always to oppose reason and right to violence and usurpation.

(Signed,)

" FRANCESCO II.
" DE MARTINO.

"NAPLES, *Sept.* 6, 1860."

ROYAL PROCLAMATION.

" Among the duties prescribed to kings, those of the days of misfortunes are the grandest and the most solemn, and I intend to fulfill them with resignation, free from weakness, and with a serene and confident heart, as befits the descendants of so many monarchs.

" For such a purpose I once more address my voice to the people of this metropolis, from whom I am now to depart with bitter grief.

" An unjust war, carried on in contravention to the law of nations, has invaded my states, notwithstanding the fact that I was at peace with all the European powers.

" The changed order of government, and my adhesion to the great principles of Italian nationality, were not sufficient to ward off the war; and, moreover, the necessity of defending the integrity of the state entailed upon me the obligations of events which I have always deplored; therefore, I solemnly protest against this indescribable hostility, concerning which the present and future time will pronounce their solemn verdict.

" The diplomatic corps residing at my court has known since the commencement of this unexpected invasion, with what sentiments my heart has been filled for all my people, as well as for this illustrious city, with a view of securing her from ruin and war, of saving her inhabitants and all their property, her sacred churches, her monuments, her public buildings, her collection of art, and all that which forms the patrimony of her civilization and of her greatness, and which being an inheritance of future generations, is superior to the passions of a day.

" The time has now come to fulfill these professions of mine. The war is now approaching the walls of the city, and with unutterable grief I am now to depart with a portion of my army to betake myself whither the defence of my rights calls me. The remainder of my army remains in company with the honorable national guard, in order to protect the inviolability and safety of the capitol, which I recommend as a sacred treasure to the zeal of the ministry; and I call upon the honor and the civic feeling of the mayor of Naples and of the commandant of the said national guard, to spare this most beloved country of mine the horrors of internal discord and the disasters of civil war; for which purpose I concede to the above-named the widest powers that they may require.

" As a descendant of a dynasty that has reigned over this continent for 126 years, after having preserved it from the horrors of a long vice-royalty, the affections of my heart are here. I am a Neapolitan, nor could I without bitter grief address words of farewell to my most dearly beloved people, to my fellow citizens. Whatever may be my destiny, be it prosperous or adverse, I shall always preserve for them a passionate and affectionate remembrance. I recommend to them concord, peace, and a strict observance of their civic duties. Let not an excessive zeal for my dynasty be made a pretence for disturbance.

" Whether from the fortunes of the present war I return shortly amongst you, or whatever may be the time at which it may please the justice of God to restore me to the throne of my ancestors, a throne made all the more splendid by the free institutions with which I have irrevocably surrounded it, all that I pray from this time forth is to behold again my people united, strong and happy.

" FRANCIS II."

THE LATE KING OF NAPLES DESCRIBED BY HIMSELF.

A late number of the " Revue de Paris" publishes a curious correspondence between Louis Philippe and Ferdinand II., the late King of Naples. Shortly after the revolution of July, Louis Philippe addressed a letter to Ferdinand II., advising him in the government of his kingdom, to relinquish a little so that all might not be lost, to give up his system of compression and severity. " Imitate," said Louis Philippe, " the system in France ; you will be a gainer in every respect ; for, by sacrificing a little authority, you will insure peace to your kingdom and stability to your house.

The symptoms of agitation are so strongly pronounced and numerous in Italy, that an outbreak may be expected sooner or later, accordingly as the stern measures of Prince Metternich may hasten or adjourn it. Your majesty will be drawn into the current if you are not prepared to stem the tide, and your house will be burst in two, either by the revolutionary stream or by the measures of repression the Vienna Cabinet may think fit to adopt. Your majesty may save everything by anticipating voluntarily and with prudence the wishes and wants of your people."

To this excellent advice and very remarkable counsel, coming as it did from a Bourbon, Ferdinand II. returned the following answer :

"To imitate France, if ever France can be imitated, I shall have to precipitate myself into that policy of Jacobinism, for which my people has proved feloniously guilty more than once against the house of its kings. Liberty is fatal to the house of Bourbon ; and, as regards myself, I am resolved to avoid, at all price, the fate of Louis XVI. and Charles X. My people obey force and bend their necks, but woe's me should they ever raise them under the impulse of those dreams which sound so fine in the sermons of philosophers, and which are impossible in practice. With God's blessing, I will give prosperity to my people, and a government as honest as they have a right to ; but I will be king, and always. My people do not want to think ; I take upon myself the care of their welfare and their dignity. I have inherited many old grudges, many mad desires, arising from all the faults and weaknesses of the past ; I must set this to rights, and I can only do so by drawing closer to Austria without subjecting myself to her will. We are not of this century. The Bourbons are ancient, and if they were to try to shape themselves according to the pattern of the new dynasties, they would be ridiculous. We will imitate the Hapsburgs. If fortune plays us false, we shall at least be true to ourselves. Nevertheless, your majesty may rely upon my lively sympathy and my warmest wishes that you may succeed in mastering that ungovernable people who make France the curse of Europe."

Here it was well remarked by a writer :

"We have the father of Francis II. exactly as he was, and exactly as his son has been after him. Out of the lips of the Bourbon it is proved that a Garibaldi was sadly wanted in Sicily. Well, the Garibaldi has come, and the necks of the people bend no more; the people have begun to have a desire to 'think;' have raised their necks ' under the impulse of those dreams which sound so fine in the sermons of philosophers,' and the 'woe's me,' which the Bourbon Ferdinand II. feared would fall upon him when the people did so rise, has fallen upon the head of the Bourbon Francis II. 'The Bourbons are very ancient,' said Ferdinand, 'and if they were to try to shape themselves according to the pattern of the new dynasties, they would be ridiculous.' Well, Francis II., penned up there in Gaeta, with a very small pattern of an army, strikes us as a very ridiculous king, and ridiculous because he did not shape himself according to the pattern of a wise and liberal monarch. This letter of Ferdinand II. is one of the most striking lessons of history that the present century has afforded."

CHAPTER XVI

" Garibaldi ! Garibaldi ! thy glorious career
Is worthy thee and Italy : thy name to man is dear,
A brighter course has never a warrior true displayed :
Unsullied in the hour of peace, in danger undismayed,
Thy heart with every virtue warm, compassion all and love,
In war resistless as the storm, in peace a gentle dove."

MS.

GARIBALDI'S JOURNEY THROUGH CALABRIA—REACHES PALERMO —ENTERS NAPLES—ENTHUSIASM AND GOOD ORDER OF THE PEOPLE—THE NEW GOVERNMENT—THE ARMY AND NAVY—VARIOUS OCCURRENCES.

GARIBALDI, after his wonderful triumph over the royal army in Calabria, made rapid marches through the wild regions of that part of the peninsula toward Naples. By rising early, pressing on and resting but little, he performed a journey of about two hundred and eighty miles to Salerno, in a fortnight from the day of his landing at Reggio.

Before Garibaldi's entry into Naples, the Sardinian admiral had threatened to fire upon any Neapolitan vessel which should attempt to proceed to Gaeta.

A *Te Deum* had been celebrated in the cathedral by Father Gavazzi, the people shouting "Hurrah for Victor Emanuel !" "Hurrah for Garibaldi !" The people were armed, some even with pikes and sticks.

General illuminations had taken place. The Papal Nuncio, a great part of the ambassadors, and Count Trapani, had followed the king to Gaeta. The king had appointed Signor Ulloa, brother of General Ulloa, as his prime minister, and had issued a proclamation.

On the morning of the 7th of September, Garibaldi was at Salerno, a town near the southern extremity of the vast and splendid bay of Naples, and about thirty miles distant from the capital, preparing to proceed to it by the railroad. The love with which he attaches his friends to him was evident, in the manner in which his personal staff clung to him at the station. Very few accompanied him ; but 25,000 troops were to follow him in four days.

The following account of Garibaldi in Salerno, is from a letter of Mr. Edwin James to a friend :

" The long roll of the ' spirit-stirring drums,' the discordant noises of the Calabrese soldiers as they were endeavoring to form their ranks, the dashing in of carriages from Naples with their cargoes of deputations to attend Garibaldi, roused me before four o'clock, September 7th, from my bed, in a wretched ' albergo' in Salerno, where I had been the prey of mosquitoes since midnight. Garibaldi was astir as early as four o'clock ; he had seen members of the committee from Naples, and was arranging his *entrée* into the city. At my interview with him yesterday at Eboli, which was a hurried one, he had requested me to see him in the evening ; he was so surrounded by crowds of admirers, all anxious for a glimpse at the ' great man,' that I delayed my interview until this morning. On entering the large rooms of the Hôtel de Ville, or ' Intendenza,' the throngs of people and their agitation and excitement were most striking.

" The national guard of Salerno lined the avenues ; priests of every denomination crowded to touch the ' hem of his garment. Officers of State of the king were in earnest conversation with him, urging his coming without delay into Naples.

" A special train of about 20 carriages was in waiting at 10 o'clock, and we obtained a seat in the carriage next to that in which Garibaldi was. Throughout the journey to Naples, in every village, at every station, the joy and enthusiasm of the people exceeded the powers of description. Women and girls presented flags, threw flowers into the carriages, struggled to kiss the hand of the general. Mayors and syndics ejaculated their gratulations ; priests and monks stood, surrounded by their wretched flocks, on the hill-side, and shouted their ' Vivas,' and holding the crucifix in one hand and the sword in the other, waved them in the air, and bawled out their benedictions. As the train passed the king's guard at Portici, the soldiers threw their caps into the air, and joined lustily in the ' Viva Garibaldi !' "

It was reported in Naples, about eleven o'clock, that Garibaldi was to arrive that day, and a great part of the inhabitants, on first hearing the news, hastened to the station. A detachment of national guards marched with the national colors flying, and in the yard assembled all the leading liberals in their carriages, the secret committee, now no longer concealed, and several foreign ministers, including the French, M. Brenier, to do honor to the hero.

"Many ladies were in the waiting-saloon, which was crowded with national guards and gentlemen in plain clothes and all sorts of uniforms.

"After waiting an hour (writes a spectator), shouts were heard, and the scream of an arriving train. 'He is come!' The train steams in. In the first carriage, standing on the roof, is a giant of a man, with a cap, a red shirt, and the handkerchief fastened on his shoulders. The cries and cheers increase. Suddenly all is hushed again, and we are down to zero. It is only a train of disarmed Bavarians en route from Salerno. At last he does come. The enthusiasm is overpowering. Surrounded by a band of soldiers, sons of Anak as to size, and dressed in the wild and travel-stained costumes of an irregular army on a campaign, comes Garibaldi. The first thing that strikes you is his face, and the deep determination of his extraordinary forehead. A face that might serve as a model for the sculptor, is softened almost to sweetness by the mildness of the eyes and the low tone of the most musical voice I have ever heard. Long, grizzly curls hang from his broad hat. He wears a red shirt with a silk handkerchief on his shoulders, like the 'panuelo' of the South American, and grey trousers. He escapes as well and as soon as he can from a reception, which he accepts rather than covets, and proceeds to take possession of his new abode.

"Garibaldi entered the private carriage of the French minister, his staff following in other carriages, and some few on horseback; the cortége consisted of about twenty vehicles. Individually I have never seen such men as his body-guard, and the picturesque dress sets off their height and the squareness of their build. Compared with these soldiers, Garibaldi is short, but very powerfully made. Along the crowded Marinelli, the headquarters of lazzaroni, now constitutional popolani, one of whom rode before Garibaldi's carriage, through the Largo del Castello, the Strada di Toledo, and finally to the Palazzo della Regina di Savoia, opposite the Palazzo Reale, which the dictator refused to inhabit, the cortége makes its way, and Garibaldi enters into what was once a palace of the Bourbons. The shouts of the

crowd now gathered together in the square penetrate the inmost re-
cesses, and presently the window opens and Garibaldi appears, followed by a large staff of officials. The others stop, and he advances
alone to the centre of the balcony that extends along the palace, and
the cheering is deafening. It is no use for the hero to speak till the
people have a little exhausted their powers ; so he stands there alone,
leaning on his hand, with his fine features in repose, and an almost
melancholy expression on his face, as if he felt that his career was a
duty which had its thorns as well as its roses ; and that, though the
end sanctifies the means, yet carnage and slaughter, tottering thrones
and crumbling dynasties, leave their impression on the brow that
caused them. I have never seen so grand a study as Garibaldi, as he
stood silently speculating, perhaps, over the true value of the people
whom he had just freed. He spoke at some length, but it was impossible to distinguish what he said, though it was easy to perceive that
he speaks with great energy. Having satisfied, for the moment at
least, the desires of the bassa-gente (the populace), it was time to re-
enter the palace and receive the welcome of the upper classes. The
stair and entrée to the dictator's levée were an extraordinary spectacle. The door leading to the suite of apartments in which the general
held his reception was kept by the national guard, who were perpe-
tually assailed by persons desiring to see the dictator ' face to face.'
Men of all nations and in all costumes seemed suddenly to have
started up in the heart of Naples.

"The reception was brief—even Garibaldi requires repose—and
after having appeared on both sides of the palace, and received the
compliments of all classes, including a Venetian deputy, who said,
' We are ready, and only await Garibaldi,' to which the dictator replied,
with a quiet smile, 'Aspetta, aspetta!' (Wait, wait), he retired from
the palazzo to his quarters in the Palazzo Angri, Strada Toledo, where
another ovation awaited him. On his way he went to the cathedral,
and was received with due honors. The generality of priests have
retired to their cells, but many are still about, and I met one in the
presence chambers in full canonicals, crossed by a tri-colored scarf,
and bearing an enormous Sardinian flag—' *Tempora mutantur et nos.*'"

On Saturday, the 8th, there was a sudden commotion in
the Castelnovo, on the shore, a description of which will
convey a just idea of the state of Naples and the garrison.
A spectator wrote :

" One of those uproarious bursts of applause which come upon us like hurricanes, called me to the window. The soldiers in the garrison at the Castelnovo had just burst out, and were running, jumping, galloping past my house like so many slaves who had burst out of the house of bondage. Some were armed with muskets; most had their sacks full of loaves of bread, which dropped from their wallets as they ran along, shouting, like so many madmen, 'Viva Garibaldi!' At every step they met with crowds of men and women, armed with naked swords, daggers, and pikes, which they flourished in the air, uttering at the same time the usual magic cries. Dirty-looking fellows, in the Neapolitan uniform, were hugged and kissed by persons as dirty as themselves, and then uniting, all surged onward to the Toledo. It was impossible to remain in the house, and escaping from my chains, which fell from me as soon as the post left, I hurried into the street. I turn round to Criatamone, and just above me, peering over the walls, I see a number of soldiers in garrison in the Pizzofalcone, and watching if the road was clear. The people about me were waving their hands to them, and inviting them to come down. There are iron doors at the bottom, and sentinels stand by them. Down come the troops in a torrent— sentinels are motionless, the doors bend, at last yield, and at length out they come like so many madmen out of Bedlam, and run after their companions from the Castelnovo. Sentinels still stand, 'pro formâ,' at the doors of both the forts, but they are abandoned, and empty walls and harmless cannon alone remain to be guarded. Meanwhile, Garibaldi is going to Pie di Grotta, like another Emperor Carlo III., on the first day of his entry into Naples. Carriages dash by me full of red jackets, or of men and women brandishing swords and pikes, whilst the rain is pouring down in torrents, and the thunder is pealing, as if it were a salute of heaven for the liberator of the Two Sicilies. The weather prevented any grand display, though the disposition was not wanting on the part of the people, as the flags which hung down lank from the windows abundantly showed. The weather brightened up toward the evening, and the town was more brilliantly illuminated than last night. There can be no mistake about the matter, the enthusiasm is very great. People are beside themselves, and scenes are witnessed which, perhaps, have never been witnessed in any other country under the sun. Two lines of carriages go up and down the Toledo filled with persons decorated with tri-colored ribbons and scarfs, and carrying the flag of Piedmont, or rather of Italy. There are people of every class : there are priests and monks, as gaily decorated as any, and some are armed ; there are women in the Garibaldian dress, and many carry daggers or pikes; there are red jackets of Garibaldi and red jackets of England; there are people from the provinces, who have scarcely dared to speak or breathe for twelve long years, who are now frantic with joy. What wonder if they have lost their senses?

"But many adjourn to San Carlo,* for Garibaldi is to be there, and, indeed, one of our autumnal hurricanes of rain is coming down. I was there when he arrived, and we knew of his approach from the shouts of the populace outside. Every one is standing and craning over his seat to catch a view of the great man, and at last he enters the stage box, while many of his followers take possession of the neighboring boxes, and a storm of applause greets him, and calls him to the front. There are few spectacles so brilliant as San Carlo when lighted up in gala fashion; and this evening particularly, with the banners waving from the boxes, and from above the stage, it showed better than I have ever before seen it; but altogether the demonstration was a failure. The theatre was not two-thirds full, and when those two magnificent pieces of music were performed, the 'Hymn of Garibaldi' and 'The Chorus of the Lombardi,' not a voice joined in. I wanted, together with my friends, to raise a chorus on our own account, for it was irritating enough to witness a number of people sitting and fanning themselves, as though they came to be amused, instead of pouring out their very souls in honor of the great man who had liberated them. I shall not say anything more of San Carlo. On my road home, a poor fellow was found not far from my door with a dagger in his body. I regret to say that several, if not many, cases of assassination have occurred during the last three days. Political fanatics have stopped every one, and threatened them with the knife if they were not prompt in crying out 'Viva Garibaldi;' and private vengeance has demanded its victims too, perhaps. But, take it altogether, the people have not been sanguinary, and, considering the immense provocation which they have received, order has been wonderfully preserved, and little blood shed."

Garibaldi, from the first, gratified the Neapolitans, by appointing natives to office. All public officers were, for the moment, retained in their old stations. The holding of several offices by one and the same person was forbidden, and pluralists were to select, within five days, which office they would retain.

---

* This theatre is one of the most splendid in Europe, and has five galleries, all entirely covered with gilding.

All military men willing to serve were ordered to present themselves at the nearest station, give in their adhesion to the actual government, and take their certificate of it.

Those officers who presented themselves with their troops were retained in their positions in full activity; those who presented themselves alone were placed in the second class, to be employed when the army is reformed; those who did not send in their adhesion in ten days were excluded.

The "Official Journal" of Naples of Sept. 9th, published a series of decrees, of which the following are the most important: All the acts of public authority and of administration are to be issued in the name of His Majesty Victor Emanuel, King of Italy, and all the seals of state, of public administration, and of the public offices, are to bear the arms of the Royal House of Savoy, with the legend, "Victor Emanuel, King of Italy." The public debt of the Neapolitan state was recognized; the public banks were to continue their payments, as also the Discount Bank, according to existing laws and regulations. Passports for the United Italian States were abolished; those for foreign states and Italian states not united were to be signed by the Director of Police. The following address to the army was published:

"If you do not disdain Garibaldi for your companion in arms, he only desires to fight by your side the enemies of the country. Truce, then, to discord—the chronic misfortune of our land. Italy, trampling on the fragments of her chains, points to the north—the path of honor, toward the last lurking-place of tyrants. I promise you nothing more than to make you fight.

" G. GARIBALDI.

"NAPLES, Sept. 10."

A series of dispatches was published from Nola, Benevento, Aquila, and a host of other places, expressive of the public joy at the arrival of the Dictator in the capital. In Arriano and Avellino there had been a reactionary movement among the liberals. Some disturbances also took place in Canosa, and in the island of Ischia.

In Naples, the castles had all capitulated, and were in the hands of the National Guard. The population gradually settled down into its usual sober state, which had recently been disturbed by the madness of exultation, and before that by apprehension.

Naples continued tranquil on the 11th of July, to the surprise of everybody ; and the means by which the public peace was preserved at that time and afterward, may well be a subject of curious inquiry. The public anticipations of mobs, violence, robbery and bloodshed were as much and as agreeably disappointed, as when the *"levée en masse"* in Turkey was disbanded after the Russian war, and the soldiers went home joyfully and peaceably. The truth is, that men who desire power, wealth, and undeserved honors, have too long accused their less ambitious or vicious fellow-beings of needing their government. Naples with her 70,000 lazzaroni, who are destitute even of shelter at night, remained quiet during and subsequently to one of the most peaceful revolutions on record.

The following accounts were reported on the 11th of September :

The tranquillity of the town had not been disturbed, and the same enthusiasm still prevailed. The Elmo and the other forts have surrendered. The English admiral paid a visit to Garibaldi, who afterward went on board the Hannibal, the English ambassador being present. On that occasion the Sardinian fleet fired a salute of seventeen guns in honor of the dictator. The Sardinian troops disembarked by order of the Dictator. It was said that the king, in leaving Naples, ordered the bombardment of the town and the burning of the royal castle, and that the original of the order has been found. The king had formed a new royalist ministry, the members of which are Caselli, Canofini, Girolamo, and Ulloa. The Austrian, Russian, Prussian, and Spanish ministers, and

Papal nuncio, had followed the king to Gaeta. The whole army of Garibaldi was to arrive at Naples in four days, and, with the revolutionary bands, the total force was 20,000 or 30,000 men. The revolution was everywhere triumphant. The Bixio and Medici brigades had just arrived in port. The entrance of Garibaldi into Naples was celebrated at Milan in the most enthusiastic manner. The whole city was illuminated and decorated with flags. The very name of the dictator inspired electric enthusiasm. A number of illuminated drums, fixed on long poles, were carried through the streets. The drums bore significant inscriptions, as follow : " To Rome !" " To Venice !" " Rome, the capital !" Most cities of Italy celebrated the annexation of Naples.

The Neapolitan navy, which had deserted, all together, to Garibaldi, he delivered to the Sardinian admiral. The Neapolitan navy is of very respectable size, taking a place in respect to materiel at least above the second rank in Europe. It does not fall much below that of the United States. The whole number of vessels amounts to ninety, carrying 786 guns, with a complement of upward of 7,000 sailors and officers of all sorts. Of the vessels, 27 are propelled by steam. Of these, one is of large size, carrying 60 guns ; 11 are frigates, armed with 10 guns each ; 8 corvettes, with 8 guns each, besides seven smaller vessels, each with four guns. Of the sixty or more sailing vessels, the largest is armed with 80 guns. There are five frigates, carrying an aggregate of 252 guns, or about 50 each. Among the rest are bomb and mortar boats in considerable number, and others armed with Paixhan guns. These latter have been found useful by the king, when he has felt inclined to indulge his propensity of knocking down the palaces and cities of his disobedient subjects.

GARIBALDI'S PROCLAMATION TO THE CITIZENS OF NAPLES.

"To the beloved population of Naples, offspring of the people ! It is with true respect and love that I present myself to this noble and imposing centre of the Italian population, which many centuries of despotism have not been able to humiliate or to induce to bow their knees at the sight of tyranny.

"The first necessity of Italy was harmony, in order to unite the great Italian family; to-day Providence has created harmony through the sublime unanimity of all our provinces for the reconstitution of the nation, and for unity, the same Providence has given to our country Victor Emanuel, whom we from this moment may call the true father of our Italian land.

"Victor Emanuel, the model of all sovereigns, will impress upon his descendants the duty that they owe to the prosperity of a people which has elected him for their chief with enthusiastic devotion. The Italian priests, who are conscious of their true mission, have, as a guaranty of the respect with which they will be treated, the ardor, the patriotism, and the truly Christian conduct of their numerous fellow ecclesiastics, who, from the highly to be praised monks of Lagracia to the noble-hearted priests of the Neapolitan continent, one and all, in the sight and at the head of our soldiers, defied the gravest dangers of battle. I repeat it, concord is the first want of Italy, so we will welcome as brothers those who once disagreed with us, but now sincerely wish to bring their stone to raise up the monument of our country. Finally, respecting other people's houses: we are resolved to be masters in our own house, whether the powerful of the earth like it or not.

"GIUSEPPE GARIBALDI."

The following were some of the occurrences in Naples immediately after the entrance of Garibaldi.

The four battalions of chasseurs whom the king had left behind in his flight, quartered here and there about the town, disbanded. Many of the soldiers went home; those who wished to remain at Naples, secure from harm, did obeisance to the new powers, by wearing a small badge with the Savoy cross on their breasts. The fortress of St. Elmo followed the example of the fleet. It fired a thundering salvo in honor of Garibaldi, hoisted the Sardinian colors, and admitted the national guards within its walls. The other forts were garrisoned by this same burgher militia. Naples, in short, was now wholly in the hands of the patriots, and Garibaldi had already pushed forward one or two brigades, which gained

possession of the royal palace of Caserta. The king had shut
the gates of Capua. There and at Gaeta he was to abide
till his enemies should come on. Meanwhile Garibaldi,
master of the seas, sent his steamers to Paola, to Sapri, to
all the small ports near which his overtasked legions lingered
behind. Every morning were shouts of a joyous landing and
a triumphant march of those several brigades. The whole
force was soon brought together, and the respite allowed to
the king at Gaeta was of no long duration.

The joy of the good Neapolitans at their cheaply-gotten ·
emancipation, became daily more noisy and frantic. Every
evening the Toledo was all alive with banners and torches,
with thronged masses of possessed people, all shouting out
with all the might of their southern throats, that favorite
cry, " *Una! Una! Una?*"—conveying their desire that all
Italy should be made *one* country. There was a grand gala
night at San Carlo, when the proscenium, the pit, and the
boxes became one vast stage. The whole performance consisted of *Io Pæans* to Garibaldi, who, calm and serene in his
homely garb, had a pleasant word for all the friends who
surrounded him in his box, and was, in fact, less insensible
to that popular demonstration than he might have wished to
avow.

One of the greatest objects of interest was the easily-won
castle St. Elmo. The whole population of Naples, male and
female, seemed bent on performing a pilgrimage to that shrine
of their patriot martyrs.

One of Garibaldi's soldiers thus described it :

" Yesterday I went up myself with a party of friends. We first
walked through St. Martin's marble church and monastery, where our
Garibaldian red shirts, I dare say, boded little good to the white-
cowled monks, who gazed at us as we passed, tall, stately, and motionless, so that we at first mistook them for statues ;—good Carthu-
sian monks, doing penance in a marble paradise, bound by vow to
perpetual silence, and affecting an easy, unconcerned air, though in
their heart of hearts, probably, trembling not a little for the visible

and invisible treasures of which their sanctuary has been, time out of mind, the repository.

"From the marble cells of the monks to the iron dungeons of the victims of Castle St. Elmo the transition is but short, but the contrast is appalling. The stone steps wind down six floors, and at every floor room was made for about half a score of victims. Some of the miserable cells had windows; but, as the view from the hill over the loveliest panorama of land and sea would have been too great a solace to the lonely captive, the window was latticed over by thick wooden bars, not intended to prevent escape—for from that height only a bird could attempt it—but simply to rob the poor recluse of the distant view of his familiar scenes. In the lowest floor there is no window to the dungeons—only a little wicket in the door, opening outwardly, for the gaoler to communicate with the prisoner if he has a mind. That wicket would be opened one moment in the morning to let in a little bread and water; then the wicket would fall to, and for twenty-four hours all would be darkness inside.

"I do not like to witness horrors, much less to dwell upon them, else I could tell you of the loopholes we were shown, through which the sentries could shoot the prisoners in their cells and their beds. I could repeat the instances of wholesale executions of Swiss and Sicilian mutineers of which St. Elmo has been the theatre, and of which the world never knew anything. The caitiffs who were but yesterday in the king's pay are eager to promulgate abroad the infamy of his doings, and I have no doubt St. Elmo will soon become the subject of books or pamphlets, yielding but little in interest to the stories of La Bastille, of which it will soon share the fate.

"The good people of Naples are bent upon demolishing St. Elmo, and are only awaiting the dictator's bidding to lay hand to the work. A tough job they will find it, I am sure. As I was walking yesterday along the upper battlements the impatient citizens were already busy pulling back the huge brass guns, each of which was most offensively pointed at some of the most densely crowded quarters of the town, and turning their muzzles inward. What a fortress that was, and what a protection to the city! It was no bad emblem of the whole sea and land might of the Bourbon—worse than useless against foreign aggression, wholly and exclusively directed to crush internal commotion."

The condition of Naples on the 12th of September was thus described in a private letter of that date :

"There is much to be done here, and Garibaldi is doing it well. It is impossible to take up a journal, or move about in the midst of

17

the vast crowds which throng the capital, without feeling that a master-spirit is here. Long before the city has shaken off its slumber, the dictator is up and driving about. Yesterday he went to visit Nisida, and surprised the British library, on his return, with a visit at half-past six o'clock A.M , wishing to purchase some books. During the day he was hard at work receiving visitors and legislating, and the following are some of the fruits of his labors :

"All political prisoners are to be liberated immediately. All custom-house barriers between Sicily and the Neapolitan continent are abolished. Twelve infant asylums, one for each quarter, are to be established in the capital at the public expeuse, and are to be municipal institutions. Secret ministerial funds are abolished. The trial by jury in criminal cases is to be established. The order of Jesuits, with all their dependencies, is abolished in the territory. Two Sicilies, and their property declared national. All contracts on property for the benefit of the order are annulled. Considering that religious fanaticism and aristocratic pride induced the late government to make distinctions even between the dead, the burial of the dead is henceforward absolutely forbidden within the walls of a city. The traffic in grain and flour with Ancona is prohibited.

"All these decrees have a history attached to them, which, if narrated, would tell of sufferings and persecutions almost incredible. They are admirable, and in themselves amount to a beneficial revolution; but the better and the more sweeping the changes that are introduced, the greater the necessity for some established government.

"His majesty, Francis II. has already formed his ministry, and placed at the head of it Gen. Cotruffiano ; and among his colleagues are Caselli, Ulloa—not the general—and Canofari, all of the legal profession.

"MM. Maniscalchi, father and son, notorious for having been the most active agents of the late king's tyranny at Palermo, were arrested on the 7th, at Caserta, and taken under escort to Naples."

Another letter, written on the same day, gave the following additional particulars :

"Troops are continually coming in and marching to the frontier. The Piedmontese admiral, with another steam frigate and the ex-Neapolitan ships, is in the harbor.

"I hear the sound of cracked trumpets, and, looking out, see the first ranks of a Garibaldi division coming down the Santa Lucia. I am struck by the youthful appearance of some, certainly not more than twelve, or at the furthest fourteen years old—fair, pretty-looking boys, who might have had a satchel instead of a knapsack on their backs. There were, however, some glorious-looking fellows, and all, whether men or boys, seemed to be animated by a spirit little known to the Neapolitan troops. The latter were a sect to defend a vile political creed, and inflict chastisement on those who opposed it; but the former are banded together to assert the sacred rights of liberty. I saw it in their march; there was an elasticity about it which denoted what was passing within. *I cannot say much for their uniforms; they were very dirty, out of order, and irregular, and I have no doubt but that so eminent a general officer as Ferdinand II. would have been much scandalized; but they were evidently working men, had an object in view, and were not going to fight for money. I have seen hundreds of them about the town to-day; they are billeted about in the hotels and lodging-houses, while the Piedmontese troops are in Castel-Ovo.

"The city is in immense confusion—crowded, picturesque, almost mad. Foreigners seem to outnumber the Neapolitans, and the red jacket every other colored cloth. Such a Babel is every public place that I imagine myself to be living some thousand years back—Englishmen just arrived, hob-nobbing with Italians, whose only common lingo is that of the fingers. Many of our countrymen came on Tuesday, and I watched some of them carrying on a most animated, though purely gesticulatory, conversation with Frenchmen yesterday morning."

After the peaceful and triumphal entry of Garibaldi into Naples, new rumors were put into circulation of a pretended disagreement between him and the King of Sardinia. These were most satisfactorily refuted by the measures which the victorious general adopted immediately afterward. On the 14th of July, he proclaimed the government of Victor Emanuel, placed all the ships of war and commerce, the arsenals and materials of marine, by decree, at the disposal of Sardinia, and put them into the hands of Admiral Persaro; the portfolio of the interior was confirmed to Liborio Romano, the only member of the late ministry who enjoyed the confidence of the people. The choice of Scialoia, who had already left Genoa to assume the ministry of finance, was very generally applauded. Two battalions of genuine Piedmontese Bersaglieri were landed from the Sardinian men-of-war,

and took possession of the Darsena.   Telegraphic orders were
sent for two more Piedmontese regiments to garrison the
Neapolitan forts.   By taking the Neapolitan marine under
its command, and occupying the strongholds, dockyards and
arsenals about this place, the Sardinian government committed itself more openly to the annexation of these kingdoms than it ever dared to do in the case of Tuscany or
Romagna last year.   And all these measures were taken
not only with the consent but by the express desire of Garibaldi, who certainly exhibited no apprehension that the
king's government would interfere with his vast undertakings.

The extreme joy with which the news of Garibaldi's
entrance into Naples was received by all classes and parties,
from Messina to the Alps, can be best understood by those
who know the detestation with which the oppression and
vindictive cruelty of the late government were universally
regarded.   This feeling was greatly increased by the disappointment of the nation in all those hopes to which the
death of Ferdinand had given birth, and the conviction that
his successor was determined to tread in his father's steps
rather than enter sincerely on any new course.   When
Francis II. ascended the throne, it was felt that a young
monarch, above all, one educated as he had been, had every
claim to public consideration, and very sincere hopes were
for the time entertained, that he would cease to follow the
beaten track of Bourbon perjury and despotism, and frankly
identify himself with the wants and aspirations of his country.   Possessing, through his mother, a considerable hold
on the affections of his subjects, and succeeding a sovereign
who was detested by his people, he had an excellent position,
and by a judicious system of even moderate reforms, might
have conciliated all parties and opposed a successful barrier
to the tide of revolution that was soon to sweep over the
landmarks of Italy.

The amnesty was followed by a " circular " which struck
at its very root and replaced thousands under the surveil-

lance of the police. Then came the infamous and illegal deportation to Capri of men who had never been put upon their trial, and upon whose liberation England had insisted, through her minister, in the strongest terms. A system was pursued that has been characterized as a perpetual violation of all law, and a practical denial of Christianity.

The general satisfaction felt by the people of Naples after Garibaldi's arrival amounted to enthusiasm. An Englishman, writing from that city on the 14th of July, thus described the aspect of the people :

"I do not know Naples now, so changed is its aspect. Faces that I have not seen for twelve years appear in every street and square. They have come from foreign exile ; from confinement in some frontier town or village ; from some voluntary lurking place, the retirement to which was their only security from persecution ; from the prison and the bagnio ; all have met together again, by hundreds and thousands, in the capital of what was once the two Sicilies. Revolution is said to turn the dregs uppermost ; yet the appearance and manner of those who now appear on the scene contradict the common proverb. In their very attitude, there is an air of self-respect and independence to which I have long been a stranger. I do not see the assumption or the swagger of the overbearing, or the timidity of the man who leaves his friend, and walks on before, because a spy is coming, or whispers and looks over his shoulder for fear that such a person is listening. No ; all this has passed away, and I meet erect, independent men. My life here has brought me, too, into frequent intercourse with them ; and, accustomed as I have been to the trivialities and the nullities rendered at first necessary, and afterward habitual, by despotism, I have been astonished at the new tone of thought and conversation. The Neapolitans now reason and talk like men, and there is a degree of self-restraint about them which is in the highest degree creditable after the sufferings to which they have been so long exposed. It is clear that the intellect of the country has for years been out of it, or in seclusion, or in imprisonment. Nor is this to be wondered at, when ignorance was rewarded and learning discouraged by those twins of darkness, the sovereign and the clergy, and the only hopes of the Bourbons and the Vatican depend upon brutalizing the national mind. Ferdinand II. it was who interrupted a father describing the acquirements of his son by

saying, 'Better he had a stone round his neck, and be thrown into
the sea;' and it was a priest who held a high public office, who
checked a person indulging in a similar style of speaking by saying
that it would be well for the rising generation to be 'little asses and
little saints.' These times are, however, passing away; heaven grant
that the light of freedom and intelligence may not dazzle the as yet
unaccustomed vision of the natives.

"We have likenesses of Victor Emanuel and of Garibaldi in every
shop window, and multitudes crowd around them to admire; in
short, there is at present a *furia* for the *Re Galantuomo* and the
Hero of Sicily."

The prisons of the police were thus described by the same
writer :

"I yesterday saw some of them. Several members of the commission appointed to close them—themselves once prisoners here—
accompanied me. A grated door led down to an ante-chamber,
which was lighted only through these bars. Stone walls, stone floor
—stone everywhere, except the ground, which was covered over with
burnt fragments of books, that had been taken in domiciliary visits
and destroyed here. 'Here one breathes,' said a pardoned prisoner;
'but bring a light,' he said to a jailer, and we descended from this
twilight room into another which received the reflection of the twilight through a hole in the door. It was small and of stone—nothing
but stone—and on the right I observed a stone bed three feet high
from the ground, with an elevation of stone called a pillow. A door is
opened and leads into another room, where no twilight, no reflected
twilight, nor a ray of light nor a breath of air can penetrate. 'I
was imprisoned here,' said one of my conductors. I looked at him
as if expecting to find that he was turned into a brute beast, for it
was a den for a wild animal, not a chamber for a Christian man, in a
country teeming with Christ's ministers, and where the holy Apostolic
Catholic religion is the only one permitted to be professed. In some
parts a man could not stand upright, so that there he lay in Stygian
darkness, without any change of air, 'and on bare ground,' said my
friend, 'unless he could afford to pay an extortionate price for a mat-
tress, to a licensed spy and denouncer, who drove a good trade in
human misery.' 'Let us leave this den,' I said, and so we groped
back into the chamber where the reflection of twilight penetrated.
'Take care,' cried the jailer, as I stumbled over a mountain of old
books and papers. On the opposite side was another *criminale*

about eleven by five palms, where five or six persons were at times confined. The smell of the prison was insufferable. Now mark, who were the men confined in these places not fit for beasts? Not condemned criminals; no! but men arrested on suspicion and waiting for an order for their committal—men of rank and education accustomed to the comforts of a home."

The following passages from a letter written at Florence, are very appropriate in this place :

"The ministry appointed by the Dictator is a liberal but moderate one. Garibaldi is in earnest in his devotion to the King of Sardinia, and in his determination to unite Italy under his rule. It is to be hoped that he will, as soon as may be, commence the work of raising the Neapolitan people out of some of the absurd superstitions which have always kept them in ignorance, and made them the serfs of juggling priests. He has not yet countenanced, by his presence at the operation, the ridiculous juggle of the liquefaction of the blood of Saint Januarius, which is held in such high esteem by the Neapolitans, that all the conquerors of the city have heretofore been obliged to respect it. Saint Januarius, according to tradition, was exposed to be devoured by lions in the amphitheatre of Pozzuoli, when the animals, instead of devouring him, prostrated themselves before him, and immediately became tame. So many persons were converted to Christianity by this miracle, that the saint was ordered to be decapitated, which was done at Solfatara, in the year 305, and the body was buried at Pozzuoli, until the time of Constantine, when it was removed by St. Severus, the Bishop of Naples, and deposited in the church of St. Gennaro. When this removal was made, the woman who is said to have collected the blood at the time of the execution, took it in two small bottles to St. Severus, in whose hands it is said to have immediately melted. After undergoing several removals, the body of the saint was brought back to Naples in 1497, and deposited with great pomp in the cathedral, and the phials containing the blood secured in a tabernacle kept securely locked with two keys, one of which is kept by the archbishop and the other by the municipal authorities. Twice a year, and at other times, on extraordinary occasions, the phials are brought out, and the clots of dried blood, by some chemical process which has been secretly preserved among the priesthood and handed down for four centuries, made to liquefy and run in the phials. Can a people appreciate and derive much benefit from free institutions so long as they permit their senses to be cheated by such a palpable swindle as this?

"But if detestation for young Bomba and his government have been heightened by his flight, how much more grandly than ever Garibaldi looms up in the light of a brave, noble, disinterested, patriotic man. Three months from the day when he left Genoa with a handful of adventurers, denounced as a filibuster and a pirate by the lovers of legitimacy and tyranny, he enters Naples with but five of his staff, knowing that his deeds had made him a home in the hearts of the people there, who welcome him as their angel of deliverance. Naples lights up with joy—the free flag of Italy waves from her windows, her long oppressed citizens shout exultingly, and crown the hero with wreaths of laurel, and fill his ears with glad cries of 'Long live Garibaldi.' Well does he deserve them. Five marvellous stages mark the progress of the hero, Marsala, Palermo, Malazzo, Reggio, and Naples, all passed over in the short space of three months—and this has been all the time which Garibaldi required, supported as he was by the national sentiment, to overthrow a monarchy deemed immovable, which, not four years since, defied France and England, and which in the face of the naval preparations of the two greatest powers of the world, had determined to persevere in its resistance. Such triumphs, such ovations, would have turned the brain of a weaker or more ambitious man, and Garibaldi has given the lie to those adherents of tyranny who have charged him with personal ambition, by immediately, upon taking possession of the capital of the Two Sicilies, proclaiming the territory and himself under the reign and rule of Victor Emanuel. In future ages, when the deeds of the Cæsars and the Alexanders and the Napoleons shall be appreciated as they deserve, according to their merits, how high above them all will rise the memory of the two greatest of the world's heroes, of the two men whose personal ambition was merged and forgotten in the welfare of their country, of two men worthy to stand ever side by side and hand in hand—Washington and Garibaldi."

CHAPTER XVII.

"Thou, Æneas' nurse, Caieta, gav'st thy name,
  In dying, to our shores, with deathless fame;
  Thy name the place shall keep, thy bones shall guard,
  In great Hesperia, if that be reward."
                          Virgil's Æneid, Book vii. T. D.

THE GOOD ORDER IN NAPLES—ITS CAUSES—GARIBALDI VISITS PA-
LERMO—RETURNS—THE KING AND HIS ARMY AT GAETA AND
CAPUA—DESCRIPTION AND HISTORY OF GAETA AND CAPUA—
PRESENT CONDITION OF GAETA.

In what a peculiar, unexpected, and unaccountable condition must the minds of the citizens of Naples have been
before and after the arrival of Garibaldi! Whoever has
visited that city, as thousands of our countrymen have done,
and, while admiring the celebrated climate and scenery,
observed the poverty, ignorance, superstition, and idleness
of the mass of the people, especially the Lazzaroni—seventy
thousand of whom, it has often been asserted, have no home
or shelter, or certain means of subsistence—must have been
ready to believe that scenes of lawless violence might be excited there with great facility, and that riots might occur if
the government were weakened even for a moment. How
strong and general, then, must have been the salutary influences at work to preserve peace and order in that population
of nearly a million, under the circumstances which have been
reviewed! What could possibly have secured such results
but the faithful care of wise and good men? The patriotic
committee must have been successful in their efforts to enlighten people of all classes, and to instill patriotic sentiments into the hearts even of the Lazzaroni themselves; and
they and the rulers must have been well acquainted with the
effects which had thus been produced, or they would never

17*

have suffered, much less invited, Garibaldi to enter Naples as he did, with only a few unarmed friends, and meet with so peaceful and kind a reception.

On the 17th of September, Garibaldi made a flying visit to Palermo, in the Neapolitan steamer Electrica. His arrival was entirely unexpected ; but, on his way from the landing to the palace, he was recognized by the crowd, who followed and assembled beneath the palace windows. He made his appearance on the balcony, and addressed them in these words :

"People of Palermo, with whom I have shared fatigues, perils and glory, I am once more among you. Your memory is dear to me, and whatever part of the world I may be in, I will always think of you.

"Those who wished to urge you to a speedy annexation, were putting you in the wrong path. If I had followed their advice, I should not have crossed the Straits and restored seven millions of men to Italy.

"They would have prostrated us at the feet of diplomacy, which would have bound us hand and foot. There would have been brothers beyond the Vulturnus, with chains on their ankles. People of Palermo, I thank you in the name of Italy for your resistance. I love Italy and Victor Emanuel; no one is a greater friend than myself of Victor Emanuel, the representative of Italy. You despised their counsels, and I thank you for it, you invincible people of the barricades."

The following proclamation was isued by Garibaldi to the inhabitants of Palermo :

"The people of Palermo, who showed no fear in face of those who bombarded their city, have shown themselves recently equally regardless of fear in face of corrupt men, who want to lead them astray.

"They have spoken to you of annexation, as if any one was more fervent than myself for the regeneration of Italy; but their object was to serve personal interests, and you replied like a people who felt its own dignity, and placed confidence in the sacred and unviolated programme which I proclaimed—'Italy and Victor Emanuel.'

"At Rome, people of Palermo, we will proclaim the kingdom of Italy, and there only will be sanctified the great family-bond between free men and those who are still slaves of the same country.

"At Palermo annexation was demanded, that I might not pass the Straits; at Naples it is demanded that I may not cross the Volturno. But as long as there are chains to be broken in Italy, I will follow my course or bury my bones there.

"I leave you Mordini, as pro-Dictator, and certainly he will show himself worthy of you and of Italy. I have yet to thank you, as well as the brave national militia, for the faith you have placed in me and in the destinies of our country.

" GARIBALDI.

"PALERMO, *Sept.* 17, 1860."

The following proclamation was addressed to the Palermitans a few days before :

"Near to you, or far from you, brave people of Palermo, I am with you, and with you for all my life !

"Bonds of affection, community of fatigue, of danger, of glory, bind me to you with indissoluble ties ; moved from the very depths of my soul, with my conscience as Italian, I know that you will not doubt my words. I separated myself from you for the common cause, and I left you another self—Depretis ! Depretis is confided by me to the good people of the capital of Sicily ; and, more than my representative, he is the representative of the holy national idea, 'Italy and Victor Emanuel.' Depretis will announce to the dear people of Sicily the day of the annexation of the island to the rest of free Italy. But it is Depretis who must determine—faithful to my mission and to the interest of Italy—the fortunate epoch. The miserable beings who talk to you of annexation to-day, people of Sicily, are the same who a month ago spoke to you and stirred you up ; I ask them, people, if I had condescended to their individual littlenesses, could I have continued to fight for Italy—could I have sent you this day my salutation of love from the beautiful capital of the Southern Italian continent ? Well, then, noble people, to the cowards who hid themselves when you fought in the barricades of Palermo for the liberties of Italy, you will say, from your Garibaldi, that the annexation and the kingdom of King Victor Emanuel we will proclaim quickly ; but there, on the heights of the Quirinal, when Italy shall count her sons in one family, and receive all as free men in her illustrious bosom, and bless them.

" G. GARIBALDI."

Garibaldi has always been humane and sympathizing, and especially with his own suffering soldiers. Of this there are proofs in the preceding pages. Few men ever knew as well as he how to make the unfortunate feel that they were compassionated. The following is an account of one of his visits to the hospitals of Palermo, from the letter of one of our own countrymen, who had offered his services as a surgeon early in the Sicilian war :

" One of the most moving sights it has been my lot to witness, was Garibaldi's visit here the other morning. As he entered the different wards, it seemed as though an electric shock had been communicated to all the inmates; after the first joyful cry: ' *E lui ! E Garibaldi ! E il Generale !*" a dead silence prevailed; all eyes were fixed upon him as he passed from bed to bed, taking the thin, wasted hands in his, or pressing his own upon many a feverish brow, making each patient feel that he was his general's favorite son, and that from him he might expect all that a father's tenderness could give. All his own men were known to him; he called them by their names, remembered where and how they were wounded, promoted this one, promised honorable employment to others disabled for military service, granting permission to others to go home, and providing them with ample means. When he came to the Sicilians, he inquired kindly into their wants and condition; ordered that the pay of one should be doubled, that another should be pensioned, and so on. But perhaps the most interesting scene of all was his visit to the Neapolitan ward, where we have eleven wounded prisoners, who have petitioned to enter our ranks. After being told that they were wounded at Calata Fimi, he said, 'Then you are brave men, truly! You have been misled; taught to look on us as enemies. I am fortunate to have you for my soldiers and for brothers.' Those men, strong and stalwart as they were, wept like little children, and in Garibaldi's eyes were tears ; none could help weeping, and one felt why it is that he is so loved, so idolized by all. When the emotion had a little passed, they tried to kiss his hands; he snatched them away. 'No, no !' he said, 'no more *Eccellenza ;* no more kissing of hands; that is servile. We are Italians—brothers—we are equals !' "

On Garibaldi's return to Naples, he had soon to turn his attention from the city toward the strongholds to which the poor king had retired, in the northwestern extremity of his late kingdom. The only territory now remaining to him of "the Two Sicilies," was the remarkable promontory of Gaeta and the adjacent range of mountainous and hilly country, extending southwesterly a few miles, near the frontier of the Pope's dominions, and along the courses of the rivers Volturno and Garigliano, to the heights of Capua. Gaeta and Capua have long been strong fortresses, and have known, at different periods, the hard fate of war. In Gaeta the present pope found a refuge, when he fled from Rome in 1848 ; thence were sent the calls to his spiritual subjects in all countries, to make contributions of "Peter's pence," and the demands on "Catholic powers," to reinstate the "Gentle Shepherd" in his sheepfold—by force of arms. That call was answered by four monarchs ; one of whom, the savage father of the now fugitive King of Naples, had his armies, too, routed by the now victorious Garibaldi ; and another, Louis Napoleon, after having his advance of 8,000 men driven back by the same hero, at the point of the bayonet, afterward, by false faith and overwhelming numbers, took the city by fraud and bombshells, and, on one pretext and another, has held it to the present time. He, however, has recently done so much for Italy, and seems resolved to do so much more, that her friends gladly indulge the hope, that he will continue a course quite the opposite of that which history was compelled to record nearly twelve years ago, and which posterity will ever be compelled emphatically to condemn.

A description of Gaeta, Capua, and Caserta will be necessary to many readers, before a connected account is given of the important military events which took place in that remarkable vicinity in October and November, 1860.

The traveller who leaves Naples for Rome, soon joins the route taken by the Apostle Paul from Puteoli. He first crosses the Campagna di Lavoro (country of labor), formerly called by the Romans, the Campania Felix (happy country), and now covered with countless fields, pastures, gardens and forests of vineyards. At the distance of about twenty miles, he reaches the foot of the bare mountain range above mentioned, where are seen the ruins of ancient Capua ; and after winding among eminences—among scenes desolate compared with those he has seen—and crossing the Volturno and the Garigliano, he stops at Castello or Mola di Gaeta. From the windows or terrace of the post-house he looks out through a garden of flowers and orange-trees, upon a fine bay, several miles across, the shores of which, low and curving round on the right, extend to a high, round mountain opposite, where a city is seen at its foot, and the zigzag walls and batteries of a mighty fortress on its sides and summit.   That is Gaeta.

When seen and sketched by the writer, not a ship or boat lay on the noble bay, and there was scarcely a sign of life on the land.   Cicero's tomb (if tradition may be trusted) is one of the large square masses of brick-work, overgrown with ivy, which stand near the road beyond the hotel ; for on his way to Gaeta was the great Roman orator assassinated, by command of the treacherous Octavius.

An old Latin itinerary of Italy gives several pages to the history and description of Gaeta, which was considered an almost impregnable fortress two centuries ago, being a peninsula connected with the mainland only by a fortified bridge, and having many forts and batteries.

We translate the following account of Gaeta with abridgments, from a celebrated work, "The History of Naples from 1734 to 1835," by General Pietro Colletta :

The first walls of this city were raised by the Trojans, according to ancient tradition ; and Æneas named it after his nurse, Caieta, who was buried there.   It soon increased and was extended.   Alfonzo, of Aragon, erected a castle ; Charles V. inclosed the city with fortified walls, and succeeding kings added new defensive works.   In 1734, it was besieged by the Spaniards, and was then almost as it is now. It is situated on a promontory, at the end of a low isthmus of the Tirrenian sea, the descent to which is very abrupt. The isthmus extends, in a narrow plain, to the mountains of Castellona and Itri.

On the summit of Gaeta is the very ancient tower of Orlando. The walls of the fortress follow the declivities of the ground, and present bastions, curtains and angles defending every point, modern science being brought into use, as far as the nature of the ground would permit. On the land side is a second inclosure within the first, with two fosses, two covered ways, and several parade grounds. The citadel is called the Castle of Alfonzo.

The Duke of Liria besieged the place with 16,000 Spaniards, well provided with ships of war, arms, machines and supplies, when it was defended by 1,000 Germans and 500 Neapolitans of the battalion formed by the Duke of Montaleone. Trenches were soon opened, and approaches made, by covered ways, toward the wall, while several cannon and mortar batteries were raised, to batter the citadel, and reply to the guns of the fortress. The Duke of Montemar and Charles V. joined the besiegers, pressed the siege, and, after some delay, the place was surrendered, after small loss on both sides. Only Capua then remained bearing the standard of Cæsar ; the Count de Traun commanding the Germans, and Count Marsillac the Spaniards, who had been, as on previous occasions, friends, enemies, and prisoners to one another, often disappointed by ill-fortune, but always with benevolent hearts. The preceding facts we have abridged from the first volume of Colleta's history.

Between the time of the surrender in 1734 and the treaty of Aix la Chapelle, and during the fears of war in the reign of Ferdinand, the old walls and bulwarks were restored, and the place surrounded by two walls, and in front were formed a fosse and two covered ways. The siege was commenced in February, by about 14,000 men against 7,000, in the form of a blockade, as the besiegers were destitute of heavy artillery and besieging apparatus. By the end of May, cannon being obtained, and batteries having been constructed at Montesecco, the trench was opened, and branches extended toward the two sides of the isthmus, and formed the first parallel. But, the soil being bare and composed of hard calcareous rock, earth was brought from a distance, and fascines and gabions from the woods of Fondi, twelve miles distant.. Much wood, however, was obtained by destroying the houses in the vicinity, which had been inhabited by nine thousand sailors and other industrious people, who had fled from the scene of war. Batteries were raised to fire upon ships approaching, and Sicilian and English vessels were several times driven off with loss. The fortress kept up firing day and night, and 2,000 shots were made in twenty-four hours without doing any injury or receiving any reply from the besiegers. By the beginning of July, preparations were made to open breaches in the citadel and the Bastion della Breccia; and on the 7th, after the long silence on the part of the besiegers, a tremendous fire was opened with eighty heavy cannon and mortars, to which the besieged promptly replied. After ten days of continued firing, the citadel was breached, but the bastion held out until the 19th. On the morning of the 20th, when the French had shown themselves ready to assault, the garrison demanded terms and surrendered. They took an oath not to fight France or her confederates, and 3,400 were transported to Sicily, some hundreds remained in the hospital, some escaped, and others deserted to the conquerors. About 900 Bourbonists were killed and wounded, and 1,100 Frenchmen. Among the former was Prince Phillipstadt, and among the latter, General Vallongue.

In 1798, Gaeta was surrendered to General Rey. While the left wing of the French army was proceeding slowly through the Abruzzi, the right wing reached the Garigliano, and summoned the Swiss commander of Gaeta, Marshal Tschiudi, to surrender. The latter being a Swiss mercenary, who had risen to rank by marriage and promotion without merit, urged by the bishop and intimidated by the first missile thrown by the French, gave up the fortress without conditions. Four thousand men, and a formidable fortress well prepared for resistance, were thus given up, with 60 brass cannon, 12 mortars, 20,000 arquebuses, a year's provisions, machines, ships in the harbor, and innumerable materials for defence. The soldiers were sent into prison, but the commander secured himself and officers the shameful distinction of liberty on parole.

General Mack still held out in Capua, and Gen. Macdonald hoped to find him also a coward or a traitor ; but his assault was resisted with vigor, after the outposts had been driven in, and the attempt was fruitless. Capua was given up to Gen. Championet by the treaty of Jan. 13, 1799.

The present condition of Gaeta is thus described by recent Turin papers :

"Gaeta is a second Gibraltar. It is armed with seven hundred pieces of artillery. All the sovereigns, from Charles V. downward, have added to its defences. Ferdinand II. fortified its most vulnerable points. Our army will find great difficulties in taking it; but this siege will not hinder the political and military reorganization of southern Italy, a task to which the government is devoting its utmost efforts. Gaeta has provisions for six months, and during the siege, the representatives of foreign powers will remain on board ships of war belonging to their nations at anchor in the port.

"The front of attack on the land side does not exceed 700 metres in extent. It is defended by works cut in the rock, and armed with three rows of faced batteries, one of which has rifled cannon. These batteries together mount about 300 guns, and their line of fire converges on the points from which the attack must necessarily be made. The ditch at the foot of the escarpment is cut in the rock, and the bottom of the escarpment itself is completely covered. The other fortified points are protected by masses of rocks, which render them unapproachable. The ground in front of the place of attack is so rocky that any approaches must be most difficult, and occupy a considerable time. Independently of those defences, Gaeta possesses a certain number of works established on the heights, among which may be mentioned the Castle, the Tower of St. Francis, and the

Monte Orlando, a strong fort, which commands both the land side and the sea. As to the port, it is defended by considerable works, which would cause great damage to vessels of war built of wood. In the situation in which Gaeta now is, and with the sea side remaining free in consequence of the non-recognition of the blockade by European powers, it may, with a garrison of from 6,000 to 7,000 men, with supplies of all kinds, defend itself for an almost indefinite period. The struggle will be confined on both sides to a combat of artillery. The besiegers may establish mortar batteries and bombard the place, but that means will only occasion the destruction of the churches, public buildings and private houses, but will not make the defenders of it surrender, for the batteries and forts are all bomb-proof. The king had put one wing of his palace into strong defence, and to it retired with his family."

Francis II. had issued the following order of the day:

" SOLDIERS : When, after two months of generous efforts, perfect self-devotion, labor and fatigue, we thought we had completed the work of crushing the revolutionary invasion of our country, there arrived the regular army of a friendly sovereign, which, by threatening our line of retreat, has obliged us to abandon our position. Happen what may from these events, the whole of Europe, in estimating and judging them, will not be able to do less than admit the valor and fidelity of a handful of brave men, who, resisting the perfidious seduction, as well as the strength of two armies, have not only made resistance, but have once more rendered illustrious the history of the Neapolitan army by the names of Santa Maria, Cajazzo, Trifisco, Sant' Angelo, etc. These facts will remain indelibly graven on my heart. To perpetuate the remembrance of them, a bronze medal will be struck, bearing the legend, 'Campaign of September and October, 1860,' and these words on the reverse, 'Santa Maria, Cajazzo, Trifisco, Sant' Angelo,' etc. The medal will be suspended by a blue and red ribbon. While ornamenting your noble breasts, it will remind every one of your fidelity and your valor, which will always be a claim to glory for those who shall bear your name.

" FRANCIS II."

CHAPTER XVIII.

" Though soft the couch on which oppressors lie,
A harder fate will meet them ere they die."—*MS.*

" Then Fingal eyed his valiant chiefs;
His valiant chiefs replied ;
The storm of battle roar'd again,
And Lochlin fled, or died.

" Never did joy o'er fallen foe
Upon my face appear
But I the feeble sav'd—the proud
Found that my rage was fire."

Ossian versified. T. D.

THE ROYAL PALACE AND GARDENS OF CASERTA—CHANGE OF TIMES
—THE RIVER VOLTURNO—POSITIONS OF THE KING'S TROOPS AND
GARIBALDI'S—THE BATTLE OF VOLTURNO.

BEFORE we return to scenes of battle, we must stop to survey the splendid and luxurious retreat of the King of Naples, where Garibaldi had now established his head-quarters.

The palace and gardens of Caserta, as we saw them in a time of peace, we may thus briefly describe : An avenue opens before us a mile in length, at the end of which is seen the palace, presenting a front of white marble, seven hundred and forty-six feet in length, with a spacious square in front. From the broad steps the visitor discovers that he has unconsciously been rising some distance above the level of the Bay of Naples, now far behind him. But his attention is attracted within the splendid palace, where a noble portal receives him, with a staircase on his right, made of the celebrated variegated marbles of the kingdom, which has had few if any equals.

It would require chapters to describe the almost innumerable apartments, ante-chambers, waiting halls, reception halls, etc. Within its vast compass are two theatres, one of which is said to be inferior only to San Carlo in the capital. The front view of the edifice gives a very inadequate impression of its real dimensions ; as it covers an area five hundred and sixty-four feet deep, with sides and a back front in the same style, and two interior ranges crossing at right angles.

The glimpses we catch of the garden, through the spacious halls, or from the upper windows, invite us to hasten through the palace ; and a charming view bursts upon us as we reach the rear portal. A tract of land a mile in extent gradually rises to the hills of Capua, covered with gardens and groves, lawns and avenues, interspersed with winding paths, cascades and fishponds, glowing with flowers and adorned with statues, whose beauties are redoubled by the shady foliage, the velvet grass and the perfumes which fill the air. Directly before the observer the main avenue of the garden opens the view up the ascent of the sloping ground, where many terraces rise behind each other in succession, by broad steps of white marble, on the right and left sides of the wide avenue, while cascades pour down between them, in the various forms of broad sheets and broken streams, intermingled with dark rocks and white statues of animals, sea-gods and nymphs, and alternately supplying and draining basins, ponds and small lakes, with grassy or flowery margins, where swans, gazelles and other harmless creatures sport in peace. On one of the lakes, formed in the adjacent fields and groves, is an island, accessible in a ferry-boat, with a pavilion, where refreshments are in waiting for the royal visitors ; and on the shore of another, a mimic fortress, with towers, battlements, moats and drawbridges for the young princes to practise the art of war. Ah ! what a pity that Caserta should so long have been the only spot in the dominions of Bomba where peace and happiness could be seen ! Had he been as mindful of the rights of his subjects as of the convenience of his brute favorites, there would

have been no need of the fortifications of Gaeta, the protests
of Europe or the invasion of Garibaldi.

A friend and admirer of that great man, while viewing, years
before his arrival, from the upper end of the grand avenue,
this garden and the adjacent " English garden " (which
alone is three miles in circuit), and seeing the campagna
stretching to Naples, with her noble bay beyond, thirty
miles wide, marked by its islands on the west and Vesuvius
on the east, exclaimed : " Oh ! this land is worthy of better
masters !" The response to this wish has been recently fulfilled in a most unexpected manner, by placing the two
Sicilies in the power of the Dictator, and giving him that
splendid palace for his head-quarters during the war in earnest, which he has so successfully waged against the tyran-
nical Bourbon, in one of the last of his strongholds.

Late in September was fought the battle of Caserta,
which forced the royal army to retire across the Volturno,
to the fortress and batteries of Capua.

THE BATTLE OF VOLTURNO

Was fought on the 1st of October, 1860, and was the
greatest, for the number of troops engaged, in which Garibaldi ever took part.

Both armies knew that Victor Emanuel was approaching at the head of the Sardinian army, which passed so vic-
toriously through the papal territories, and was unopposed
in those of Naples ; and, while it was the policy of Garibaldi
to wait for his coming before fighting, it was that of the
royalists to gain a victory, if possible, before the arrival of
his powerful reinforcement. The Neapolitan generals had,
therefore, brought together all their available forces, and
supplied the losses caused by sickness and desertion.

The heights of Sant' Angelo and Bosco di San Vito form
a long range, reaching from the northwest of Caserta toward
the river Volturno, two miles northeast of Capua, passing to

the left of the plain of Santa Maria. This range descends precipitously to the rapid and narrow Volturno, leaving room only for the road toward the Scafa di Carazzo. It commands the country around and has much brushwood, while there are many trees on the plain. Garibaldi oftened examined this ground ; and he erected several batteries to sweep the road on the opposite bank ; dug a trench near the shore to cover riflemen, and brought barges from Naples to cross with if necessary. There he stationed several corps of troops. The left flank and communication with Santa Maria were rather exposed. On the right the position was pretty well guarded by the ground and the troops.

The positions formed a semicircle of nearly thirty miles along the hills to Limatola by the river's course, and then curving back. Along the chord of this arc, nearly ten miles long, lie Santa Maria, Caserta and Maddaloni.

"October 1st at dawn," writes an officer, "the Neapolitan army of forty or fifty thousand men, who were strongly fortified in the fortress of Capua opposite, and its numerous outworks, attacked all parts of this line at once. But, before that hour, Garibaldi had left Caserta by railroad for the line. When he arrived, the firing had already begun. The three places, Capua, Santa Maria, and the Spur of St. Angelo, form almost an equilateral triangle, which is indicated by the three roads which connect these places. They run with little curves almost straight—that from Capua to St. Angelo, close to the river ; that from Capua to Santa Maria, parallel to the railway ; and that from Santa Maria to St. Angelo, at some distance from the hills till close to this latter place, where it is joined by the road coming from Capua.

"This triangle, which is in most parts thickly wooded with olive, and other trees, and has only few open spots, the Neapolitans had chosen as their field of operations on our left, and as the chief attack of the day. During the night all the troops stationed in the Polygon behind had passed through the town and had collected in the Campo, a large open space before the fortress. Here they opened out in two directions—one column, the left, toward St. Angelo, and the right toward Santa Maria.

"I shall first speak of the left column. Besides the great road from Capua, alongside the river, there is a by-road, which, leaving the main road at a little distance from the town, strikes across the country and goes straight toward the village of St. Angelo, which lies on the retreating slopes of the heights. This was chosen by the Neapolitans as the centre of their operations against this point, while they sent one column by the main road toward the right, and another to the right across the country to take the village in the other flank.

"The by-road which runs direct from Capua to St. Angelo, intersects the road from Santa Maria to the river, just where the road turns up to St. Angelo. In order to guard this position a barricade was constructed a little beyond this point, and armed with four guns. The country near the river is so low that every morning the exhalations of the ground cover it with a thick white mist. Besides this, the torrents which come down from the hills have artificial beds of 15 to 20 feet in depth, very steep, and covered with brushwood, which are dry now, and serve as roads. The Neapolitans, advancing by these, and taking advantage of the mist, approached quite close to the barricade, and carried it at the first onset, driving our men across the main road toward St. Angelo. Having taken this position, they came out and formed in an open field which lies along the road, in regular order of battle. Their left had been equally successful, driving ours from the trench near the river, and forcing them back on the heights of St. Angelo. The column to the right again had not only passed the road, but had gone up a little hill commanding St. Angelo.

"It was at this critical moment that Garibaldi arrived. He had taken, with his staff, carriages at Santa Maria, and was coming on in the main road toward St. Angelo. The balls and grape were flying about, but the carriages still proceeded. When they arrived in the neighborhood of St. Angelo they were in sight of the Neapolitans, who were drawn up there in line of battle. Fortunately, close to this spot was one of the torrents dammed, which formed a covered way. In this the carriages turned down, except the last, which was struck by a cannon ball, and remained on the road. Through the road Garibaldi advanced, revolver in hand, toward St. Angelo, and arrived just in time to give new courage to the defenders. The object was to drive away the column in the rear of the hills to the left of St. Angelo; this was easily done by throwing some skirmishers on the heights above those occupied by the intruders. There was, fortunately, some artillery in front, which was turned to good account, but as usual, it was the bayonet which decided. The Neapolitans tried to penetrate by a cavalry attack, but were beaten back, chiefly by the coolness of the Calabrese, who behaved splendidly. After three or four hours' fighting, whatever could be got together of available men were carried forward, and the Neapolitans not only driven back from their position on the great road, but likewise the barricades retaken. This was about nine o'clock.

"During this time the fight had been equally hot at Santa Maria. General Milvitz, who commanded there, was obliged to confine his defence to the immediate vicinity of the town, holding the main road to Capua and the space between- it and the railway. Some light earthworks which he had thrown up lately were of good service. But the enemy brought up fresh and fresh troops, which he kept in reserve in the Campo before Capua. The shells and shot flew into the houses of Santa Maria, and the inhabitants left in masses. Dispatch after dispatch was sent to Caserta, where the reserve was, to ask for reinforcements. But the reinforcements were likewise claimed on another side. Early in the morning a column had shown itself toward Castel Morone, but was easily driven back, and did not renew its attack. More serious was the advance agains Maddaloni, where a column of four thousand or five thousand men attacked Bixio. It was a hard fight, for there were not more than two thousand to two thousand five hundred men to oppose on a long line where the hills had to be kept on both sides. But the struggle was soon decided. By noon the news came that the enemy had not only been driven back from their position, but had likewise been followed up to the river. A part of their forces were cut off, and threw themselves into the mountains between Caserta and Maddaloni.

" Then there was a little breathing time, at least on our side, and the whole effort could be directed against Capua. There were but two brigades remaining in reserve, both weakened by detachments sent in different directions. The first was sent on by rail; the second went by the road, and both arrived almost at the same time, about one P.M. And it was time. The Neapolitan bullets and balls were coming freely into Santa Maria, while Garibaldi sent orders to let any disposable troops advance as quickly as possible toward St. Angelo. The defence of Santa Maria was quite confined to the outskirts of the town, where the Piedmontese artillerymen were behaving beautifully. The first thing was to oppose this, and a battalion of Bersaglieri and one of the regiments of the Brigade Eber, were sent to advance, while the Brigade Milano was sent by the Porta St. Angelo to take the enemy on the left flank. But before this occurred, the newly-formed Hungarian Hussars had been sent out by the Porta Capua to drive back the enemy's cavalry, which ranged close to the gate. Although not more than sixty horsemen, they charged and drove back the two squadrons, cutting them down and taking a number of prisoners.

"The infantry soon followed, and General Turr took the command of that side. Although mostly fresh troops, with the exception of the *cadres*, composed of the Cacciatori of the first expedition, they went on like old soldiers. The enemy, who had evidently all day long the idea of intimidating our troops with his cavalry, charged: but the Picciotti, guided by the soldiers of Calata Fimi, formed groups, and not only stood firing, but bayoneted the horsemen. After this it was almost nothing but advance with the bayonet, till the Convent of the Capuchins and the Cemetery, the two chief positions of the Neapolitans, were permanently taken.

"While this was going on on that side, the rest of the Brigade Eber, the last reserve, was called by the Dictator toward St. Angelo. Scarcely out of the gates, it fell in with Garibaldi, who, accompanied only by a few officers, was waiting for further reinforcements to fall on the flank of the enemy, who, on withdrawing from St. Angelo, had taken to the woods, and occupied some houses with his artillery.

"After the first defeat in the morning, the enemy had returned with new forces to carry St. Angelo. Not only did all his field guns scatter death in every direction, but likewise three batteries from the opposite bank, and the mortars from the fortress, began to open a tremendous fire, under the protection of which the Neapolitans advanced between 10 and 11 A.M. They carried once more the position of the barricade, and occupied even the first houses leading up toward St. Angelo. Medici and Col. Spangaro, besides Garibaldi, did everything to steady the wavering troops, who, seeing themselves so much outnumbered, and attacked by such formidable artillery, began to think the day lost. For hours the fight lasted, a continual advance or retreat on both sides, but still the Neapolitans could not gain much ground. This was, perhaps, the most strongly contested spot on the whole line, and only in the afternoon the advantage began to show on our side. The Neapolitans had again to clear the road, but they still held our barricade and the woods on both sides of it. With great trouble two skirmishing lines were formed, and sent to threaten their left and right, and then a hundred men were collected behind the first house, and these made a rush, at the cry of 'Viva Garibaldi!' and carried the position about 2 P.M., which was kept, as well as the guns which were in it.

"Garibaldi returned to Santa Maria and brought on the rest of the Brigade Eber to complete the success which had been gained. Scarcely half a mile from Santa Maria, an open space lies on the left of the road, through which a detached barrack is visible. Here the

Neapolitans had placed some guns, while their infantry lined the woods. As soon as they saw the column, they opened fire. Garibaldi, not heeding, still advanced, until he came to the first body. Here he gave orders to the Hungarian legion and the Swiss company to advance and drive them away. The two threw themselves into the woods, and, scarcely using their arms, advanced with the bayonet, driving the Neapolitans before them like sheep. A cavalry charge of several squadrons followed, and did a good deal of harm to the little body of brave fellows, but did not hinder them from following up their success and pushing forward to the very edge of the Campo before Capua.

"Garibaldi still advanced with the few remaining companies in the direction of St. Angelo, sending off one after another to continue the work of the Hungarians. Medici had, in the meantime, also pushed in advance, and by 4 P.M. the Neapolitans were flying in all directions, and our men had occupied the edge of the wood at half a mile from Capua, where they remained all night.

"It was as complete a defeat as ever an army suffered.

"They had on the whole line quite 30,000, to which we could scarcely oppose 15,000.

"The losses were not so serious as might have been expected. Many wounded, but few dead.

"The column which was cut off by Bixio showed about Caserta, and next morning Garibaldi went to give them the finishing stroke.

"We have five guns which were left by the Neapolitans early in the day, but could only be secured toward evening. Two British sailors distinguished themselves in removing them."

The king's troops had erected strong defensive works along the right bank of the Volturno, where they had, besides the formidable fortress of Capua, on the margin of the water, every favorable point occupied with forts or batteries. They entirely commanded the river, which is there only a ditch, with bridges crossing from the castle. From San Clemente to Cajazzo their bank was covered with well masked batteries, redoubts and barricades of trees; while the low parts of the shore were full of impediments and dangerous, concealed obstructions; and the whole was supplied with numerous chosen troops, well intrenched, excited by the promise of rewards.

We here translate *Garibaldi's Order of the Day*, after the battle of Volturno :

" On the 1st of October, a fatal and fratricidal day, when Italians fought, on the Volturno, against Italians, with all the energy which man displays against man; the bayonets of my companions in arms found also on that occasion the victory in their gigantic footsteps. With equal valor they fought and conquered at Maddaloni, St. Angelo and Santa Maria. With equal valor the courageous champions of Italian independence led their brave men to the conflict.

" At Castel Morone, Bronzetti, a worthy rival of his brother, at the head of a handful of Cacciatori, repeated one of those deeds which history will surely place by the side of the combats of Leonidas and the Fabii. Few, but splendid with the crown of valor, the Hungarians, French and English, who attended the southern army, worthily sustained the martial fame of their countrymen. Favored by fortune, I have had the honor, in the two worlds, of fighting against the first soldiers; and I have become convinced that *the plant Man grows in Italy not inferior to any country;* I have been made to believe that these same soldiers whom we have fought in southern Italy would not be placed behind the most warlike, when assembled under the glorious standard of emancipation.

" At dawn on that day, I arrived at Santa Maria from Caserta, by the railroad. While entering the coach for St. Angelo, Gen. Milwitz said to me : 'The enemy have attacked my outposts of San Tamaro.' Suddenly, beyond Santa Maria, toward St. Angelo, was heard a lively fusilade ; and near the posts of the left of the said position, they were powerfully engaged with the enemy. A coachman and a horse of the coaches in my train were killed. I might, however, pass freely, thanks to the bravery of the Simonetta brigade, Division Medici, which occupied that point, and courageously repulsed the enemy. I thus reached the crossing of the Capua and Santa Maria roads, the centre of the positon of St. Angelo, and there were the Generals Medici and Avezzana, who, with their accustomed courage and coolness, made their arrangements to repel the enemy, breaking in upon their whole line. I said to Medici, 'I am going alone to observe the field of battle. Defend the position at any cost.' I had hardly proceeded toward the heights behind, when I found the enemy were masters of them. Without loss of time, I collected all the soldiers at hand, and placing myself on the left of the ascending enemy, I endeavored to prevent them. I sent, at the same time, a company of Genoese Bersaglieri toward Mount St. Nicolas, to prevent the enemy from gaining possession of it. That company and two of the Sacchi brigade, which I had demanded, and which made their appearance opportunely on the heights, arrested the enemy.

"Then moving myself toward the right, on their line of retreat, the enemy began to descend and fly. Not until some time afterward, I learned that a corps of the enemy's Cacciatori, before their attack in front, had got to our rear by a covered way, without being known. In the mean time, the battle was warm on the plain of St. Angelo, now favorable to us, and then compelling us to retire before so numerous and tenacious an enemy. For several days unequivocal signs had announced to me an attack; and therefore I was not left to be deceived by the different demonstrations of the enemy against our right and left; and this was of much importance, because the royalists had collected all their disposable forces against us on the first of October, and attacked us simultaneously in all our positions.

"At Maddaloni, after varying fortune, the enemy had been repulsed. At St. Maria equally; and at both points they had left prisoners and cannon. The same happened at St. Angelo, after a fight of more than six hours; but, our forces at that point being very inferior to those of the enemy, he had remained, with a strong column, master of the communications between St. Angelo and St. Maria. I was, therefore, obliged, in order to get to the reserve which I had asked of General Sistori from Caserta, to pass to the east of the road leading from St. Angelo to the latter point. I reached St. Maria near 2 p.m., and there found our troops commanded by the brave general Milwitz, who had bravely repulsed the enemy at all points. The reserves sent for from Caserta reached us at that moment; and I placed them in column of attack on the St. Angelo road; the Milan brigade, at the head, followed by the brigade Eber; and I ordered in reserve part of the brigade Assanti. I then pressed to the attack the brave Calabrians of Pace, who were in a wood on my right, and fought splendidly. The head of the column had hardly issued from the wood, about 3 p.m., when it was discovered by the enemy, who began to fire grape. This caused a little confusion among the young Milanese Bersaglieri, who marched in front; but those brave soldiers, at the sound of charge from the trumpets, rushed upon the enemy, who had begun to retire toward Capua. The lines of the Milanese Bersaglieri were soon followed by a battalion of the same brigade, which fearlessly charged the enemy without firing a shot.

"The road from St. Maria to St. Angelo forms, in the direction of

St. Maria to Capua, an angle of about forty degrees; so that, while the column was proceeding along the road, it must always be on the left, and alternate forward.   When, therefore, the Milanese brigade and the Calabrians were engaged, I sent forward the brigade Eber against the enemy on the right of the former.   It was fine to see the veterans of Hungary march under fire with the tranquillity of a parade-ground, and in the same order.   Their fearless intrepidity contributed not a little to the retreat of the enemy.   With the movements in the front of my column and on the right, I soon found myself joining with the column of Medici, which had bravely sustained an unequal contest through the whole day.   The courageous Genoese carabiniers, who formed the left of the division Medici, did not wait for any command to charge the enemy again.   They, as always, performed prodigies of valor.   The enemy, after fighting obstinately all day, toward 5 P.M., reëntered Capua in disorder, protected by the cannon of the place.

"At evening I had noticed in St. Angelo, that a column of the enemy of 4,000 or 5,000 men was in Old Caserta.   I ordered the Genoese carabiniers to be ready at two in the morning of October 2d, with 350 men of the corps of Spangaro, and 60 mountaineers of Vesuvius.   I marched at that hour on Caserta by the mountain road and St. Lencio.   Before reaching Caserta, the brave Colonel Missori, whom I had directed to discover the enemy, with some of his brave guides, informed me that the royalists were on the heights between Old Caserta and Caserta, which I was soon able to verify.   I went to Caserta to concert with General Sistori, and not believing the enemy bold enough to attack that city, I combined with him to collect all the forces at hand, and march against the enemy's right flank, and attack him by the heights of the park of Caserta, thus placing him between us and the division Bixio, which I had ordered to attack him on that side.

"The enemy still held the heights; but discovering only a small force in Caserta, had projected its capture, ignorant, no doubt, of the result of the battle of the previous day, and, therefore, pushed half his force upon that city.   While I was thus marching under cover, on the right flank of the enemy, he attacked Caserta in front, and would, perhaps, have gained it, if General Sistori, with his accustomed bravery, and a band of valorous men, had not repulsed him. With the Calabrians of General Stocco and four companies of the northern army, I proceeded against the enemy, who was charged— resisted but little, and was driven almost at a run to Old Caserta. There a small number of the enemy sustained themselves for a moment, firing from windows, but they were soon surrounded and made prisoners. Those who fled in advance fell into the hands of the soldiers of Bixio, who, after fighting bravely on the first at Madda-loni, arrived on the field of battle like lightning. Those who remained behind capitulated with Sacchi, whom I had ordered to follow the movement of my column ; so that, of all the enemy's corps, few were able to escape. This corps, it appears, was the same which had attacked Bronzetti at Castel Morono—and that his heroic defence, with his handful of brave soldiers, had restrained them the greater part of the day, thus preventing them from getting into the rear all that day. The corps of Sacchi also contributed to detain that column beyond the Park of Caserta on the first day by repulsing it bravely.

"G. GARIBALDI.

"CASERTA, *October*, 1860."

GARIBALDI'S PERSONAL HEROISM.

A correspondent of the Paris "Journal des Débats" says :

"The most brilliant episode of the action of the 1st of October was the recapture of the battery at the foot of Mont St. Angelo. When I left Santa Maria, I knew that this battery had been very much dis-abled in the morning. Garibaldi arrived at nine o'clock, when the enemy was thundering at it with all his strength, because it took him in flank, and was causing him severe loss. The triple battery cour-ageously resisted the attack, and never slackened fire, when all at once the one situated at the foot of the hill became silent. The royalists, to the number of 2,500, got round the hill, and rushing upon the guns, spiked five of them, and killed several of the men at their pieces. Garibaldi, on the San Tannaro side, soon observed the silence of his favorite battery, and an aid-de-camp from General Milwitz soon informed him of the disaster, which would probably have lost him the battle. Garibaldi at once started off, crossed Santa Maria, followed by Medici and his staff, and collecting what men he could, cried out in a voice which caused all to shudder, 'We are going to die, but the Italians must win the day : at all other points we have conquered.' Followed by one hundred men, at a rapid pace, Garibaldi leading the way in a small, disabled carriage, went right forward. But just as they got near the Casino of St. Angelo, some Neapolitan Chasseurs, who were lying on the ground, rose and fell upon them. The coachman drove his horses into a ditch and formed a barricade of the carriage. Garibaldi jumped up, indignant, and went up to the Chasseurs, shouting, 'Viva Italia!' Some of his men coming up at the same time, the enemy became demoralized and took to flight. Garibaldi was slightly wounded in the stomach, and his trousers were riddled by two or three bullets. 'If I only had another pair,' he said, and without further remark he continued his march toward a battalion of one hundred and fifty Hungarians, commanded by General Mogyorady. He pointed to the Neapolitans who were in possession of the battery, and cried out to them, 'Forward, my lads, disperse that rabble for me!' This 'rabble' consisted of a regiment of the line, a squadron of Cavalry, a company of Chasseurs, and a company of Artillery. The Hungarians, without waiting to count the numbers of the adversary, rushed forward and charged with the bayonet. After a contest of twenty minutes, the battery was retaken, and once more it poured its storm of grape on the Neapolitan troops, who fled in confusion across the fields. The Hungarians, in this encounter, had thirty men put *hors de combat*, the Neapolitans about two hundred. Garibaldi did not wait to dress his wound, but hurried elsewhere. The day, however, was now won."

CHAPTER XIX.

> " This Pius the Ninth for us, Romans, has made
> Short joy and long grief by his treacherous trade.
> Beguil'd and oppress'd, we have lost ev'ry hope:
> Then unpope him, unpope him, unpope the false pope."
>
> *G. Rossetti.*

" Priests of Italy ! we can conquer without you, but do not wish to. Are you not our brothers ?"—*Mazzini.*

" Have the Roman people submitted quietly to the Popes' temporal power ? History records more than one hundred and sixty rebellions against it in ten centuries."—*An Italian writer.*

" Curia Romana non petit ovem sine lana."—*Modern Roman proverb.*

THE POPE URGED BY FRANCE AND SARDINIA TO DISMISS HIS FOREIGN TROOPS — INCONSISTENCIES OF LOUIS NAPOLEON — MARKED CHANGES OF TIMES, DOCTRINES, AND MEASURES — VICTOR EMANUEL'S DEMANDS PRESSED ON THE POPE—CONSPIRACIES AND INSURRECTIONS IN THE POPE'S REMAINING DOMINIONS — THE ULTIMATUM REFUSED — GENERAL CIALDINI MARCHES—BATTLE OF CASTELFIDARO—CAPTURE OF SPOLETO, ANCONA, PERUGIA, AND OTHER PLACES—VICTOR ENTERS THE KINGDOM OF NAPLES.

WE must now leave Garibaldi for a time, and devote a chapter to the affairs of the Pope and Sardinia.

The Emperor of the French and Victor Emanuel had long since advised and urged the Pope to dismiss his foreign troops, with which he garrisoned his fortresses, and not only kept the people in awe, but oppressed them intolerably ; but he, under the influence of his prime minister, Antonelli, stubbornly refused, as well as persisted in denying every proposition for the removal of abuses. Adhering to the old and impious claim of divine right, as the vicegerent of God on earth, and hoping, no doubt, that Austria would be able to come to his aid with her armies, when every intelligent eye saw that Austria was hardly able to stand alone, the pope had excommunicated Victor Emanuel, and even Louis Napoleon in fact, though without naming him, at a time when the latter was still upholding with his army the papal power in Rome, which he had restored by besieging that city in 1849. There was an abundance of inconsistencies and self-contradictions on all sides ; and it would have been difficult to point out any way in which either of the three sovereigns could consistently move, speak or even stand still. But good men rejoice when good is done, and some-times the more when it is effected in an unexpected quarter. In 1849 the Roman republic was overthrown by French can-non, though created by the free suffrage of the Pope's sub-jects ; and, in 1860, most of the Pope's territory and for-tresses were to be captured in siege and battle, in order to drive out foreign troops, whose presence was "an insult to Italy," and to allow the inhabitants freedom to vote for annexation to Piedmont.

England had often protested to the kings of Naples against their inhumanity toward their subjects ; and thus she was prepared to approve, as she has done, of the invasions of her territory by Garibaldi and Victor Emanuel.

We can find here but little space to notice the events which followed the Pope's final refusal to accede to the demands made upon him. How unreasonable soever they appeared to him, or however inconsistent they may have seemed to the world, especially the appeal to free, universal suffrage, which would be hardly submitted to in any other country in Europe, no alternative was left.

After the iniquitous overthrow of the republic by Louis, the occupation of Rome by his army in fact conciliated the entire papal priesthood of the world, and the population which has remained under their spiritual influence ; and it has prevented Austria not only from taking that place, but of every excuse and possibility of aspiring to obtain it. While the Pope has been surrounded by French troops, he has appeared to be under safe guardianship, even although during the few months which have passed since the fulmination of the Bull of Excommunication against Victor Emanuel, Louis Napoleon himself has also been, by plain innuendo, laid *under the ban* by the same instrument, and has been transformed from " the eldest son of the church—the beloved in Christ," as the Pope used to denominate him, to an enemy, delivered over to Satan, and anathematized, in every part and member of his soul and body, from the crown of his head to his accursed feet.

But now things have changed wonderfully, and we have indications that the French emperor is about to change his position accordingly. If events take such a course as we may anticipate, the Pope's temporal power will soon be entirely gone, and his respectability in the eyes of the world will be only such and so much as can be bought with two millions of dollars a year, and by a train of cardinals, with ten thousand dollars apiece. This is the plan now proposed for the future position of Pius IX., which Victor Emanuel seems likely to carry into operation, with the approbation of Louis Napoleon. There is now no longer any danger from Austria, weak as she is by bankruptcy, the loss of most of her Italian possessions, threatened with the invasion of the remainder by Garibaldi on " the ides of March," and with Hungary ready to rise at the first signal. The Italians can now take charge of the Pope and of Rome, without fear of Austria or assistance from France ; and, either before any more fighting in Lombardy and Venetia, or, if need be, after it, the kingdom of all Italy is likely to be proclaimed, according to Garibaldi's announcement, from the Quirinal, one of the seven hills of Rome.

When this shall have been done, the anticipations of the Italian patriots will be realized, who have long regarded the loss of the Pope's temporal kingdom as surely involving the destruction of his spiritual ; and many of them were early advocates of the doctrine preached by Gioberti twenty years ago, although he was a devotee of popery and they were its radical enemies, because they had sagacity to foresee the necessity of this act, which was beyond his perception. They knew full well, what millions of the unwilling subjects of the papacy have known for centuries, that nothing but severe and cruel oppression could ever keep the human mind submissive to such a system of tyranny, spiritual and physical, and that, whenever force and fear were removed, individuals, communities and nations would throw·off the galling and degrading yoke.   This the world has seen proved within the past few months, in ways and modes, in a degree and to an extent, which only those who were acquainted with popery, with human nature and with Italy would have expected.   As soon as freedom of speech and action was granted to the people of Lombardy, the Duchies, Tuscany and Emilia, and a free, universal suffrage was proclaimed, the inhabitants rose in a mass in city, villages and country, and proceeded, with banners, music and acclamations, to the election urns, and voted unanimously for immediate annexation to the constitutional kingdom of Victor Emanuel.   And this expression of the universal and enthusiastic popular will was greatly enhanced by the circumstance that the king had just before been excommunicated by a Bull of the Pope, which consigned him to outlawry, persecution, torture and death in this world, and to eternal misery in hell ; and yet many Italian archbishops, bishops and priests, of all degrees, have openly approved the rejection of allegiance to the papacy, and urged and even led their people to the polls, themselves, in many instances, putting in the first votes.

But not only have the hopes of good Italian patriots been gratified : the prophecies of God himself have been fulfilled, by the recent astonishing course of events in Italy.   So striking is the resemblance between those changes and the scenes recorded in the Bible, that the mind is filled with solemn awe and grateful adoration while contemplating them in comparison. "The souls under the altar" introduced to the reader of the book of Revelation, with their purity, faithfulness, patience, but earnest inquiry: "How long, O Lord, holy and true, dost thou not avenge our blood?" how much do they resemble the victims of the Inquisition, whose horrible secrets were disclosed by the opening of that infernal edifice in Rome by the republican government in 1849! And how much does the present period resemble that described in chap. xviii. ver. 13 of that book, where the destruction of Babylon the Great is described, and one of whose chief articles of traffic were not "the persons of men," as in Tyrus (Ezekiel xxvii.), but their "souls!"

And how Garibaldi appears like the agent by whom that destruction is to be accomplished, when we hear him repeat his open and tremendous denunciations against the papacy, now, recently, standing in Naples, almost in the same words which he wrote in New York in 1850, for this volume, and recorded on page 233.

Before the war with Italy the States of the Church were divided into four legations, not counting the district of Rome. The first comprised the provinces of Bologna, Ferrara, Forli and Ravenna, and was called Romagna. This is the portion which had been already annexed to Piedmont. The second, which separates the Romagna from the Neapolitan states, is composed of the provinces of Urbino, Pesaro, Macerata, Loreto, Ancona, Fermo, Ascoli and Camerino. It is this portion of the Roman territory which is commonly known under the name of the Marches, and is bounded on the north by Romagna, on the east by the Adriatic, on the south by the Neapolitan territory, and on the west by the provinces of Spoleto and Perugia. The third legation was composed of the provinces of Spoleto, Perugia and Rieti. The first two corresponded to what is generally known under the name of Umbria. The fourth legation comprised Velletri, Frosinone and Benevento, the last province being surrounded by Neapolitan territory. The district of Rome was placed under a special *régime*, and consisted of that city, of Viterbo, Orvieto and Civita Vecchia.

The course of policy recently adopted by Sardinia had now been made known by what was deemed a semi-official announcement by a Turin gazette, under the direction of Cavour. It was this : that the cabinet of Turin, in placing itself in the position of the representative of Italian nationality, had a right to reproach Austria for not having given to Venetia, either a separate government or an Italian army. This violation of the treaty of Villafranca had very naturally disquieted the Sardinian government, which, however, had no intention of provoking an imprudent war. On the contrary, it desired to prevent this, and demanded to this end, the dismissal of the foreign hordes which had been united by General Lamoricière. "It cannot be permitted," says the paper in question, "that Italy should be made the camping ground of twenty-five thousand foreign mercenaries, who entertain toward the Italians feelings of hatred and aversion." The Sardinian government cannot look on with indifference at the renewal of the massacres of Perugia. It owes protection to the populations of Umbria and the Marches, who are subjected to a military dictation which they hate, and it is better for the government to take the responsibility of energetic measures, which will be too late if it waits for the attack. Such was the substance of the article written while the people of Umbria and the Marches were in a state of insurrection. For, before that time, the following accounts had been received from different parts of the Pope's dominions. At Fano, Sinigaglia and Ancona, the government of Pius IX. were in serious danger. The last-named town in particular, which had revolted, and had been brought back to obedience rather by stratagem than by force, was said to be the centre of agitation and the hotbed of revolutionary incendiarism. A correspondence had just been discovered which compromised a great number of per-

sons. Many had been arrested. It was connected with a
conspiracy, the ramifications of which were said to be so
widespread, and included men so high placed in society, that
the authorities admitted that they were incapable of guarding against the storm without the assistance of an armed
force. Advocates, officials, private individuals, and even a
certain number of Roman officers, were compromised in the
affair, but no general arrest could be attempted for fear of
leading to a most dangerous collision. The mass of the people only waited as a signal the arrest of some eminent person-
ages to rise in insurrection, and the police were well aware
that a large depot of arms existed, but they were ignorant of
the spot. Such was the situation of Ancona, which, it would
appear, regulated the movements of the towns on the coast
of the Adriatic, such as Sinigaglia, Fano and Pesaro, and of
those in the interior, as Osimo, Loretto and Recanati, and
as far as Macerata. In this state of things the Roman
government had just ordered troops to proceed by forced
marches on Ancona from Pesaro, Perugia and Rome.

At length Count Cavour gave notice to the Pope, in the
following letter to Cardinal Antonelli, that he must immediately decide on what course to pursue.

"TURIN, *Sept.* 7.

"EMINENCE: The government of his majesty, the King of Sardinia, could not without serious regret see the formation and existence
of the bodies of foreign mercenary troops in the pay of the Pontifical
government. 'The organization of such corps not consisting, as in
all civilized governments, of citizens of the country, but of men of all
languages, nations and religions, deeply offends the public conscience
of Italy and Europe. The want of discipline inherent to such troops,
the inconsiderate conduct of their chiefs, the irritating menaces with
which they pompously fill their proclamations, excite and maintain a
highly dangerous ferment. The painful recollection of the massacre
and pillage of Perugia is still alive among the inhabitants of the
Marches and Umbria. This state of things, dangerous in itself, be-
comes still more so after the facts which have taken place in Sicily
and in the kingdom of Naples. The presence of foreign troops,

which insults the national feeling, and prevents the manifestation of the wishes of the people, will infallibly cause the extension of the movement to the neighboring provinces. The intimate connection between the inhabitants of the Marches and Umbria and those of the provinces annexed to the states of the king, and reasons of order and security in his own territory, lay his majesty's government under the necessity of applying, as far as in its power, an immediate remedy to such evils. King Victor Emanuel's conscience does not permit him to remain a passive spectator of the bloody repression with which the arms of the foreign mercenaries would extinguish every manifestation of national feeling in Italian blood. No government has the right of abandoning to the will and pleasure of a horde of soldiers of fortune, the property, the honor and lives of the inhabitants of a civilized country.

" For these reasons, after having applied to his majesty, the king, my august sovereign, for his orders, I have the honor of signifying to your eminence that the king's troops are charged to prevent, in the name of the rights of humanity, the Pontifical mercenary corps from repressing by violence the expression of the sentiments of the people of the Marches and Umbria. I have, moreover, the honor to invite your excellency, for the reasons above explained, to give immediate orders for the disbanding and dissolving of those corps, the existence of which is a menace to the peace of Italy.

" Trusting that your eminence will immediately communicate to me the measures taken by the government of his holiness in the matter, I have the honor of renewing to your eminence the expression of my high consideration. " CAVOUR."

The following is the reply of Cardinal Antonelli :

" ROME, *Sept.* 11.

" EXCELLENCY : Without taking into account the manner in which your Excellency has thought proper to have your letter of the 7th inst. conveyed to me, I have directed my whole attention calmly upon the subject you lay before me in the name of your sovereign, and I cannot conceal from you that it has cost me an extraordinary effort to do so. The new principles of public law which you lay down in your letter, would be, indeed, sufficient to dispense me from giving any answer at all, they being so contrary to those which have constantly been acknowledged by all governments and nations. Nevertheless, feeling deeply the inculpations cast upon the government of his holiness, I cannot refrain from at once noticing the blame, as odious as it is unfounded and unjust, pronounced against the troops belonging to the Pontifical government, and I must add, that I find the pretension of denying the right belonging to the Pontifical government as well as to any other, of having foreign troops in its service, utterly unjustifiable. In fact, many governments of Europe have foreign troops in their pay. On that subject it may be expedient to observe that, owing to the character with which the Sovereign Pontiff is invested as the common father of all believers, he ought to be less subject to criticism than any other for receiving in the ranks of his troops all who come and offer themselves from the various parts of the Catholic world, for the defence of the Holy See, and of the States of the Church.

"Nothing is more false or insulting than to attribute to the Pontifical troops the disorders which have taken place in the states of the Holy See. There is no necessity for asking, for history has already enregistered whence came the troops who have violently constrained the will of the people, and the artifices which have been made use of for throwing into perturbation the greater part of Italy, and ruining all that was most inviolable and most sacred, both in right and in justice.

"As to the consequences which it has been sought to make weigh on the legitimate action of the troops of the Holy See, to put down the rebellion of Perugia, it would truly be more logical to throw that responsibility on those who, from abroad, have excited the revolt; and you know perfectly well, M. le Comte, where that outbreak was concerted, whence were derived money, arms and means of all kinds, and whence instructions and orders were sent to the insurgents.

"There is, consequently, reason for representing as calumnious all that has been said by a party hostile to the government of the Holy See, as to the conduct of its troops, and for declaring that the imputations cast on their chiefs by the authors of proclamations of a nature to excite dangerous ferments, are not less. Your excellency concludes your painful dispatch by inviting me, in the name of your sovereign, to immediately order the disarming and disbanding of the said troops. This invitation was accompanied by a sort of menace on the part of Piedmont in case of refusal, to prevent the action of said troops by means of the royal troops.

"This involves a *quasi* injunction which I willingly abstain from qualifying. The Holy See could only repel it with indignation, strong in its legitimate rights, and appealing to the law of nations, under the aegis of which Europe has hitherto lived, whatever violence the Holy See may be exposed to suffer, without having provoked it, and against which it is my duty now to protest energetically in the name of his holiness. With sentiments of consideration, I am, etc.,

"G. CARDINAL ANTONELLI."

The occupation of the Roman States by the King of Sardinia was one of the most important and unexpected steps in the war, which soon followed the preceding announcement. The above note was sent by Count Cavour to Cardinal Antonelli, minister of the Pope, in compliance with the urgent demand of the people of Umbria and the Marches, in which the Sardinian government had demanded the immediate dismissal of the papal mercenaries, affirming that the presence of upward of 20,000 foreign troops in the centre of Italy was incompatible with the treaty of Villafranca. The note threatened that unless this demand should be agreed to in 24 hours, the Sardinian army would enter those territories. No reply was received within that time, and then Victor Emanuel issued the following proclamation :

"SOLDIERS: You enter the Marches and Umbria to restore civil order in their desolated cities, and to afford the people the opportunity of expressing their wishes. You have not to combat powerful armies, but to free unhappy Italian provinces from foreign bands of mercenaries. You go not to avenge the injuries done to me and to Italy, but to prevent the bursting forth of popular hatred and vengeance against misrule. You will teach, by your example, forgiveness of injuries, and Christian tolerance to him who in his folly has compared to Islamism our love for our country, Italy.

"At peace with all the great powers, and without any idea of provocation, I intend to remove from the centre of Italy a perpetual source of disturbance and discord. I desire to spare the seat of the head of the church, to whom I am ready, in accord with allied and friendly powers, to give all those guarantees for independence and security which his blind counsellors have vainly imagined they could obtain from the fanaticism of that mischievous party that conspires against my authority and the liberty of the nation.

"Soldiers; They accuse me of ambition! Yes! one ambition is mine—that of restoring to Italy the principles of moral order and of preserving Europe from the continual peril of revolution and of war.   "VICTOR EMANUEL."

Before the middle of September, General Cialdini had taken the town of Pesaro, and captured twelve hundred of the German troops, being a portion of those bands of foreign soldiers, against the keeping of which France and Piedmont had so long protested, and the retaining of which was the chief ground of the war. Orvieto was also taken. Fossombrone had risen in insurrection, as Pesaro had done before Cialdini's arrival ; but Fossombrone, being unsupported, had been reduced to obedience, by such savage punishment as had been suffered by Perugia.

The " London Times " remarked, on receiving this news, and in reviewing the manifesto of Victor Emanuel :

" We freely admit that nothing but the extremity of the evil could justify the step which Sardinia has taken, but we think that step is justified. The evil would not cure itself. For all these reasons, we think the King of Sardinia is entitled to the sympathy of Englishmen in the war in which he has engaged. We wish him cordially success, and that his success may be rapid as well as decisive."

The war, in fact, was begun by the rulers and their hired butchers against the people, before the Sardinian troops crossed the frontier. The presence of those troops was also an insult to Italy, as their express object was to oppose the movement in the free territories. The same writer added the following remarks :

" Then there is the intolerable oppression of the Pope's government, The best proof of that oppression is the fact that the Pope dares not trust his own subjects with arms, but places himself, like Dionysius of Syracuse, in the hands of foreign mercenaries. The spectacle of a people kept down by such means is an outrage on the civilization of the age, and a danger and menace for all the rest of Italy. Till some government be established in the centre of Italy, which can be maintained without ten thousand French troops to garrison the capital, and five and twenty thousand foreign mercenaries to sack insurgent towns, it is in vain to hope for peace."

General Cialdini approached Ancona, and a naval squadron was to coöperate. The battle of Castelfidaro was

fought on the 18th of September, when Lieut. General
Cialdini was furiously attacked by General Lamoricière, with
eleven thousand men and one hundred and forty cannon.
Four thousand other papal troops made a sortie from Ancona, to support the latter. The contest was short but
bloody. Many of the wounded papists used their daggers
against the Piedmontese, who went to assist them. The results, said Cialdini's report, were as follows :

"The junction of Lamoricière's forces with Ancona has been prevented; we have taken six hundred prisoners, among whom are more
than thirty officers, some of them of high rank; we have taken six
guns, among others those given by Charles Albert to the Pope in
1848, one standard, and numerous ammunition wagons, etc. All tho
wounded, including General Pimodan, who led the attacking column,
are in our hands, and a great number of killed."

General Cialdini conceded the honors of war to this corps,
and officers and men were allowed to return to their homes.

General Lamoricière, accompanied by a few horsemen, fled
from the field of battle on the 18th, and, following the road
by the sea through the defiles of Conero, succeeded in reaching Ancona. All the prisoners and troops were indignant at
his conduct. Nothing remained of Lamoricière's army except the troops shut up in Ancona ; all the rest were in the
hands of the royal troops, with the exception of two thousand
men dispersed in the mountains. The Sardinian government
offered to the English government to set all the Irish prisoners at liberty. The latter sent a courteous reply, leaving
it entirely to the Sardinian government to take such resolu-
tions as it might deem most suitable. The Sardinian government ordered the release of all Frenchmen taken prisoners
from Lamoricière.

"The mercenary army of General Lamoricière (as the "London
Times" remarked) was the last hope of the Pope. Lamoricière, whom
the last accounts had described as seeking a junction with the Royalist
Neapolitan troops, and threatening a southward movement upon the
Garibaldians, had appeared suddenly before Ancona. Cialdini ac-
cepted the offered battle, and the event has been that the African

general was totally and entirely routed. Those bands, from whom so much was expected, seem to be of no avail whatever against the Sardinian soldiers. This fire-eating and pious soldado, who had fulminated such dreadful threats, and who was known to have done such strong deeds among the Arabs, has really done nothing in Italy which might not have been done by one of the College of Cardinals. With eleven thousand men, and the vigorous aid of the garrison of Ancona, he has simply marched up to a signal defeat."

Ancona was soon after besieged, blockaded, bombarded, and captured. The Sardinian navy and army displayed great skill as well as discipline and courage in this operation. The particulars of this must be omitted, as well as most others connected with the march of Victor Emanuel on his triumphant course toward Naples.

The city of Spoleto was besieged and soon taken. The besieged had three guns, two on a platform above, overlooking the town, and one below, placed in an embrasure on the left of the outer gate of the *enciente*, so as to command the road leading up to it. They were iron guns of no great range, but still serviceable. The smallest of the three, in the embrasure by the gate, was the only one that did any execution.

The Piedmontese arrived at Spoleto in the morning. They were between two thousand and three thousand strong, and had one battery of field artillery, consisting of six guns. The fact is, that the whole thing was a farce ; there was very little attack, and still less defence. The report of the commandant of Spoleto is an enormous exaggeration.

The Piedmontese, on their part, did not press the siege with much vigor. The Italians were positively disaffected, and threatened their foreign comrades to blow up the powder magazine if they did not give in. Most of the Irish asked nothing better than to escape from the service and from the country, and the rest of the garrison—the motley crew of German, French, Swiss, and Belgians—they were few in number and of little worth. The whole loss of the Piedmontese was, according to the evidence afterward obtained, under one hundred men. The loss of the garrison is stated at three killed and ten wounded.

Nothing, certainly, says a visitor, could be more complete or miserable than the failure and break-down of the Irish contingent to the Pope's harlequin army. It would be very unjust, however, to consider this to be in any degree a stain on the gallant Irish nation, whose impetuous courage and many excellent military qualities, every one must recognize and admire. The same ignominious disasters might, and no doubt would, have fallen to the lot of any body of men, no matter of what nation, similarly recruited, and deceived, and neglected, and sent into the field without the training and education which make the soldier. The shame falls not on Ireland, but on those who insnared unwilling recruits to prop a bad cause.

Perugia, which was the scene of an inhuman butchery last year, committed by some of the horde of foreign wretches who formed the Pope's army, was now held by about three thousand of them, who made a strong resistance. The garrison had raised barricades in all parts of the town, and occupied the houses, from which they fired upon the Sardinians. Every street was the scene of a conflict ; but the assistance afforded to General Fanti by the inhabitants made the struggle much shorter than it would otherwise have been. A considerable portion of the Pontifical carbineers contrived to escape out of the town—the others retired to the citadel, which could not hold out long. Toward evening the fort capitulated, and the whole of the garrison, consisting of 1,600 men, were made prisoners, as well as General Schmidt, who commanded them. He was the worthy chief of the adventurers whom the Italians so cordially detested. Switzerland refused to acknowledge him. He was one of the heroes of that impious war of the Sonderbund, which caused much bloodshed in the Swiss cantons. He was subsequently exiled.

Victor Emanuel's address to the people of Southern Italy, dated at Ancona, October 9th, 1860, concludes thus :

"PEOPLE OF SOUTHERN EUROPE : My troops are advancing among you to establish order. I do not come to impose upon you my will, but to cause yours to be respected. You will be able to manifest it freely. Providence, which protects just causes, will inspire the vote which you will deposit in the urn. Whatever be the gravity of events, I wait tranquilly the judgment of civilized Europe and that of history, because I have the consciousness of having fulfilled my duty as king and Italian. In Europe my policy will not be useless in reconciling the progress of the people with the stability of monarchies. In Italy I know that I terminate the era of revolutions.
                                        " VICTOR EMANUEL.
                                        " FARINI.
"Given at ANCONA, Oct. 9, 1860."

In the middle of October Victor Emanuel entered from the north the kingdom of Naples, which Garibaldi had now won for him, though by expressly disobeying him, as we have before seen. The Piedmontese army, approaching by two columns, was now drawing, as a writer remarked, " the iron circle, out of which there is no outlet. One column has already passed Foggia on its way to Benevento and the Upper Volturno ; it has landed at Manfredonia, and is making its way through the plains of the Capitanata. The other, under the personal command of the king himself, has landed at Giulia, and has pushed forward to Pescara, whence a branch leads into the main road from the north through the Abruzzi into the rear of Capua.

" As for the Piedmontese troops landed at Naples, they have already taken up their position in line. It was high time, for the fatiguing service, in the heavy autumnal rains, with the cold winds, the heavy dews, and chilly mornings, was fast thinning the ranks. For the most part in the open air, or with but indifferent huts, constructed of branches and straw, without camp fires at night, and with continual alarms, it was a wonder that these young volunteers could resist as they did."

CHAPTER XX.

" Our Tricolor, not as in days that are gone,
    Shows Italia disjoin'd, but united in one;
    The *White* is the Alps, our volcanos the *Red*,
    And the *Green* the rich fields over Lombardy spread,"
                                    Dall' Ongaro. T. D.

THE PRESENT POSITION OF THINGS — DOUBTS RESPECTING GARI-
BALDI—DESCRIPTIONS OF THE CAMP AT CAPUA—ENGLAND
DECLARES FOR VICTOR EMANUEL—GARIBALDI'S PROCLAMATIONS
—MEETING OF GARIBALDI AND VICTOR EMANUEL.

AND now the short but momentous drama of the year was
drawing rapidly toward its close. Whatever opinions may
be entertained respecting the original intentions of Louis
Napoleon, Victor Emanuel, or their counsellors, or the period
when they were expected to come to their accomplishment,
it seems certain that the steps taken by them not only hastened the epoch, but secured its success. The world may
perhaps never know what part was performed by individuals in plans and councils, nor be able to judge of their comparative merits or abilities. But of Garibaldi we have much
better opportunity to form our opinion, and on most points
there is little room for doubt or misapprehension. One
question still remained to be solved to those who had not
attentively observed his career in former times ; and some,
probably, expected to see him ultimately break the promise
which he had made, to resign his power and possessions to
Victor Emanuel ; while more, it is natural to believe, expected
to see him claim a high reward, or at least to accept such
splendid honors and permanent powers as the King of Sardinia would, of course, be ready to bestow. Anxious fears
were expressed, and eager inquiries were made, by many
well-wishers of Italy and admirers of her hero, especially
about the epoch at which we have arrived.

The siege of Capua was pressed.   A Scotch gentleman, who had visited Garibaldi's camp and hospitals, thus wrote on the 6th of October :

" Let any man go to the hospital--what cruel wounds, what horrific sights! and how cheerfully some of the sufferers bear their troubles. We have heard much of the noble way in which our English heroes in the Crimea conducted themselves. Truly many of the common soldiers of this patriot army might take rank beside them. Again, as to the officers. If Garibaldi has thought it advisable to break some of their swords, how many instances can be cited of a heroism in others which cannot be surpassed. There is a young Sicilian nobleman, Baron de Cozzo, commonly termed 'The Flower of Sicily,' and beloved by Garibaldi as a son, now lying cruelly wounded and suffering in the hospital of Caserta. He had fought untouched all through the campaign, from Palermo to Capua. He was in the thick of the battle of the 12th at Capua, and was still unhurt, but he observed a private of his company in the front struck down wounded ; he returned, put the man on his back, and was carrying him off, when he received his own wound, and such a one as will most probably render him a painful cripple the rest of his days, if, indeed, he survives it. Hundreds of wounded men, and many others mere boys, came into Naples yesterday, after the battle; and we must reflect how many more must have fought bravely to render such an account.

" Yesterday morning, Captains Smelt and Davidson started early for the batteries situate on the hills of St. Angelo. On arriving at the camp at the base of the hill, they joined Lieutenant Cooper, of Major Pietuni's brigade, and proceeded to the batteries where the guns had been put into position in order to prevent the royalist army from getting round to Caserta, as they had previously succeeded in doing. On gaining the summit of the hill they perceived a body of artillery with a couple of guns advancing from the right of Cajazzo, with some cavalry on the left. The officers having been granted the use of the guns, opened fire upon the enemy as they gradually approached. Although the first trial shots fell somewhat short, they had the effect of checking the artillery. The cavalry, however, advanced notwithstanding, when another shell fell in amongst them, and sent them flying. Captains Davidson, Smith, and Cowper, finding that they were now making tolerably good practice, and seeing a house on the other side of the river where there appeared to be something stirring, they dropped a shell right into the centre of the said mansion, and out came the contents like so many bees disturbed in their hive.

" We started this morning for Santa Maria. The havoc amongst the avenues of trees on the roads shows how severe the contest must have been.

" The view of the field of operations from the top of Mount St. Angelo toward Capua, is most commanding. Garibaldi, in a round black hat turned up at the rim, and in a light brown cloak, lined with Rob Roy tartau, was coming down the hill with his staff, and we joined in. He held a sort of standing council at the bottom of the hill with one or two officers who met him, but he spoke so low, that only those quite close to him could hear a word. We then returned to Caserta with Colonel Peard, Major Wortley, Captains Sarsfield and Davidson."

An American gentleman who visited the camp before Capua, and the Palace of Caserta in October, thus spoke of them in a letter :

" In company with two English gentlemen and Madame S., of Naples, I visited the camp before Capua. As we drove down the road leading to the River Volturno, we reached the extreme point where the road turned round the base of St. Angelo, when a sentinel stopped us, saying, ' You are in great danger from the batteries from the other side, which command the entire road you have just come down, and they have been firing upon us this morning.' We at once halted, and sent our carriage back, and under the conduct of one of Garibaldi's men, ascended the mountain till we reached the summit of the rising ground, and had a good view of Capua and its defences. While thus standing at gaze, aided by glasses, a gun was fired from a small battery we had not before observed on the side of the opposite mountain. In an instant the ball flew over our heads, and chanced to fall in the camp beyond, near a group of officers, and killed a horse. With this notice to quit, we descended and reached the road of St. Angelo, just as Garibaldi and his staff were ascending, and soon saw him standing alone on the highest point, scanning the enemy's position with his glass. One of his aids who had joined us, and who was known to Madame S., said it was the general's custom to remain for hours upon the mountain ; so we were compelled to give up all hope of seeing him. As we were walking toward the place where our carriage was, we were addressed by an English gentleman, such a one as we have in our minds when we hear the song sung of ' The fine old English gentleman, all of the olden time.' His dress and bearing were alike the type of a landed gentleman out of the agricultural

counties. He begged us to avoid the road, as we were within the
range of the enemy's guns. Thanking him for his kindness we left
him, and among our guesses we thought he must be no other than
Colonel Praed, who is to command the English contingent—a regiment of men just arrived, and who had been that day sent forward as
far as the king's palace at Caserta.

"When we reached the palace, whose magnificent courts and
rooms we found filled with English, we there met this gentleman (Col.
Praed), and asked Lieutenant Campbell, whom we knew, if that was
his colonel. 'Oh no! that gentleman came down with us, and has
offered his services as a private. He has declined a commission, and
will act only with us as a common soldier.' We mixed with the soldiers, who told us that they were to be sent to the front that night,
and expected to be in action the next day. They were as joyous as
they would have been going out to a May party. While thus occupied,
Lieutenant Campbell called our attention to a lady in a military costume, just entering the court, attended by a gentleman. Her dress
was a velvet cap, with a feather, a grey suit, the full skirt of which
hung in many folds to her knees. She wore military boots with spurs,
and a sword hung by a waist belt. Her face was handsome—a dark
brunette, with fine flashing eyes. The English clustered around her,
and she addressed them a few words of welcome, whereupon the
cheers of the soldiers made the walls of the palace vocal with strange
music for such a place. The lady was the Countess de la Torre, who
commands a company, and has greatly distinguished herself by her
courage and coolness. In the battle of the 1st instant a shell fell
near her, and those near by, thinking as most persons do at such
times, that 'discretion is the better part of valor,' fell upon their
faces awaiting the bursting, but the countess, following the example
of the great Frederick under similar circumstances, stood with her
arms folded, and when it exploded, she uttered the most fierce re-
proaches on those who cowered."

On the 11th of October, Lord John Russell, in an official
dispatch to the British minister at Turin, declared that
although the Emperor of the French had expressed his dis-
pleasure at the invasion of the Roman territory, the Emperor of Russia that of Naples, and the Prince of Prussia
had also objected, the British government could see no cause
sufficient for those objections. He closed with these
words :

" Her majesty's government will turn their eyes rather to the gratifying prospect of a people building up the edifice of their liberties, and consolidating the work of their independence, amid the sympathies and good wishes of Europe. I have, etc.,

(Signed)   "J. RUSSELL.

" P. S.—You are at liberty to give a copy of this dispatch to Count Cavour.

" To Sir James Hudson, etc., etc."

Garibaldi, on the 15th of October, issued the following proclamation :

" Italy and Victor Emanuel !

" To satisfy a wish cherished by the whole nation, I, the dictator, decree as follows :

" The Two Sicilies, which have been redeemed by Italian blood, and which have freely elected me their dictator, form an integral part of one and indivisible Italy under her constitutional king, Victor Emanuel, and his descendants.

" On the arrival of the king, I will depose in his hands the dictatorship conferred upon me by the nation.

" The pro-dictators are charged with the execution of the present decree.

" G. GARIBALDI.

" CASERTA, *Oct.* 15."

After this decree, both parties which had been vying with each other to destroy Garibaldi, saw that there was an end to their calculations. His enemies felt that, in spite of all intrigues and ingratitude, he rose higher than ever at the moment they thought of crushing him, and his false friends understood that his noble nature will always find out the right way, in spite of the abuse which is made of the sacred name of friendship, to lead him where their interest might wish him to go. Indeed, this time they fell into their own snare, for this announcement was accelerated by their last effort to divert Garibaldi from the right path.

The day was now at hand, when an end was to be put to doubts and fears, and the mouths of calumniators were to be stopped forever. How can the enemies of Garibaldi look upon their aspersions without mortification ; or even the greater part of the first journalists of Europe as well as of America, reperuse their evil prognostications, without a desire to recall or to make some amends for their unworthy suspicions ? How must the character of Garibaldi rise in the view of those who were unacquainted with his previous life, and allowed themselves to attribute to him the weakness of judgment, the selfish aims, or the uncontrolled passions of common men, since they have found him exalted far above the ordinary level of soldiers and statesmen ! How must his willful calumniators turn, not only in bitter disappointment, after the defeat of their criminal efforts, but with self-loathing, from the contemplation of a character which makes their perfidy appear doubly hideous by contrast.

Can we not imagine, in some just degree, what must have been the feelings of his own heart, even through the periods of his greatest darkness, when, independently of the opinions or fears of friends, and the aspersions and intrigues of foes, he proceeded on his gigantic task with unshaken resolution, undeviating step, and unfailing success, from the beginning to the end ? The difficulties, dangers, delays, obstacles and opponents continually around him, far from overpowering, impeding or disheartening him, never seemed to agitate or excite him. Self-possessed, as if in tranquil scenes, he appears never to have lost, even for a moment, the full exercise of his judgment or the perfect control of his passions. He entered every new scene with a consciousness of these extraordinary faculties, and came out of it confirmed, by new experience, in his ability to do everything necessary in future. With such conscious integrity and powers, how lofty must have been his feelings during every stage of his career ; and how exalted and delightful when he arrived at its close !

The contemplation of such a character cannot fail to be useful as well as delightful to every virtuous mind and heart ; and the new model which he has bequeathed to the world by his pure and splendid example, must be extensively and long appreciated, and have great and blessed effects. And one way in which it must most naturally act, will be by encouraging men possessing traits like his own, in different spheres of life, duly to estimate those humble virtues, which have been so much underrated in our country in late years, because thrust aside or trampled down by the empty vanity of wealth, or the impudence of corrupt party power. Indeed, we may hope that the example of the pure and noble Garibaldi, since it has been so displayed as to strike all eyes, and to engage all minds, will impress upon good citizens a sense of the duty which they have so long neglected, of combining to cast bad rulers from the seats designed for better men.

A letter from Naples, dated the 29th of October, gave the following affecting account of the interview between Victor Emanuel and Garibaldi :

"I was on my way to the head-quarters of Victor Emanuel, at Teano, and took a cut through the mountains. While waiting for a conveyance, I met Major Cattabene, commandant of Garibaldi's head-quarters. He was coming from Teano, and to him I am indebted for the following account of the interview between Victor Emanuel and Garibaldi. Garibaldi had taken up his quarters at a small inn, about four miles and a half between Teano and Speranzano, on the 25th. He ordered his column to advance and take up positions, and sent Count Trecchi to see the king. On the following morning, Count Trecchi and Missori came to inform him that Cialdini was within an hour's march, and the king not far behind. Garibaldi left immediately with his staff, and three-quarters of an hour afterward he came in sight of the head of the Piedmontese column. He put spurs to his horse. The Piedmontese advanced as follows: the 23d and 24th regiments of the Como Brigade; the 26th and 27th of Pinerolo's Brigade; and then a battery of rifle cannon. The columns presented arms to Garibaldi, and opened to allow him to pass through. Cialdini rushed forward, and Garibaldi, jumping from his horse, embraced him affectionately. After exchanging a few words, Garibaldi remounted to meet the king. Victor Emanuel was not far behind, leading on his own division. Seeing the red shirts, the king took his telescope, and, recognizing Garibaldi, put spurs to his horse and galloped toward him. Garibaldi did the same. When they were within ten paces of each other, the officers of the king and of Garibaldi shouted, ' Long live Victor Emanuel!' Garibaldi advanced, took off his hat, and in a voice somewhat hoarse with emotion, said, ' King of Italy!' Victor Emanuel put his hand to his kepi, then held it out to Garibaldi, and equally moved, replied, ' Thank you.' They stood thus, hand in hand, nearly a minute, without uttering another word.

" Garibaldi and the king, still holding each other's hand, followed the troops for about a quarter of an hour. Their suites had mingled together, and followed at a short distance behind them. Passing a group of officers, Garibaldi saluted them. Among them were Farini, minister of war, in the foraging cap of a staff officer, and General Fanti. The king and Garibaldi were conversing. After the king followed the 17th, 18th, 19th, and 20th regiments of the line, then sixty guns, and four regiments of cavalry. His majesty was at the head of 30,000 men.

" Before reaching Teano, King Victor Emanuel halted, and ordered a portion of his army to file off in presence of Garibaldi, that every one might observe the good feeling which prevailed between him and the chieftain. He then reviewed Bixio's Brigade, which was posted a little beyond Calvi. He was received with the enthusiastic and unanimous shout of ' Long live the King of Italy!' Garibaldi has 7,000 men divided between different positions. The king remained at Teano; Garibaldi returned to Calvi to give orders."

CHAPTER XXI.

"Rest in thy shadowy cave, O sun !
   But soon return with joy,
For Crona's bloody strife is done :
   Let songs the night employ,
For Fingal there, on Crona's banks,
   His foes had triumph'd o'er,
And backward turn'd their foreign ranks,
   Like surges from the shore."

"Now spread the sail ! said Morven's king,
   And catch the winds for home.
We rose upon the wave with joy,
   And rush'd through Ocean's foam."
                   Ossian Versified. T. D.

GARIBALDI'S ANNOUNCEMENT OF VICTOR EMANUEL'S APPROACH
TO NAPLES—THEY ENTER TOGETHER—GARIBALDI RESIGNS HIS
DICTATORSHIP—CAPITULATION AND SURRENDER OF CAPUA—
HIS ADDRESS TO THE HUNGARIAN HUZZARS—HIS FAREWELL TO
HIS TROOPS—HE SAILS FOR CAPRERA—UNEXPECTED CHANGES
—LETTERS DESCRIBING THEM.

THE siege of Capua was now pressed; and, during its con-
tinuance, the besiegers were joined by the Sardinian army,
which had already, after its victorious career through the
territories of the Pope, approached Naples.

Garibaldi announced the approach of Victor Emanuel in
the following terms :

PROCLAMATION OF GARIBALDI TO THE INHABITANTS OF NAPLES.

"To-morrow, Victor Emanuel, the king of Italy, the elect of the
nation, will cross the line which has divided us from the rest of our
country for so many centuries; and, listening to the unanimous voice
of this brave population, will appear here among us. Let us receive,
in a becoming manner, him who is sent by Providence, and scatter in
his path, as a pledge of our rescue and of our affection, the flower of
concord, so grateful to him, so necessary to Italy.

439

"No more political distinctions! no more parties! no more dis-
cords! Italy one, as the people of this metropolis have expressed it,
and the gallant king, be the perennial symbols of our regeneration
and of the greatness and prosperity of the country.

"G. GARIBALDI."

Victor Emanuel and Garibaldi entered Naples together,
on the 7th of October. The following animated description
of the scene is from a letter of that date.

"King Victor Emanuel and Garibaldi entered Naples together, for
it would have been a grievous thing if, as had been feared, the apostle
of Italian liberty, the man of a century, had not been united with the
sovereign on this great occasion. When they left the railway *en route*
for the cathedral, there were Victor Emanuel and Garibaldi on his
left hand, and the pro-dictators of Sicily and Naples sitting opposite
them in the same carriage. The suite followed, and all along the
railway to the Duomo there was a perfect ovation. The streets, which
are very narrow, and scarcely wide enough to admit of more than
two fat persons abreast, were festooned with flowers and evergreens,
hung from window to window; pictures, tapestry, banners, and all
the adjuncts of a great *fête* in Naples were there, but looking as *triste*
and downcast as heavy rains could make them. On arriving at the
Duomo, or the cathedral, the piazza of which was beautifully decorated, his majesty was received by the authorities, and conducted to
the high altar, amidst such a storm of shouts and applause as could
only be compared to the storm which was raging outside. 'Viva Victor Emanuel!' 'Viva Garibaldi!' 'Viva Italia Unita!' Such were
the cries which rose, not from one, but from a united body of many
thousands, who waved their hats, and handkerchiefs, and flags, as the
royal party advanced to the high altar; and this in the cathedral
church of San Januarius, the special protector of the Bourbons, whose
favor (the saint's) Baron Brenier not long since requested as an honor
for M. Thouvenel.

"The king did not take his seat on the throne, but stood a little
below it, and wiped his hands, and then his face, with his pocket-
handkerchief, and then looked round with that bold, undaunted aspect
which indicated an iron nerve. Shortly after, the ceremony began,
and his majesty knelt at the *prie-Dieu* (a stool for kneeling), whilst
Garibaldi, the pro-dictators, Farini, and others, stood behind him.
The *Te Deum* was sung in magnificent style.

"As soon as the ceremony was over, they came down the aisle, and

I had an admirable view of the king and the Liberator face to face, and as a gleam of .sun shone out on the monarch, every line was visible. ' Humanity ' came first, and ' Divinity ' after. The difference in the two expressions could not fail to strike the most insensible. I looked at Victor Emanuel's unvarying face and bold glance, and said, he is the *Re Galantuomo*, true to his word, and ready to maintain it with his sword; but I looked on Garibaldi, and felt all the moral grandeur of his character—not a statesman, because he is something much higher—he carries in his face his character: an amiability which wins all hearts, and an energy which overcomes all difficulties. The crowd around each was immense, though the soldiers round the church on either side did all they could to keep the path open, but it was all of no use; one of the poorest of the poor laid hold of his sovereign's hand and walked with him; and the people clung to Garibaldi and kissed and embraced him as a father. He was the greater idol in a temple of idols; and so the royal party walked down the church, and entered their carriage in the midst of the bursts, and long-continued storms of applause, as heretofore. The king was dressed, let me say, as a general of division, and Garibaldi in the same simple dress in which he had conquered the Two Sicilies and given away a kingdom.

" As the cathedral clergy refused to officiate on this occasion, the clergy of the palace offered their services."

On the 8th of November, the day after his entry into Naples with the king, at eleven o'clock, Garibaldi, followed by the ministry, presented to his majesty, in the throne-hall, and in the prescribed form, the *Plebiscitum*, or Vote of the People. The Minister of the Interior and Police thus addressed the king :

" Sire : The Neapolitan people, assembled in Comitia, by an immense majority, have proclaimed you their king. Nine millions of Italians unite themselves to the other provinces governed by your majesty with so much wisdom, and verify your solemn promise that Italy must belong to Italians."

The king answered in a few noble words. The act of union was performed. The ministry then offered their resignation, the dictatorship having expired from which they had received their powers. The enthusiasm of the people of Naples continued to be expressed in the highest degree.

The Capitulation of Capua was signed November 2, and, abridged, was in these terms :

" Convention on the capitulation of Capua, arranged by mutual agreement, by order of his excellency, Gen. Della Rocca (commander of the corps of the Sardinian army), commanding the besieging corps, and by order of Field Marshal De Cornet, commanding the place, by the undersigned commissaries, and afterward ratified by the respective generals in command.

" 1. The place to be given up in twenty-four hours to the troops of Victor, with the entire armament, arms, clothes, provisions, bridge equipage, horses, carts, and all else, civil and military, belonging to the government. 2. The gates and fortifications to be immediately given up. 3. The garrison to march out with the honors of war. 4. The forces to go with banners, arms and baggage, 2,000 men hourly, laying down their arms outside (officers retaining their swords), and proceeding to Naples on foot, embark for a Sardinian port. The generals to go to Naples by railroad. The families of soldiers not to follow the column. The sick and wounded to remain in Capua. 5. A mixed commission to superintend affairs, and an inventory to be made," etc.

The scene presented at the surrender is thus described by an American who was in Garibaldi's army.

" At 7 A.M. we took up the line of march for Capua. The sun rose in all his glory, after having hid his face for three days. The troops were in the finest spirits, and decked their arms and colors with branches and flowers, and as they marched up the road the bands played the opera of ' Don Giovanni,' the troops joining in the chorus, the gay Calabrese dancing with very joy. With such music as this, with glorious mountains, and a beleaguered city lying prostrate before us, you can imagine that we do not sigh for the Academy of Music. At 11 A.M., 12,000 men laid down their arms in the beautiful plain in front of the city. A sadder sight I have not witnessed since the surrender of Vera Cruz to Lieutenant General Scott. The city is now in the quiet possession of our troops, and all the cities in the valley are illuminated. General Avezzana's division marched tonight for Caserta, the palace of the king. Captain Warwick, the young Virginian, is now with Colonel Wyndham, the gallant commander of General Dunn's brigade (General Dunn having been severely wounded). General Jackson, a major general of the English army, has been here for three weeks past, lending his sympathy and his presence, even upon the field of battle, to this glorious cause.

"The palace and hunting park at Caserta are said to be the most magnificent in the world."

After the surrender of Capua, the battalions of volunteers were disbanded, to be reorganized in the regular Italian army, if they wished to remain in service.   They were to be sent to Northern and Central Italy, and disposed as follows : The Medici division in Parma; the Turr division in Palermo; the Cosenz in Bologna; and the Bixio in Florence.

Garibaldi asked of the king amnesty for all the soldiers who had deserted from the Sardinian army to join his expeditions, and the request was immediately granted to both regulars and volunteers.

Garibaldi decreed as follows on the 15th of October :

"That the Two Sicilies, which owe their rescue to Italian blood, and who have freely chosen me as Dictator, form an integral part of Italy, one and indivisible, with her constitutional king, Victor Emanuel, and his descendants."   ·

GARIBALDI'S ADDRESS ON DELIVERING FLAGS TO THE HUNGARIAN

HUSSARS IN NAPLES.

"NEAPOLITANS : This is a fine day—a great day !   It is fine and great, because it reunites, with a new chain, the brotherhood which binds Italy to Hungary.   The peoples are consolidated together. The free Italians cannot, ought not, to forget it—nor will they forget it." (Here the people broke out in overwhelming applause, " *Viva Garibaldi !*"   The general replied:)   " Italians free !   Yes, they shall be—all, and soon.   To a life wholly consecrated to the cause of liberty—to the thought of our nationality—nothing else have I added; nothing else do I wish to add, but the right to speak the truth—to speak it equally to the powerful and the people.

" Hear me, then, generous people of this great and beautiful metropolis, and, if I deserve anything of you, believe my words.

" The canker, the ruin of our Italy, has always been personal ambitions—and they are so still. It is personal ambitions which blind the Pope-king, and urge him to oppose this national movement, so great, so noble, so pure—yes, so pure—that it is unique in the history of the world. It is the Pope-king who retards the moment of the complete liberation of Italy. The only obstacle, the true obstacle, is this.

"I am a Christian, and I speak to Christians—I am a good Christian, and speak to good Christians. I love and venerate the religion of Christ, because Christ came into the world to deliver humanity from slavery, for which God has not created it. But the Pope, who wishes all men to be slaves—who demands, of the powerful of the earth, fetters and chains for Italians—the Pope-king does not know Christ: he lies to his religion.

"Among the Indians, two geniuses are recognized and adored—that of good and that of evil. Well, the Genius of Evil for Italy is the Pope-king. Let no one misunderstand my words—let no one confound Popery with Christianity—the Religion of Liberty with the avaricious and sanguinary Politics of Slavery.

"Repeat that. Repeat it. It is your duty.

"You who are here—you, the educated and cultivated portion of the citizenship—you have the duty to educate the people. Educate them to be Christian—educate them to be Italian. Education gives liberty—education gives to the people the means and the power to secure and defend their own independence.

"On a strong and wholesome education of the people depend the liberty and greatness of Italy.

"Viva Victor Emanuel! Viva Italia! Viva Christianity!"

Garibaldi's proclamation to his troops, when about to retire to Caprera, commences thus:

"*To my companions in arms!*

"We must consider the period which is now about to close as the last step but one in our regeneration, and prepare ourselves to finish splendidly the stupendous conception of the choice men of twenty generations, the fulfillment of which Providence has assigned to this fortunate generation.

"Yes, young men! Italy owes to you an enterprise which deserves the applause of the world. You have conquered, and you will conquer, because you are now trained to the tactics which decide battles. You have not degenerated from those who entered the

Macedonian phalanxes, and struck to the heart the proud conquerors of Asia.

"This stupendous page of our history must be followed by one more glorious still ; and the slave will finally show to the free brother a sharpened iron which belonged to the links of his chains.

"To arms all!—all!—and the oppressors, the supremely powerful, shall be turned into dust."

Garibaldi embarked in the small steamer, Washington, for his island, and was so eager to be once more in retirement, that he cast off the hawser with his own hands.

The following account of his arrival at Caprera we translate from a letter dated :

"MILAN, *Nov.* 16, 1860.

"By the return of the steamer Washington to Naples, we have received direct news from the Island of Caprera, where Garibaldi has established his winter quarters. As soon as he placed his foot on shore in the island, the dictator felt himself free as from an incubus weighing on his mind and heart. As Garibaldi never could remain inactive under so seductive a sky, like Victor Emanuel, he is in his element only when in the field of battle, or hunting among rocks. In fact, he speaks of the re-conquest of his own individual liberty, which he wishes to divide with his three war-horses, which, when he had first stepped on the sand on the island, he unbridled and left free among the fields.

"But a pleasing surprise came, on his arrival, to enliven the mind of the Italian hero. The modest cottage which had served him as an abode the past year, during his absence had been changed for a handsome and elegant *casino.* The avenues were well marked out, and, instead of the nakedness of the ground, the wild and uncultivated aspect in which he had last seen it, he observed marks of recent cultivation, plantations of trees and hedges, well arranged convenient and well-made roads.

"Garibaldi, full of wonder, went about trying to imagine and divine what magical hand could have made so great a change. He even almost began to doubt whether it was the Island of Caprera. Entering the house, and looking about in every part, he found in the centre a rich and commodious hall, and, supported from the wall, a large and beautiful portrait. It was one of Victor Emanuel!"

The following is from a letter of the Rev. J. Newman, dated "Naples, November, 1860 :"

AN INTERVIEW WITH GARIBALDI.

It was my good fortune to have an interview with General Garibaldi, in the royal palace at Caserta, a day or two before his departure. When I arrived at the palace, the dictator was in the king's garden, sitting for his photograph —a pretty Italian lady acting as artist. General Turr, and the other officers of his staff, were present ; also the wife of the mayor of Palermo, and two other ladies. As in ordinary cases, the artist had great difficulty in arranging the general's head and hands, but still more in getting him to keep them arranged, according to order. And after the picture was finished, he was the first to look at it, which he jocosely pronounced *good*. He then walked with one of his staff, and again with the mayor's wife, through the broad avenues of the garden, and finally strolled off alone, with his arms thrown behind and his head inclined forward, like one in deep reflection.

He kindly received me into his private apartments in the palace, where, by a most winning manner, he made me feel myself quite at home. Learning that I was an American, and having himself travelled through North and South America, the conversation turned upon the United States. He indicated his comprehensive and penetrating mind by a marvellous familiarity with our history and prosperity. Nothing can exceed the grace and dignity with which he conversed. He was mild in his manner.till I suggested the great want of railroads in Italy, when he immediately grew animated, and drew a striking contrast between Italy and America, as to material greatness, and concluded with expressions of hope that a brighter day is dawning upon his native land. Garibaldi is so justly proud of his 'American antecedents, that it is not egotism for me to claim for our country an important agency in the Italian Revolution, by the impressions our institutions and greatness made upon his mind while there. My previous admiration for the man was increased by this brief interview. He seemed to me to be a man of exalted purpose and of generous sympathies. He is now in the prime of life, and in the enjoyment of robust health, which he preserves by his simple mode of living. He is above the medium height, and has a powerful muscular frame. His complexion is florid ; his hair and beard sandy; his brow lofty, and his eyes are of a light chestnut hue, and when at ease they have that dreamy expression so peculiar to many great men. He is not particularly dignified in his address ; his gait is even careless ; his carriage might be thought uncourtly, yet there is that indefinable something in his presence which, while it does not overawe you, yet impresses you with a profound respect for the man. He is certainly an extraordinary character, and the most popular man now before the world. He is honest in his principles, unselfish in his purposes, unalterable in his decisions, lasting in his friendships, bitter in his enmities, and magnanimous to all. When I saw him he was attired in grey pants, a red shirt, and a grey mantelet, lined with a red and black plaid, the sides of which were looped upon his shoulders, giving free play to his arms. He wore a Chinese cap, common in England, and a serviceable sword was dangling at his side, which constituted his uniform. His mode of living is extremely simple, so much so that his staff joke him by saying they do not expect to get much to eat where he is. He never takes wine, and generally breakfasts upon a cup of coffee and a few Italian chestnuts. He had formed the decision to retire to his island home. If you will turn to your map, you will see a little island on the northern coast of Sardinia, near the entrance of the Straits of Bonifaccio, and opposite to the southern point of Corsica. This is Caprera, where the famous Garibaldi, with his son and daughter, together with a few choice friends, is now residing. The island is less than six miles in length and not two in breadth. It consists of two rocks, which belonged to an Englishman and the general. The former is now dead, and Garibaldi is left alone in his rockland glory. But on reaching his island, he was most agreeably surprised ; the appearance of his home had been so changed since he left. Well cultivated fields and beautiful plantations, with shady groves and spacious avenues, had taken the place of a stony desert. It looked as if a magician had been there, and struck the island with his wand, bidding nature forthwith to lavish her treasures on this chosen spot. But the general was still more surprised when, instead of his humble cottage, an elegant villa stood before him ; but on entering it the mystery was solved, for on the wall hung the portrait of his friend Victor Emanuel, whose generosity had anticipated his happiness.

The following extract of an unpublished letter from a gentleman in Piedmont to a friend in New York, contains a most particular description of Garibaldi's arrival at Caprera :

" TURIN, *Nov.* 24, 1860.

" What do you say of all that has been passing here, and of Garibaldi, the king-maker ? You will have heard that this true patriot refused the rank of first marshal of the kingdom of Italy, which would have made him the first person after the king ; and the order of Annunziale, which is equal to that of the Golden Fleece, and generally only given to born princes.

" Garibaldi lives near the Island of Sardinia, on the small Isle of Caprera, right in front of the Pass of Bonafaccio. It is a mere rock, uninhabited or nearly so, where he has a small house and a little garden, where he lives with his daughter, spending his time fishing. To this hermitage he has retired, after having made a present to Victor Emanuel of the kingdom of Naples. But you may fancy his surprise, when, on arrival, he found his little garden had given room for a park, with large trees, more than a century old, with flower-beds, etc., etc. He entered his house. The outer walls were as he left them ; but the interior had become a palace, with magnificent furniture and velvet hangings, with gold fringes, etc. He passed into the study, and there above the massive mahogany table, hanging against the wall, upon the velvet tapestry, a large painting, made by one of the first artists of the day, in which he could not but recognize himself, sitting at a table, his head bent over a drawing of a plan of battle he was forming, while the king standing next him, his right arm leaning familiarly on his shoulder, was looking, in a bending position, at what he was doing.

"Was this not a pretty surprise which the king prepared for his faithful follower, the fisherman's son, who had given him a kingdom and would accept nothing—neither rank, nor honors—in return?"

THE END.

www.ingramcontent.com/pod-product-compliance
Lightning Source LLC
Chambersburg PA
CBHW022028110726
47901CB00006B/1691